THE PILGRIMS
OF THE
DAMNED

THE PILGRIMS OF THE DAMNED

STEVE McHUGH

Podium

Podium

LIST OF CHARACTERS

The Assembly
Miles Watson: Arbiter
Church: Vampire-enhanced Doberman; best girl
Mordecai Balderas: Assembly Justice

House Venator (The House of Justice)
Drest: First Lord of House Venator
Charlotte Henry: First Counsel of House Venator

House Idolator (The House of Faith)
William Fuller: First Lord of House Idolator
Thomas Reed: First Authority of House Idolator
Pedro de Moxica: First Priest of House Idolator
Arvid Holmlund: House Idolator familiar
Jenny Lewis-Palmer: House Idolator pilgrim

House Phalanx (The House of One)
Samuel Austin: Works with the FBI as a liaison
Major Alan Parker: Formerly of House Phalanx, now of the Maine First
vampire militia

The Free City of Bangor
Joseph Davies: Ex-Assembly; lead doctor for the Free City of Bangor
Carol Walters: One of the leaders of the Free City of Bangor
Bethany Parker: Scientist working at the Free City of Bangor

No Affiliation
Stuart Murphy: Ex-Special Forces; human; seeks a cure for his illness
Liam White: Friend and longtime ally of Stuart
Amelia Roberts: Journalist for the *Independent*; reporting on the pilgrimage

The Pilgrims of the Damned

PART ONE

Stuart Murphy woke up in much the same way he had done every morning for the last year, full of misery and anger. Life had not gone the way he'd wanted it to, most of which seemed to be completely out of his control.

He hadn't asked to grow up in a dysfunctional home. He hadn't asked for his wife of ten years to run off with their two children. He hadn't asked for her to file divorce proceedings from across the country as she hid with her parents, citing his increasingly aggressive and cruel tendencies. He hadn't asked for the stage four cancer diagnosis a month later. He hadn't asked for those damn vampire blood pills to stop working a year later. He hadn't asked for the company he worked for to be involved in some kind of attack on Assembly personnel.

The last one he was still confused about. It had been six months since Templar International had lost its Assembly accreditation, meaning the security company was no longer used by the vampires. The business was, in all effect, persona non grata, and a big chunk of their worldwide clients vanished overnight.

Stuart had run the Boston branch and, along with a dozen of his most trusted employees, had started to move their clients over to a new company. One that would be ready to go once he was better. He'd grown tired of waiting, though, and had set a plan in motion to ensure that where modern medicine failed, he would not.

Within five minutes of waking up, he had heard his phone buzz with a notification. He picked it up from the kitchen counter in his almost empty four-bedroom house and read the message. It was from one of his friends, Liam White, someone he'd served with. They'd continued to work together when they left their CIA Special Forces unit, where, before all the bureaucracy had kicked in, they were given the freedom to do what needed to be done. The message read, *Ready to go.*

Stuart smiled. He'd been waiting for this day for two years. Ever since he first heard rumours about it, he knew it was for him. He *knew.* Stuart replied, *It's a go. Meet me at the church. Two hours.*

With a happiness he hadn't known in a long time, Stuart finished off his morning coffee, had a toasted bagel, showered, and dressed in a navy blue three-piece suit, with tan leather shoes. He removed the black velvet pouch from his chest of drawers, tipping the contents onto his hand. It was a silver pendant in the shape of a teardrop with a blood-red jewel set in the middle. He'd been told it was a talisman. An item of great power, and that when the time came, he should wear it always. Now was the time.

The pendant was hung on a thin silver chain, and Stuart slipped it over his neck, placing the cold metal against the skin of his chest.

He looked at himself in the mirror, at the stubble covering his head, sunken eyes, at the loss of weight, the loss of muscle, the cane he had to use. He missed his beard, his long hair; he missed being able to go to the gym, to go to the gun range. Not long now.

Stuart had errands to run in his neighbourhood first. Something he'd needed to do for a long time, and now was the right time. He wasn't coming back to this house. He had wanted to make a life here, it had been his perfect home, but now it was just a reminder of all he'd lost. All that had been taken from him.

He removed two of the vampire blood medicine tablets from the container in his pocket and popped them both in his mouth, swallowing them with a glass of water, immediately feeling the surge of warmth rushing through him. In the beginning, they'd stopped the cancer from growing, and in some lucky people, they actually reversed the effects. In others, the effect of the pills quickly lessened, only slowing the cancer's growth and having even less of an effect over time. But they still made him feel good, sharp, alive. He knew it was short lived, maybe four or five hours at best, but that was all he needed.

The errand only took a few minutes, and he was soon in his black Mercedes GLA, driving into Boston. He parked the car outside of the Church of the Holy Trinity near Boston Common, and sat there looking up at the red brick building, adorned with a golden cross high upon its steeple. Stuart didn't know much about the church, or much about religion in general, but he knew his wife had come here for many years.

Opening his car door, he swung his legs out, grabbing the dark wooden cane as he stepped out into the spring morning in Boston. It was busy out with people going about their day. He wondered idly how many of them knew how far down the food chain they were. Vampires were well-known, of course; they lived and worked alongside humans, and while some humans hated and distrusted them, Stuart was not one of them. He found vampires fascinating, dangerous but fascinating. Vampires had spent a great deal of time and money showing the world that they were no threat to humanity, but Stuart knew otherwise. He'd seen what vampires could really do. But to him, it was just another part of the mystique, something to admire, not be afraid of.

He crossed the street slowly, the metal band on the bottom of his cane clicking on the tarmac as he walked along the sidewalk, and up the ramp to the church door. A young woman who was just leaving held the door open for him, and smiled kindly when he thanked her.

"You have a good day, now," Stuart said, wondering what she would think in a few hours when the news came through.

He stepped into the church and looked up at the sanctuary at the far end of the nave. There was an altar table atop it, upon which sat several candles, and a foot-tall golden cross. A large wooden Jesus on a crucifix was on the wall behind it. Next to it was the pulpit, where Father Noah O'Brien stood and preached sermons to his adoring congregation.

There were several people sitting in the church pews, some praying, heads bowed, and some just sitting there quietly, looking up at the stained glass windows that sat on either side of the nave.

Stuart walked down the nave, ignoring the people, and over to the door on the left-hand side of the room. He pushed the door open, revealing a small kitchen and lounge area. There were windows on one side that overlooked the green garden behind the church, and let in a large amount of light.

"Oh, I'm sorry," the man inside said. He sat on a wooden chair at a glass-and-wood round table, between the kitchen area and the twin sofas in the lounge. He placed the cup of coffee that was close to his lips back onto the table, before smiling disarmingly. "This is a private area."

"I know, Father O'Brien," Stuart said, taking a seat on a chair opposite the priest, his cane resting against the table. "But I feel like this is something we need to discuss."

"We?" Father O'Brien asked with confusion. "I'm pretty sure we've never met."

"We have, actually," Stuart said. "I got married here. To my wife, Alice. Do you remember Alice Murphy, Father O'Brien?"

The priest nodded slowly, still unsure where this conversation was going. "Why are you here, Stuart?" Father O'Brien was a large man. He was the same six-two as Stuart, but he had a significant advantage of body mass. In his youth, Father O'Brien had been a boxer, and a good one, having won several competitions while in the military. He'd maintained those skills over the years in a local gym, although he didn't do more than spar these days. At nearly sixty-five, Father O'Brien looked a good ten years younger, with a full head of short dark hair, and piercing blue eyes.

"Father, I want to tell you a tale," Stuart said.

"You want to confess your sins?" Father O'Brien asked in all seriousness.

"Yes," Stuart said, brightening up. "That's *exactly* what I want to do."

"We should go to the confessional," Father O'Brien said, standing.

Stuart removed the Beretta M9 from the holster against his back and placed it on the table.

Father O'Brien eyed it with no fear. He'd seen guns before; he'd used guns before. He looked from the weapon back to Stuart. "Are you threatening me, Stuart?"

Stuart shook his head. "I just want you to understand my state of mind. I want you to sit down and listen to me speak."

Father O'Brien obviously saw no need to antagonise the man opposite him and sat back down. "So, what do you want to confess to me, my child?"

Stuart nodded and made the sign of the cross. "Bless me, Father, for I have sinned. It's been . . ." He paused as he did the maths in his head. "Thirty-three years since my last confession. Don't worry, I'm not going to confess it all. We'd be here all week, and I have a schedule to keep."

"Then please continue," Father O'Brien said, still keeping an eye on the gun.

"Father, I can't claim to have been a good man," Stuart said. "I joined the Marines, joined the Special Forces, Force Reconnaissance, did some good work. Joined the CIA when I was thirty-five, did ten years, did some dirty work. Left to work for Templar International. And left a lot of bodies in my wake. But that's not why I'm here. I'm here because two years ago my wife took my children from me. Flew them to California to her parents. You want to know what the kicker is? Her daddy works for the FBI, or worked, either way, I can't very well just fly out there and force them home. I considered it at the time. Before I got sick. And then sicker, and sicker, and then better, and then the vampire tablets stopped working, and I got sicker again."

There was a pause for a moment. "I'm sorry," Father O'Brien said eventually. "You have had a terrible time."

"You're right, I have," Stuart continued. "But that's not why I'm here. Well, it is, but we'll get to that. You see, after a year of hoping I was going to get better, of doing all of the right things, of trying to maintain a positive outlook, despite the fact a judge said I wasn't allowed within two hundred feet of my wife and children. You know, I haven't even spoken to them on the phone. They don't want to talk to me. Apparently, I scared them by being *aggressive*. Fucking youth of today have no idea what life really is, Father. Life is aggression, for fuck's sake. Sorry for swearing."

"It's fine," Father O'Brien told him, fully aware that it didn't sound like Stuart was sorry at all.

Stuart smiled, although there was no happiness in it. "Anyway, nearly two years ago, I got a call from a friend of mine. Liam. We grew up together, went to the military together, joined the CIA together. When I got sick, he was the first person to visit me. Told me he knew someone who might be able to help. I asked him if it was a vampire. I mean, turning me into a vampire would cure me, but no vampire worth anything is just going to turn someone they don't know into a vampire. And I didn't want to be saddled with some no-name, no-power pussy for my vampire master, or whatever they're called. I told him I needed someone with actual power, I *deserved* that.

"Well, long story short, he said he'd look into it, but in the meantime, there was another way. A way that not even the vampires know about. *Magic*."

Father O'Brien raised a disbelieving eyebrow. "Magic?"

"That was my initial thought too, at first. I thought Liam was just trying to make me feel better, give me something to *hope* for while this fucking disease destroyed my body. But no, it's not fake. Actually, there's two types of magic."

"And what are they?" Father O'Brien asked, despite himself.

"You don't really need to know all of the details, Father," Stuart said. "All you need to know is all magic has to have a cost. No matter what you do, there needs to be payment for it. Harmony magic, well, that's all a bit wishy-washy, if you ask me. They use their own energy to do something. Harmony witches tend to be gardeners, or healers, or something like that."

"So it kills them by using their own life force?"

"No," Stuart almost snapped; he hadn't intended this to turn into a conversation about the types of witches. "We're getting off track here."

"I understand," Father O'Brien said. "And the second type of magic?"

"Chaos," Stuart said, with a little more glee in his voice. "This is magic where you *take* from things around you to feed into your magic. So you might create a fireball in your hands, but to do so, you take the life force from others—humans, animals, plants, doesn't really matter—and you feed that into your power."

"That sounds dangerous," Father O'Brien said, now more than a little worried about the sanity of the man before him.

"Oh, it is," Stuart said. "You can kill people, or you can leave the ground a barren wasteland. You could make plants wither and die. Obviously, you don't *have* to do that; you could take just a small amount of energy, killing a flower, or a bug, or whatever. The more power you take, the more powerful your magic."

"And how do you perform these spells?" Father O'Brien asked, hoping to stall for time, hoping to figure out how to get Stuart as far away from his church as possible. To use the time to call the police. "Is there a book? A . . ."

"Grimoire," Stuart said, removing a leatherbound book about the size of a paperback from his inside coat pocket and placing it on the table. "This tells us how to use that power. How to shape it, how to create it."

"So you need the book forever?"

Stuart opened the book, showing the blank pages. "No, the witch bonds with the grimoire. The information, the essence of the magic transferring into the witch. It's an unpleasant experience, and a slow one, but eventually . . ." Stuart flicked through the rest of the grimoire, showing that all of the pages were blank.

"You've learned it all?"

"I've had a lot of time on my hands, Father," Stuart said, feeling the weight of the talisman that hung around his neck. He felt the power it contained, power that helped enhance his own gifts. He once wondered if he could have learned all he had without it, but it didn't matter. All that mattered was what he'd achieved, with or without help from the pendant. "Time, and a need to ensure that those who did me wrong aren't allowed to get away with it."

"And who did you wrong?"

"I know what you're thinking," Stuart said. "And I'm not going to go after my wife. I don't want to hurt her, I don't want to hurt my children, or their grandparents. They've moved on, and so have I. You see, I've been waiting for over a year to get the message I got this morning. My friend has been searching, so I'm going to Maine to find the person who can help me."

"Maine?" Father O'Brien asked. "That's a very dangerous place. It's walled for a reason."

Maine had been the scene of one of the worst outbreaks of the desolate in the modern age. The outbreak had spread out to New Brunswick, and thousands had died before the plague of monsters had been brought under control. Unfortunately, by the time the desolate had been stopped, Maine was little more than a pariah state. A walled reminder of what could happen should the monsters that dwelled in the darkness be let loose.

"I know all about what happened there," Stuart said dismissively. "We've got someone who knows the way. I may be gone for some time, so I've been cleaning house, so to speak. Did I tell you about my neighbours?"

Father O'Brien was almost afraid to ask.

"No matter," Stuart said as he started to tap his fingers on the table. "You see, they moved in a few years ago. They're *awful* people. A couple, both in their mid-thirties maybe. The man, let's call him Lloyd, constantly smells of weed. I used to come home from the hospital and sit in my garden hoping for some peace, and all I'd hear was Lloyd loudly talking about the amount of cocaine he had to sell. Or arguing with the lady, let's call her Jill.

"And that doesn't even begin to include the number of times they had music blaring at all hours of the day and night. People had asked him to quiet down, and he'd told them all to fuck off. Told me to fuck off. When I was healthy, I would have fucked that little nobody up, buried him in the woods so no one ever found him. They were both little more than degenerate criminals. A waste of oxygen."

"Unruly neighbours are always a problem," Father O'Brien said, looking down at the gun again.

"Oh, I didn't *shoot* them," Stuart said with a dry chuckle. "That's insane. Do you know how many people in my neighbourhood would have heard that? I'd never have made it to the car before the police showed up."

Father O'Brien allowed himself a smile. "So what did you do?"

"I took Jill's life force and used it to burn Lloyd from the inside out," Stuart said matter-of-factly. "First time I'd ever done that, and I've got to tell you, it was a rush."

"You killed two people?" Father O'Brien asked, shocked at what Stuart had said.

Stuart waved away the accusation as if it were nothing. "Of course. There was just a little screaming from Lloyd, because Jill was out cold already; she was high as a kite. Oh, well. You want to know something funny? If my wife hadn't come here every week, and if she hadn't started talking to someone who works for you, Father, about our lives—if they hadn't told her that maybe she should consider leaving me, which I thought went against the Catholic ethos—then I never would have been alone when Liam brought me the grimoire and talisman that now sits around my neck. I never would have practiced every day until I could barely read the words anymore. I never would have just murdered two people in their own home and smiled as they died. Your church gave me the opportunity to do better."

"You can't possibly think that," Father O'Brien said with horror. "You were an abusive husband and father; your wife fled because of that abuse. We didn't put you on a path to murder people. *You* did that."

"Huh," Stuart said, thinking to himself. "Maybe you're right. Let's go see what your congregation says about it."

Stuart popped two more pills, sighed, grabbed the gun, and was up and out of the door, grabbing the key from the hook beside it, moving quicker than a man in his condition would have usually.

Father O'Brien ran after the younger man, taking the cane with him in case he had to incapacitate the clearly mentally unwell Stuart. A man whose wife and children had been afraid of him, a man who had refused to seek help for his own problems, and had used alcohol and drugs as a way to deal with them.

Stuart stood at the front of the nave, looking out over the four people who were staring back at him with confusion. He'd put the gun back in its holster against his back, his hands held out to the sides, showing the tattoos on the palms. He lowered them and turned to Father O'Brien. "Come join us," he said, waving the Father over. "Now, people of the congregation. I want you all to know that I truly believe that we are in dangerous times."

"Stuart," O'Brien said sternly. "Stop it."

Stuart walked between the pews until he reached the door. He locked the door with the key he'd stolen from the break room. He walked back down the pews until he was halfway and stared at the priest. "Thanks for the talk." The skin on Stuart's hands cracked and started to glow as several of the congregation who were closest to him tried to climb over the pews in an effort to get to the door. Stuart waved a hand at them, balling the hand into a fist, and they screamed out in pain, falling back onto the pews.

Several of the congregation started to cough and wheeze, their bodies pulled apart, the energy flowing through to Stuart.

"Stop it!" Father O'Brien shouted. He ran at Stuart, the cane raised high, but Stuart caught it with one hand, slamming his other into the priest's chest, sending him reeling, and leaving a burned handprint on the cassock.

"You should have minded your own business," Stuart said as he went back to funnelling the life energy he'd stolen directly into the priest, setting him on fire from the inside out.

The priest fell to his knees, and a look of comprehension filled his face for a moment before his entire body shimmered with the heat and light inside of him. After what had only been a few seconds, his body burst into flames. Stuart spun around as fire leapt from his hands, setting everything aflame.

When done, the nave and all that surrounded it was an inferno. "Say hi to your boss," Stuart said, picking up his walking stick and slowly moving to the exit. He unlocked the door, tossing the key back into the flames, and walked down the steps, across the road, and to a waiting parked black BMW M3. Stuart opened the door and got into the passenger seat, feeling his energy draining out of him. Magic took a lot of stamina to perform, and he hadn't all that much to begin with.

"You ready?" Liam asked in his South Carolina accent, with a beaming smile. "The team is all at the border."

Stuart looked over at the church as the windows began to shatter from the heat. There was no saving the building. "Let's get this done, then."

CHAPTER TWO

For years, Miles had wondered how long it would be before he got to spend quality time at his own house. He'd purchased the house and surrounding land the century before, expecting it to be a place he visited often. Unfortunately, his work for the Assembly at the time meant his ability to actually come home had dwindled more and more as he moved around the globe sorting out vampire issues that appeared never ending.

Until four months ago, since the events with Templar International, when he'd told the Assembly that he needed a break. Time away from them, from his job, from *people*. The last year or so had been far busier than he'd liked: having to put down an internal uprising led by the corrupt First Captain of House Umbra, Vedran Vinko. Vedran had died hard for his crimes, but that had been just the start of the madness. Next up had been finding and stopping a group intent on murdering several Assembly employees, himself included, barely surviving a massacre at a holiday resort, and tracking down illegal vampires, serial killers, and even rampaging desolate. Then dealing out punishment to all those who'd caused death and destruction. It was not exactly restful.

Miles wasn't particularly concerned that he'd killed—he was a vampire, an arbiter, and killing rogue murderous vampires was part of the job description. But he'd killed *a lot* of people, and seen those he'd liked and cared for cut down. He needed time to himself.

Lying in a hammock in the large, well-maintained garden of his Highland home, he finally felt he was starting to relax. The five-bedroom home was north of the town of Dingwall, a few minutes outside of a small village known as Evanton, about half an hour drive north of Inverness.

The red brick house was nestled in a wooded area, with the rest of the land just beyond. It was near Alness Bay, which itself was next to the shores of Cromarty Firth, an inlet close to the North Sea. Miles had spent many a day sitting on the shore as the night rolled in, watching the occasional harbour porpoise or Eurasian otter as they played in the deeper waters.

Miles looked up at the stars and closed his eyes. He wasn't tired, he'd barely been up for five hours, but he liked to listen to the bats and owls as they hunted. Church's bark made him open his eyes and look over at her.

"Aye?" he asked as Church placed her head on the hammock and licked his hand. "Were you out in the fields again?" Miles asked, looking down at Church.

The large dog made a slight whining noise and tried to look as innocent as possible. Other dogs reacted to Church with fear or aggression, but wolves and foxes weren't fazed by her. There were several fox dens in the area, and Church had set about making friends, spending the nights running through the woods and fields with them.

"You know that those fields don't belong to me, right?" Miles said. He was grateful that his nearest neighbour, who did own the fields, was fine with Church and her friends using them as some sort of off-road racetrack. Despite the fact that she wasn't exactly a "normal" dog.

Church looked like a Doberman pinscher, although she was considerably larger. Her mother had been experimented on by her owner in an effort to extend her life. It hadn't worked, but as one of the two pups she'd given birth to who survived the experience, Church had been imbued with vampiric blood. She wasn't a vampire, she didn't drink blood or have any aversion to UV light, but she was considerably larger and stronger than any usual Doberman. She was also frighteningly intelligent and easily capable of understanding anything Miles said.

Above all, though, Church was Miles's constant companion. His best friend and confidant. Miles had killed those who had tried to hurt her in the past and would do so again. Going for him was fine, it was part of the lifestyle he'd chosen, but going after his dog was not something Miles would tolerate. As several people—vampire and human—had discovered to their cost.

Church barked again.

"You smell something?" Miles asked, sitting up and looking out across the woodland. Like all of his senses, his night vision was excellent, better than most humans during the day, but it paled in comparison to Church's sense of smell and hearing. If Church could smell someone, then there was someone to smell.

Miles swung his legs out over the side of the hammock as the sound of a car engine could be heard in the distance.

The car was coming closer, and Miles quickly climbed up the exterior of his three-storey home, to the slanted tiled roof. He looked out across the landscape, but there were far too many trees in the way to get a good look at the approaching motorcade. Four cars, all moving in concert, all with their lights on.

"Ah, do you think they're friends or foe?" Miles said.

Church barked once in reply. *Yes.*

"Thanks, lass, very helpful," Miles said, dropping off the roof and landing softly on the patio at the side of his property. "Now *that* is weird."

In the distance, flying over the hills to the west of his home, was a helicopter.

"Coincidence?" Miles wondered aloud.

Church barked twice.

Miles looked down at the dog and stroked the back of her neck. His phone vibrated with a message. Miles picked up the device, and saw the name *Charlotte,* followed by the message: *We're in the helicopter.*

Did you nae think to call? Miles replied.

I told you I was going to come see you.

A time would have been good, Miles said. *Or a date.*

I'll explain, Charlotte said.

I was only expecting a car. You with them?

Miles watched the little *replying . . .* indicator on his messaging app. *Sort of.*

"I guess we're about to have guests one way or another. I'll go put the kettle on."

Taking the door at the side of the property, Miles stepped into his kitchen, filled the kettle, and switched it on. He removed a mug, putting in a tea bag and single cube of brown sugar. By the time the kettle had boiled, the helicopter was almost overhead. He poured the hot water into the mug, gave it a stir, and left it alone as he walked back outside in time to see the four-car motorcade pull up on his driveway, just as the helicopter flew overhead.

All four cars were identical in colour, make, and model—black Volvo EX90s—and Miles waited as the doors to the first and last cars opened, whereupon four guards in black suits stepped out into the cool night air. They stood by the middle two cars, opening the doors from the outside and stepping back to allow the passengers space to get out.

"Miles," Mordecai Balderas, an Assembly Justice, said, walking the short distance to shake Miles's hand.

The middle-aged man had dark skin, a bald head, and a short beard. He wore a plum suit with black shirt and black shoes, polished to a mirror shine. Justice Balderas carried a walking cane made from a dark mahogany, with a jade dragon's head atop it.

"It's good to see you," Miles said with a surprised smile. He quite liked the older vampire, although exactly *how old* Justice Balderas was, Miles couldn't say. "I wasn't expecting any of you."

The Justice looked back at the cars and saw that the helicopter had landed in a nearby field.

"Ah, yes," the Justice said. "That's sort of why I arranged to come see you."

"Oh, new friends?" Miles asked. "Well, you know how I just *love* company."

The Justice gave him a wry look as two more men got out of the third of the four SUVs. The first was tall—more than Miles's own five-ten—with a bald head and piercing gaze. He wore a well-fitting light grey suit, a midnight blue shirt, and no tie. He had a full black beard which he rubbed with one muscular hand as if in thought. Several golden rings adorned his fingers, and he wore a bronze bracelet that hung from his wrist. He looked over at Justice Balderas and Miles and smiled, walking over and waving away the guards who tried to follow him.

The second man was five-five and wore a black suit that was probably a size too small for his muscular frame. His arms bulged from the effort of being contained inside the jacket, and Miles wondered why anyone would want to look as if they were being inflated beyond their packaging instructions. He had long blond hair that fell over his broad shoulders, and he constantly adjusted his jacket sleeve, presumably to show off the Rolex on his wrist.

"Guten morgen," the first man said, offering Miles his hand.

Miles looked over at the Justice, who gave the barest nod, and Miles shook the hand of a man he'd only ever known by reputation. "First Lord William Fuller," Miles said. "A pleasure to meet you."

"The pleasure is mine," First Lord Fuller said. "House Idolator is honoured to meet you in your home. Thank you for having us."

"Sure," Miles said. "Why are you here?"

First Lord Fuller looked over at Justice Balderas and back to the other man, before looking back at Miles. "No one told you?"

Miles shook his head. "I'm making tea, though, if you'd like a cup?"

"Do you have coffee?" the German asked.

"I do," Miles said. "You might have to wait for it to brew, though."

"Ah, that will be fine," First Lord Fuller said with a renewed smile.

Miles looked beyond the First Lord to his companion, just as Charlotte and First Lord Drest walked onto the driveway, accompanied by three guards—two men and a woman—all wearing burgundy suits. All First members of a House had their own Blood Guard, although Charlotte had been trying to get out of it for as long as Miles had known her. She'd finally relented after the mess from a few months previously.

"Ah, we're all here," Justice Balderas said.

"Yay," Miles said, looking beyond everyone he knew to someone he'd never met before. "Sorry, but who are you?"

Everyone turned to the second man who had arrived with First Lord Fuller. "First Authority Thomas Reed," he said, his voice placing him from one of the southern states, although Miles couldn't have said more than that.

"American?" Miles asked.

"From Georgia," he said with a nod of his head.

"Would you like a tea or coffee?"

"Coffee," the man said and received a glare from First Lord Fuller. "Please."

"Are these your Blood Guards?" Miles asked First Lord Fuller.

"They are," he confirmed. "They will be staying out here. I assume that is also the case with yours, Charlotte."

Charlotte, who had now made it to the front door with Drest, nodded. "Oui," she said with a French accent.

"You didn't bring any, Drest?" First Lord Fuller asked.

Drest shook his head. "No room in the helicopter. Besides, I think we're all about as safe as anyone can possibly be. How are you, Miles?"

"Very confused," Miles said. "I'm going to make my tea now."

Miles left the driveway and didn't look back at those following him as he walked through his home to the kitchen, where he poured the now stewed cup of tea away and re-boiled the kettle, fetching five more mugs from the cupboard. He set about putting tea bags and sugar in mugs as required, and started on the coffee. Everyone else sat at the birch circular table, taking up five of the six available chairs.

"And I never thought I'd need so many chairs," Miles said.

"You have a lovely home," Justice Balderas said. "It's very out of the way."

Miles laughed as Church entered the room, drawing a wide-eyed expression from Thomas Reed. "I was told you had a dog, but I did not expect her to be so imposing."

Church licked Miles's hand and walked around the table, getting her needed attention from everyone she knew, before stopping at First Lord Fuller.

"Magnificent," he said, getting a lick on the face for his compliment, which made him laugh. It was a deep, throaty noise, full of genuine joy.

Church barked and moved on to Thomas, who gingerly patted her once on the head. Church looked back over at Miles with an expression of contempt, and walked out of the room.

When all of the drinks were made, Miles found a selection box of Scottish shortbread and placed it between his guests. He took a chocolate chip one for himself and dunked it in his tea before taking a bite.

"I should have brought lebkuchen," First Lord Fuller said, taking a bite of shortbread. "I could have left you with a gift for having us."

Miles got up and opened a nearby cupboard, removing a bag of the German gingerbread, and put them on the table to the obvious joy of the First Lord.

"A man of refined taste," First Lord Fuller said, taking one of the small gingerbreads and popping it whole into his mouth. "Delicious."

"No offence, but you didn't all come here to talk to me about sweet treats," Miles said. "I assume there's a point to this meeting beyond an appreciation of Scottish and German baked goods."

First Lord Fuller, his mouth full of more of said baked goods, motioned to anyone else to start.

"Miles," Justice Balderas said, "we know that you're taking time away from your role as an Arbiter. We all understand that."

"But?" Miles asked.

"But we need your help," First Lord Fuller said after swallowing his mouthful of shortbread.

"Okay, which one of you needs my help?" Miles asked.

"Both of us," Drest said, motioning to himself and First Lord Fuller.

"Oh," Miles said.

"I'm here, along with Thomas," Charlotte said. "As seconds to our First Lords. Just to ensure that there are witnesses to this meeting."

"And you?" Miles asked Justice Balderas.

"I'm here for the shortbread and tea," he said with a grin. "Also, First Lord Fuller asked me who would be best for him to talk to regarding this matter, and I suggested you."

"Thanks," Miles said, with a hint of sarcasm. "Appreciate it."

Justice Balderas and Drest both tried to hide their smirks, and did a terrible job of it.

"Is that how you talk about a First Lord?" Thomas asked with shock. "With so little respect that your name was put forward?"

"I could talk to him how I speak to Drest, if you'd like," Miles told him with a smirk.

"I don't think that would help things along," Drest said quickly as Charlotte stifled a laugh.

"Okay, just tell me," Miles said.

"It will take some explaining," First Lord Fuller said.

"And yours?" Miles asked Drest.

"Oh, that's *definitely* going to take explaining," Drest said. "But as they're both in the same place and involve the same thing, I'll let First Lord Fuller go first."

Miles knocked back his tea, got to his feet, opened a cupboard, and withdrew a glass tumbler and bottle of fifteen-year-old Dalmore whisky. He poured himself a large measure and drank it back in one swallow. He poured a second, similar-sized measure, removed four glasses from the cupboard, and took the glasses and bottle back over to the table, placing the latter in the centre.

"What do you know about the pilgrimage?" First Lord Fuller asked.

Miles barely stopped himself from knocking back his second whisky and pouring a third. He looked over at Drest, who had already poured himself his first whisky, and sighed. "Which one?"

"Maine," First Lord Fuller said. "You start at Portsmouth, New Hampshire, and you walk through to Kittery, Maine. From there, you pass through the Walls of Maine, to Brunswick, and then up to

Bangor, where you pay your respects to the first great towns to have been destroyed."

Kittery was the start of the Walls of Maine. It was a town that had once been a part of the state of Maine and was now one of several neutral cities—those along the border of New Hampshire or Canada that were now mostly full of military personnel. Kittery was one of only a handful of towns that was left untouched during the trouble that happened there back in the 1980s. Trouble that was still a sore spot for a lot of people, both human and vampire. The Walls of Maine started from close to Seaport Beach, and went straight up to South Berwick, before continuing north, skirting the border of New Hampshire, before reaching Canada and going east, doing the same thing. The Wall itself wasn't always a physical thing, with large parts of it being patrolled by guards—both human and vampire—but there was no way to get into what remained of Maine without someone noticing. In theory, anyway.

"If I remember correctly," Miles said. "Some of your more . . . senior members continue on to Blue Hill, the epicentre of what happened back then. The latter is a symbolic journey for the most part, although you do make sure to kill as many desolate as you find on the way. That sum it up?"

First Lord Fuller nodded. "Although you have missed out several of the more religious aspects of the pilgrimage. And also, why we do it?"

"It's a rite of passage for House Idolator members," Miles said. "And you also spend time in the various villages that still exist, providing help to those who need it. The whole trek to Blue Hill to carve your name on one of the wooden posts in the village there isn't my cup of tea, but the rest of it does actually help people, so I get it."

"You think that's all we do in Blue Hill?" Thomas asked, a little too tersely for Miles's liking.

"Oh, that's right, you talk to the First Priest of House Idolator," Miles said, deciding to ignore the tone of the First Authority. "A position that isn't in any other House, and was created after what happened. Let me see if I've got this right—it's mostly symbolic in regard to actual power within the House. A new priest is selected every few pilgrimages. They're expected to stay there and help, to commune with those who came before, so to speak. Those who do it usually come back and take up an advisory role within the House. I think you're on your fourth priest, but I could be wrong about that."

"Fifth," First Lord Fuller corrected. "Otherwise, that's spot on. Although the current First Priest, Pedro de Moxica, was actually in Maine for decades before the fall. Left a few months before it happened, thankfully. He has waited a long time for his chance to return and do good there."

"Fortunate timing on his part," Miles said.

"Sometimes fortune favours us. Since the fall, we do the pilgrimage every few years but only change the priest when necessary. This will be our twenty-eighth time performing the pilgrimage since the Maine incident happened in 1984. Our first pilgrimage was sent in 1986, when the incident had only just been dealt with. When the walls surrounding the state of Maine and parts of New Brunswick were still being built. We go there to help those who could not leave, or refused to. You know that there are several flourishing towns still within the area of Maine, as it currently stands. Thousands of people—mostly vampires—still live there. Most who remained behind refused to leave. They either want to put things right, or they consider it their home and won't have the Assembly or US government tell them otherwise. They are self-sustaining, but they still need aid, people to come in and help as needed. That is why we do what we do."

After the desolate outbreak in Maine, and subsequent fall of the state, the US government had been advised by humans within it to nuke the whole place and call it a day. Thankfully that hadn't happened—in part because the humans in charge had realised that nuking your own country-men during an election year is a terrible idea, but also because a deal had been struck between the humans and the Assembly. The vampires stayed in Maine, it was walled off—New Brunswick, too—and it was up to those who remained to keep the place safe. Over forty years later, the area still wasn't what Miles would have called *safe*, and the human politicians usually ignored its existence, but it wasn't a radioactive wasteland, so most people considered it a stalemate, if not a win. And sometimes, you take what you can get and make it work.

"And what does any of that have to do with me?" Miles asked, already dreading the answer.

"Allow me to show you," First Lord Fuller said, motioning for Thomas, who removed his phone and sent a message.

A few seconds later, the front door of Miles's house opened, and a voice called out, "Hello?"

"In here," First Lord Fuller called out.

Miles listened to the footsteps as the newcomer walked through the house to the kitchen, until she stepped into the room itself. She was a little under five and a half feet tall, with shoulder-length light brown hair that was tied back in a ponytail. She had pale skin and a tattoo of a snake around the forearm of her right arm. Her left arm had several tattoos from various pop culture icons, and Miles noticed both the Wonder Woman and Batman logos among their number. There were several piercings in each ear, and as she stood in the mouth of the kitchen in her jeans and black hoodie, with a pale brown leather satchel over one shoulder, she gave the impression of someone who wanted to be elsewhere.

"Whisky?" Miles asked, raising the bottle.

"Oh God, yes," she said, walking over to the table, where Miles poured a measure into one of the still unused glasses.

"Miles Watson," he said, offering his hand as she picked up the glass and took a drink.

"Amelia Roberts," she said, her accent placing her from somewhere in Yorkshire.

"Amelia here is from York," First Lord Fuller said. "Although she lives in Liverpool."

Amelia nodded and sipped more of her whisky as Drest stood and motioned for her to take a seat.

Liverpool was a vampire-controlled city and had been for centuries. A lot of large port towns the world over had vampire control, at least in part.

"Thank you," Amelia said.

"And why are you here, Amelia?" Miles asked. "You're human, which I definitely wasn't expecting, so I'm genuinely interested."

"Are you the Arbiter?" Amelia asked.

Miles nodded.

She offered her hand for Miles to shake. "I'm a reporter for the *Independent.*"

﹠ CHAPTER THREE ﹠

Miles ignored Amelia's hand. Instead, he frowned. "Whatever this is, the answer is no."

Amelia retracted her hand.

"Miles," Drest said warningly. "It's important."

"A human reporter usually means something bad," Miles pointed out. "No offence meant."

"A little offence taken," Amelia said with a shrug. "I don't know what you've dealt with in the past, but I'm not here to cause trouble, or do some stupid hit piece on vampires. There are enough idiots doing those already."

The amount of venom she placed in that last sentence made Miles believe that she was telling the truth. At least inasmuch as her not liking the hacks whose job it was to do little more than stir up old fears and give those who already hate something to shake their fists at with impotent rage.

"Okay," Miles said, raising his hands in surrender. "Let's start again. Apologies. You're a journalist, you're here to do a story on vampires. I assume you want me to take you to Maine."

"I want to do a story showing that vampires and humans still live together, in harmony, inside Maine," Amelia explained. "I went to Lord Drest to pitch the story and ask for help in gaining entry to Maine, in a safe way that doesn't interfere with the people living there. It's not a huge surprise that a lot of vampires distrust human journalists. Sadly, they have a long and storied history of writing nonsense to make people afraid. Unfortunately, fear sells. He suggested I talk to the Assembly, and Justice Balderas put me in contact with Lord Fuller.

"First Lord Fuller was very helpful and suggested we go along with one of the pilgrimages, which is due to take place in a few days. Lord Drest, who was present at the meeting, put forward the idea of sending a body-guard in with me. Someone who could protect the pilgrimage and knows how to survive in a hostile environment."

"Me," Miles said.

"Yes," Amelia said.

"Okay, I have questions," Miles said, looking over at Drest. "One, why me? There are hundreds of vampires who could do this."

"I trust you," Drest answered. "Justice Balderas trusts you, and we know that no matter what happens, you will do all you can to keep Amelia safe."

"Okay," Miles said, certain there was more to it, but wanting to move the conversation on. He looked back to Amelia. "How'd you get in contact with Drest?"

"I know someone who works within House Venator," Amelia said. "He's a friend of mine, and he kindly told me he could help."

Miles looked over at Drest for confirmation.

"True," Drest said. "Her friend has been a member of Halime's group for several years now. Good guy, good soldier, and trustworthy. Besides, I'm always looking for positive vampire PR, and Amelia had a good story. It's not like you're currently doing anything."

"So this isn't Assembly official?" Miles asked Justice Balderas.

"Nope." He shook his head. "If I asked you to go in on official business, we'd have to involve a handler, and honestly, the fewer people in the Assembly who know everything, the better. Doing it that way might alert others in the Assembly who might have opinions on sending an Arbiter to Maine, and right now that wouldn't be helpful."

"I didn't realise that Maine was such a hotbed of issues at the moment," Miles said.

The Justice sighed. "The Magistrate are making it one."

The Magistrate were a group in the US who were *officially* meant to investigate vampire-on-human crimes, and work alongside the Assembly to ensure that everyone was safe. *Unofficially*, they wanted to hunt and exterminate vampires out of a combination of hate and fear. The Magistrate were backed by billionaires and politicians, and like all hate groups, preyed on the stupid, the gullible, the angry, and the easily afraid to bolster their numbers.

"How?" Miles asked.

"They're lobbying to have Magistrate forces sent into Maine to carry out . . . *inspections*," Drest said grimly. "They suggest that vampire numbers linked to the Assembly are increasing in Maine, and that they're building an army of our kind. It was decided to keep Assembly numbers to a minimum."

"Are you?" Miles asked. It wasn't out of the realm of possibility.

"No," Justice Balderas said. "But for now, the Assembly has agreed to step back from Maine while this is all dealt with. The likelihood is nothing will happen. The Magistrate are just shouting the loudest in an effort to stir up trouble, but after what happened in Seattle—which was no fault of your own—we are erring on the side of caution."

The Seattle Magistrate branch had been shown up for what they really were, and the subsequent investigation had proved them to be a well-funded law unto themselves, who were quite happy to kill vampires should they get the chance. And weren't averse to murdering humans if it meant using those murders to further their own bigotry.

Public perception of the Magistrate had shifted after that, and more pro-vampire groups had started to gain traction in the Congress and Senate, exposing those corrupt members who accepted *donations* from the billionaire founders of the group.

Membership in the Magistrate had plummeted since, but those who remained were ardent supporters, extremists who wouldn't listen to the possibility that they were in the wrong. It made a lot of remaining members dangerous, but they were small in number so overall, the vampire community took the win. There was a long way to go, but it felt as though the US was turning a corner in human-vampire relations.

Miles stared at the Justice for a moment before he said, "Right, so what else is going on? Am I being asked to go because there's Magistrate shittery afoot? No offence, but House Idolator could keep an eye on Amelia."

Everyone else at the table had the good grace to look uncomfortable.

First Lord Fuller got to his feet. "I asked them to tell you about the pilgrimage first," he said.

"I told you we should have just laid the cards out on the table," Drest said to First Lord Fuller.

"Yes, well, officially, I'm not meant to be involved in this bit," First Lord Fuller explained. "So, I thought I'd just stay here for the pilgrimage part. The rest of it is something you all need to discuss."

"What are you getting out of it?" Miles asked him. "You didn't agree to be a cover story for no reason. None of this is ever getting out to the wider public, so I may as well know now."

"House Idolator gets to put forward a proposal at the next meeting of the Houses," First Lord Fuller said. "A new settlement in Maine. North of Brunswick. Using Assembly and House personnel. Currently we have to keep to the coast, go from Kittery to Portland, to Brunswick, Rockland, and up to Bangor. It's a long, but ultimately a relatively safe, route which we have done many times. We want to clear out Augusta and Waterville and make an alternative, and much faster, route to Bangor."

"Waterville isn't there anymore," Miles said. "It was firebombed because there wasn't a single living soul in the city by the time the desolate turned up. There's nothing left but several hundred craters, and the remains of buildings that are still full of any desolate that managed to survive. Augusta isn't much better, it was just never firebombed. Mostly because by the time they flew to Waterville, the military discovered that electronics don't work in Maine when at low altitude, and they lost several aircraft as they tried to fly home."

"I never said it would be easy," First Lord Fuller said. "But it can be done."

"The start of reclaiming the state of Maine," Miles said. "I did wonder how long it would be."

"The state has a lot of work that needs to be done," First Lord Fuller explained. "When were you last in Maine?"

Miles thought back. "Mid-nineties."

"Things have changed in the time since you last went," First Lord Fuller said. "Like I said, there's a lot of work still to do."

"That proposal is already passed, I assume," Miles said, wondering just how bad the state had gotten in the more than three decades since he'd last been there.

"No vote has taken place yet," Thomas Reed said. "But the backing of House Venator would almost certainly mean it would pass through to the Assembly."

Miles nodded that he understood.

"We will wait outside," First Lord Fuller said.

When Lord Fuller and Thomas had left Miles's home, Drest said, "How much have you been paying attention to the American news over the last month?"

"Nae much," Miles said. "I mean, a little, but nothing too intensive."

"You heard about Stuart Murphy?" Charlotte asked.

Miles tried to remember if he knew the name. "Is he from the Magistrate?"

"Possibly," Amelia said. "We're not entirely sure, although we do know that he's ex-military, ex-CIA, worked for a group called Templar International."

Miles couldn't have kept the shock from his face if he'd tried. "Seriously?"

"The American branch," Charlotte said. "They split from the European part of the company shortly after their Assembly accreditation was removed. I've been informed that you know about that."

"A little," Miles said, not wanting to get into the fact that the Assembly accreditation—given to companies who can offer something to the vampire world—was removed because it turned out they were involved in some pretty shady stuff. Shady stuff that got them and a lot of other people killed. "Can I assume that Stuart was also involved in some pretty . . . morally ambiguous things?"

"Before Templar, he worked in a black ops CIA-run six-person unit that did protection detail," Drest said. "But he just happened to be in countries that had uprisings put down, or assassinations of people who may or may not have been about to testify before a government. The coincidences are, frankly, staggering."

"And you're investigating him?" Miles asked Amelia. "That's the real reason you want to go to Maine? That's probably more dangerous than going to Maine for a bit of a walk."

"Stuart Murphy was an abusive husband and father, and two years ago, after his family fled from that abuse, he was diagnosed with stage four prostate cancer. He was placed on vampire blood medication, which appeared to slow down the disease, although not stop it. What no one knew was that he was looking for a vampire to turn him the whole time."

"Illegally?" Miles asked. "I assume anyway."

"No one would," Amelia said. "I interviewed several people at a vampire club in Boston, and they all said that he'd tried to pay them a lot of money to do it. Kept coming back for about six months, and then he just stopped."

"So far, so karmic retribution for being an arsehole," Miles said.

"Then, two weeks ago, he murdered his neighbours, a priest, and everyone in the church at the time. Seven people in all. He used magic to kill them."

Miles felt his mouth drop open. "Witches are meant to be extinct. Have been for close to a century now."

Amelia picked up her satchel from the floor beside her, opened it, and removed a black velvet bag that contained an old and well-read book. She passed the bag over to Miles, who read the gold-leaf lettering on the front: *Grimoire.*

"Bollocks," he whispered.

"We are not extinct, Mister Watson," Amelia said staring at him.

Miles looked up from the grimoire at Amelia. "*We?*"

"I am a witch."

Miles looked over to Drest and the Justice. "You knew witches weren't extinct?"

They both nodded.

Miles looked back at the grimoire. "Of course you did. Who did this belong to?"

"A friend of mine," Amelia said. "Her name was Heather Croft."

"You speak about her in the past tense?"

"She left her job one night, got into her SUV, and was never seen alive again," Amelia said. "They found her body hanging from a tree branch three days later. She'd been drowned first. That was eleven days ago."

"I'm sorry for the loss of your friend," Miles said. "I assume you think Stuart Murphy is her killer?"

"I do," Amelia said.

"Why?"

"What do you know about witches, Mister Watson?"

"Miles is fine," he said. "There are two types," Miles said, trying to remember everything he knew. It had been a long time since he'd met a witch, and even longer since he'd needed to consider one of them a threat. "Harmony witches are just people who use their magic to better others and the world around them. Chaos witches are the opposite. I assume Stuart falls into the latter category."

"You would assume correctly," Amelia said. "You can open the grimoire, it won't explode."

"Did you steal this from a crime scene?" Miles asked, opening the velvet bag and gingerly removing the book.

"It was in Heather's will that it be given to me," Amelia said. "It was in her safe. I put it in the bag to keep it . . . well, safe."

Miles studied the grimoire on his kitchen table. It was mostly words and hand gestures, about how to tap into a magical power. Should you be able to.

"The pages become blank when a witch learns the magic," Amelia said. "And they refill upon the death of the witch."

Miles flicked through to the end of the grimoire, where there were pages a slightly different colour from the rest. "The pages make themselves?"

"No, a witch will add new pages when they take possession of the grimoire," Amelia said.

"So these writings here, this is everything Heather learned during her life?"

Amelia nodded.

"Why would Stuart want your friend dead?"

"Witches police our own," Amelia said. "When covens—yes, we do actually have covens—get wind of a chaos witch, or any witch willing to hurt others, we find and stop them. Heather had no coven. I guess, I mean, except me, maybe."

There was a slight stumble in Amelia's voice that made Miles look up. There was no point in asking if she was okay; it was pretty obvious that she wasn't.

"What did she do for a living?" Miles asked.

"She was an artist," Amelia said. "A good one. She wanted to work in comic books."

"How did she find out about Stuart?"

"Fourteen months ago, a witch was murdered," Amelia said. "They were attacked in their home, at night. Two bullets to the head, one to the heart. Officially, nothing was taken. Just a senseless attack, but the witch was a friend of Heather's. Heather took it upon herself to look into it, discovered the grimoire was missing. Started looking into it and was led to Stuart Murphy. Actually, first she found an employee of Templar International, who she thinks did the robbery and murder on the orders of someone else, possibly Stuart. We're not sure."

"What happened to the employee?" Miles asked.

"He accidentally shot himself in the head while cleaning his gun," Amelia said.

"Seriously?" Miles asked.

"It's officially an accident," Amelia said.

Miles rolled his eyes. "What makes you think that Stuart has this grimoire?"

"The victims he murdered were all cooked from the inside out," Amelia said. "I have a friend in the police, let me go to the crime scenes. The amount of magical energy still there made me feel dizzy. He killed his neighbours, a priest, and several members of the congregation. The police have him listed as a *person of interest*, although with Stuart having fled to Maine, no human cop is going to go rushing off to track him down."

"Okay, so Stuart is a witch," Miles said. "A murderous witch. A murderous witch with stage four cancer. I think time is just going to finish the job for us at this rate."

"I don't think we can wait around for him to die," Amelia said. "He's already killed people. And there's a possibility that his magic is, at the very least, slowing the advancement of the cancer."

"Valid point. Do we know for certain that he killed your friend?"

"I don't know," Amelia admitted. "What I do know is that Stuart has ties to some seriously dangerous people. That he fled to Maine with a man by the name of Liam White. There's CCTV footage of them in a car together after Stuart torched the church."

"And Liam White is?" Miles asked.

"Ex-CIA. Current Templar International," Amelia said. "I got a friend of mine to call up a contact in the CIA, and when Liam's name was mentioned my friend was told never to say that name again."

"Oh, that can't possibly be good news," Miles said.

"What we could find out is that he has ties to several Magistrate members."

Miles considered pouring another drink. "So, Liam and Stuart fled to Maine, but with Liam's ties to the Magistrate, it's likely that Liam has a plan. Otherwise, he's just aiding a known murderer. You're going into Maine to track down Liam and Stuart, and then what? Photograph them, write a piece about them? What's the plan here?"

Amelia's gaze hardened. "I want to find the people who murdered Heather. I want them to see justice."

Miles looked up at that. "Justice or vengeance?"

"Justice," Amelia said with conviction. "Stuart Murphy was last seen going into Maine with several others, two weeks ago. They were allowed in by a guard friend at the northern tip of where it meets New Hampshire, the guard was arrested a few days after Heather was found."

"When was she killed?"

"She was taken the same day that Stuart and his friend fled into Maine," Amelia said.

"How do they know it was this guard who did it?"

"One of the other guards ratted him out. He set up hidden cameras and had been filming Stuart's guard friend for several weeks. After Heather's murder, all of the footage was sent to one of the guard stations in New Hampshire, who had Stuart's guard friend arrested. They got him taking bribes and found footage of him allowing the driver of Heather's SUV through the checkpoint. No clue who the driver is, unfortunately. The SUV was found near Heather's body, burned out. The guard has ties to the Magistrate, and he's not talking."

"Why kill Heather?" Miles asked, wondering how long it would take to get the guard to crack. "She's not really a threat to a bunch of people who used to do what Liam and Stuart did."

"I don't know," Amelia said. "I think she found something out, but I haven't been able to discover what it is. Heather deserves justice, Miles. And from a witch's point of view, they murdered one of our own."

"Stuart's wife and children?" Miles asked. "They safe?"

"In California," Amelia said. "They're all safe."

"Why aren't more witches in the area looking into Stuart?" Miles asked. "I assume there are more. I mean, I've just learned you're not actually extinct, so I have no idea of your numbers."

"There are several thousand witches across North America," Amelia said. "Most are gardeners and doctors, people whose use of magic is barely noticeable. To answer your question, Heather's murder has freaked them all out. Witches who have had combat experience aren't exactly in abundance."

"Okay, I have a few questions."

"Sure," Amelia said, putting the book back in her satchel.

"How do you know where Stuart and his people are? I mean specifically?"

"I think they're headed toward Brunswick," Amelia said.

"Why Brunswick?"

"The CIA friend of a friend," Amelia said. "Said that Brunswick is the epicentre for Magistrate activity in Maine. With Liam's links to people in the organisation, I think he's gone there to hide out. The pilgrimage goes close to it; I figure I can head inside and ask around."

"And I'm there so you don't get killed in the process, but then what?" Miles asked. "You never gave me a full answer earlier, so what's the whole plan? You going to be putting their faces all over the papers?"

"Not entirely," Amelia said. "Stuart has a stolen grimoire; it needs to be found and recovered. It wasn't his, wasn't passed down through blood, so his link to it is still breakable. Losing it will not end well for him."

"You're going to kill him?"

"I'm going to retrieve what isn't his," Amelia said. "And that might kill him."

"You ever killed someone before?"

"No," Amelia said, never taking her eyes off Miles.

"Or maybe he meets an unfortunate end?" Miles suggested.

"I won't let someone else find that grimoire," Amelia said.

Miles looked from Drest and the Justice back over to Amelia. "So, officially, your plan is to outwardly write a nice piece about the pilgrimage and all it does to help the humans and vampires, while at the same time, you're only there to retrieve this grimoire from a psychopath? You're not planning on writing an exposé about Stuart, Liam, or their connections to the Magistrate. That about sum it up?"

Amelia nodded. "There won't be a story about Stuart. Although if we do find evidence of the Magistrate's unlawful behaviour, we can pass it on to those who need it. Otherwise, I'd rather the world never knew Stuart existed, never mind what he's capable of doing."

"I thought you wanted justice for your friend," Miles said.

"I do," Amelia said. "But I also need to ensure that Stuart does nothing to hurt anyone else. That means getting the grimoire back. If that means that justice for my friend is unofficial, then so be it. The witches will know; that will have to be enough."

"Do we know *why* Stuart is headed to Maine?" Miles asked. "I get that he's dying, but he and his friends have burned their old lives to go to a place that is best described as hostile to anyone who doesn't know their way around. What's he hoping to achieve?"

"I don't know," Amelia admitted again.

"We get to Maine, we go to Bangor with the pilgrimage," Miles said. "We do nae go straight to Brunswick. We need intel, nae a battle with a witch and a bunch of murderers, and whatever we might find between Bangor and Brunswick. It's bad enough that House Idolator wants to go to

Blue Hill, but they're vampires, even young ones, and can at least nae die easily. You are, and I mean this without disrespect, squishy by comparison."

"You'll do it?" Amelia asked, more than a little hope in her voice.

"Aye," Miles said. "I'll take you on your trip, I'll play bodyguard. Can I assume no one else on this pilgrimage knows about it?"

"It's between those of us here tonight," Drest said. "No one else."

"You got any combat experience?" Miles asked Amelia.

"I once headbutted a man who wouldn't take no for an answer," she said, letting the silence hang in the air before she continued. "I did some self-defence classes, got my brown belt in Muay Thai."

"But any actual fighting experience?" Miles asked. "Apart from the headbutting, which is a nice touch, by the way. Any experience in a combat zone? Of being attacked by people who are trained? Any weapons training?"

"I've done some gun range stuff in America, but that's about it," Amelia said.

"Right, you wear a bulletproof jacket at all times," Miles said. "I don't care if you're awake or not, you wear it. You will carry a weapon, nae a gun, I don't want you to shoot at shadows, and guns are going to be useless against desolate or vampires. But a volt baton and heat dagger will do the job. I have both. You are nae to walk away from me, or Church. One of us will be with you at all times. And if we're nae there, there will be an appropriate person with you who is trained to keep people safe."

Amelia looked to Drest and Charlotte, who both pointed at Miles as if to say *it's his rules*. "Okay," she said after looking back at Miles.

"If I find out that you're bullshitting me on any part of this, the agreement is off," Miles said. "You can't begin to understand how much you do nae want to be left alone in the middle of some of the parts of Maine. You won't be making it out of there except in something's belly."

"Yes, sir," Amelia said.

"Miles is fine," he corrected. "Keeping you alive, and relatively scathe-free, is now my job. So you're going to make it easy on both of us, by letting me do that job. If it all goes to shit, and I'm incapable of getting you to safety, you stay with Church."

On cue, Church entered the kitchen. Amelia's eyes grew wide as the dog went over to say hello.

"Church, Amelia," Miles said. "You're her new protector."

Church stared at Amelia and barked.

"That is a very large dog," Amelia said slowly, as if speaking at a normal speed might startle Church somehow.

"She's also smarter than most people," Miles said. "She understands English perfectly. One bark yes, two no. She barks at you, move. She tries to drag you away somewhere, you go. She can literally crush a man's skull in her jaws. Trust me when I say that if she wants you to move, do it. Or get a broken arm. At best."

"Hi, Church," Amelia said.

The large dog circled around the table, sat in front of Amelia, and gave her one paw, which Amelia shook. Church stood, licked Amelia's hand, and rested her head on the reporter's lap for Amelia to stroke.

"She likes you, that'll help," Miles said.

"That is very good," Amelia said, stroking Church, whose tail was moving fast enough to threaten liftoff.

"Right, you two," Miles said, looking over at Drest and Justice Balderas. "What is it you want that you're sending me to help a witch?"

"If the Magistrate are taking control of Brunswick, it puts us in a difficult and potentially dangerous position," Justice Balderas said. "We need to know more. We need to know what they're playing at. Frankly, it sounds like whatever is going on, Stuart and Liam are involved somewhere, but we don't know exactly what their involvement is. They wouldn't have burned their lives for nothing."

"We need to find these people," Drest said. "Witches are one thing, but magical murderers who also have alliances to a hate group could cause a lot of trouble for a lot of innocent people."

Miles nodded. "I agree, let's nae make a bad situation worse. So, what's the chance of Stuart going to Maine to look for a cure? Anyone know what happens to a witch if they do get turned into a vampire? Seeing how Stuart seemed keen on being turned into one nae too long ago."

"Nothing," Justice Balderas said. "You can't be both. You're one or the other."

"Weird that someone with Magistrate ties is helping someone else who wanted to be turned into a vampire," Miles said.

"The Magistrate have always been selective in their hatred when it comes to our kind," Charlotte said, speaking for the first time in several minutes. "They want our power, our longevity; they just hate that we won't give it to them. If Stuart has gone there for a cure, it won't be from a vampire. If he's gone there to go out in a blaze of glory, a lot of people are going to get hurt."

"And you're sending me on this little mission because you want to know what he's doing, what the Magistrate are up to, and if necessary, to stop them before they hurt more people. That about sum it up?"

Everyone nodded.

"I'm off to hunt down an exceptionally powerful witch with nothing to lose," Miles said with a sigh. "So that a second witch, Amelia, can steal the grimoire that he stole first, before more people, quite possibly, die. This trip is sounding like less and less fun."

Chapter Four

With all the details of Miles's new position as bodyguard sorted out, Miles drank the remainder of his whisky and, along with everyone else, left via the front door.

First Lord William Fuller stood outside of the car he'd arrived in. The Blood Guards who had accompanied him and Thomas Reed were close enough to do their jobs, but far enough away not to be seen as interfering. Charlotte's own three Blood Guard members were off to the side, closest to the entrance to the drive. A respectful distance from the House Idolator personnel, but close enough to Miles's house, so that they could get inside quickly should they need to.

"So is this agreed?" First Lord Fuller asked.

Miles nodded and offered the man his hand, which the First Lord shook.

"When and where do I need to be?"

"Kittery, Maine," First Lord said. "One week from today. The pilgrimage will have already left Portsmouth, New Hampshire, but it's a safe passage from Portsmouth to Kittery, so you'll join them there. I will inform those going that they are to have additional security."

"How many?"

"Sixteen," the First Lord said. "Twelve of our members, and four guards. All four guards are members of House Idolator's Authority. Hence Thomas being here."

The role of First Authority was to be in charge of the administration of the House. They were usually people who were smart, capable, and like all Firsts completely loyal to their House above all. However, despite them being vampires of considerable age, those who took the job of First Authority weren't known for their martial prowess or level of power.

Miles looked over at Thomas. "How good are your people? Honestly."

First Authority Reed bristled a little at anything he considered to be slur on his team, even if Miles hadn't meant it so. "They are handpicked by me," he said eventually. "All four have been vampires for at least a century. All of them have prior military training. They are good at their jobs."

"I'm sure," Miles said. "But I had to ask. And the twelve?"

"All turned within the last twenty years," Reed said. "We require new vampires to wait some time before being allowed to take the pilgrimage. Sending newborn vampires to Maine would not be wise."

"Sensible," Miles admitted. "How many of them have military training?"

"A few are ex-military," Reed said. "None of this matters to you, Mister Watson. You are there to guard the human."

"While that's true," Miles said, noticing the disdain Thomas had used on the word *human*, "I'm also travelling with *your* people. If there is trouble, I assume I'm expected to help, nae just stand back and wait for it to blow over. I'd like to know how many of the pilgrims can be counted on to help out with any situations that might arise."

"Two," First Lord Fuller said. "One male, one female. The male was an Army Ranger, the woman was a combat medic. The former American, the latter British. You'll have to ask the others yourself. They are not our tales to tell."

"Fair enough," Miles said. "One week, I'll see your people in America. I'll get them to Bangor. You never said anything about getting them out."

"That won't be necessary," First Lord Fuller said. "The pilgrims will be staying there for some time, as it is part of their trial. Thank you for agreeing to do this. I feel like Amelia's report on our people in Maine could go a long way to soothe concerns about the region."

Miles hoped the First Lord was right, although he knew it would take a lot more than a nice new article to make people comfortable. Although, if the end goal was to reopen Maine, he assumed clearing out two large cities and reestablishing them would signal the start of it.

"I'm going back with First Lord Fuller," Justice Balderas said, slapping Miles on the shoulder. "I'll send you up anything you need. While this isn't sanctioned by the Houses or Assembly, and this isn't *official* Assembly business, you're still an Arbiter. Should you need to throw your weight around a little, you won't get any pushback from the Assembly. I'll make sure of it."

"Good job I'm on holiday," Miles said. "Gives me time to stretch my legs and visit the world. And honestly, I've never been able to resist the opportunity to help out my fellow vampires. It all works out quite well."

"Oh, and Rosa sends her best," Justice Balderas said. "She wishes she could go with you, but a handler travelling with someone who isn't meant to be on official business might be seen as . . . well, official business."

"I get it," Miles said. "I'll need flights. First class, because you're paying, and Church will need her own seat. We'll need somewhere to get weapons in America, because while I *could* supply Amelia with what she's going to need, I'd rather nae have to explain why I'm nae on official business, but have armed the human who is with me."

"We'll arrange everything when we start the pilgrimage," Reed said from behind him.

Miles turned toward him and nodded. "Okay." He turned back to Justice Balderas, who had an envelope in his hand. Miles plucked the envelope from the Justice's fingers, opened it, and discovered three first-class tickets to fly from Heathrow to Boston on one of the vampire modified planes used by British Airways.

"We knew you'd agree," Justice Balderas said smugly.

"Tomorrow night?" Miles queried. "I guess that means we need to get to London. Why so early?"

"I'll explain," Amelia said. "I promise."

"Where are you staying?" Miles asked her.

"We are going to be flying from Inverness to London in about two hours," Drest said. "You have hotel rooms booked near Heathrow, and a car waiting to drive you from the hotel to the airport tomorrow afternoon. Seven PM UK time."

"And how do I get from here to Inverness?" Miles asked.

Drest checked his watch. "A car will be here in about an hour."

"Everything planned out in advance," Miles huffed, feeling a little annoyed that the natural assumption would be him agreeing to help.

A short time after, Justice Balderas and the House Idolator people were gone, leaving Miles, Drest, Amelia, Charlotte, and Charlotte's three Blood Guard out on the front driveway.

"I should be really offended," Miles told them, waving the tickets at everyone. "You all knew I'd say yes."

"We did," Charlotte admitted.

"Time is of the essence," Drest said.

"Why?" Miles asked. "Why do we need to fly out in eighteen hours?"

"We're going to see the crime scene," Amelia said. "Scenes, hopefully. I want you to see if you can find something I didn't."

"Where are we going first?" Miles asked.

"We're going to talk to the guard who let Stuart and his buddies into Maine," Amelia said. "And we're going to Stuart's home, I've arranged for a Boston Detective to meet us there to answer any questions. He wasn't thrilled about it, but he also wants this case solved, and can't do that while his main suspect is hiding in a place no one will go."

"Do you need to go get stuff for the trip?" Miles asked. "A bag, clothes, phone charger, whatever?"

"Everything I need is on a private jet in Inverness," Amelia said.

Miles turned to Drest. "That you, too?"

Drest's smile confirmed everything.

"Okay, anything else I should know before I go pack for me and Church?" Miles asked.

"I have a friend in Bangor," Drest responded. "Used to work for the Assembly, was in Maine about two months after it all went to shit. Name is Joseph Davies, he's a doctor in the city. Actually, he's the lead doctor. Smart man, and a good man, too. When you get there, go speak to him; he knows the area well. He's also an expert on magical energy, maybe one of the best I've ever met. If this Stuart has gone anywhere near there, he'll have an idea where it could be."

"Will do," Miles said. "I'll have a witch with me, though, can't she help track Stuart?"

Drest shook his head. "I've had Joseph keep an eye on magical energy in the state for a few years now. Just in case anything else happened there. He's spent a lot of time looking into any places in Maine with a high amount of magical energy. He's a bit . . . obsessive about things. If anyone will have an idea where a powerful witch will have gone in Maine, it's him."

"How does he track magical energy if everyone thought witches were . . ." Miles trailed off. "You told him they weren't extinct."

"Actually, he figured it out on his own." Drest shrugged. "He can track magical energy. That's his secondary ability. He always considered it to be fairly useless, but he sensed a build-up of it in Maine in the eighties, and then it all went to shit."

Miles frowned. "Are you telling me there's a possibility that magic was involved in the fall?"

Drest nodded.

"How bad is Maine now?"

"There are still plenty of desolate," Drest said. "While their numbers have gone up in the last year or so, they're not much more than a nuisance. Oddly, despite how many are killed, their numbers never seem to go down, and honestly no one knows how or why. They've killed thousands of them over the years, but it feels like they're respawning or something."

"That would be bad for everyone," Miles said.

"I've heard tales of monsters," Charlotte said. "Out to the east of the state. Not sure how accurate they are, but after we found that gigantic desolate back in the Templar International building, I'm willing to bet a few desolate might have cocooned themselves, and been left that way for a long time."

"Nae ideal, but we'll figure it out," Miles said. "We get to Bangor first, we ask around. Actually, first, we go do some crime scene investigating, like Amelia wanted. You know, I was just beginning to learn how to relax? I hope you all realise that. I was going to learn to play the flute."

"Then we've saved the world from that horror," Charlotte said.

"Just for that, I might learn something louder," Miles said. "Nae enough bagpipe players in the world for my liking."

Charlotte laughed.

Miles packed light, both for him and Church, making sure that he only really needed a carry-on bag for the whole trip. Anything else he needed, he'd buy in America, and seeing how all Church needed was a few bags of her favourite treats, and a squeaky toy in the shape of a turtle, it didn't take Miles long to get everything ready.

Before he left, he checked the weather forecast for the area he was travelling to. He'd expected it to be warm considering the time of year, but apparently it was going to do little more than rain and be windy once in Maine. Although, considering the forecast only covered ten days, he hoped it might be somewhat less soggy by the time they got there.

"You ready?" Drest asked Miles and Church, the latter of whom barked with a lot more enthusiasm than Miles felt.

Miles was about to reply when a black Audi Q7 pulled onto the driveway. The car stopped beside everyone, the driver's door opened, and a dark-haired human woman of about fifty got out.

"Diane," Miles said, remembering Drest's driver from the last time he'd had to go from Inverness airport to the House Venator estate a few years ago.

"Pleasure to see you again, sir," Diane said, smiling. "Sorry, Miles."

Miles and Amelia put the bags in the boot of the car, before Miles walked around the house, making sure he'd left nothing on, or open. He locked up and placed a hand against the wooden front door, letting out a small sigh.

"You'll be back soon," Drest said.

"I never get to spend much time here," Miles told him, turning around to see Amelia climb into the rear seats of the car, with Church practically bounding in after her.

"This is important," Drest told him.

"We never would have come here if it was anything else," Charlotte said. "I'm sorry we've sort of ruined your holiday."

"I always knew something would," Miles said. "Probably better it's you than someone I dislike."

"Ah, at least you still like us," Charlotte said, pushing Miles on the arm.

"Things can change," Miles said, which made Charlotte laugh.

Miles hugged both Charlotte and Drest, saying his goodbyes, before seeing there was little room in the rear of the Audi, so getting into the front passenger seat instead.

"You ready to go?" Diane asked.

Miles was about to answer when he felt an unease grow inside his gut. He didn't know what it was, or where it had originated from, but there was something about the whole situation that bothered him.

He was going to hunt down dangerous people, in a dangerous place, while trying to keep a group alive. That should be enough to give him goose bumps up the back of his neck, but it was something else. Something deep inside made him feel . . . concern. It was an abstract feeling, with nothing to pinpoint it toward, except Maine as a whole. He'd been back since it had fallen, and hadn't enjoyed the experience, but the revelation that witches weren't actually extinct put a new spin on what might have otherwise been a straightforward assignment. Magic could be unpredictable, and downright dangerous. Maybe that was it.

"You ready?" Diane asked again, gaining Miles's attention as his mind continued to wander.

Miles pulled on his seatbelt; just because he was a vampire didn't mean he wanted to go headfirst through the windscreen should there be an accident. When secure, Miles told Diane he was ready. He leaned back in the comfortable leather seat, using the controls on the side to move the seat back, and looked out of the window at the darkness around him. He wondered if the fear was an overreaction to having to go back to Maine for the first time in decades, or something more sinister.

❧ CHAPTER FIVE ❧

Miles, Church, and Amelia landed at Heathrow, where a second car waited for them. It drove the trio to a nearby hotel where, despite the fact that dawn was an hour away, Miles decided it was best to get some sleep. They had over twelve hours before their flight to Boston Logan International Airport, and Miles wanted rest, food, and a shower before he set foot on that airplane.

He was asleep on the hotel room's king-sized bed seconds after having showered and changed. As usual, Church slept lightly on the floor next to the bed, awake the moment anyone came to the door. As far as alarm systems went, Church was second to none.

Miles opened his eyes, feeling rested, and looked over at the red numbers on the clock next to the bed, the only light in the otherwise pitch-black room. Two PM, which meant they had time to get something to eat before they were taken back to Heathrow and left at the vampire boarding area to await their flight. Sunset wasn't going to be until after the plane had taken off and, according to his phone, the UV index for after four PM was a zero, so he wasn't concerned about going outside even before nightfall.

Teaching humans that vampires weren't scared of the sun, and that sunshine didn't kill them, was something that was still ignored for Hollywood films or books. The UV index, heat, or decapitation killed vampires. Although to be fair, decapitation killed pretty much everything. Vampires didn't like being in temperatures of anything over about eighty Fahrenheit—about twenty-six Celsius. Anything over a hundred Fahrenheit would kill a vampire just as surely as a UV level of over three would for most vampires. Miles had once seen a vampire walk out into bright midday sun, rather than be handed over to the Inquisitors. The UV levels had been up near seven. The vampire had survived for about twenty seconds. Miles occasionally recalled the look of horror on their face before they were turned to ash.

Miles left the thick curtains closed and switched on the bedside reading light, sitting up in bed as Church jumped up beside him, lying down to get her morning ear rub. "Sleep well?" he asked her.

Church let out a contented growl.

After picking up his phone, he scrolled through to Amelia's contact information. They'd exchanged numbers before going their separate ways.

Miles dialled her number, which she answered immediately. "Ah, you're up," he said.

"I think we may have different sleep patterns," Amelia said.

"Humans and the nighttime sleeping," Miles said. "I vaguely remember having done it."

"Do vampires get jet lag?"

Miles chuckled. "Sort of, but once we've had a feed and sleep, we're usually pretty good to go. It's why a lot of us sleep on the flight. And why we usually only fly if we can be in darkness when we get to our destination. Should be about ten PM when we reach Boston, so we're all good on that front."

"I want to show you Stuart's house," Amelia said. "The police have already taken all of the evidence they found, but I think you should see it anyway. We're going to meet my Detective contact there."

"When we land?" Miles asked.

"A few hours later," Amelia said. "I wanted to give you and Church time to acclimatise yourselves to a new city."

Miles put the call on speaker and got off the bed, stretching as he stood. The fact that all of this had been arranged well in advance of anyone coming to Miles's home should have annoyed him, but he found the idea of having an actual plan ahead of time to be something of a rarity in his life.

"I've been to Boston before," he said. "Many times over the years. There's a large vampire population there. New York, Delaware, Virginia, North and South Carolina all have big vampire populations. Goes back across the northern states to Michigan and Minnesota too."

"I heard there was a large exodus of vampires from America after Maine," Amelia said.

"Officially?" Miles asked.

"We're not on the record, we're just talking."

"In that case, yes probably," Miles said. "I can't tell you the figures, but a lot went north to Canada. By a lot, we're talking a few thousand. There might be half a million vampires all across the United States, but probably three times that in Canada. Maybe more, I don't keep track of who does what. You'd have to ask a Justice, or someone from the Assembly Administration."

"That's a lot different from the Magistrate numbers," Amelia said. "They think it's closer to ten million vampires."

Miles laughed. "I heard thirty-five million once. I don't even think there's anything close to thirty-five million vampires on the planet. If I'm honest, I'd say ten million was probably every vampire who lives right now. Like I said, I don't know the exact figures."

"Ten million is a lot," Amelia said.

"The vast majority of vampires who are turned die within the first century. They are either illegal and are hunted down for doing something awful, or they cross the wrong person at the wrong time. Eight billion people live on this planet. Ten million of them being vampires is just over zero-point-one percent."

"And now you can add witches to the number of nonhumans," Amelia said. "Again."

Miles pulled on a T-shirt and pair of jeans. "I'm happy to know I was wrong about your kind being extinct. How many witches are there?"

"Officially?" Amelia asked.

Miles smiled. "I'm nae on the record either."

"No idea. Maybe a million, and of those, maybe a hundred thousand know what they're doing and use magic on a regular basis. From that, maybe ten thousand are someone to keep an eye on."

"Witches managed to keep a million magic users from the Assembly and human governments," Miles said. "Impressive."

"Like I said, only a fraction of those know what they are, and a fraction of those have any real power," Amelia said.

"So, do you have covens and the like?"

"We do," Amelia said. "The coven keeps its area clear of problem witches."

"What if the coven itself is the problem?"

"Then a neighbouring coven deals with it," Amelia explained. "There are nomadic witches who do any dirty work that needs doing. Removing problem witches, or making sure the authorities find evidence of any human crimes they've been involved in. It's worked that way for centuries."

"Do you have any contact with other species?"

"Other species?" Amelia asked. "You mean like werewolves?"

"You know of werewolves?" Miles asked.

"Met a few," Amelia said. "None were exactly fun experiences."

Werewolves tended to keep to themselves, and for the most part weren't really a big problem for vampire or human populations. The werewolves usually knew what they were, and they either took steps to ensure that their wolf side wasn't allowed free rein, or they did something stupid and got killed by werewolves who would rather their species not be front page news.

"You know any?" Amelia continued.

"Werewolves?" Miles asked. "I've met a few. They've always been pretty chilled out. They don't hunt the moors at night looking for lost Americans to bite. Werewolves in their beast form don't hunt humans, just like wolves don't. There's easier prey. Although I wouldn't want one hunting me through the dead of night."

"I tried to do a story about one a few years back, but couldn't find her," Amelia said.

"You know, we could just have this conversation face-to-face," Miles said. "It's a little odd chatting while I'm trying to get dressed."

"Sorry, brain ran away with me," Amelia said. "Anyway, I'm having food in the restaurant, if you care to join me. The glass here is specially designed to stop UV light."

"I'll be down shortly," Miles said, ending the call. He finished getting dressed, packed up his things, and left the room with Church beside him, taking the stairs instead of waiting for the lift.

The stairwell opened into the large foyer and reception area, which Miles and Church walked through to the restaurant, where they were greeted by a pleasant young man who seemed completely at ease with both vampires and large dogs.

Miles was shown where Amelia was and walked over, taking the seat opposite her. Amelia put down her pen on top of her notebook as a waiter arrived. Miles asked for a pot of coffee, some oat milk, and a bacon sandwich.

"No blood pouch?" Amelia asked, after the waiter walked away. She wore a forest-green hoodie which wasn't zipped up, revealing the plain white T-shirt beneath.

"I'll get one at the airport," Miles said. "They have different vintages there."

"Is it ever weird ordering blood?"

"No," Miles said, nodding a thank-you to the waiter who brought over his drink and explained that the sandwich would be a few minutes.

"You were just used to it from the very beginning?"

"We didn't have blood pouches back when I was turned," Miles said. "You went out and found someone to drink from. It was a more dangerous time to be a vampire for a host of reasons."

"Is the oat milk because you can't eat dairy?" Amelia asked. "Sorry, I don't mean to pry, I just don't know many vampires, so I'm getting all the questions in."

"I don't like milk," Miles said, then corrected himself. "Actually, that's nae true, I don't mind milk, but I prefer not to drink it. For centuries, I'd just suck it up and use milk, or drink tea and coffee black. But now, humans have come out with dairy alternatives. It's been a bit of a revolution for my coffee drinking."

"You settled on oat?"

"Is this really the conversation you want to have with a vampire?" Miles asked with a grin, as he poured the milk into the coffee, put in a tablespoon of brown sugar, and started stirring.

"No," Amelia said. "I just don't know you. At all. I've heard a lot about you from Drest and Charlotte, but I'm trying to get a read on the kind of person you are."

"And you think that the type of milk I drink might give you that read?" Miles asked, laughing, as his bacon sandwich arrived along with a selection of sauces. Miles selected the brown sauce and opened the sachet. He removed one slice of bread, selecting a piece of bacon and tossing it to Church, who caught it before it touched the ground, after which he poured brown sauce onto the rest of the bacon before taking a bite. "Is the brown sauce a strange thing, too?"

"No, that's the only sauce that should ever go on bacon," Amelia said firmly. "Ketchup is disgusting. It's like eating tomato sugar."

"On that, we agree," Miles responded, enjoying his food. "So, what do you want to ask me? Preferably not about food or drink."

"How bad was Maine?" Amelia said. "Honestly."

"Oh, it was bad." Miles sighed, wiping his mouth with a napkin. "Humans and vampires spending decades experimenting on the desolate, keeping hundreds of them for testing. And then they got free, and tens of thousands of desolate were created in a few hours. More than a hundred thousand people—human and vampire—were either displaced or killed. I've been to war. I've seen people die. A lot of people. Some horribly. Some peacefully. No one who died in Maine did so peacefully. If the desolate caught you, you were either turned into a desolate, or you were food. No middle ground. No one was injured and survived. Thousands of people died in the first day. Tens of thousands in the first week. Vampires and humans couldn't handle the exploding number of desolate.

"I went in about a month after it happened. I was helping to rout out and exterminate the more stubborn desolate populations who had gone north and were being held back by the humans and vampires who had come down from Canada, trying to stop the spread. By this time, New Brunswick was in danger of falling totally, and it felt like we were fighting a losing battle. Thankfully, we managed to stop the horde of desolate and contain them farther south, but not before we lost Maine in its entirety, as well as a portion of New Brunswick."

"You haven't been back since the nineties, yes?" Amelia asked.

Miles nodded and finished his cup of coffee, before pouring a second, making sure to get the last dregs out of the coffee pot.

"What do you think of House Idolator's plans to reestablish Maine?"

"Is this an interview?" Miles asked, pointing to the open notebook.

Amelia closed the notebook. "Sorry. Look, I just want to know what you think about it all. To me, it seems sensible to have a permanently open road from Bangor to Portsmouth."

"While I agree in principle, I've heard about Augusta," Miles said. "It was overrun with desolate during the breakout. They were mostly destroyed, although there are still some hiding in long abandoned buildings, or trapped underground. At some point, it was declared free of desolate and an expedition—a combination of vampires and humans—was sent to look around. Found no desolate, so a second expedition was sent to see if it was possible to repopulate the area. Only two people of a ten-strong team came back, both humans, both babbling incoherently about giants and desolate.

"After that Augusta was kept an eye on, but no one was sent there. Out of sight, out of mind. There's the occasional desolate, from what I hear, but mostly it's a ghost town that creeps everyone out who goes there."

"No more people screaming about giants?" Amelia asked.

"Can I assume you'd like to go there?"

"I'm not sure that *like* is the right word," Amelia said. "And hopefully it won't be necessary."

"So we go with the pilgrimage to Bangor, and then we try to figure out where Stuart and his friends have gone, so you can go reclaim a stolen grimoire," Miles said. "I don't think he's going to give it up willingly. You going to kill him for it?"

"I hope not," Amelia said, although her tone suggested she would do whatever it took.

Miles finished off his bacon sandwich.

"Stuart went there for a reason," Amelia said. "He's dying, and from all I've heard, desperate for a cure. At this point, the magic might be the only thing keeping him alive. If there's someone in Maine capable of curing his cancer, they're not going to do it for free. The kinds of people who would have use for someone who burns a priest and his congregation to death are probably people the witch and vampire world should know about."

"I can't disagree with that," Miles said, unsure if Amelia was withholding something from him. "Tell me about Heather."

"We met in college," Amelia said sadly. "She studied at St Andrews near Edinburgh, just like I did. We've been friends ever since. Nearly eighteen years now. I went to her wedding when she was twenty-two and married the completely wrong person, I went to her divorce party two years later. She was my friend, Miles. And some fucking asshole took that light from my world."

"And she thought that Stuart ordered the theft and murder?" Miles said.

"Yes," Amelia said.

Miles nodded. "I mean, we don't know for certain that the grimoire that Stuart has is the same one stolen from the murdered witch. And we can't ask the killer because he's conveniently dead. I guess we get more answers when we find Stuart."

Amelia got to her feet. "I'm going to get all of my stuff together and we'll get the car to the airport. I know vampires don't have to check in as early as we do, but it would help to make sure we were ready."

Miles nodded. "I'll meet you in the foyer in, what, ten minutes?"

"Sounds good," Amelia said, leaving the restaurant.

Miles paid his bill, thanked the staff, and left with Church beside him. He opened his phone, went to *Kentucky* on the contacts page, and dialled the number.

"Miles Watson, as I live and do not breathe anymore," the male voice said, his voice full of warmth.

"Samuel Austin," Miles said. "You still causing trouble everywhere you go?"

Samuel Austin was a friend of Miles's from back when the latter worked for House Venator, and the former for House Phalanx. Samuel had gotten into some hot water with his First Lord and had been sent to be a liaison with the humans in America. He'd started work for the FBI not long after and had been a big help in bridging cooperation between the human and vampire worlds.

"For a hundred and fifty years," he said. "Now, as lovely as this conversation is, I'd like to know why an Assembly Arbiter is calling me on this fine morning."

"You still up?" Miles asked.

"Miles," Samuel said, a little more *get on with it*, in his Kentucky accent.

Miles smiled, enjoying speaking to his old friend. "You know anything about a Stuart Murphy?"

"Should I?" Samuel asked.

"He's ex-CIA," Miles said. "Friends with a man by the name of Liam White."

"Oh, that son of a bitch," Samuel said. "Him, I know. Why?"

"They've killed some people and fled into Maine."

"Good, let the desolate eat them," Samuel said.

"Stuart used chaos magic to kill a bunch of people," Miles explained.

"Witches?" Samuel asked in a tone that suggested it had better not be.

"I thought they were extinct," Miles said. "Apparently, I was wrong. Did you know they were still around?"

"Not concrete," Samuel said. "I've heard rumours over the years, but they thankfully keep to themselves. What did this one do? And how does it involve you?"

"I'm flying into Boston with a reporter. They killed her friend, Sam. Maybe nae personally, but it sounds like they have reach. Sounds like they're up to no good, too."

"Goddamn it, Miles," Samuel said. "Can't I never just have a little peace and quiet on my vacation?"

"You on vacation?" Miles asked. "Where'd you go?"

"New York," Samuel said. "Got tickets for the theatre. You know how long you have to wait before you can see some of these shows? You want me to come up, say hi? Maybe do a little digging on your Stuart friend in the meantime?"

"You still have contacts in the CIA?" Miles asked.

"I still have people who owe me a favour," Samuel said. "That's pretty much the same thing. If you played nicer with them humans over there, you might have contacts, too."

"Aye, but why bother when I have someone with as sparkling a personality as you do to help?"

Samuel's laugh was deep and full of genuine warmth. "Damn you, Miles, you're going to get me in trouble. Message me when you land with an address. I'll see what I can do. Oh, and Miles, Liam is a bad guy. He did some seriously dark stuff that there are no official records of, if you get my meaning."

"I do," Miles said. "Thanks, Sam."

"Be safe, my friend," Samuel said, ending the call.

Miles pocketed his phone as Amelia walked over to him. "You ready?" she asked.

Miles nodded. "Let's go fly to Boston."

❧ Chapter Six ❧

The flight was uneventful, which gave Miles time to read up on what Amelia had found on Stuart Murphy and Liam White. She'd written several notes about Stuart, each of them a scathing indictment of the man, and gave multiple sources and detailed information on his activities as someone for whom violence was second nature. It was a well-written, well-researched piece, and it poured a lot of fuel on a man who didn't seem that bothered about seeing things on fire.

Her information on Liam White was less detailed but included a few photographs and some information about the time he beat a man half to death in a drug-fuelled need for vengeance over the matter of twenty dollars. None of it was on record, with several mentions by Amelia about how people refused to talk to her about him if there was a chance it would come back on them.

The flight was a pleasant experience, as was getting through the vampire side of passport control, and out to the black BMW i7 that was waiting for them in the nearby underground parking area. The keys had been waiting for them at the manned guard area, along with a note from Charlotte that told Miles the car was to be returned in the same condition it was found in.

"Well, now, this is going to get totalled," Miles said, rolling his eyes, as he opened the door behind the driver's side and let Church in, who immediately made herself at home on the burgundy leather seats.

"Because she wrote not to?" Amelia asked.

"I don't make the rules," Miles said, closing the door behind Church and opening the driver's side. He paused. "You want to drive?"

Amelia was already halfway into the car when Miles spoke, and she climbed back out, looking over the roof. "I heard you like to drive."

"I do." Miles nodded. "I trust my driving more than anyone else's, but I've also been told I have control issues, and you know where we're going better than I do."

"I'll put the address in the satnav," Amelia said. "You drive, I'll point out when you're doing it wrong."

"Teamwork," Miles said with a smile and got into the car, adjusting the seating and mirrors until he was comfortable.

"They never show that bit in movies," Amelia said. "People just jump in and go."

"Probably nae the most exciting way to build tension," Miles pointed out, satisfied that he could now see out of the wing mirrors. He pressed the starter button, letting the car come soundlessly to life.

"I would have assumed vampires would have a hard time adjusting to new things," Amelia said.

Miles drove the car out of the underground parking lot, following the satnav. It was only a thirty-minute drive to the destination that Amelia had put in, but considering the power of the car, he figured he could do it quicker.

"Vampires have to adapt," Miles said as he took the electric car onto I-93 and gave it a little more power, smiling as the car sped through the night.

A few minutes later, they were off the interstate and driving through a dense wooded area. They came out the other end, and Miles followed the instructions on the computer for a few more miles until he pulled up outside of a house opposite a large pond.

"Whipple Hill," Amelia said, pointing to the pond area. "It's a big conservation area. That's Heather's house."

"We're staying at your friend's home?" Miles asked, switching off the car.

"She left it to me," Amelia said, and was silent for several seconds before she opened the door and stepped out into the still, cool night air.

"She left you a house?" Miles asked as he and Church followed Amelia up the drive to the forest-green painted building.

"She didn't have family," Amelia explained, removing a set of keys from her bag and opening the door. "I was like a sister to her."

Amelia quickly moved into the building as something inside started to beep rhythmically.

Miles stepped into the darkness of the building and stroked Church's head as she pushed up against his leg. The small area just beyond the front door was big enough to put coats and shoes and a set of keys on a rack, and that was about it. In front of him were two sets of stairs, one on the left leading down, and one on the right leading up. Miles chose to stay where he was until called.

The beeping stopped and the lights in the tiny hallway came on. Amelia stood at the top of the right-hand staircase. "Alarm," she said, which explained the beeping. "Down there is a bathroom, office, and exit to the side of the house. Come on up."

Miles let Church go first, and he followed into a long living area that stretched the length of the house, ending with a large window that, even from where Miles stood, he could see led to the decking at the rear of the property, and presumably the back garden. There was a patio styled sliding door next to the window. Between him and the door was a sofa large enough to fit a dozen people, opposite a TV that probably should have been in a cinema screen.

"Heather had a passion for old movies," Amelia said sadly.

Miles stepped into the room and looked to the side, where a floor-to-ceiling set of cabinets sat, full of old movies on several different mediums. "That's quite the passion," he said, wondering if once this was all over he might have time to watch a few of them. He stepped back out as Amelia continued the tour. "Front room," she said, pointing to a small room which had two comfortable chairs, and an entire wall which consisted of books on shelves.

"Second bathroom through there," Amelia continued. "Bedrooms are upstairs. There's a bedroom downstairs in the basement, next to the bathroom, it only has one window and blackout curtains. I thought you might like to use it."

"Sounds good," Miles said, placing his bag on the floor beside him and looking around. "You okay?"

Amelia gave him a thumbs-up. "Why are you wearing your torc?"

Miles looked down at the bronze bracelet on his wrist that identified him as an Arbiter for the Assembly. He chuckled. "Force of habit. I guess I won't be needing it this time around, nae being official and the like, but I figured for now I'll leave it on. I don't have to tell people it's nae official if they decide that it *looks* official. You avoided my question."

"I am not okay," Amelia said, shaking her head. "Not even a little bit. This was my friend's house. And someone murdered her, and now I'm here. Owning her house and trying to find her killer, to take back what he or his friends stole from another witch they also murdered. So, yeah, I'm dealing with some shit. And I don't really know what I'm meant to do with a house I don't live in, in a country I don't want to move to. It's a lot."

Church went up to Amelia and licked her hand.

Amelia looked down, smiled, and quickly looked away, wiping at her eyes. "Damn it."

"You want some time?" Miles asked.

"No," Amelia said, turning back to him. "We need to get to Stuart Murphy's house in a few hours. I'm going to make coffee and have a shower. You're welcome to use the bathroom downstairs."

"Do you have the address we're going to?" Miles asked. "I wanted to ask a friend to look into something."

"Sure, I'll send it to you," Amelia said.

"Thank you," Miles said.

"Can you let Church out into the back garden?" he asked.

"My pleasure," Amelia said, motioning for Church to follow her through the long living room.

Miles picked up his bag and took it down to the basement, office, bedroom, bathroom area. He removed his phone as Amelia's text came through, which he forwarded to Samuel with the message, *two hours.*

Miles's phone vibrated a few seconds later with a message: *Already in Boston. See you there.*

He put his phone down on the nearby table and walked through the office to the adjacent bedroom, which had a pull-out sofa bed, already made up with fresh sheets, pillows, and a blanket on top. Blackout curtains were also in place. Amelia had prepared, or had someone come in and do it for her. Miles wondered how long in advance Drest had let her know that he would become involved. Miles moved the curtain slightly to see that the window on the wall was high up and was small enough that it wasn't going to be a huge problem with the curtains closed.

There was an AC control on the wall just outside of the bedroom, and Miles turned the temperature down to cold, had a shower using the fresh lilac-coloured bath towel provided, and put on a fresh pair of jeans and a clean T-shirt. Feeling more like his usual self, he lay on the surprisingly comfortable sofa bed until Church bounded into the room and jumped up beside him.

"I don't like this," Miles said. "Dead witches, a stolen grimoire, a magic user who may or may not be utterly psychotic from what I've seen so far. Stuart is dying, so he must have a time scale, unless, like Amelia suggested, the magic is keeping him alive, in which case, who knows."

Church let out a soft whine.

"Aye, I know," Miles said, scratching her under the chin.

Amelia arrived at the door a few minutes later, having changed into a pair of jeans and new T-shirt. "You ready?"

Miles nodded and sat up. "How long is the drive?" he asked.

"Forty minutes, maybe," Amelia said. "I went there just after Stuart's name came up in Heather's murder. It reeks of chaos magic."

"How so?" Miles asked.

"Chaos magic draws out living force from everything around it and leaves a sort of greasy residual energy in the air. Feels like you've walked through somewhere a horrific thing took place. You can drive. I'm going to sleep on the way."

"Why not go to the church in Boston?"

"The Detective suggested we meet at the house," Amelia said. "We can always go to the church too, if you need to."

It wasn't long after that they were on their way once again, with Miles driving through the darkness to the destination where Stuart had murdered his neighbours and burned down his and their homes. Amelia fell asleep almost immediately, and Miles made sure to follow the speed limit to the exact mile per hour, letting her rest a little longer.

There was a lot about being human that Miles had forgotten, but he remembered being up for days at a time, exhausted, his brain clouded with fog. Desperate for sleep. Vampires got a similar feeling if they hadn't drunk blood for an extended period. Although that came along with headaches, and a disposition that would tentatively be described as *crabby.*

Miles pulled over at his destination behind a dark grey Ford Expedition that may as well have had *police* emblazoned across the back.

Amelia woke when the car stopped, yawned, and stretched.

"We're here," Miles told her, motioning to the car in front. "Your cop friend?"

"Not sure *friend* is the right word," Amelia said and opened the door.

Miles got out of the car, letting Church out too, and together they followed Amelia a short distance toward the two burned-out shells of what clearly used to be houses. A lone man stood between the two buildings. He wore a badly fitting black suit—his arm muscles bulging out of it—and, as he turned to see Miles, an expression of wishing to be elsewhere. He was white, with short hair, almost in a military style, and dark goatee.

"Amelia," he said, his accent pure Bostonian. He walked over and shook her hand. "This your vampire friend?"

"Miles, this is Detective Payton Hauser. I'll sit back and listen, if that's okay?"

"Detective," Miles said, offering his hand, which the Detective shook.

"Sorry, this place gives me the creeps," he said with a sigh, his eyes widening as he took in Church. "That your dog?"

"This is Church," Miles said. "She's harmless."

"She's a big girl," the Detective continued. "She must eat like a lion or something."

"It costs a lot in wildebeest," Miles said.

"Seriously?"

"No," Miles said with a smile. "She does eat a lot, but so far no wildebeest. Which one of these is the Murphy house?"

"Oh, that one," Detective Hauser said, pointing to the building on the left. "Stuart left his house, went to his neighbour, killed them both by . . . means unknown, and set fire to their building."

"Amelia said that there's proof to back that up."

"Neighbour saw him walk across to that house, go inside, lots of screaming, lots of flames," the Detective said. "He then walked out and got into his car and drove to Boston. He entered the Church of the Holy Trinity—CCTV shows him going inside—where five people were killed, including the priest, before CCTV shows Stuart Murphy leaving, followed by the church bursting into flames."

"Any ideas why?" Miles asked.

"According to the neighbours and constant police reports, the couple who lived here were playing loud music at all times of day, and were dealing out of the house," the Detective said. "The police were called several times, and each time the couple received warnings. The male occupant had previous drug offences. We got a warrant to do a search, but found nothing except completely legal amounts of pot."

"How long did they live there?" Miles asked.

"Three years," the Detective said.

"Three years of pent-up resentment at his neighbours, combined with anger at his wife and kids leaving, and his cancer," Miles said. "And his already unpleasant temperament. Nae adding up to good things. You ever get a call about him hitting his wife or kids?"

"There was some concern at the local school when one of the kids had bruising, but Stuart explained it away. Report says they were riding, kid fell down a hill, dad grabbed him, hurting his arm to stop him from serious damage. Kid and wife agreed, although we all saw how they were around him. After that, no more problems at school. Local neighbours say the wife had an occasional bruising on her neck and arms, but after it was pointed out, she wore long sleeves all the time. Murphy beat his wife and kids for a long time is my guess. He's a piece of shit, and if I had my way, I'd drive into Maine and drag him out by his fucking ears, but I don't. And no one else wants to get involved either."

"No one?" Miles asked.

"Amelia said her friend Heather was poking her nose into Stuart's business," the Detective said. "They drowned her and hung her from a fucking tree. Outside of my, or any, police force's jurisdiction, I might add. Found her in Maine, so officially, she's Maine's case. Want to know how many police forces there are in Maine to deal with stuff like this?"

"Zero," Miles said. "It's why I'm here."

"You really gonna go in that place?"

Miles nodded. "And drag the fucker out by his ears if given the chance. If Heather's murder doesn't fall under anyone's jurisdiction, why was her body allowed to be recovered?"

The Detective let out a sigh. "There are guard stations all up the east side of Maine. Most are manned by the army, or your guards, but a few have gotten themselves manned by the Magistrate. They allowed Heather's body to be brought back to Boston, although frankly, if they're not helping Stuart and his people I'd eat my fuckin' hat."

"Nae a fan?"

"Of the Magistrate?" the Detective asked, making sure his tone suggested exactly what he thought of them. "No. They're bigoted little dipshits. Fuck 'em."

Miles was beginning to warm to the Detective. "May I look around?"

The Detective motioned for Miles to go ahead.

"Quick question before I do," Miles said. "You found any links between Stuart and the Magistrate?"

"Officially, none," the Detective said. "But the guard who got grabbed at the border has a lot of links. And that guard knows Stuart pretty well. His name is Patrick Rodgers. He's got friends in the Magistrate, and he's an asshole. That's my official Detective term for him. He's got a record of violence, mostly alcohol enabled. Frankly, I don't even know how someone with his record gets a job as a guard anywhere near the border."

"He mentioned Stuart?" Miles asked.

"Not by name," the Detective said. "He asked if we'd be interested in information about the person who set a church on fire in Boston. Said he knew the guy, said they both had friends in the Magistrate. Said we needed to make a deal. Then a lawyer arrived and he shut up quicker than I've ever seen."

"So it's possible that the Magistrate is working with Stuart, too," Miles said.

"Working with, working for," the Detective said. "We tried looking into any connection, and we were informed that it was an avenue we needed to leave alone."

"Who warned you?"

"My boss," the Detective said. "Technically, my boss's boss."

The overwhelming thought rattling around Miles's head was: Why would the Magistrate want to help Stuart? He'd seen firsthand that the Magistrate would happily hold their collective noses and work with those who weren't human, if it meant they got something out of it. So, what were they getting out of all this? The possibility of creating witches? They'd need a lot more grimoires, and from what Miles could remember, they weren't the sort of thing that were just put together by anyone.

"Thanks," Miles said, as he walked over to the closest house, which had belonged to Stuart's neighbours, and stepped inside. It had been about a month since the fire and murders inside, but as Amelia had said, there was a weird atmosphere to the place. Chaos magic was not something you got to use and walk away from without making sure the world knew it had been used.

With Church beside him, they moved through the ruined building to the living area, which according to Amelia had been where the bodies were found. The sense of *wrongness* was at its peak in what had been a large room. There were no floorboards above, and the contents on the bedroom above had fallen through the destroyed floor. Someone had placed a green tarpaulin over the large hole in the roof, but it had done little to stop the rain getting in, and from the smell of it, local vermin too.

Church let out a low growl, and something small scurried off into the darker recesses of the building, splashing water from the inch deep puddle the room now sat in.

Miles wasn't interested in seeing if he could find anything; he just wanted to get a feeling for what had happened. And that feeling was nothing good. He left the house with Church beside him, who shook herself the second they were outside, as if exorcising something unpleasant from her fur.

"Find anything?" Amelia asked, taking Miles's attention away from his thoughts.

"Evil," Miles said. "No other word for it. Evil was done in that house."

"Chaos magic can't be used for anything else," Amelia said grimly. "It quite literally tears out life force to use it. It stains the world. My advice would be to knock that house down, salt the earth, and never build here again."

"Seriously?" the Detective asked.

"It makes my skin crawl," Miles said. "You ever come across it before, Detective?"

The Detective nodded, although his expression suggested he'd have rather not. "Some incel piece of shit decided to use it to try and kill a woman who turned him down. He was practising, lost control of it, tore himself in half after he froze the moisture all around him and it exploded. That moisture included his blood. Was a bit of a mess, but the place where he did it still feels weird even after seven years. That was my first time dealing with the wonderful world of magic. You'll be shocked that no one put *magical fuckery* as the cause of death. Not just because no one would believe them."

"Everyone on this planet should be glad that chaos magic is so rare that the vast majority of people will never have to deal with someone using it," Amelia said.

"I doubt we'll be so lucky that Stuart is stupid enough to set himself on fire," Miles said. "Unfortunately."

"Would save us all a lot of time and effort," the Detective said. "He worked for Templar International. You know it?"

Miles nodded. "Little bit."

"Big-time private security place," the Detective continued as if Miles hadn't said anything. "They look after a lot of rich and famous people. We went there to ask about Stuart, you know, before the boss told us to drop it. Model employee. Everyone really surprised he would ever hurt anyone, must have been all the trauma from having cancer. It's sad when some people can't talk about their problems. Wife and kids left him too, very sad. Anyway, we have nothing to show you, do you have a warrant? Please leave and contact our lawyers in future."

"Judging by your chat with your boss's boss, he has friends in high—or low, depending on your point of view—places," Miles said.

"I think you're spot on there," the Detective said.

"What's happening with the guard now?" Miles asked.

"He's being held without bail until we can get him before a judge, which should be in a day or two. Unfortunately, his lawyer is making loud noises, and there's a possibility if we can't get something to stick involving his part in Heather's murder, we may have to cut him loose."

"Can I talk to him?" Miles asked.

"Officially? Hell no."

"Maybe unofficially then," Miles said.

"I'll see what I can do," the Detective said with a shudder, and offered his hand to Miles. "In the meantime, I'm going home. I'll let Amelia know what's going on with Patrick. I wish you all the luck in the world. Get these bastards, because whatever they've gone to Maine for, it can't possibly be good."

"I'm going to do everything in my power to make sure we get them," Miles said.

Detective Hauser nodded a goodbye to Amelia, got into his vehicle, and drove off.

"So, what do you think?" Amelia asked when they were alone.

"I think Sam needs to come tell us what he found out," Miles said with a smile.

"Who's Sam?" Amelia asked.

"That would be me," Samuel said as he walked out of the darkness behind the burned-out neighbours' house and strolled over to Miles and Amelia.

He wore a checked black and red suit, white shirt, red waistcoat, and matching tie, along with dark brown shoes and a black fedora that had a peacock feather in it. He was a tall, thin man with dark skin and several earrings in both ears. He looked as if he'd been created explicitly to wear the items of clothing he had on, as though he'd just stepped off a catwalk in Milan.

"Sam," Miles said, hugging his friend.

Sam removed his hat, revealing his short-cropped black hair, and nodded hello to Amelia. "My name is Samuel Austin." He removed a badge from his inner coat pocket, flashing it to her. "I'm with the FBI, but mostly I'm here because I'm a *really* old friend of Miles's."

"What are the FBI doing here?" Amelia asked.

"Mostly wonderin' how Miles here managed to get himself neck deep in shit," Samuel said, turning to his friend. "Again."

CHAPTER SEVEN

Miles, Amelia, Church, and Sam all travelled back to Heather's house, where Amelia had immediately gone to make coffee. Miles let Church out into the sizeable garden, which she set off exploring while Miles and Sam sat on the decking.

"So, this is a dead woman's house," Sam asked. "I get the feeling your journalist friend finds that weird."

"I think she's having difficulty adjusting," Miles said, not bothering to correct the use of the word *friend*. He still didn't quite trust Amelia, she was a journalist, after all, but he did find that he enjoyed her company.

"On the subject," Sam continued, "what the good goddamn hell are you doin' with a journalist?"

Miles gave Sam a more in-depth run-through of his position and what the plan was. Sam didn't interrupt once, just sat and listened, occasionally nodding.

When Miles was done, Sam said, "House Idolator. So, they're lookin' to move back up to being one of the Great Houses. They lost their spot a long time ago, but they're always lookin' for a way back. What do you think of their plan to make a more direct route through Augusta and Waterville?"

"I think it's a good plan," Miles said. "Mostly."

Sam laughed. "Mostly? That one word is doing a lot of work there. What do you really think?"

"I think there's more to it than just making Augusta safe," Miles admitted. "Waterville is a desolate wasteland now. Clear out any outlaws who are dumb enough to call it home, clean it up, and move in. I don't see an issue with it, although if that's the case, why wasn't it done already? Augusta is apparently clear of desolate these days, at least those on the surface. I heard there's a lot of them trapped underground. So anyone trying to clear that place out is going to need an army. A lot of body bags for them. You know anything else?"

"From what I know," Sam said, "a few desolate get out here and there, but there are *a lot* of them under the city. If House Churchy starts doing renovations, they're going to unleash a goddamned horde back onto Maine."

"House Churchy?" Miles asked with a slight laugh. "Seriously."

"The House of Faith," Sam said, in mocking tones. "Praise the vampire gods and their ways."

"Miles mentioned about the desolate trapped underground before," Amelia said from the doorway as she carried out a tray of empty cups and a large pot of coffee. "They that big of a problem?"

"Yeah," Sam said. "Maybe a few thousand desolate, if I'm honest. There's a bunch of old caverns under Bond Rook, they go deep, and there's a lot of them. Used to be an archaeological dig down there because they found some old stones all under Maine, no one could figure out what they were for. Now no one wants to go look at them again."

"Stones?" Miles asked.

Sam nodded. "I remember hearing about them from someone, can't remember who. Apparently one of the scientific groups working there found them. Anyway, while the initial outbreak was at Blue Hill, there were several secondary outbreaks. Augusta had a laboratory in the caverns; it's how the desolate spilled out into the city so quickly. When the Assembly and US government sent people to clear it up, they just left the multitude of desolate still in the caverns where they were and sealed it up. Too dangerous to go into those caverns to hunt desolate."

"And they're just sitting there?" Amelia asked as Miles poured coffee for everyone. "How do they feed?"

"The desolate go into a cocooned state if left without sustenance for long enough," Sam explained. "If there's enough desolate in one place when the process starts, they sort of cannibalise one another. It makes whatever survives bigger, tougher, meaner. No one is going to want to go down there and see what's waiting for them. It would be suicide, even for vampires."

"I didn't know that," Amelia said.

"I only found out about it last year when I fought a cocooned bastard for the first time," Miles said, thinking back to the time in Templar International when he along with Charlotte, Church, and Rosa had fought one of the giant desolates that had been kept inside a laboratory there.

"Vampires and humans are all good, but we don't share everything," Sam said. "Leavin' desolate alone is a bad idea for a lot of reasons; it's why I have my job at the FBI, after all. But getting down into those tunnels under the city would be next to impossible, and blowing the place to hell could release more somewhere else. Safer to just monitor it all."

"What is it you do?" Amelia asked.

"Officially, I am a liaison to House Phalanx and the Assembly," Sam said with a flourish of his hands. "Unofficially, I'm put out of the way, so I don't get under the skin of the House Phalanx First Lady."

"You don't get on?" Amelia asked.

Miles sprayed his mouthful of coffee all over the decking.

"You could say that," Sam said with a glare Miles's way.

Amelia looked between Sam and Miles.

Sam sighed. "First Lady Töregene of House Phalanx is a wise and even-tempered woman."

Miles stared at him.

Sam's sigh was longer than the first. "I killed her First Captain. He was a bully, a thug, and I didn't go through the right channels to duel him. I just challenged him in front of the whole court. I knew he wouldn't back down, wouldn't be able to live with his dented pride, so he accepted. And he died. Töregene understood what I did, and why, and that's why I got to keep my head. Instead, she would rather I was out of sight, out of mind. Which is a short way of explaining why I'm back in America as a liaison, until such time as she lets me back into court."

"Am I allowed to ask why you challenged him to a duel?" Amelia asked. "If that's too personal, I'm sorry . . . I just don't know much about vampire politics. I don't think anyone not a vampire does."

"I had a . . . relationship with a man which the First Captain decided was inappropriate," Sam said. "The First Captain was a bigot. It happens, even among vampires, although less so now. And it's definitely not something you would do openly, but like I said, the First Captain was a bully. And now he's dead."

"And your gentleman dalliance?" Amelia asked.

"Works for the new First Captain," Sam said. "A lady who was very happy with her promotion. This was fifty years ago now. I was sent to America to stay here and work with the FBI to help improve vampire-human relations. Mostly, I work with a team to hunt down the desolate.

Occasionally, we work with the Assembly to track rogue vampires. We're good at our jobs. I'm very proud of the work we've done. Also, no one on my team is bothered whether I have sex with men or women, or both, or neither. I think that works out well for all concerned."

"I didn't mean to pry," Amelia said.

"Yes, you did, you're a journalist," Sam replied with a warm smile. "But I don't mind. You should ask Miles about that time he had his own . . . dalliance, with the First Lady of House Nebula."

"We should not," Miles said, frowning.

Sam's grin suggested the mischief he was happy to impart should he be given the chance.

"I also didn't know you knew about that," Miles continued.

"FBI, baby," Sam said.

Miles laughed. "You work on that a long time? Didn't know the FBI kept track of my exceptionally short-lived love life."

Sam chuckled. "I heard from someone, who knows someone, who may have been drunk. It's not like it's illegal for an Arbiter and a House Lord or Lady to engage in . . . whatever dirty little things you and First Lady Adile did."

"Please stop talking," Miles begged.

Sam laughed. "I'm just messin'. Anyway, moving onto more serious matters. Namely, this man Stuart Murphy you're both keen to find."

"You found out something about him?" Miles asked.

"He worked for the CIA, along with Liam White," Sam said. "He did some bad things that are not taught about in history class. He made some people go missing, made some other people take the blame. None of it was official, you're aware. Stuart left the Company, or Agency, or whatever you want to call it. Went to Templar and continued his shady work. Only now there was no CIA bureaucracy to keep them in check. Liam White was the same. These are not *good* men, Miles. These are the kinds of men who do horrible things and are never held accountable for their crimes. These are the kinds of men who should not be allowed to breathe the same air as everyday humans."

"What aren't you telling me?" Miles asked.

"Liam was in a unit in the CIA called the Helsings. Want to guess what those fuckers did?"

"Hunt vampires," Amelia whispered.

"The lady got it in one," Sam said.

"And Stuart went to vampires to ask them to make him one?" Miles asked.

"I don't think they were killing vampires for any political ideology," Sam said. "They just got paid well to do it. They became experts at it. If you're going after them, they ain't gonna be going down easy. Not just because there are some definite links to the Magistrate."

"What kinds of links?" Miles asked.

"The kind they went to great lengths to hide," Sam said. "But they exist. Liam is friends with several members, and from what I've heard did some off-the-books work for them. I've got a friend still looking into them; hopefully I'll learn more soon."

"How good were Liam and Stuart's people?" Miles asked, and sighed before he finished the sentence. "The Helsings."

"I assume you don't approve of the name," Sam said with a wry smile. "And they were very good. Highly trained and motivated to do whatever needed to be done to finish the job. When I looked into them, I was told to do so quietly and without making waves. I met Liam before all of this, before he left the company to go to Templar. It was only a brief meeting, and it was several years ago, but he was a very intense man."

"Can I ask something?" Amelia asked, looking between the two vampires before she said, "What are the vampire gods you were talking about?"

Miles and Sam turned to look at her.

"Wait, is that nae common knowledge?" Miles asked. "I forget what the humans—and I guess witches—do and don't know."

"If it's common knowledge, I've never heard of them," Amelia said.

"You want this one?" Sam asked Miles.

"Vampires, as you know them, come from a group of individuals known as the Dusk," Miles said. "Those of us who were turned from human to vampire by them are known as the Dark."

"The Dusk brings the Dark?" Amelia asked. "That's it, right?"

Miles nodded. "It was never a particularly original idea even five thousand years ago. Anyway, the Dusk were twenty vampires, or creatures, or whatever they were, and their blood made the first vampires. If you've been turned by one of the first vampires, you're usually more powerful than those who proceed you. The level between first turned and five hundredth isn't particularly large, but it is there. So the Dusk made a bunch of vampires, and in roughly five hundred BCE, they nearly all just up and disappeared one by one. No one has any idea where they are or why they left."

"Can't people just ask the Dark members?" Amelia asked.

"None of them know," Miles said. "There are only a few Dark members left in the world, and none of them remember. I know because I spent a year when I was First Librarian trying to figure out how a bunch of vampires could go missing and no one know about it. When you get to the thousands of years old part of life, you tend to spend a lot of time asleep, in a sort of vampiric stasis. It's suggested by some that the Dusk are all in deep sleeps across the world, or maybe they all got so old that they simply died. People have come up with some weird theories over the centuries."

"And this leads to House Idolator, how?" Amelia asked.

"They think the Dusk are all gods," Sam said. "That they brought vampires to this world, and with their job done, they went off to live their lives in the reward of the afterlife. However, one day, when we need them most, they will return."

"House Idolator are pretty much the only people who believe any of this nonsense about gods and the Dusk," Sam said, mockingly. "They think that their bloodline gift is based on their faith and link to the Dusk. That their faith, quite literally, gives them power."

House Idolator's bloodline gift was the ability to use their vampiric energy as a physical manifestation. They could create shields or weapons with it that were capable of withstanding, or dealing, an incredible amount of force. A lot of them believed that this power was linked to their faith in their religion, although Miles was unaware of any actual proof that this was the case. Unfortunately, the manifestations didn't last long, but while they were active, they were a formidable weapon.

"You don't approve?" Amelia asked Sam and Miles.

"Couldn't care less," Miles said. "Believe whatever you like. But some in House Idolator have a tendency to look down on those who don't believe as they do. There's a part of the House whose sole job is to try and bring people to their way of thinking. Not to bring them into the House itself, that would be sacrilege, but to convert them to spread the word among the Houses."

"Does that work?" Amelia asked.

"Some Houses are more tolerant than others," Miles said. "Drest is tolerant of the individual people, but less tolerant of House Idolator's wish to spread their word. You tell him the Dusk were gods to be worshipped, and not doing so makes you a heretic, and there's a good chance he's going to punch you."

"What are your thoughts, Sam?" Amelia asked.

"On House Idolator?" he asked, with just enough venom to make sure Amelia and Miles knew *exactly* what his thoughts were. "Holier than thou bullshit artists. If they want you here to document the pilgrimage, you can be damn sure they want to try and show the world just how holy they are."

"You think they're going to try to convert me?" Amelia asked. "I haven't been to church since I was seven. Not about to start now."

"You, no," Sam said. "They don't care about you. But that piece you write—about their pilgrimage, about their holy land—you'd better believe they'll try to use that as a recruitment drive. They care about the possibility of new initiates to their House. They lost their status as Great House because the First Lord believed that no one else could become a member without a bunch of hoops being jumped through. The new House First Lord, he wants to bring their numbers back up, and that means recruitment."

"I'm not going to write with any kind of bias about the pilgrimage," Amelia said with a touch of irritation that anyone might think otherwise.

"Oh no," Sam reassured her. "They'll want it as a warts-and-all kind of piece. Only those truly committed to their cause will read it and think, *I want some of that.* I don't know for sure that's what they're thinking, but House Idolator is always looking for a way to spread the word of Heavenly Dusk."

"Heavenly Dusk?" Amelia asked.

"It's what they call the gods," Sam said. "Their . . . *pantheon*, if you will."

"I spent time with the First Lord," Amelia said. "He seemed like a pious man, a believer in his faith, but he didn't really talk about anything to do with Heavenly Dusk, or even mention that his gods were old vampires."

"Members of House Idolator talk about their faith a lot, but they don't usually mention specifics unless they trust you," Miles said. Being a member of House Venator, and then an Arbiter for the Assembly, had ensured that he was left out of the preaching process. Hopefully, that wasn't about to change. "I'm sure you'll hear more about it once we're on the pilgrimage."

"Speaking of which, are you ready for it?" Sam asked Miles, who shrugged in response.

"Have you done it before?" Amelia asked.

"Not the pilgrimage, no," Miles said. "No phone lines in Maine, and for some reason it's a gigantic black spot when it comes to getting a signal. Radios are spotty unless within close range. Satellite phones work, but otherwise, getting information in and out is hard work, and done via letters and couriers who work with, or at least alongside, the pilgrimages. The last time I went there, it was like going back in time, and it doesn't sound like much has changed in the decades since. It's a bit of a culture shock, so I understand. Have you had all of this explained to you?"

Amelia nodded. "No phones, no signal, no Wi-Fi. Drest said that there's a satellite phone in Bangor, but otherwise, once in Maine, you're on your own."

Miles stood and stretched.

"What else can you tell me about the Magistrate?" Amelia asked.

"After Seattle, the Magistrate were hit hard," Sam said. "Lots of investigations, lots of arrests for people who helped those involved there. It's made those who stayed a little hardened. These are the *believers*. Those who think that vampires are nothing but a threat to the human way of life. Who have bumper stickers that say things like *A good vampire is a dead vampire,* or *Ashes to ashes is the only way.* There are rumours of Magistrate hit squads moving in Maine and New Brunswick, hunting down any lone vampire who wanders away from one of the settlements. Don't know how true it is, because we can't get reliable news in and out of the place in a timely fashion."

"Also, the Magistrate are still backed by powerful people," Miles said. "If this guard killed Heather, and if he's a Magistrate member, there's a possibility that they ordered her death to keep her quiet."

Amelia nodded. "I know, and I also know that if they did kill Heather, I want to ruin them. I'm not scared of going after the Magistrate. Some people just need to be reminded that they're not gods, and they don't get to do whatever they like without some form of recompense."

Sam laughed. "I like you," he told Amelia, pointing at her. "I wish there were more people who thought like that, but thinking like that is also more likely to get you killed."

"Which is why I'm here," Miles said.

Amelia yawned. "I'm going to go sleep. It was lovely to meet you, Sam. Thank you for your time."

Sam nodded his head toward Amelia, who said good night and turned in.

"You think she's for real?" Sam asked after several seconds of silence. "She'll go after anyone if it means getting her friend's killers?"

Miles nodded. "I think she's got a lot of anger about how her friend was killed. About *why* her friend was killed. But she's also keen to return the grimoire to its rightful owners. The fact that the people we're after are responsible for both hopefully makes it a little easier for her. Whatever happens, this group with Stuart and Liam isn't going to be arrested and tried by a jury of their peers. If they're linked to the Magistrate, they're never gonna let them get to a position where they can spill secrets. It would end up being a political hot potato, at best."

"That also why you're here?" Sam asked.

Miles looked over at his friend and shrugged.

"You might have to make sure there's no evidence that any of those who killed Heather are ever found again," Sam said. "That they just vanish. You think that's why Drest asked you to help Amelia?"

Miles nodded again. "Partially."

"And what's the other part?" Sam asked.

"That I keep an eye on the Magistrate," he said. "It's possible that they're gaining power in Brunswick. And if that's the case, it could cause long-term problems for everyone in Maine, especially vampires."

Sam stared at Miles for a moment before he said, "You ever hear about the Maine curse?"

"Really?" Miles asked. "A curse."

"People say that if you were there when it fell, you feel compelled to return," Sam said.

"People say that, do they?" Miles asked with a smile. "What people and how much crack have they been smoking?"

Sam chuckled. "I figured that might be your response, but I've heard from a few Agents who have links with people in Maine that no one *wants* to leave. That they're fixated on the early 1980s, the poor bastards, and those who do feel compelled to return. I'm just saying, it might be a lot stranger than we first thought."

"Superb," Miles said. "I'll keep an eye out for people who are compelled to stay in Maine for reasons they don't understand. I'll also keep an eye out for monsters, psychopaths, werewolves, witches, and I assume roaming gangs of delinquents."

Sam slapped Miles on the back. "Man, I don't envy you."

"If it helps," Miles said, "I don't envy me either."

CHAPTER EIGHT

Sam went back to his hotel in Boston an hour before dawn, and Miles crashed on the bed in Amelia's basement. Just before he fell asleep, he reminded himself of the need to stop at an emporium and get some blood. He wasn't sure what the pilgrimage did for food while on the road, and he had little desire to be hunting rats and mice on the trip. He'd done that in the past, but it wasn't what he'd call a fun experience. Vampires could live on the blood of vermin, as their biology destroyed any pathogens that might exist, but it wasn't what Miles would call a good life.

Sam was already at the door of the house when dusk started. He greeted Church with his usual exuberance, passed Miles a file and a blood pouch, and went to make himself some coffee.

Miles drank the blood pouch, savouring the feeling of how it made his body relax. He hadn't realised he'd been so tense.

"You needed that, I assume," Sam said as he brought out a pot of coffee onto the decking.

Miles nodded. "Thank you."

"You're going to Kittery tonight, yes?"

Miles nodded again, leaning back against the chair and operating the lever at the side to move to a more comfortable lounging position. "Whenever Amelia gets back from talking to her Detective friend. Apparently, whoever had Patrick Rodgers—the guard who let Stuart and his little party of friends into Maine—in custody doesn't have him anymore. They're moving him to somewhere more appropriate, or something. Amelia got a call about an hour ago. Seemed pretty flustered."

"You know I'm not coming with you to Maine, right?"

Miles looked over at his friend. "You're on holiday, sorry, vacation. You've got those tickets for Broadway. Can't be missing that. In all seriousness, thanks for your help. It's good to get a sense of the people we're looking for."

"Do we actually know who killed Heather, though?" Sam asked. "Like, a name, or photo?"

"Well, someone kidnapped and killed her," Miles said. "There's CCTV of her car being driven into Maine. But we don't know who did it yet. I was hoping the guard they arrested might have more information."

"I'm thinking it was on the orders of Liam, rather than Stuart," Sam said. "He's used people in the past to do dirty work for him."

Miles considered it for a while before he said, "You know what bothers me? Why would Liam help Stuart? Stuart asked around about being turned into a vampire to save his life, and Liam hunted vampires."

"You're thinking that maybe their aims aren't quite aligned?" Sam asked.

Miles nodded. "Stuff isn't quite all adding up. Is there magic that can cure cancer?"

Sam didn't even have to consider it. "No."

"So what's his plan?"

Sam took a little longer to reply. "Nothing good."

"That's all I've got so far, too," Miles told him, looking over at the nearby glass table as his phone began to vibrate. He picked it up, noticing Amelia's name on the screen, and answered it.

"Can you come to the address I'm sending you?" she asked before Miles could speak.

"Sure, what's going on?"

"Patrick escaped from custody," Amelia said.

"What?" Miles almost shouted.

"He had help," Amelia continued. "Patrick's lawyer wanted his client moved to an Assembly facility, and he escaped mid-move."

"Fantastic," Miles said with a sigh.

"Also, the person who sent in the footage of him was found dead this morning. Drowned himself at World's End."

"Do we have any idea where Patrick is?" Miles asked. "And did the second guard die before or after he was released?"

"Before," Amelia said. "Patrick was caught on CCTV walking toward the address I sent you. He stole a car with GPS in it, dumped it close by. We'll find him." Amelia hung up.

"Oh for fuck's sake," Miles said, getting to his feet and checking his messages, then copying the address and adding it to the navigation app on his phone. "You hear that?"

"I'm a vampire," Sam said. "Of course I heard it. We going then?"

"Church!" Miles shouted out, and a second later there was the sound of the dog running through the nearby greenery and up the stairs toward the decking.

They were in the car two minutes later, with Miles driving as he followed the fifteen-minute journey to the address Amelia had sent him in Burlington.

"Humans just can't help but get in trouble, can they?" Sam said as the little blue car on the BMW's computer screen edged ever closer to its destination.

Miles had nothing to say to that, but there was a pit of fear in his stomach that he couldn't shake. He took a corner a little too fast, and the vehicle fish-tailed slightly before he got it under control.

A few minutes of tense driving later, and they'd reached their destination in Burlington. It was a grey stone, two-storey office building, with a small parking area out front and well-maintained lawns on either side. The building had lots of large windows and a flat roof, with a welcoming presence. It looked to Miles like the kind of place that would have *bring your pet to work* days.

Miles parked out front and got out of the car, letting Church out, who sniffed the ground and set off at a steady pace as Sam followed them slightly down the dark, badly lit road to where Detective Payton Hauser and Amelia sat inside his Ford Expedition.

Amelia got out of the car first, with the Detective following shortly after.

"So, what's going on?" Miles asked, looking between the pair. "You found our escapee yet?"

"We know he was here," the Detective said, pointing to a CCTV camera outside a nearby building. "Security guard there is ex-job and was very helpful. Found the abandoned car a block away; he was caught on camera running at speed."

"From something, or toward something?" Sam asked.

"You sure he went in there?" Miles asked, pointing to the building closest to them.

The Detective removed his phone, typed in his passcode, clicked on the correct file, and passed the phone to Miles. The picture quality was excellent, which Miles was grateful for, but while it showed the man running, it didn't show who or what he was running from. The man removed a key from his pocket, opened the door of the nearby building, and darted inside. Miles continued to watch the feed and caught a glimpse of a shadow in the distance. He paused the film, rewound it, and played it again.

"What is that?" Sam asked, over Miles's shoulder.

"I have no idea," Miles admitted, passing the phone back to Detective Hauser. "The time stamp says that was forty minutes ago, that right?"

The Detective nodded.

"So Patrick has been in there for forty minutes," Sam said. "What's in there that's so important?"

"We should go find out," Miles said.

"It's his lawyer's office. Stupid thing is that he might have been released anyway," the Detective said. "His lawyer quoted the fact that Maine isn't under US law anymore, and would actually come under Assembly law."

"I'm Assembly law," Miles pointed out.

"Me too, sort of," Sam said.

"Well, this man is now your problem," Detective Hauser said. "Captain said that maybe we should let some Assembly people know where Patrick was last seen so that he can be someone else's problem. Here's me, letting you know. Enjoy."

"Was he really going to get released because no one wants to deal with Maine?" Miles asked. "Seems short-sighted."

"Not the first time," Sam said. "There's a law that states all crimes in Maine, human or otherwise, come under Assembly jurisdiction. It's not exactly something used regularly, but some law enforcement pull it out when the humans don't want anything to do with something that happened in Maine. Maine is the talking point no one wants to talk about. The last presidential election felt like it was trying to see which one of them would bring it up first. You know what the official policy for Maine currently is? Ignore it and hope it goes away."

"That's just magnificent," Miles said.

"No one said it was a good policy," Detective Hauser said.

"Like the murder of a young witch, and the letting in of a group of highly trained murderers," Miles said, feeling as if his involvement in the whole situation had been a lot longer than the few days it had actually been. "Love political bullshit. So, this Patrick guy is in there?"

"Seems to be," Amelia said.

Miles turned back to look at the offices. From where he stood, there were no lights on, no parked cars, no semblance of anyone actually being inside.

"Church, do a sweep," Miles said.

Church set off at a gentle run and was quickly gone from sight.

"What happens if she runs into trouble?" Detective Hauser asked.

"She gets fed," Miles said without looking back at him.

Fortunately for anyone stupid enough who might have designs on hurting a large Doberman, Church made it back to everyone without getting covered in blood and gore. She licked Miles's hand and whined a little as she pawed the floor.

"She smelled something she didn't like," Miles said. "Let's go check."

Detective Hauser placed a hand against the holster at his hip.

"Not you two," Sam said. "Humans can stay here and not get eaten."

"This is my—" Amelia said.

"If it's nothing, we come get you," Miles said. "We find something, we come get you. Right now, my exceptionally fierce dog, who is capable of taking down vampires, smelled something she didn't like. And both Sam and I noticed movement on that footage we can't confirm the identity of. If there's another vampire out here, that's nae good news for the squishy species among us."

Amelia didn't say anything, and Miles and Sam ran off with Church in front. The vampires followed the dog around to the rear of the building, which consisted of a large piece of lawn in front of the beginnings of some woodland. There was a pond between where the three stood and the start of the woods.

Miles walked up to the pond, which was large enough to have three wooden benches around it comfortably, and looked up to the woods. Something made the hairs on the back of his neck stand up on end, and he took a long, deep breath through his nose, trying to smell what was bothering him. He let the breath out slowly through his mouth, and tasted something on the air. Blood. New blood. He looked around on the grass, and spotted the droplets of blood on them.

"I smell blood," Sam said from closer to the business premises. "Fresh."

"Me too," Miles told him as he rejoined his friend. "There's drops here. That's nae what Church was worried about."

Church pawed the ground again and let out a slight bark.

"There's something *exceptionally* bad here," Miles said, licking his lips, the taste of blood still in the air.

Miles looked up at the building beside him and made out a mark on the top, by the roof. "What is that?" he asked, pointing to it.

"Let's go look," Sam said, turning into his vampire self. His face gaunt, his eyes two dark pools of red, the hands growing long talons which he used to scale the side of the building as if it were nothing.

Miles did the same, arriving just after Sam. The scent of blood was considerably stronger on the flat roof. He looked down on Church, who remained where she was, looking up at them, whining. "Be right down," Miles told her. "Do another circuit and go back to Amelia."

Church barked that she understood.

"You're gonna wanna see this," Sam said.

Miles turned toward his friend who was crouched down by a smashed skylight. Glass was scattered around it, as was a smear of blood.

Sam touched the blood and licked it. "Human. Fresh. Probably happened around twenty minutes before we got here."

Miles walked back to the edge of the roof and looked down at Church. "Be careful, there's something out there."

Church barked, and turned to the woods. If there was something out there, it wasn't going to have a fun time if Church got hold of it.

Miles looked back to where Sam had been standing to see him drop through the smashed skylight. He ran over and dropped through after, landing next to a pool of blood that was smeared across the wooden floor. The room was thirty feet by thirty feet in size, with several identical wooden and metal tables, along with plastic chairs around them. At one end was a kitchen, with microwave, oven, and fridge.

"A canteen or dining area," Sam said from next to a set of double fire doors that had blood across them. "Whatever it is came from out there in here, and then jumped up through the skylight."

Miles looked up at the ceiling fifty feet above his head. "That is quite the jump."

"Could you do it?"

Miles nodded. "Probably. If a vampire did this, they sure left a lot of mess. Also, whatever did it isn't here anymore. We should get out and look around."

"We'll go through the front," Sam said, pushing the door open and stepping over more blood that was puddled behind it.

The pair walked down the hallway beyond, past the bathrooms to an identical door at the end. The trail of blood stretched all the way down the hallway to the second door. Beyond the hallway was the reception area. A door sat to the right of where Sam and Miles had entered, next to the receptionist's desk, on the opposite side to where the front door was. More blood covered the floor, and the door next to the desk had a large dent in it.

Sam moved through the reception area and pushed the door open a few steps as Miles went to the front door and found it to be unlocked.

"Oh, fuck," Sam said.

Miles was by his friend in a moment, regarding the scene before them. "That Patrick Rodgers?"

"Guess it used to be," Sam said.

The room beyond was long and empty, with wooden floors and blinds covering the windows. There were three doors at the far end, and between them and where Sam and Miles entered was the body of what had once been a person, though considering how many limbs it was missing, it now resembled a lump of torn-apart meat.

"That's a hard way to go," Sam said as he stood over the remains.

"Something quite literally tore him apart," Miles said grimly, removing his phone and taking a photo to show the Detective. "His throat, his chest, his limbs, fucking hell, I've seen some sadistic vampire shit in my life, but this is . . ."

The gunshot followed by a bark from outside brought Miles's attention away from the body. He turned and ran back through the room as a loud crash could be heard from outside, followed immediately by a car alarm. Miles ignored the noise and continued on until he sprinted through the front door, smashing it open as if it were nothing. Church ran toward him, barking.

"What's going on?" Miles asked as he followed Church back toward where the Detective and Amelia had been waiting. Amelia knelt on the soft grass next to the Detective. She was covered in his blood from the wound that had cleaved him from shoulder to hip, as she tried in vain to stem the constant bleeding. He was already dead by the time Miles reached them.

"He's gone," Miles said softly to Amelia while Church stood by as guard. It was only then that he saw the massive dent in the side of the car the Detective and Amelia had arrived in. It had been shunted away from the kerb, the windows shattered along the passenger side of the vehicle. There was no way the passenger side car door was ever being opened again. Something had impacted it with incredible force, all but writing the car off in the process.

Bits of bark littered the ground, and Miles picked one up, sniffing it. He looked back at the tree which sat near the kerb. He'd ignored it when first arriving, because there was nothing about it that looked out of place, but now that he studied it, the branches appeared to be . . . wriggling. It was as if they'd been forced to grow, and had been allowed to ping back to their normal size.

Miles looked over at Amelia, who was still kneeling by the dead Detective. "What happened?"

"We can save him," Amelia said weakly.

Miles noticed the grass moving up around the Detective's body. "Amelia," Miles said, putting a little bit of power in his voice. He hated to do it, but he needed answers.

She looked back at him, tears in her eyes.

"He's gone," he said softly, and noticed the grass beginning to retreat from the Detective's body. "What happened?"

"It came out of nowhere," Amelia said. "I was looking down at my phone, and standing here, and when I looked up . . ."

"What was it?" Miles asked, suddenly very aware of just how exposed they all were.

"Werewolf," Amelia said.

Miles took in a long, deep breath. The scent of the werewolf was strong, but it was almost overpowered by the scent of freshly cut grass and flowers. He considered going after the scent, following the werewolf, but right now he had no idea if that would lead him into a trap, or if getting him away from Amelia would leave her open to another attack.

Sam exited the building and ran over to the others. He looked down at the body of Detective Hauser. "Fuck. I'd better make a call."

Miles nodded as he continued to look out into the darkness of the street, then took Amelia to the rear of the car. He popped the boot and removed a bottle of water and a medical kit. "Are you injured?" he asked.

Amelia blinked again. "I'm fine. I'm . . ." She looked back at where the Detective's body was, turned to the side, and vomited onto the road.

The emergency services arrived a short time later, covering the whole street in blue and red flashing lights. Miles let Sam sort it all out, as he sat with Amelia a little way from the crime scene and gave her the bottle of water to wash the blood off her hands. Two Detectives took her statement while Miles sat beside her, which didn't please either of the investigators, but Miles didn't much care.

An hour later, as the bodies of Detective Hauser and Patrick Rodgers were removed, Amelia was taken into an ambulance for the medics to look her over. Miles played back Amelia's statement in his head. She'd been standing beside the Detective, looking at her phone, and the next thing she knew, he shouted something. As Amelia looked up, she saw a blur of movement, and she'd been splattered with the Detective's blood. She didn't remember what had happened after that.

When everyone had left, and Miles and Amelia were sitting alone beside each other on a low brick wall, Miles said, "So, you used magic to stop the werewolf." He pointed to the ruined car. "Powerful magic."

Amelia looked straight ahead. "I'm not some new witch fresh out of the coven."

"You're also not a chaos witch," Miles said. "No decay anywhere. And I didn't think harmony magic was powerful. Yet here we are."

"My mum was a chaos witch," Amelia said. "My dad a harmony witch. I got a little of both. I'm not as powerful as a chaos witch, but I have more power than a harmony witch. I just get tired quickly when I use it."

"You made that tree attack the werewolf," Miles said.

"I used it to shield me," Amelia corrected. "Tried to shield Detective Hauser, too, but it was too late. I may have gotten angry."

"You launched a werewolf into the side of a car with enough force to write the vehicle off," Miles said. "What was with the grass?"

"I was still upset, angry. I wanted to protect Detective Hauser," Amelia said, wiping her eyes with the back of her hand. "The grass moving was my desire to protect him from further harm."

"A hell of a first impression," Sam said as he walked over to them. "Detective Hauser looks like he died instantly. He was slashed across the chest and down over the stomach, looks like five claws, one punctured his heart. We have ourselves a genuine werewolf problem."

"It spooked Church," Miles said, a feeling of dread in his chest. "I should have known it was something else then, but I was focused on finding Patrick. Didn't expect anything to attack the Detective or Amelia."

"It tore off body parts, but there's no evidence of it drinking or feasting on the body of Patrick," Sam said. "This was a hit."

Miles nodded. "And this wasn't some newborn werewolf either."

Sam whistled briefly. "It can jump fifty feet up with little problem. It scares a dog who frankly terrifies everyone she's ever smiled at, and it moves fast enough to get a seasoned Detective before he can even pull his gun. And it ran off after Amelia practically pancaked it against the car. You want to take Church out to the woods to look for it?"

Miles shook his head. "It'll be long gone by now. Also, don't know if it's just a werewolf out there."

"They hunt alone," Sam said.

"Usually," Miles said. "But if this werewolf was after Patrick because of what he knew, then it's a good guess that it's working with Stuart and gang."

Sam nodded, too. "Fucking hell, Miles. What have you and Amelia gotten into?"

Miles looked over at Amelia. "You okay?"

Amelia nodded, although she didn't seem convinced. "Never seen someone killed right in front of me before. He didn't deserve that."

"No, he didn't," Miles said. "You still want to go ahead with this?"

Amelia looked over at Miles, determination written over her face. "Do werewolves scare you?"

"You ever seen one before?" Sam asked.

Amelia shook her head.

Miles considered Amelia's question for a while. "Anyone nae afraid of a werewolf is someone who has never met a werewolf. These aren't like the werewolves you see on film and TV. They're nae mindless killers, they're nae humans who are sad that they turn into a monster once a month and start eating people. Most werewolves live alone, don't really care much for company, and when they turn—which they can only do at night, with or without a full moon—they usually do so far away from populated areas. They don't like to draw attention to themselves, and they don't, normally, kill humans.

"This one isn't like that. Clearly. Werewolves are about as close to a perfect killing machine as exists on this planet. And I'm including vampires. They're about as strong as vampires, but faster, and they heal up quicker than they can be hurt. Silver and decapitation will kill them. That's it. Although they're nae fans of fire, but then nothing is."

Amelia swallowed but said nothing.

"So, I'll ask again," Miles said. "You still want to go ahead with this?"

Amelia looked over to where the Detective's body had been not long ago and nodded. "I need to do this. More so now than ever before."

Miles got to his feet. "Right, then tomorrow we get some stuff to help with the werewolf situation, we head to Kittery, and we go get justice."

"Thank you," Amelia said.

Miles looked toward the blood-slicked road. If Amelia had said no, if she'd decided it was enough, he'd still have gone. There were some things you just can't ignore, can't leave for someone else to clean up. And there were some people who needed stopping. Rogue werewolves fell under both of those categories.

CHAPTER NINE

Before they could go anywhere, Miles made a statement to the local police and gave his condolences for the death of Detective Hauser. The Detective talking to him asked if he was going to go after whatever had killed him, and Miles assured him he would, which seemed to go some way to giving comfort to him.

"Werewolves, witches, a pilgrimage," Sam said as Amelia drove them back to Heather's house. "Probably some other stuff I've forgotten. It's been an eventful few days with you. I'm beginning to wonder if you're this busy all the time."

"Technically this is me on holiday," Miles said as he sat next to Church, whose head was rested on his lap.

Amelia pulled the car onto Heather's, now Amelia's, driveway. She switched off the engine and everyone sat in silence as Amelia removed her phone and stared at the blank screen. "If I'd been paying attention . . ."

"You can't think like that," Miles said.

"Let's all get inside," Sam said softly. "I'll make tea."

Everyone disembarked into the house, where Sam went to make tea, while Church lay on the floor in the living room next to Miles, who sat on the edge of the sofa. Amelia sat next to him. Sam arrived shortly after carrying a tray, three mugs, a sugar bowl, and a teapot. He placed everything on the coffee table and took a seat on the other side of the sofa, opposite Miles.

"I'm going to make a call," Sam said, getting back to his feet. "Back shortly." He left without another word.

"So, a chaos witch and at least one werewolf are working, if not together, then for the same people," Miles said. "No point in killing Heather unless she was a threat. She was investigating Stuart, and by extension Liam."

"Yeah," Amelia said, her voice with an elsewhere tone to it, as if she weren't really sitting beside Miles.

"Not ideal," Miles said.

"I didn't know about the werewolf," Amelia said apologetically.

Sam walked back into the room, looked between Miles and Amelia, and said, "So, seeing how we've all had a terrible evening, allow me to make your lives worse."

"You know who the werewolf is," Miles said.

"Kind of jumping the gun there," Sam said.

"Okay, what's happening?" Miles asked.

"I don't know who the werewolf tonight was," Sam said. "But I do know that Liam and his team are werewolves."

Miles narrowed his eyes. "Seriously?"

"Yeah, but there's more to it than that," Sam said. "Liam wasn't a werewolf when I met him, and his whole team was human then. Seeing how so much of his file was redacted, I left someone digging, you remember?"

Miles nodded.

"Yeah, well, turns out, on one operation something happened, one of them got bitten, and the others decided that becoming werewolves sounded awesome. Stuart was already gone by that time, so he missed out on turning hairy on a regular basis."

"And this was all allowed?" Amelia asked.

"*Allowed* is a strong word," Sam said. "He did good work, his team did good work, so *ignored* is probably a better description."

"How many are in the team?" Amelia asked.

"Six," Sam said.

"And you're sure they're all werewolves?" Miles asked, already knowing the answer but wanting confirmation.

Sam nodded.

"Werewolves don't tend to work in packs," Miles said.

"Werewolves don't tend to be highly trained Special Forces operatives," Sam pointed out.

"This is bad on a number of levels," Miles said.

"Maybe werewolves work together better if they all knew one another before they were turned?" Amelia suggested.

Sam shrugged. "Plausible."

"Who knows," Miles said. "Maybe the desolate in Maine are controlled by a Desolate King or Queen, and we can have all the shitty stuff happening together."

"You think that's possible?" Amelia asked. "A Desolate King or Queen?"

Desolate Kings and Queens were, in Miles's experience, some of the worst monsters he'd ever met. Unlike normal desolates, who were creatures only interested in feeding and killing, the desolate royalty maintained some semblance of their human intelligence, and could control the desolate. Until his time in Seattle, he'd assumed all Desolate Royals were creatures whose base nature was to sow chaos and death, with little interest or concern about *who* that was aimed at. He'd continued to believe that right up until he'd met Lauren Gibson, who'd proved him wrong. A Desolate Queen, who controlled the desolate as usual, had gone after those responsible for her creation instead of taking innocent lives to feed a bloodlust.

"I'm just being facetious," Miles admitted; the very idea of having to deal with all of them at once was not something he wanted to entertain.

"Heather really got in over her head with these people," Miles said. "There's no way she could have known about the werewolves, even if she knew that Stuart was using magic."

"We got more than a little lucky tonight," Sam said.

"I don't feel lucky," Amelia said softly. "I don't think the Detective's family would consider what happened to be lucky."

"No, probably not," Sam conceded.

"You should have told me," Miles said. "That you're actually a powerful witch, I mean. You said you were a witch, but you didn't say that you were capable of the kinds of things you did tonight. You kept your true power from me, and I asked you not to keep secrets about anything that will have an effect on this mission."

"I'm sorry," Amelia said. "I wasn't sure how you'd take knowing I've got actual power. Some people don't deal with it well. Vampires included."

Miles opened his mouth to reply, quickly thought better of it, and nodded. "Just . . . is there anything else you haven't told me?"

"No," Amelia said, keeping eye contact with Miles. "Nothing."

"Good." Miles smiled. "Look, tonight has been a lot," Miles told them. "I think it would be best if we all got some rest and then tomorrow we headed to Kittery. We'll be a bit behind schedule, but it'll be fine."

Amelia nodded her agreement and looked over to Sam. "Thank you, Sam." She got to her feet and hugged him.

"You be careful," Sam said. "And don't you worry about Miles leaving you anywhere. I know the man—he'll follow you to hell and back if that's what he has to do."

Amelia glanced back to Miles and smiled weakly before going to bed.

"I think she's a little shaken," Sam said, finally pouring a cup of tea. "You want some?"

Miles shook his head.

Sam took a sip. "Not bad at all. She's dealing with her near-death experience better than I'd expected. She's a little shaken, but that's probably normal. It's been a while since my first near-death experience."

"She stood next to a man who was almost cut in half," Miles said. "I'd be a little shaken, too."

"I also think she's scared of you," Sam said. "Or at least, nervous about the idea of someone knowing her secret."

"Aye," Miles said. "She shouldn't have lied. I'm meant to be keeping her safe."

"I don't think she lied out of malice," Sam said.

Church snorted her agreement with Sam, let the vampire pet her for a few seconds, and walked downstairs.

"The dog agrees with me," Sam said.

"The dog is smarter than both of us," Miles pointed out. "You going back to New York?"

Sam nodded. "Just so you know, Miles, I'll be talking to some people in my office about all this. We'll have my team in Kittery should you need it. If you have to send Amelia out of Maine, we'll be there to help. I don't think she's going to leave willingly. There are parts of Maine that a witch, even one as capable as Amelia, shouldn't be walking around."

"There are places in Maine that a vampire shouldn't be walking around either," Miles said. "But thanks for your help. If there's trouble, I'll get word to Kittery. Somehow. Drest told Amelia something about a satellite phone in Bangor. We'll get a message to you if needs must."

Sam walked over to Miles and offered his hand, which Miles shook after standing. The pair embraced. "Be careful, Miles," Sam said, slapping him on the shoulder. "None of this sounds like a fun time."

Miles said his goodbyes and walked Sam out, before closing and locking the door. He sat on the step next to the doorway for a moment, then went upstairs and knocked on the bedroom door that Amelia was using.

"Can I come in?" Miles asked.

"Sure."

Miles opened the door to the master bedroom. The only light in the room was the bedside lamp, illuminating Amelia as she lay in bed reading. She'd changed into an oversized black T-shirt with a picture of Gonzo from the Muppets on it.

"I shouldn't have been so harsh when we met," Miles said. "It's nae your fault I have issues with journalists. It's nae your fault the First Lords of two Houses decided to involve me in something with no prior warning. I'm sorry."

"I should have told you everything," Amelia said, putting the book on the bed beside her. "I'm scared, Miles. I don't get scared very often, and after tonight, I . . ."

"It's difficult to see someone die," Miles said.

"Is it still difficult for you?"

Miles considered it for a moment. "It depends on the person. Someone I care about, or like, yes, it's hard. Someone who wants to hurt me or someone I care about, no, not really. I've always been this way, which is probably a damning indictment of my upbringing."

Amelia looked down at her hands, turning them over as if expecting to see them still covered in blood. "The Detective was a good man. He wanted to help. I couldn't stop him from being killed."

Miles tried to think of something that might offer Amelia some comfort and came up empty. "I don't think there's anything I can say or do that will make what happened better," he said eventually. "You are alive. That's all that matters. So while, yes, what happened tonight was horrific, and Detective Hauser didn't deserve it, it happened, and we need to concentrate on the fact that you didn't die. I know that's difficult. I wish it wasn't. If you need to talk, I'm here. And if you need someone to hug, so is Church."

Amelia laughed but quickly placed her hands over her mouth as though she'd done something awful. "Not a hugger?"

Miles smiled. "I don't mind the occasional hug. Church is a lot better at it, though."

"Would Church come and sleep in here?" Amelia asked.

Miles turned around. "Church," he called and, within moments, the large dog was in front of him. "You want to keep Amelia company tonight?"

Church wagged her tail and bounded into the room and up onto the bed, giving Amelia's face a lick.

"Good night, you two," Miles said.

"Thank you," Amelia called after him as he closed the door.

Miles made his way back to the front room and out onto the balcony. He mentally figured out what time it would be in Scotland, decided he didn't much care whom he woke up, removed his mobile phone, and called Drest.

Drest answered on the second ring. "How's America?"

Miles gave a brief rundown of everything that had happened since he'd arrived. Saying it out loud made it all feel like a lot to deal with for such a short space of time.

"Werewolves *and* witches," Drest said. "I didn't know about the first of those two being involved. A pack of werewolves is unusual, to say the least."

"Whatever is happening here, with Stuart taking a grimoire and running off to Maine with a werewolf pack, it all feels like a precursor to something much worse."

"Keep safe in Maine," Drest said. "I'll get in contact with Sam, I've met him before. We'll coordinate getting people in Kittery ready to go should you need help. You're just going to have to get word to us that you *need* help. So, until you get that satellite phone, you're on your own. Be careful, Miles. Nothing about this feels good."

"I'll be in contact when I can," Miles said and ended the call. He stood looking out over the darkness of the surrounding neighbourhood for a few minutes, before deciding to go get some rest. Judging by his time in America so far, tomorrow was going to be an *exceptionally* long day.

Chapter Ten

The journey to Kittery was done the following night, setting off at dusk with Amelia driving. There was little conversation on the hour-long journey, with Miles mostly spending the time running through everything in his head that he'd seen or dealt with in the last few days. Witches and werewolves, neither of which filled him with much joy.

Before he knew it, Amelia was driving over the Piscataqua River bridge and continuing on through what had once been a town with nearly ten thousand people. Despite the buildings still being there, the population was now closer to two or three thousand mostly US military and their families. It was better than some places along the border that were now little more than ghost towns. She stopped the car a few minutes later by what used to be a shopping centre, which had been all but demolished and replaced with a sizeable military outpost. Due to the destruction of several roads—including large parts of the Maine turnpike—it was the only way through Kittery to the rest of Maine.

The entire road, which Miles guessed was technically still called Route 1, was blocked off with thirty-foot-high concrete walls, topped with razor wire. There were four guard towers, each one equipped with a high-calibre weapon. An identical checkpoint sat on the opposite side of Spruce Creek—which was where the wall separating Maine and the rest of America officially started. That checkpoint faced out into the wilderness that was Maine.

Amelia stopped at the checkpoint—which was large and imposing enough that it would have given Communist Berlin envy—and spoke to the marine who walked to the car. Three more marines stood back beyond the barricade, and next to a tank. An actual tank. Miles didn't know the make or model, but you didn't really need to when faced with a tank. Before they'd arrived, Miles had wondered if a checkpoint would be enough to stop the desolate, and having seen the amount of firepower at their disposal, he figured that at the very least it would give the humans and vampires enough time to sound an alarm. Amelia used the controls on the arm of her door to lower both driver's and passenger's windows down and show her credentials to the marine.

A second marine stood by Miles. "And you, sir?" he asked.

Don't say on vacation, Miles reminded himself, remembering that the guards in places like this tended to have very little in the way of a sense of humour. "I'm with her," he said.

"And your ID," the marine said.

When Miles removed his wallet, the marine caught a glimpse of the torc on his wrist. "You're an Arbiter," he said.

Miles mentally cursed himself, but smiled all the same. "Aye, I'm her bodyguard. She's doing a story on the pilgrimage."

"Just you?" the marine asked.

"And Church," Miles said, pointing toward her.

"What's a church?" the marine asked.

Church's head appeared next to Miles, and the marine took a step back.

"That's a big dog," he said slowly.

Miles scratched Church under the chin, never taking his eyes off the marine. "Yes she is."

"I'm still going to . . . to need a name," he said, his voice trembling slightly.

"Miles Watson," he said. "And you don't need to worry about Church. She only hurts vampires and desolates."

Judging from the expression on the marine's face, that little fact did not actually help the anxiety he was currently feeling. Instead, he took another step back, and turned away and spoke into his radio. "We've got a Miles Watson and a really big fucking dog. Like she's fucking huge."

"I can hear you," Miles told him.

The marine turned back to Miles.

"I'm a vampire," he said, explaining. "Good hearing."

Let them through, came the gruff-sounding voice on the other end of the radio.

"Go on through," the marine said immediately.

Church returned to sitting on the back seat as Amelia drove through the checkpoint, going past the tank and through into a large area where there were more tanks and marines. One of the marines directed her to drive through the centre of the military base.

"Apparently we follow the yellow line," Amelia said, nodding a thank-you and continuing on.

Miles looked around at the hundreds of personnel going about their work. There were Apache helicopters, APCs, several dozen other vehicles all ready and waiting to go. He wondered if any of them had ever been deployed in Maine proper.

"Why haven't they ever retaken Maine?" Amelia asked as they continued along at the ten-mph speed limit.

"There was talk of it in the early nineties; it was one of the reasons I was sent here," Miles said. "A few reasons why they didn't, in the end. Firstly, it was deemed that it would be a massive cost of lives. And the president at the time did nae like the idea of losing a lot of people to reclaim Maine. Secondly, it would cost a fortune to rebuild everything, and to remove the wall that was still mid-construction in some places. It was already costing a lot to build it all in the first place. Thirdly, it was deemed to be an Assembly issue now, so the humans could ignore it as best they could, and the Assembly were quite happy to just let the vampires still living in Maine deal with any problems. A short-sighted way to attack the issue, but no one wanted to actually make it a priority."

"So, they just walled it off, put troops and guards everywhere, and let everyone inside stay there?" Amelia asked.

"Pretty much," Miles agreed. "Only a certain number of people inside Maine are allowed out. Usually the large truck convoys that collect supplies and bring them back to the towns. People make a lot of money doing that job."

"Just driving around Maine, delivering supplies?"

Miles nodded. "Aye. And the people who stayed here have made it their home without the need to worry about the outside world. Yes, it's dangerous in Maine, but they survived the collapse of society, and most figure they aren't going to let the desolate win."

"People do leave, though."

"They do," Miles admitted. "A lot have left. Mostly those with family. If humans want to leave, they can so long as they're willing to sit through six months of interviews, tests, examinations, and the like. There's still a genuine paranoia that humans are carrying some kind of desolate gene that's just waiting to come out. It's nonsense, they know it's nonsense, but some in Congress are going on about it still, and the Magistrate are using it as a beating stick."

"Are we going to see one of those convoys?"

"Maybe. Some people come along to travel through Maine to see family, usually staying with the monthly convoys. Safety in numbers. There are a hundred vehicles sometimes. Maine is a no-fly area, so you can't get in via helicopter or plane, unless you're Assembly or human military. And even then, you can't actually fly into Maine itself. Whatever is happening in the sky above, it screws around with electrical signals."

"So we couldn't have flown in anyway?" Amelia said. "You looked annoyed when the marine knew you were Assembly."

"I'm nae meant to be here officially, remember," Miles said, removing the torc and placing it in his pocket. "Not everyone here will know why you're here. I would like to keep it that way. Reporting on the pilgrimage is all we're doing, and I'm only here to keep you safe."

"I remember," Amelia said as they drove toward Spruce Creek, where there were signs along the road about where to go for the pilgrimage.

It didn't take long to arrive at what had probably been an idyllic little cul-de-sac called Cottage Way. Considering the number of vehicles and people milling around in the dark, it was pretty clearly now the staging area for pilgrimages.

Amelia parked and took a deep breath.

"You'll be fine," Miles said, opening the car door and letting Church out. "You've got ten minutes, don't go far."

Church bounded off into the nearby trees.

There were four vehicles in the cul-de-sac, not including Miles's car. Two of them were repurposed military trucks, each with the badge of House Idolator—an orange Dusk-like sunset, with a bright white moon in the left corner—adorning several parts of them, as well as sewn on the sleeves of several armed guards.

The other vehicles were two matching black Winnebagos that looked geared to go off road, with metal bars around the windows and huge tyres. There was also a large orange-and-black bus that resembled something a rock star would go on tour in, although this too had metal bars around the windows. All of the vehicles had the same House Idolator badge on them somewhere and were currently being loaded with the belongings of those who would be travelling in them soon enough.

"Amelia!" one of a group of four shouted over to her.

"Jenny," Amelia said, walking over to her and hugging the tall blonde vampire. "This is Miles. Miles, this is Jenny Lewis-Palmer."

Miles nodded a hello to the small group.

"So, you're a member of House Idolator?" Jenny asked. She had a posh English accent and wore designer clothing that had the approximation of ruggedness, but in reality probably wouldn't hold up to anything that might be considered *off road*. Miles wondered how many people going on this pilgrimage had ever been somewhere like Maine before. Probably not many, he concluded.

"I'm her bodyguard," Miles said with a warm smile.

"She doesn't need a bodyguard," Jenny said with an equally warm smile. "She has us."

"That's good to know," Miles said as the other three members of Jenny's group came over and introduced themselves. They were two men and a woman; all of them wore jeans and a sweatshirt with the badge of House Idolator on it, making them look like the kind of people who might knock on someone's door and try to talk to them about *believing*.

The two men were both about six feet tall, and that was where the similarities ended. One had dark skin and a faded haircut and was cleanly shaven, while the other was white with long blond hair and a beard long enough that he'd plaited it.

"This is Jeremy," Jenny said, motioning to the black man. "And Travis."

Both men offered Miles their hands, which he shook in turn.

"And this is Maeve," Jenny continued, giving the second woman a big hug that didn't appear to have been needed or wanted. Maeve was just over five and a half feet in height, with pale skin and long red hair that went to her waist.

"Nice to meet you both," Maeve said, her accent Irish. She looked over at the bus, and someone was waving to the group.

"You the combat medic?" Miles asked.

Maeve nodded. "Although more the medic part than combat."

"So, are you all vampires?" Miles asked.

Jenny nodded enthusiastically. "House Idolator through and through."

Miles noted a touch more than just pride in Jenny's tone. She was a believer. "Your first pilgrimage?" he asked.

Jenny smiled. "The first day of a new dawn. A pilgrimage to spread the word of our House and help those in need. A great day."

"I think we need to get on the bus," Maeve said. "See you both later."

"It's lovely to see you again," Jenny said, giving Amelia another hug.

"You too," Amelia told her.

Jenny walked by and hugged Miles, who was a little taken aback, as he hadn't been expecting it. "And you, too."

Miles watched Jenny walk over to the bus and climb aboard.

"First Lord Fuller put me in contact with Jenny," Amelia said at Miles's confused look, "when he found out I wanted to write this article about the pilgrimage." She gave him a wry smile. "She's a true believer in House Idolator and its doctrines."

"She's very . . . what's the word?" Miles asked, trying to be diplomatic.

"Exuberant?" Amelia suggested.

"Sure, let's go with that," Miles said. "Young."

"She's about fifty in human terms, but she's been a vampire about twenty-five years," Amelia said. "She may or may not have been brought into the House because her parents died and left her several hundred million dollars."

"She's filthy rich," Miles said.

"She is," Amelia said. "She's lovely, but she has no clue. About anything. I hope she doesn't get herself into trouble, because she will have no idea how to get out of it. I know she's a vampire, but I'm pretty sure I'm more equipped to get lost in Maine than she is. I get the feeling that she thinks her faith in House Idolator will protect her."

"She ever mention the Dusk to you?"

Amelia shook her head. "No. Until you and Sam told me, I'd never heard of it."

"What about the others?"

"Jeremy is ex-military," Amelia said. "All I know. Travis, I have no clue, Maeve either. I'm not even sure that any of them knew Jenny before she sort of brought them all together. There are a few more members of their little group. If Jenny has one power, it's making friends. It's genuinely incredible to watch her just make people like her."

"Any sort of relationship stuff there that might bring friction?"

"With Jenny?" Amelia asked as if it were the oddest question ever. "God, no. She doesn't date people, she sort of *acquires* them. I don't even know if she's ever had any kind of romantic entanglement. She doesn't seem to care about it, and no one seems to be all that bothered about trying."

"Miles Watson," a familiar voice said.

Miles looked over at First Authority Thomas Reed as he walked toward them. He wore an outfit similar to everyone else, jeans and grey sweatshirt with the House Idolator badge on it.

"Amelia, can you go see the organiser over there? You'll be travelling in the Winnebago with Miles and Church," Thomas said when he reached the pair. "We made sure you three have your own place so that you can write without the constant revelry that can happen. We'll be taking regular stops so that you can have people come on board and you can interview them about the trip. I believe Jenny is especially excited."

When Miles and Thomas were alone, Thomas said, "Any trouble?"

"Nae yet," Miles said. "Everyone seems very happy to be here. Anyone not House Idolator?"

"Oh, they're getting picked up from Portsmouth and brought here," Thomas said. "Should be only a few minutes away. There are twelve of us from House Idolator, another six human guards, who are all familiars to either myself or the First Lord, and I believe another eight from outside of the House. It's going to be quite the few days."

"Few days?" Miles asked.

"We stop at several places along the way, to refuel and stretch our legs, to help those who might need it," Thomas said. "The quickest we've done it is six hours. Ah, that was quite the whirlwind. Usually it's closer to thirty. We don't drive during the day. It's a bit of a different place since you were last here."

"So I gather," Miles said as two black Range Rovers pulled into the lot.

"They going to be okay over rough terrain?" Miles asked, pointing to the Winnebagos.

"Both of them are equipped with four-wheel drive," Thomas said. "Anything else?"

"What's in the two army trucks?"

Thomas looked over. "Supplies. Mostly medicines, equipment, and the like. Food comes in the convoys, so we don't have to worry about anything spoiling. We've done this before, Miles."

"I know," Miles said, feeling as though he was being chastised for questioning anything. "You ever lost someone?"

Thomas's stare bored into Miles, but eventually he said, "Yes. We've had a few fatalities over the years. Not in a decade, though. We know where we're going, we know how to get there, we know how to do it safely. All vehicles will have a familiar stationed in them during the day, including the one you will be staying in. Besides, if there's any trouble this time, we have an Arbiter among our ranks. Aren't we lucky."

"You don't like me much, do you?" Miles asked Thomas.

The First Authority opened his mouth to talk, closed it again, and eventually said, "No. It's not you personally, but I know your type."

Miles raised his eyebrows in question. "My type?"

"Don't believe in anything, don't believe that we might actually have looked into our faith, and we're not just barmy idiots praying to the sky," Thomas said. "Those who mock who we are and what we believe in. Those who think we're all loons."

"I don't think either of those," Miles said with a shrug. "I don't believe in what you believe, but I have no issue with your own belief. I don't mock you for it, but I don't like being preached to. By anyone. From any religion. Avoid that and we'll all get along famously. I'm nae here to piss on your bonfire, Thomas. I'm here to make sure Amelia gets her job done and leaves in one piece."

Thomas was silent for a moment. "I spoke out of turn," he said eventually. "I apologise."

"None necessary," Miles told him. "Like I said, we don't believe the same things, but that's fine with me. You all crack on and do whatever you need to do."

Thomas stared at Miles for several heartbeats before turning and walking away.

Church came over for a stroke as Amelia shouted, "You ready?"

Miles waved over to her, grabbed his stuff from the boot of the car, and took it to his new, albeit temporary, home. He hoped beyond all else that it was going to be a much easier trip than the first few days of being back in America had proved to be.

PART TWO

It wasn't that long ago that Lauren Gibson had been the human wife of a police Detective. To a mean, cruel man, who had thought little of her in the long term, and who had decided that aligning himself with a group of people—the Magistrate—whose sole aim was to hate someone else, was better than being a good husband. Hell, better than being a good human.

When Lauren had decided that enough was enough, and had set about exposing her husband's friends, he'd arranged for her to be kidnapped and killed. It hadn't gone according to plan. A vampire by the name of Oliver had saved her just before she died. He had tried to turn her into a vampire to save her life, but it had gone wrong, and she'd been turned into a Desolate Queen instead. A monster. A creature that even vampires considered a nightmare. And with good reason. Not only could a Desolate Royal control the desolate they created, but they could also control any vampires whose blood they drank. It made them a frightening prospect to many vampires.

Lauren hadn't wanted to be considered frightening, she'd only wanted revenge on her husband, on the Magistrate and its leader Blake Summers. All of them were dead now. Some by her hand, some by the hand of Miles Watson, the only vampire she'd met who had treated her like something other than a monster. He'd even let her escape, to try and find a way to come to terms with what she was. He'd warned her that should she start killing to create an army of desolate, he would come for her. She knew it wasn't an idle threat, and was pretty sure she did not want Miles and Church hunting her.

She'd moved north, up through Canada, and kept going until she found small villages, but she didn't stay anywhere long. A Desolate Royal was almost as strong and fast as a vampire, and healed fast, but sunlight killed them just as quickly, as it did any normal desolate, and there was always a *need* for her to create desolates to command. A need that grew the more humans were around her.

Over the last two-ish years, Lauren slowly moved east, across the north of the Yukon and the Northwest Territories, keeping away from human and vampire populations for longer than necessary. The former of which she was starting to see as food, and the latter of which could smell that she was something "other." She'd skirted around Hudson Bay through Manitoba and into Ontario. She figured that she'd travel the entire length of the country, stop, and go back the other way, taking a different route. She wasn't really sure why she was walking, other than a need to keep distracted, keep distant from any human populations, avoid the temptation to feed, to see humanity as her prey.

Miles had told her that every Desolate Royal he'd ever heard of had been a monster in every sense of the word, using their desolate to murder and plunder. Lauren was determined not to become that person. Determined to keep who she was when she'd been human, but it was difficult. She wasn't human anymore. It was something she was still coming to terms with.

She'd reached Quebec when she'd decided to take a detour to visit Maine. She'd heard the tales, seen the documentaries about what had happened, about the people still living there, and had decided that if there was one place she might feel safe, it was somewhere where the majority of the population were desolate.

The plan was to continue on down through to Quebec City, and on into Maine. She couldn't function during the daylight hours, so had gotten used to spending nights in caves or disused buildings. The days of a comfortable mattress and Egyptian cotton sheets were seemingly at an end for her.

By the time she'd reached Quebec City, she'd needed to feed. She'd decided soon after her change into Desolate Royalty that she would only kill those who weren't deserving of their lives. Before hunting, she visited a cheap hotel or motel, showered and changed into whatever clothes she'd managed to acquire and kept in her backpack for such needs. She made herself look something close to how she'd looked when she'd been human. She made sure her multitude of tattoos on her arms were covered, as she didn't want anyone identifying her by them. Her blonde hair, which had stopped growing after her turn from human to Desolate Royalty, was still at shoulder length, and usually bunched up under a hat or baseball cap, but she allowed it to fall free. She applied makeup, grateful that neither vampires nor Desolate Royalty had a problem with mirrors. Once ready, she went out to a bar, making sure to pick places where there had been a lot of stories about women being drugged. She had a few drinks alone, and usually caught the attention of at least one scumbag.

Lauren picked people who saw a young, pretty woman, alone at a bar, and decided she was someone who could be preyed upon. She let them drug her, let them take her wherever it was they needed to take her, and then she showed them what real fear was. Their screams didn't last. She fed well. It seemed there was no shortage of scumbags, which she figured was a damning indictment of many things, but she only knew that it was one less piece of shit out there.

Each kill rose as a desolate, and each time she took her new minion out somewhere secluded to practise commanding them, before she had them write a confession of their crimes and send it to the police. The desolate would kill themselves then, their ashes making sure that no one ever found the body.

So far, she'd killed fourteen men this way, and it had unfortunately gotten easier with every kill. She sometimes wondered if one day she'd kill and her humanity would be gone forever. She wondered if she'd even know when it happened.

Lauren moved north from Quebec City, crossing over into Maine next to a small town that she didn't even bother to remember the name of. She'd watched the guard stationed next to the boundary for two nights before finally deciding they weren't worth the trouble of concern. No one was expecting a Desolate Queen to move through the forest, evading their human senses with ease.

Once in Maine, she continued on at pace, putting a lot of distance between her and the guards. There were patrols who came into Maine looking to hunt desolate, thinking they could bag themselves a trophy. After easily avoiding the first few of them, Lauren had discovered they were often loud and drunk, and had no idea the real danger they would be in should she decide to show them.

It took her a few days to get down toward Augusta. She couldn't say why there. But then she wasn't sure why she felt such a need to come to Maine in the first place.

The closer she got to her destination, the more she was able to feel the hum of power that vibrated through the landscape. There were so many desolate that it practically overpowered her senses to be so close to them all at once. She'd expected Augusta to be teeming with them, practically sardines in a can, but as she'd reached the outskirts of the once vibrant city, looking down on part of it from the vantage point of the nearby rocky cliff, and seen the walls that had been erected around part of it, she saw only a few desolates milling around. She needed a closer look.

She took the long way around the cliff, down into what had once been North Augusta, although it was now little more than a burned-out shell. She continued on, keeping to the shadows, moving at pace through what had been residential and business areas alike. There was little sign of life anywhere; not even small animals called the place their home.

Avoiding the desolate was easy enough, seeing how they weren't interested in her. It gave Lauren the time to take the occasional detour to look through ramshackle buildings, trying to find anything that might tell her why the town was so full of energy yet there were so few desolate.

After a few hours, she arrived at the Maine State House. It was a large granite building that Lauren assumed had been white at some point, or at least grey, and was now covered in a layer of dust and grime. The local plant life, which had done a wonderful job of reclaiming a lot of the city and covered the front garden and steps of the State House, stopped short of the building itself.

Lauren stopped at the pillars and pulled up part of the flora from the ground, discovering that it had been partially cut, and recently. "Someone is keeping this place tidy," she said to herself, before dropping the plant and walking up to the front door of the State House.

She pushed the door open, which moved without a sound. Forty years of decay had besieged Maine, yet the State House was well-maintained and looked after. The floor inside the grand foyer was clear of debris, although it was in desperate need of a polish and tidy. Thick dust covered everything, and part of the ceiling had collapsed, showing the floor in plaster, brick, and wood.

Every footstep echoed around the large open area, and the power thrummed inside her chest. She placed her hand against the nearby wall as a gasp left her body. There were so many desolate somewhere nearby. It was overwhelming.

Lauren hurried out of the State House, her body immediately thanking her for it. She looked down across the steps, into the town itself. Something was wrong. She needed to get away from the State House, needed to find out why it felt as though there were so many desolate. Were they all underground, hibernating? If that was the case, how long had they been down there?

A scream suddenly tore through the stillness of the night. She moved quickly down the steps and out onto the street, where there was a second scream.

Lauren found herself walking up to Memorial Bridge, which was still intact, but was also a large stretch of road with no cover and excellent lines of sight on either side. She wondered if the screaming was a way to bring her to them, to set a trap for her. Although she had to admit she had no idea who might want to trap her, or even who might know she was in Maine.

There were cars on the bridge, long since abandoned. Some rusted away to skeletons, leaving jagged pieces of metal frame in their wake. Lauren moved from cover to cover, never staying in one place for longer than necessary as she crossed the bridge. Once at the other side, the smell of blood hit her first, followed by a low growl in her stomach. The desolate were insatiable feeders, and she had wished that trait wasn't also true of Desolate Queens. Ignoring her stomach, she quickly ran over to a set of trees, moving through them as a third scream froze her in her tracks.

The scream came from a large red-brick building a hundred feet to her right, just beyond the edge of the trees. The smell of blood was strong in the air. She sniffed, but there were no desolates near her, no vampires, no humans. The building was odd in that the windows on the first two floors were still there, and the door looked secure and well taken care of. She got the impression the building was still in use.

Lauren moved cautiously toward the edge of the trees, keeping low, the smell of blood increasing as she followed it along the tree line until she found the dead man. He had been torn apart and partially eaten. She wondered if he'd been the person she'd heard scream. Lauren pushed down the urge to feed on the fresh kill, forcing herself to look away, over at the red-brick building. Whatever was going on, it was happening inside.

She ran over to the door, reached out to the handle, and paused. She wasn't some trained soldier; she didn't have the instincts of someone who had fought in a war zone, she was just someone who was strong, fast, and *exceptionally* difficult to kill. All of that said, she felt as if opening the front door to the place where someone had been screaming was an invitation to trouble.

Lauren pulled her hand back as though she'd been burned. She glanced up and down the street, judging it empty, before her features changed. Her fingers elongated, ending with talons. Her hands and arms grew longer, and her jaw split open around each side of her mouth, allowing it to unhinge. Her ears grew into something resembling that of a wolf, and her eyes turned to a bronze colour, with black pupils like an owl. Her teeth, now piranha-like, were capable of rending flesh from bone. There was no mistaking a Desolate Royal for anything else.

Her talons were sharp enough to puncture the red brick if needed, but her strength was such that she could launch herself up to the first window with ease. Within moments Lauren sat atop the flat roof of the building. She turned back into her human-looking self and strolled across the roof toward the only door there. She tried the handle, but it was locked. A little pressure and the lock snapped loud enough to make her wince. She paused, using her incredible hearing to listen out for anyone or anything inside who might decide to investigate, before she stepped into the dingy stairwell beyond.

Lauren took the stairs down to the first floor, to an emergency fire door, which she pushed open, revealing a large open floor. The windows had all been smashed, and whatever the floor had contained was long gone, leaving only the remnants of wooden desks and rotting carpet. Parts of the concrete floor had holes in it, showing the wiring inside.

Apart from the door Lauren had just entered through, there were three more, one on either side, and another in between them that, after a quick inspection, showed two elevators and a second set of stairs. She checked both doors inside the room, finding that beyond them was a large office, or meeting room, although they were barren, tattered wastelands now.

She went back to the stairwell and took it down to the floor below. She was about to open the door when a scream sounded out from somewhere below her. Lauren decided to find the source of the screaming first, and returned to the stairs, taking them down to the building entrance.

The foyer was as empty as everything else Lauren had found. What had once been a receptionist's desk had long since collapsed under its own weight and was now just a bunch of rotting wood on the floor. The whole place smelled of rot, mildew, and, more recently, blood.

She took a long sniff and followed the scent through a set of double doors and down a hallway to another fire escape. The smell of blood was overwhelming, and as she passed two closed doors in the hallway, she had to stop and regain her composure. She reached the fire escape door and pushed it open with a little more force than she'd meant to, leaving a dent in the wall of the small room beyond.

Lauren crouched by several fresh blood drops just beyond the fire door and looked up at the metal door in front of her. There was a keypad beside it, and a bloody smear on the door itself, as if someone had tried to grab hold of it when they were dragged through.

The smell of the newcomer reached her despite the scent of blood, and she turned to see two men in the hallway beyond. One was tall, muscular, with broad shoulders and huge hands. He had a smirk on his face that told of something unpleasant. The second was shorter, skinnier; he looked ill, as though he should be in a bed resting, not out in the middle of the most dangerous state in the country. He wore a silver pendant in the shape of a teardrop with a blood-red jewel set in the middle.

"My name is Stuart," the sickly man said, stroking the pendant with one finger as he spoke, as if it gave him comfort.

"Whatever you're thinking of doing, it will end badly for you," Lauren said. "I promise."

"Not here to fight," Stuart said, his hands up, palms out.

"He is," Lauren said, nodding toward the man behind Stuart.

Stuart turned a little as if seeing his companion for the first time. He looked back at Lauren and shrugged. "I figured it was better to bring backup."

"You knew I was here?" Lauren asked.

"We knew since you arrived in the state," Stuart told her. "You've been drawn to this place, yes. We were told that you would arrive, and that we were to take you to Ellsworth."

"What's at Ellsworth?" Lauren asked. "And what's behind this door?"

"Honestly?" Stuart asked her before he started to cough. He held up a finger for Lauren to wait as he removed a bloodstained handkerchief from his pocket and coughed into it, before replacing it back in his pocket. "It's a bunch of scientific labs where a group of idiots who didn't know what they were playing around with decided to piss off a god. There's nothing down there but death and pain. We were told to come here and wait for you, that this place was better for you to get to rather than traipsing across the rest of Maine to Ellsworth. The person who wants you here has spent a long time making sure that people are afraid of this place. Ellsworth is close to where the initial outbreak happened. We're going to take you there so we can go see the person who wanted you here."

"That's all very cryptic. Who?"

"It's probably better we show rather than explain," Stuart said.

"Why do you smell strange?" Lauren sniffed the air. "Both of you. Not human, not vampire. Not desolate. What are you?"

Stuart slapped the stomach of his companion. "My friend here is a werewolf. I am a witch. A chaos witch, I guess is the technical term."

"You're sick."

"I'm dying," Stuart said. "I came here looking for a cure, but that is a conversation for later."

"Am I the cure?" Lauren asked; she did not like the sound of that.

Stuart shook his head, pushing aside the frustration he was feeling. "No, you're just important to someone who once made people like you."

"*Made people like me?*" Lauren asked. "What does that even mean?"

"You *needed* to come here," Stuart said. "You're a Desolate Queen; you had no need to ever come to Maine, yet you did. I was told that you've been expected for a long time. I assume at some point you decided to just make your way here."

Lauren opened her mouth to argue and closed it again. "Yes," she said softly.

"I assume you'd also like to see the person who put that idea in your head," Stuart said.

Lauren was about to say something when she felt the air behind her change slightly. She turned just as a third man plunged a needle into her neck, injecting her with . . . something that made her feel terribly sleepy. She threw a punch at the man, who caught her hand easily in his open palm, and with his second hand injected another needle into her neck.

Lauren wobbled, her legs going out from under her as she crashed down to her knees.

"She was coming along willingly," Stuart said.

"We don't have time for this," the third man said.

"Liam," Stuart argued.

"No," Liam snapped. "She needs to come now. We'll use the tram, it'll be safer."

Lauren lay on the cool floor. It was quite comfortable, all things considered; she was so sleepy. It felt as if she hadn't slept in years. She needed to sleep. She *welcomed* it. Part of her brain screamed at her to fight it, to stay awake, but another part liked the idea of a long rest.

"Hello, Lauren," a man's voice said. He sat on a throne of skulls, wearing a pair of black trousers, shoes polished to a mirror shine, a white shirt, and a black waistcoat. He had pale skin, a short dark beard, and long dark hair that fell over slender shoulders.

Lauren looked around the crypt that she found herself in. It smelled of old water and decaying plants. There was a stone sarcophagus in the middle of the room, next to a small waterfall. It made her feel calm. There was a throne made from black stone at the far end of the crypt. "Is this a dream?" she asked the man who sat on the throne.

The man leaned forward in the throne. "Yes," he said softly. His accent had a heavy Scandinavian quality to it. "But soon, you will wake up, and we will get to work."

Lauren looked over at the seated man. "What work?" she asked. She felt no fear or concern about what she was seeing, just a need to know what was going on.

"We're going to finish what these idiots started here all those years ago," the man said with a warm smile on his handsome face.

"And what was that?" Lauren asked. "What did they try to do?"

The man clapped and got to his feet. He walked over to Lauren and dropped an arm around her shoulders. "Oh, they tried to use me to change the world. I aim to show them how it's done properly. I need you to learn how to control the desolate you didn't create."

"And how am I meant to do that?" she asked, feeling lightheaded and strange. It was as if being in the presence of the man before her calmed her, made her trust him. Somewhere deep inside her, a part of her screamed not to give in to it. She tried to hold on to that part of her as she turned to the man and smiled.

"With practise," the man said, his own smile never wavering. "And if there's one thing in Maine we have a lot of, it's desolate. Before then, rest. You're going to need it."

Chapter Twelve

The first night of the drive through Maine had been uneventful, with the lights of the military camp giving way to open stretches of dark countryside. Miles sat up to watch the darkness turn to morning and saw the devastation to the town they'd reached. The buildings had been all but flattened, and there was nothing to see in all directions but the remains of a civilisation that had been gone for decades.

The roads that hadn't been completely reclaimed by nature were bumpy to drive along, and Miles was grateful for the four-wheel drive capabilities of the vehicle they were in.

The Winnebago interior consisted of two bedrooms at the rear which were, in reality, little more than a double bed. But there was also a bathroom, with shower, and a small kitchen area next to the comfortable sofa bed, which was where Church had slept the first day as the House Idolator familiar had stood watch outside.

The convoy had pulled over during the morning at Scarborough and the vampire contingent had hunkered down to rest. Miles had left the familiar to watch over the Winnebago and had quickly fallen asleep in the rear bedroom of the vehicle.

Miles realised he hadn't said two words to the familiar when he'd woken up on the second night and found himself alone in the kitchen with the man who had started the engine for the convoy to continue on into Maine.

"What's your name?" Miles asked. "It feels rude to nae know."

"Arvid Holmlund," he said.

"You're Scandinavian?" Miles asked, picking up on the accent.

"From Norway," Arvid told him without looking back from his position as driver.

Arvid was a large, barrel-chested man, with long plaited light-blond hair and a matching beard—also plaited—which had several silver charms in it. Miles had to admit, there was a definite Norse characteristic to his look.

"So, how long have you been a familiar?" Miles asked him as the kettle boiled.

"Ten years now," Arvid said.

"You're familiar to which member of House Idolator?" Miles asked.

"First Lord Fuller," Arvid said.

"Is that why you do this?" Miles asked, pouring a cup of coffee and taking a seat behind the driver.

Church looked up from her place on the floor, decided it wasn't worth moving for, and promptly went back to sleep.

"This?" Arvid asked.

"Drive the pilgrimage?" Miles clarified.

"It is my way of helping the pilgrimage," Arvid said.

"Are all the familiars from the First Lord?"

"No, some are from the First Captain, or First Authority," Arvid said, seemingly more at ease not talking about himself. "Only the First members of House Idolator have their familiars run the pilgrimage."

"In hope that you'll be turned full vampire," Miles suggested.

"That is the aim, yes," Arvid said. "This is . . . our testing of a sort. To prove that we are trustworthy and capable. To prove that we can aid the House in its aims."

"What aims are those?" Miles asked, blowing on the hot coffee.

"To spread the Word of the Dusk," he said proudly. "In time, it is hoped that we can ascend back to our rightful place as a Great House."

"I hope you achieve it," Miles said.

Arvid looked in the rearview mirror. "Really?"

"Of course," Miles said, taking the first sip of coffee and letting out a little sigh. "I hold no ill will against any of the Houses, Great or Minor. I only hope that the Great Houses have the needs of vampire kind at heart and nae just the needs of their House. Everyone's job is easier if no one is trying to fight for supremacy within the vampire world all the time."

One of the bedroom doors at the rear of the vehicle slid open and Amelia walked out. Miles pointed to the freshly brewed coffee.

"Oh, I could marry you," she said as she poured herself a cup.

"I didn't realise coffee had that effect on women," Miles said. "I should make it more often."

Amelia laughed and sat down beside Miles.

"Sleep well?" he asked.

"Changing my sleep patterns to be nocturnal is a weird thing to do," Amelia told him. "The bed was comfortable, though, so I won't complain too much. Did I miss anything exciting?"

"No," Miles told her. "I was just talking to our driver, Arvid, about his time in House Idolator. He drives the pilgrimages for them."

"Oh, that must be exciting," Amelia said, with no hint that she thought otherwise. "How many times have you done it?"

"This is my fourth," Arvid said. "In six years."

"So, you're an old hand at this," Amelia said. "How is this one comparing so far?"

"We have only just started, so it's about the same as any of the others. It won't be until tomorrow night that we start to see the real changes to the state. The desolate here don't seem to die. They're relatively small in number, thankfully, but we kill a few, and the next time we go through, there are still more. We don't know where they're coming from. The weather swaps and changes on a dime—I think the expression is. We aren't due any storms, but then, that means little here."

"What about a food source for the desolate?" Miles asked. "There can't be enough people or animals for them to sustain large numbers."

"There is certainly an abundance of small animals, and some deer, but how the desolate are feeding is just another mystery we haven't solved."

"Someone else mentioned that the desolate numbers haven't fallen," Amelia said. "I wonder why that is. The desolates can be killed, right?"

"Fire, sunlight, decapitation," Miles said. "They definitely die; I've seen my fair share of them turn to dust."

"Where do we stop in the morning?" Amelia asked.

"The fort of Falmouth," Arvid said. "Just on the other side of Portland."

"That's nae a long journey," Miles said. "And don't you ever sleep?"

"I had a few hours during the day," Arvid said. "My familiar physiology means I don't need as much rest as a human. It's one of the benefits I'm most thankful for. And we stop in Falmouth because it takes a while to get through Portland. There are pockets of desolate there, and we stop and deal with them, so they don't become an issue."

"You have to keep stopping every time?" Miles asked.

"Yes," Arvid said.

"So, they're really not dying?"

"I'm pretty sure they are," Arvid said. "We've killed them, burned them, just to be sure. I've seen a few catch fire from the sunlight. I've seen them turn to ash. I just think they have numbers to replenish. Although we don't know exactly where those hidden desolates might be. No one has offered to go search."

"No one has checked where they're coming from?" Miles asked.

"There are rumours that there was an underground lab beneath Augusta with tunnels that ran all around the state. Apparently there were tens of thousands of desolates down there when Maine fell."

"So they are dying," Amelia said. "There's just a huge number of rein-forcements, not to mention all of the humans who were turned during the mess. Potentially hundreds of thousands of desolates could remain in this state. I didn't realise it was so bad."

"House Idolator tends to be the only House that deals inside the state," Arvid said as the Winnebago slowed, and he turned the wheel to exit the road. "Sometimes I think it's a little bit of out of sight, out of mind with this place."

"So, you stop off in Portland and decapitate a few desolates," Amelia asked, making a note in her book. "How many do you kill?"

"A few dozen, maybe more," Arvid said. "I think last year was the most, it was nearly a hundred."

"That's a lot," Miles said.

"It was a big jump from previous years," Arvid admitted.

Miles looked out of the window as if half expecting to see a horde of desolate ambling along the road.

The vehicle pulled to a stop and Arvid unbuckled his seatbelt and turned back to Miles and Amelia. "I'll go check on the others; if you need blood or food, now's the time. If you're planning on helping out, that is."

Miles waited for Arvid to leave before he said, "Something really weird is going on in this state."

"Weirder than it being overrun by the desolate?" Amelia asked.

Miles turned back to her. "I guess we're going to get our first look at just how bad this place is." He didn't bother to wait for anyone to come to the vehicle and opened the door, letting Church out into the cool night air. She immediately ran off into the nearby woods as Miles looked around the large clearing that they'd all parked in. It looked as if it had once been a parking area for those who wanted to spend some time in the woods. There were the remains of a sign that said you had to *pay to park*, although the red lettering was faded to barely anything.

"Miles," Thomas Reed said as he walked over to him.

Miles nodded hello and paid attention to those getting off the tour bus at the front of the convoy. Everyone was stretching their legs, and there was an air of excitement and nervous energy around.

"What's about to happen?" Miles asked Thomas as Amelia stepped out of the Winnebago.

"Portland was once a big place," Thomas said. "Relatively speaking. We like to clear out the desolates who have gathered here. It's usually only a few dozen, and we don't go through the buildings as some are borderline about to fall down, and some probably are a danger to anyone stepping aside, but those desolates wandering about at night are fair game."

"They just stay in the town limits?" Amelia asked.

"There has been precious little work done on desolate behaviour, which is a pity," Thomas said, the excitement in his tone suggesting it was a favourite topic of his. "Oddly, the desolates in Maine behave a little differently to those outside of it, inasmuch as they don't appear to be leaving the towns and villages. We tagged a few, tried to follow them, but they don't do much. They've never even made an attempt to get at the checkpoints. Pretty sure they wouldn't care about being outnumbered; they'd just see the people there are food. It's a little odd, almost like they don't want to leave Maine."

"And New Brunswick?" Miles asked.

"From what we can tell, it has a close to zero desolate population," Thomas said. "We've seen their numbers walking into Maine, but not the other way. Almost like there's something in this area that they're drawn toward, although for the life of me I can't think what it is."

"Strange," Miles said.

Thomas nodded. "We're not sure why, but until they get a whiff of blood they just amble about at night. Once they get that scent, though, they're like wolves and will hunt over large distances. Still won't leave a rough approximation of the state, though. They stop several miles before the northern border. Like there's a gigantic invisible barrier there."

"That's exceptionally unusual," Miles said. "Why hasn't anyone mentioned this before?"

"Because right now it's conjecture and guesswork," Thomas said. "No one wants to go study the desolate. There's no such thing as a *safe distance* from them. We tagged a few, monitored them for a short time, before whatever screws with the electronics in this place destroyed the chips."

"Can they smell us here?" Amelia asked, looking around into the darkness that surrounded them.

"No," Thomas said. "Not unless you're wounded. Once they smell blood, they are like sharks. I assume Miles had experienced that firsthand."

"More than once," Miles said, making sure that his tone told everyone that not a single one of those experiences had been fun.

"Okay, so what's the plan?" Amelia asked.

"We'll be going in groups," Thomas said. "My Blood Guard and I will take point, with the familiars staying back with the vehicles. Would you like to join me and my Blood Guard, Miles?"

Miles realised it would probably be beneficial to ingratiate himself with the House Idolator people, and nodded. "Love to," he lied. "Church, we're going hunting."

Church bounded out of the woods a moment later, as Thomas went to get everyone else ready.

"This safe?" Amelia asked.

"Hell no. Put your stab vest on," Miles told her. "Make sure the collar is up, covering your neck. Make sure you wear your jacket, too. Stay behind Church at all times; she'll keep you safe. You see desolate, you hang back behind us."

Amelia nodded once and reentered the Winnebago.

"You watch her like a hawk," Miles told Church. "Whatever happens out there, she's your primary care."

Church barked once.

Amelia exited the Winnebago a short time later all geared up and ready to head off into danger.

"You okay?" Miles asked her.

Amelia nodded. "Been to war zones before."

"This ain't like that," Miles said. "Desolate don't much care about any credentials or conventions that say you should be kept safe."

"Neither did the people who were shooting at the unit I'd been placed with," Amelia pointed out.

Miles nodded. "Fair enough. Let's go do something stupid."

"You think this is stupid?" Amelia asked as they walked toward the gathered vampires.

"We'll see by the end of the night, I guess."

Thomas was busy explaining what was going to happen while the vampires on the pilgrimage all spoke with excited tones. They were given a machete each and told to use it to decapitate any desolate they came across.

"Can't we just turn to our vampire sides?" one of the men—Jeremy—whom Amelia had introduced to Miles asked. Miles remembered that he'd had military experience.

"Some of the people here are young vampires," Thomas said. "There's a danger of too much blood making someone attack with their fangs. If you drink desolate blood, you die. It's as simple as that."

"And it's nae a good death," Miles said. "Weeks of slowly going insane as the desolate worms its way into, and eventually takes over, your mind. You'll lose whatever part of you made you who you are. If you drink desolate blood, wait until the morning and let the sun take you. It's kinder than what will happen otherwise."

Whatever good-natured mood that had bubbled among the pilgrims changed in an instant.

"Seriously?" Maeve asked Miles, who nodded.

"You ever killed someone who did that?" Jeremy asked him quietly.

Miles thought back to Sara Bakos, who had fed from a desolate, who had become one and had aimed her need at vengeance towards him and those he cared about. He thought back to her dying scared of who she might kill next, in a moment of clarity brought on by Miles's bloodline power to disrupt the vampire and human sides of a person. Or in her case, the desolate and human. "Yes," he said without looking over at Jeremy. "Trust me when I tell you, you don't want that."

"Ummm, who are you?" the other man Miles had been introduced to asked.

"Travis," Thomas said. "Miles here is an Arbiter, although he's not here on official business, as you can see form the lack of torc on his wrist. He's long since been someone who has excelled in hunting desolate. His words of warning ring true, but they are just that, a warning."

There was a low-level murmur among the pilgrims, but Miles ignored it and walked by the group, pretending he didn't see the stares they threw his way. He hadn't wanted everyone to know he was an Arbiter, but apparently that had lasted all of a few hours. He continued on to the front of the line of vehicles, where Thomas and his Blood Guard stood, all three in something resembling a cross between modern military gear and plate armour, albeit made with Kevlar, steel, and silver. They all wore plain golden full-face masks, black mesh around the eyes.

"You scared them," Thomas said without looking up, as he studied a paper map that had been laid out on the flatbed of the truck.

"Good," Miles said. "They thought we were off for a jolly. They think like that, they aren't all coming back. Where are we?"

Thomas placed a finger on the map, moving to the side to let Miles take a look. "We've come up that way," he said tracing his finger along what had been I-295. Up ahead is the Fore River. We continue on, around Back Cove, across the bridge, and we stop to clear out the area. We can't use the I-295 to go straight up to Falmouth as it's partially destroyed, so we need to cut through Portland and go up, out the top of it. It's an hour and a half walk, or it was before the desolate made the place their home. Takes closer to six now, and we're all going to be working for that time. We tried not clearing it out for a few years and ended up losing people to the desolate. So now we thin their numbers every time we come here, like a deer cull."

"What about going across the river?" Miles asked, pointing to the bridge that went over Presumpscot River.

"Bridge is destroyed about halfway up," Thomas said. "We don't know who did it—wasn't us, wasn't the humans who used it as an evacuation route. Our best guess is someone is living up on the other side and didn't want visitors."

"You ever checked?"

"Nope," Thomas said. "No time to make the detour. We go up to Falmouth fort, which is, as the name suggests, a large walled fort, and has a number of our people inside. They help clear as much of Portland as possible, but they have their own issues with the desolate that come out of the park to the north. We rejoin the I-295 and continue up to Brunswick, which has a large settlement. Or large in Maine terms."

"Okay, you let everyone know the plan, and we'll get going," Miles said as he studied the map. "You figured out where the desolate keep coming from?"

Thomas shook his head. "Best guess is they're trapped underground and dig their way out over time. There are probably a few hundred, maybe a little more, under there. The idea of napalming the place gets brought up every few months, but no one wants to go down there and check what we're dealing with, so while the desolate numbers are small, we just cull them as we find them."

"I heard that there are people who think they don't die."

Thomas laughed. "Well, that's just hyperbole, I imagine they do die. They're desolate, not the Terminator."

"Terminator still died," Miles said. "That's a maze of roads and streets, lot of alleyways, lots of places to hide. And we're going to drive right into it."

"We've done it dozens of times," Thomas said. "Maybe this time there won't be so many desolate there."

"I think you're playing whack-a-mole," Miles told him. "The root of the problem is left alone; you're just putting a Band-Aid on a gaping wound."

"I agree with you," Thomas said, shrugging. "But this is what we do. We go there, we clear it out, and we continue on. It's what we've always done."

"Tradition."

Thomas nodded. "Some of that, certainly. But also, it's relatively safe there. Lots of those houses were destroyed in the cleansing after the fall of Maine. There's a lot of open terrain, and since we actually started to clear it out every year, we've never had an issue. It might seem like busy work to you, or a pointless tradition, but it prepares these people for what we're going to see the rest of the journey. Most have never had to fight a desolate, most have never had to deal with a horde of them. This is the safest way to ease them into what they might have to contend with the rest of their time in this state."

Miles looked down at the map one last time. "Okay," he said, looking up at Thomas. "We do it your way. But I want you to know that if at any point I think one of those people back there is a liability, I'm going to tell them."

Thomas folded up the map. "Good," he said. "Hopefully you won't have to."

Miles glanced back at the group. A bunch of vampires who had never seen anything like a horde of desolate, only one with actual military training. Miles closed his eyes and inwardly groaned. *What could possibly go wrong?*

❧ Chapter Thirteen ❧

Miles, Church, and Amelia went back to their Winnebago and sat around the sofa as the House Idolator familiar, Arvid, drove to their destination. Miles watched out of the tinted windows at the landscape of partially destroyed buildings and the occasional piece of movement within the darkness.

"There are desolate out there, aren't there?" Amelia asked.

Miles nodded. "It's a bit weird that they don't stop to clear out all of this but only do so in the towns. They have their prearranged tradition and they're nae going to deviate from it. Thomas said that it's safer across the bridge, but the desolate keep coming back, so I'm unsure exactly how safe *safe* is."

"I'm going out with you," Amelia said. "I didn't come here for nothing."

"I know," Miles said. "Church will stay with you. You'll be safe. Or as safe as anyone, witch or otherwise, can be out here."

Amelia was quiet for a few minutes as they looked outside the window together. "Did you ever come to Maine before it fell?"

Miles nodded. "A bunch of times. It was, at least on the face of it, a sort of vampire-human paradise. I had no idea what was going on beneath the surface, so to speak. I'd like to think very few people did, and that's why it caught everyone unaware. Experiments on humans, on the desolate. Trying to find ways to control the desolate. Trying to find out how they work, why they come about. It's all a litany of horror stories, and it ends with the deaths of tens of thousands of people."

"And the creation of the Magistrate," Amelia said.

"Aye, the whole thing is a mess I'd rather nae see repeated."

"You think it might be?"

"Repeated?" Miles shook his head. "I doubt it. Lots of vampire-controlled cities all over the world, and there's no problems there. At least, none we know about. Do I think there are still people out there who are experimenting on desolates, on humans, on vampires? Sure. I've met my share before and after Maine happened, but I'd like to think that whatever happened here has made a lot of people, especially the Houses and Assembly, pay a lot more attention to places where vampires are in charge."

"When I spoke to First Lord Fuller, he was full of praise for what they wanted to do in Maine," Amelia said. "How they wanted to return it to its former glory, how they needed to remove the stain of what had happened here. I got the feeling he's passionate about it. If they can do it, if they can clear out Augusta, and stop the constant influx of desolate from wherever they're coming from, it's possible that Maine could be reclaimed."

"Maybe." It was a nice dream, but to Miles that's all it was. Maine was gone. No matter what House Idolator, or anyone else, did to reclaim it, to remove the desolate, it wouldn't really change anything. The *stain* of what had happened would always remain.

"You don't agree."

Miles shrugged. "I think there's something weird going on in this state that no one wants, or has the capability, to investigate. The desolate should all be dead or at least decreasing in number by now. Even the ones we know are trapped under Augusta should have just been a few thousand in total. I know people who say they should just use drones to bomb it all, but drones won't work because of the electrical interference, same reason they can't just napalm it from the air. They would need boots on the ground. And there's no guarantee it'll work, even then. No one wants to be known as the person who sent his people to die in a lost cause."

"It's only a lost cause if you fail," Amelia said.

"They might reclaim Maine, but the cost would be astronomical in terms of people. A lot of the desolate under Augusta have been stuck there for decades, just waiting. Probably cocooned down there. I fought a desolate which had been cocooned for only a few weeks or months, and it was the most terrifying desolate I've ever come across. It was practically a giant among them. Can you imagine how bad it would be to send a few thousand vampires down there, only to come across a few hundred desolate who had literally been feeding on each other, getting bigger, more dangerous?"

"So, Maine stays lost," Amelia said. "Those responsible died in the initial attack, or were tried and executed by the vampires. And then everyone looked the other way and pretended like it wasn't happening."

The vehicle was beginning to slow down, and they soon turned off the interstate and started to move through what had been a residential area, although like everywhere else, the houses were falling apart with disrepair.

"It's raining," Miles said, unsure how to proceed with the conversation about Maine. It was lost; it would take too much to get it back. And if it ever came back, would anyone ever want it to be vampire-run again? The American political landscape changed a lot after Maine, and despite the fact that the Magistrate had been given a bloody nose after Seattle, they were still backed by rich, powerful opponents to vampire kind.

"I was told the weather changes quickly here," Amelia said. "Even more so since the eighties. Any idea why?"

Miles shook his head. "Nae a clue. I don't think that what happened in the eighties had any effect on the weather, but who knows. I've heard of weirder stuff."

"Aren't there vampires who can control the weather?"

"House Nebula," Miles told her. "They can change the weather a bit, make fog, drop or raise the temperature, make it snow, make it windy, or have it rain, but it's all in isolated areas. Not full-on storms hitting a whole town, or hurricanes or anything like that. Not that I've ever heard of. We're vampires, nae the X-Men."

The vehicle stopped just behind the large bus, and Miles remained seated for a moment, watching those inside the bus disembark. There was an aura of muted excitement in their mannerisms that Miles didn't like. He wasn't sure that *excited* was ever what people should be feeling before they went on a desolate hunt.

"You okay?" Amelia asked. She'd gotten to her feet and was busy making sure her vest was still okay as she zipped up a slate grey rainproof coat over it. She held her arms out to the side and moved them around. "This is a bit big."

Miles stood and stretched. "You'll be grateful for it if any of those desolate get too close."

Amelia placed a microphone on her lapel and removed her phone from her pocket. "I'm going to film this. I've already checked with First Lord Fuller, and he okayed it. Everyone else had to sign a disclaimer to say that they might be in photos or footage."

"I didn't sign one."

"You're not going to be in any of the photos or footage," Amelia said with a smile.

"Too handsome for your readers?"

Amelia laughed.

Miles smiled. "Well, that told me."

"Yes, your obviously masculine charms might be too much for some of the people watching it," Amelia said, a smile on her face the whole time. "I don't want you to be the cause of a mass fainting."

"Smart," Miles said. "Vampires don't need any more bad press."

Amelia let out a chuckle. "You're an Arbiter. Can't have you on film."

"Aye, I assumed as much," Miles replied. "Though I prefer the idea of me being far too manly for the population of this world."

"If you like, you can tell people that," Amelia said.

Church let out a derisive snort.

"Don't you start," Miles told her.

Church made a huffing noise, and turned to Amelia, licking her hand.

"Nae appreciated in my own time," Miles said. "That's my problem."

Church barked just as there was a knock on the door, which Amelia opened, letting in a slightly damp-looking Thomas.

"It's raining," Miles said.

"I can see why you're an Arbiter, with observation skills like that," Thomas replied with a good-natured grin. "We are ready for the hunt. Amelia, please do hang back far enough that you're in no danger. One of my Blood Guard will be standing nearby."

"As will Church," Miles said.

"I think you're probably safer than the rest of us put together," Thomas told her. "If you're ready, Miles."

Miles rolled his shoulders.

"Be careful," Amelia said to Miles as Thomas exited the Winnebago first.

Miles turned back to her as he descended the steps to the outside. "I'll be fine. You two keep an eye on each other."

What had started outside as a persistent drizzle was quickly turning into the kind of rain that Miles would best describe as pissing it down. The ground the vehicles were parked on was mostly broken tarmac, as it had been a main road back when such things had been needed in the town, but he knew that outside of the town the roads got less and less usable in bad weather, and he didn't want to get bogged down—literally—in the middle of nowhere.

The pilgrims were all standing in a group, each having been given a machete of some kind or other. Two of the Blood Guard stood over to the side, their hands on the broadswords sheathed at their hips. The third Blood Guard stood at the front of the Winnebago as Amelia and Church exited, nodding toward them both as everyone walked a short distance down the ramshackle road toward the remains of what had once been a street of homes.

Most of the houses still looked vaguely house-like, although quite a few of them had partially collapsed from disuse, or being so open to the elements. Vines wrapped around porches and tufts of grass and weeds poked through cracked concrete garden paving.

"Where are they?" Miles asked Thomas. The two had set off at the front of the pack, with one Blood Guard on either side just behind them.

Thomas pointed up toward a several larger buildings in a row with a parking area out in front. "Used to be some shops," he said.

"A pharmacy," Miles said, reading the names of the shops that still had names. Five of the shops had metal shutters installed out front, which would need to be lifted up to allow anyone into the buildings themselves, which did beg the question, how did the desolate keep getting inside? "A 7-Eleven, too. Why do the desolate come here?"

"Is that a rhetorical question?"

Miles nodded. "Sorry, just wondering to myself. There's a lot of buildings that they could hide in."

"Maybe this one is just easier to get into?" Thomas theorised. "It's more derelict than a lot of others. You know, when we found out what they were doing in Maine, we found they had done so much research about the desolate, but they didn't actually learn an awful lot that survived the fall. So much lost."

Miles stopped by the remains of a Mercury Cyclone GT, its original bright red paint mostly faded or worn away. The windows were smashed, the interior all but destroyed from time, weather, or if the smell was any indication, whatever had decided to use it as a toilet.

Miles looked across the road at an old church. "You ever go in there?"

Thomas nodded. "We're going to clean it out, too. Feels like we should always make sure that places like that aren't tainted with the evil of the desolate."

Miles walked over the road to the church. It still stood tall, though the tiled roof had seen better days, and the cross that had once adorned it was now on the overgrown lawn at the front of the building. It was big enough that the downstairs would be a good place for desolate to hide during the day.

Thomas gathered the pilgrims together and walked through the plan. They were going to open the doors of each building in turn, and draw out any desolate inside. No one was to go into a building alone, and no one was to try and compete for most kills. If desolates were spotted alone outside of this area, the kill was made quickly, and reported in case there was a horde coming. After they were done there, they would move over to the church and flush out any inside.

Thomas started showing people how to decapitate a desolate, which honestly in Miles's mind you should either already know, or stay on the bus out of everyone's way. He kept that notion to himself, though, in case it upset some people.

Miles saw Amelia walking around some of the houses, filming content as she, Church, and the Blood Guard made their way slowly over to the shop area.

There was a rattle of chains as the two Blood Guard went over to the first of five shops with the metal shutters. One of them lifted the shutter as the other stood nearby, their hand on their sword hilt. As the shutter moved up, it made enough noise to presumably wake the dead.

There was a silence for a few seconds as the Blood Guard moved back from the shattered pharmacy windows. It didn't take long for the desolates to come stumbling out of the shop. There were four in total, all of whom saw the pilgrims and sprinted toward them, roaring in a need to feed and rend flesh from bone.

Miles strolled toward the group as the pilgrims set about decapitating all four desolates, before Thomas poured fluid on their bodies and set them alight.

"You do that for all of the desolate you kill?" Miles asked, the heat of the burning bodies forcing him to keep his distance.

Thomas nodded as more desolates were released from the next two shops. Shops four and five were devoid of anything except a few exceptionally irritated rats and a metric ton of cockroaches.

When it was clear that nothing more was coming out of the shops, the pilgrims walked over to the church, where Thomas and the two Blood

Guards opened the door after removing the chains. There were several desolates inside, which ran out at the waiting pilgrims.

Amelia recorded the whole thing, and went into the church with Thomas and the Blood Guard, leaving the pilgrims outside. Miles remained with the pilgrims, far enough back to not get in the way, but close enough to intervene should there be an issue.

"Hey!" Jenny shouted, pointing down the road. "It's a lone desolate."

"Must have come from around here somewhere," Jeremy said.

"I'll deal with it," Travis told them, puffing out his chest and waving his machete about as he strolled down the moonlit street toward the desolate. The latter noticed the vampire when he was about forty feet away and rushed toward him, but one vampire against a single desolate who probably hadn't eaten more than vermin for months on end was only ever going to have one outcome.

Travis stepped to the side of the desolate, knocking it back toward the crowd who cheered.

Miles didn't like where this was going, and pushed himself away from the wall he'd been leaning against. He started a slow, leisurely stroll toward the desolate, who had fallen to the floor and was scrambling to get back to its feet.

It wore the tattered remains of what had once been a pair of trousers and a shirt, although neither had much in the way of material left. It was shoeless and bald, and its ribcage looked as though someone had sucked all of the contents out of it. Its grey skin hung from its emaciated body, but it still hissed and growled, looking for its next victim.

Travis kicked the desolate in the head, sending it back to the ground. He stomped on its leg, snapping the bone.

"Let me have a go!" Jenny shouted with a lot more enthusiasm than Miles was happy to hear.

Travis gave a bow and motioned for her to continue the assault. Jenny brought her boot down on the back of the desolate's head, smashing its face into the concrete road with a noise that made several of the pilgrims wince.

"Come on!" Jenny shouted at the desolate, stepping back to give it some room. "Come show me what you can do. You abomination."

Travis whooped and hollered as several of the pilgrims began to turn away, uninterested in watching someone's idea of fun when it intersected with needless cruelty.

The desolate was back on its feet, and Jenny swiped her machete across its chest, bringing it back down onto the outstretched hand of the desolate, severing the limb. She kicked the desolate back, and laughed. "Let's get that other hand, shall we?" she asked, bringing the machete up.

Miles caught her hand as it reached its highest point, and tore the weapon out of her hand.

"Who the fuck do you think you are?" Jenny shouted at him, regaining the attention of everyone who had been happy to let her do her own thing.

Miles brought the machete down onto the neck of the desolate, decapitating it, before tossing the weapon at Jenny's feet. "We don't torture for fun."

"They're desolate," Jenny said, picking up the machete. "Who gives a fuck?"

Miles turned back to Jenny, anger in his eyes. "We do nae torture for fun. We kill, we move on, we don't linger, we don't inflict needless suffering on those we deem lesser than us. We're vampires, nae monsters."

Jenny laughed in Miles's face. "I'll do as I please. You can't do shit to stop me."

"Jenny, enough," Thomas called out.

"No, this . . . man thinks he can tell me not to enjoy myself."

"We don't torture the desolate," Thomas said.

"I am of House Idolator, and I will rid this world of vermin in whatever manner I please."

"You will not!" Miles's words were mixed with his power, slamming it into Jenny's mind with enough force to cause her to stumble back to the ground, dropping the machete.

She looked up at him with genuine fear, which was quickly replaced with rage.

Travis ran toward Miles, who avoided the punch and slammed his hand into the younger vampire's chest, breaking his ribs, lifting him off his feet, and smashing him down onto the ground with ease.

Miles turned to Jenny, who had the machete in her hands and nothing but contempt on her face. "You do *not* talk to me like that," she growled.

"If you come at me with that weapon, you die," Miles said loud enough for everyone to hear. "No games, no second chances, I'll take your life and forget you ever existed."

"Miles," Thomas said, with more than a little pleading in his tone.

Miles looked down at Travis, who remained on the ground. "Goes for you, too."

"Miles, please don't execute the pilgrims," Thomas said as he strode toward the rapidly escalating incident. "Back to the bus, all of you."

Jenny tossed her machete on the ground with a hiss of annoyance and stormed off, with Travis running after her, while everyone else stared at Miles with a mixture of horror, fear, and outrage.

"Go," Thomas called off. "Back to the bus."

The all did as they were told, with Jenny the last to go.

"They were torturing desolate," Miles said by way of explanation. "They're mindless husks, but that doesn't mean they get to be tortured for fun, Thomas."

Thomas let out a long, weary sigh. "I agree. Although I think Jenny and Travis might not be best pleased with what you've done here today. They might form a little group intent on causing you harm."

Miles watched the pilgrims go back to their vehicles, and knew it wasn't the last he'd hear from the kinds of people who thought that torture was a fun way to spend time. He turned to Thomas. "What else is new?"

❧ CHAPTER FOURTEEN ❧

I want to check something," Miles said before he returned to the bus.

"What?" Thomas asked.

"The shops where the desolate were," he replied. "Just take a minute."

"You want assistance?"

Miles shook his head and jogged away to the buildings, which two of the Blood Guard were busy closing the shutters on.

"Do you ever go inside and check them out?" Miles asked.

"No," the first Blood Guard said. "We are not allowed to perform a search and clear here. We protect the First Authority before all else."

"I'm going into that pharmacy," Miles said. "Don't lock me in."

"You have five minutes," the Blood Guard said. "I don't want to have to come in after you."

"You won't," Miles assured him as he turned to find Amelia outside of the pharmacy, Church beside her.

"You've found something?" she asked as Miles joined up with her.

"I don't know," he admitted. "I just want to look."

"At the inside of where desolate keep appearing from."

"Never said it would be a fun look," Miles told her as he stepped over the broken glass into the pharmacy itself. He was about to tell Amelia and Church to stay, but they were already inside the building with him by the time he'd turned around.

"No, I'm not waiting," Amelia said.

Church barked once in agreement.

"Fine, don't wander off," Miles said.

"This place stinks of shit," Amelia said, covering her mouth with her sleeve, while she turned on a flashlight with her free hand.

"Desolate aren't exactly the cleanliest of creatures," Miles said as he continued through the pharmacy, stepping over the remains of old medicine boxes.

"What do you expect to find in here?" she asked.

"The answer to a riddle," Miles said without looking back.

They reached the pharmacy counter at the rear of the shop. Miles stepped around it, and through one of two doors behind it. It took him into an L-shaped hallway with four doors. He started at the end, checking the door, which led to a small bathroom. The next door led to a stockroom that was mostly a mass of cardboard boxes and shelving units with well-expired medicine on them. The third door was a coffee room, with table, chairs, a TV, a small kitchen, and a fridge.

"What are you expecting?" Amelia asked.

"I'm nae sure," Miles said, trying the final door, which led to a docking area at the rear of the pharmacy. There was a metal shutter at the far end, and a truck in the middle of the floor, next to a large sinkhole.

"Jesus fucking hell," Amelia said, her voice muffled as she tried to cram as much of her arm over her face as possible. "It smells like everything died in here."

"Desolate," Miles said, dropping down from where he stood at the top of a ramp onto the docking bay floor. There were several crates, the contents of which were spilled over the floor, moving down into the ten-foot-diameter sinkhole.

Miles crouched down beside the hole and peered in. Even with his excellent night vision, he couldn't see the bottom. He listened to see if there was anything crawling up, but he heard nothing. Even so, the hairs on the back of his neck stood at attention, and he quickly walked away, back to where Amelia and Church stood.

"What is that?" Amelia asked.

"That is how the desolate keep coming back," Miles explained. "Don't ask me how it got there, because there's no way it was dug by hand, it's too smooth, but I think we found the cause of the problem."

"Maybe it's just a natural sinkhole?" Amelia asked.

"Maybe," Miles said, hoping they were all that lucky.

They returned into the main pharmacy room, and Miles checked the other door behind the counter, which was ajar. He pushed it open with his foot, half expecting something to run out at him, but all it did was swing harmlessly open, revealing a large hole in the wall.

"The desolate dug that?" Amelia asked.

Miles nodded. "Looks like it. Probably rats in the walls or something, they tried to get at them, ended up making a hole in the wall. My guess is these five buildings are all joined together with similar holes, or partially collapsed walls. I don't plan on going through each to find out. They probably went through there after food, and either smashed some windows to get out farther along, to keep tracking prey, or they got stuck. If it's the second option, I don't want to go searching for what we might find. We should leave."

Along with Church and Amelia, Miles left the shop without another word.

"You find anything?" one of the Blood Guard asked.

"Nothing good," he told them. "Thomas on the bus?"

The Blood Guard nodded, but continued to stare at Miles.

"What?" Miles eventually asked.

"You stopped the girl from torturing that desolate," the Blood Guard said.

"And I shouldn't have?" Miles questioned, ready to hear how it was *just a desolate* again.

The Blood Guard shook his head. "No, it was the right thing to do. The desolate were human once, they didn't ask for this. Didn't ask to be turned into monsters. End their suffering and move on is the right thing to do. Thank you for stopping her."

Miles nodded and walked back to the Winnebago, only to find Thomas sitting on the sofa inside, a pot of tea on the table, along with three mugs, a small jug of milk, and some sugar cubes. "I didn't know how you liked it," he said by way of explanation.

Miles smiled as Church lay on the ground between the dining-living area and the bedrooms at the rear of the vehicle. Her eyes were only on Thomas, as if expecting something she needed to be ready for.

"Your dog doesn't trust me," Thomas said.

"He's fine," Miles said to Church. "He's no threat. Right?" The last word was directed at Thomas as Miles looked his way.

Thomas held his hands up. "I am not here to harm anyone. I don't even like the *idea* of harming someone. I am an Authority. A First Authority, but still. I am an administrator, a man who would rather be overseeing the House coffers than fighting off a horde of desolate, or even fighting other vampires. My House didn't allow me to become a vampire because of my incredible physical prowess in combat. Besides, who pours tea if they're going to be a threat? This isn't *The Princess Bride*, and I haven't poisoned any of the cups."

"It's always weird when vampires who are centuries old are fans of something modern," Amelia said, taking a seat at the table as Thomas poured three cups of tea.

"I like movies," Thomas said by way of explanation. "I think the world of cinema might actually be humanity's greatest invention. Or at least the one I'm most grateful for."

Miles took a seat and dropped two cubes of brown sugar into his tea, before stirring it slowly with a teaspoon. "So, are you here to discuss what happened with that rich brat and her friends, or what I found in the shop?"

"Both," Thomas said. "Firstly, I want to thank you for stepping in with Jenny. Several of the pilgrims were unhappy with the way she and her friends were dealing with the desolate. Like it was a game. Like it was fun. Taking the life of something shouldn't be fun, even those who for all intents and purposes are dead compared to what they once were. She isn't happy, by the way. I would be careful of her."

"I got the impression she was just a combination of devout believer of all of what House Idolator offers, and a rich woman who needed people to be at her beck and call," Amelia said. "I saw a new side of her today."

"As did I," Thomas admitted. "An unpleasant side. I'll be keeping my own eye on her. I would appreciate it if you didn't kill her, or her friends should they try anything stupid. They are true believers in House Idolator, as are all of our children, but some of us can lean toward fanaticism, and I fear that Jenny might be among them."

"You want me to ask them nicely to stop?" Miles asked, taking a sip of tea.

"No, just don't go all Arbiter on them," Thomas asked. "Unless it's strictly necessary, while on the pilgrimage. I would like *all* of the pilgrims to reach Bangor."

"I will do my best to stay out of their way," Miles conceded.

"That will suffice," Thomas said with a nod of thanks. "So, what did you find?"

Miles told him all he found inside the shop.

"A giant hole in the ground?" Thomas asked. "How would the desolate have dug it?"

Miles shrugged. "No clue. It's a few hundred feet deep at least, but whoever, or whatever, dug it, did a good job. Any chance there are old tunnels under the city?"

Thomas leaned back on the sofa and considered the question. "Possibly. There could be some old caves under there; maybe it's a sinkhole."

"Maybe," Miles admitted.

"You don't think it is?" Amelia asked.

Miles shrugged. "I have no idea *what* it is. It's a giant hole that the desolate are using to climb up. I assume you haven't seen anything like that before?"

Thomas shook his head. "No. Never even heard of anything like it. I guess we don't exactly go exploring too much in Maine these days, no telling what you're about to unearth. If there are caves under the state and they house desolate, that begs the question, where did they come from?"

"You said there were lots of desolate under Augusta," Amelia said.

"They're trapped under there," Thomas said. "Caves. Actual caves. Vampires uncovered them in the seventies, but to my knowledge they don't go this far from the city."

"What were they using the caves for?" Miles asked.

"No clue," Thomas said. "Maybe someone at Bangor will know, but no one has ever told me. I assumed they were just old caves. I think they used to give tours of them, *come see the stalagmites* and the like. The desolate took shelter there; it acted as some kind of natural nest that offered them protection. Especially after the entrance was blocked. If they found a way out, that might count for why whenever we come back we find more, although I was always told it was only a few thousand desolate, so I figured they'd have run out by now."

"Could it have been a lot more than a few thousand?" Amelia asked.

Thomas took a drink of tea. "Honestly, I don't know. When we get to Bangor, talk to Joseph Davies, he might know."

"Drest's friend," Miles said.

Thomas nodded. "He's a good man, and he's been here since the nineteen fifties, so he should know a lot more than I do. He helped save lives when Maine fell."

"He was a part of the teams experimenting on the desolate?"

Thomas shook his head. "He's quite literally a doctor; he didn't have anything to do with it."

"And next we're on to Falmouth, yes?" Miles asked.

"A little ahead of schedule, too," Thomas explained. "Should be in Falmouth within the next half hour or so."

"That's longer than I expected," Miles said.

"Yes, but we can't go above ten miles per hour because some of the roads are unsteady," Thomas said. "Also, we had desolate problems the last time we were here, so we're going to take it nice and slow this time, and hopefully not have a trail of things that want to eat us by the time we reach Falmouth. They already have a hard enough job there as the I-295 was partially destroyed, so we have to come off and go through the town before rejoining farther up the coast."

"Maine is falling apart, isn't it?" Amelia asked.

Thomas nodded and got to his feet, swigging down the last of his tea. "Can I have a word outside, Miles?"

Miles noticed the slight surprise on Amelia's face, but she said nothing as he left the vehicle with Thomas, the pair walking a few hundred feet away from the pilgrimage before the First Authority stopped.

They stood in quiet for a moment looking out across the destroyed city. The sounds of things crawling around within its ruin were easy to hear for vampires.

"You wanted to talk privately," Miles said.

Thomas nodded. "Something doesn't feel right."

"Meaning?"

"I don't know," Thomas said, looking back out across what had been a street. "I've shared my concerns with my Blood Guard, who have all assured me they are keeping us safe, but that's not what I mean. I don't feel any less safe here as I've ever done, but something feels . . . *off*."

"What did you see in the church?" Miles asked.

Thomas turned to look at the Arbiter. "Ah, yes, the church. There was a destroyed back door; I think the desolate had managed to get in through there. Someone had been inside the church within the last few months. There were the remnants of supplies in there, and a small fire."

"Human?"

Thomas shook his head, paused, and shrugged. "No clue. No smell. Any scent had long since gone. Any chance they're the reason Amelia is here? Don't say anything. I know she's not really here to document the pilgrimage, I'm fine with that. I didn't, and still don't, want to know why she's really here. My First Lord didn't want to know either. All I want to know is, will it put us in danger? And by us, I mean the pilgrims."

"I don't know," Miles said honestly, because he saw no reason to be anything else. "Her story is investigating some bad people who fled into Maine, but I don't actually know how much of a threat they are to anyone who isn't human."

"They're not human?"

"Nope," Miles said.

"Vampire?"

"Werewolf and a chaos witch."

Thomas let out a long breath. "Fucking hell. I don't want to know anything else about them, do I?"

"Probably not," Miles said. "It's a bad case, with bad people doing even worse things. And no one seems to understand why they'd come here, unless it's to flee the authorities."

"Maine doesn't strike me as the kind of place you want to come to live your days on the lam," Thomas said. "The big towns find out you're murdering people, they're going to lock you up until someone like you comes along. And the smaller settlements will just stoke a big fire, or dig a big hole. Or chain you outside of a building and wait for the UV levels to do the job for them."

"You're all safe as far as I can tell," Miles assured him. "They're nae after vampires, or House members, and they're nae going to want to pick a fight with a bunch of Blood Guard and First Authority. They don't need the heat of a House, Great or Minor, coming after them."

"Maybe that was what was tingling at the back of my neck," Thomas said. "We should get going before anyone starts to decide to just walk to Falmouth instead of waiting."

Miles and Thomas went their separate ways, with the convoy of vehicles setting off the moment everyone was on board.

Amelia had remained seated at the sofa and waited for the Winnebago to start before she said anything. "He knows why I'm really here, yes?"

Miles nodded. "He's nae an idiot. He obviously knew that you were here for something more than just to cover the pilgrimage, but he wanted to know if it was something that might impact everyone's safety.

I told him the truth, that it wasn't. I think your quarry may have been in Portland."

"Why?"

Miles told her what Thomas had found.

"This could be the way they came to get to Ellsworth," Amelia said. "I guess we'll find out when we catch up with them."

They sat quietly for the twenty minutes it took to make the journey from Portland to Falmouth, with Miles looking out of the window at the passing woods, which was a lot more pleasant than the ruins of towns he'd seen so far.

The Winnebago stopped suddenly, jerking Miles back into the sofa seat.

"You okay?" Miles called to the Arvid the driver.

"Everyone has stopped ahead," Arvid told him. "Thomas and the Blood Guard are getting out."

"Church," Miles said as he got to his feet.

Church was by his side in a second.

"I'll go check," Miles told Arvid and turned to Amelia, who was also on her feet. "You're nae gonna stay here, are you?"

"What do you think?" Amelia asked, clipping the camera to her lapel again.

Miles opened the door and stepped out into the night once more. The rain had picked up in the last half hour, and the wind whipped along the dirt-covered road. "What's going on?" he called out to Thomas.

"No one is answering," Thomas shouted back, pointing off to the front of the convoy at the fifty-foot-high metal gates that sat in what had once been a road. There was a wall that jutted out from each side of the gates. They ran a hundred feet in each direction, with three gun turrets on either side.

Miles reached Thomas and the Blood Guard. Between them and the gates were the two military trucks and a second Winnebago. "How do they usually respond?"

"We drive up, park here, they come out, check each vehicle in turn, fire a flare when all safe."

"Have you tried knocking?" Miles asked.

"We're meant to stick to the plan," Thomas said. "It's safer that way."

"I'll go check," Miles said, aware of the eyes of the bus inhabitants on him. "You all wait here."

No one argued, and Miles set off with Church and Amelia behind him. He stopped at each of the military trucks, and checked on the two-person crews who were manning them, but they were all fine. The second Winnebago only had a driver and guard, neither of whom had any idea what was going on.

The metal gate was shut, so Miles knocked once, but there was no response. He slammed his telekinesis into the steel door, making a loud noise in case something meant they couldn't hear him, but still there was no response.

He took a step back and looked at the walls on either side of the gate. They were covered in spikes, each one a foot thick.

In the middle of the gate was a small hatch which could be opened from inside Falmouth Fort to check on who was outside their gates. It was shut, but it was also the weakest point of the gate. Miles smashed his telekinesis into it, trying to use his power mixed with his own strength to budge the hatch. The hatch tore free, revealing a small courtyard just beyond the gate, but no actual people manning it.

Miles went back to Thomas with the news.

"So, how do we get in?" one of the pilgrims asked from the bus steps.

"We're figuring it out," Thomas said cheerily. He moved Miles away from the bus before saying, "We can't sit out here."

Miles looked around the woods which surrounded the convoy on either side. "Desolate."

"No doubt they'll be aware we're here," Thomas said. "We need inside that fort."

"Can you get around those walls?" Miles asked.

"They stretch a few hundred meters before they join buildings. The walls sit in between the buildings in what used to be the main centre of the town. It's basically two blocks of fort with a road going through the middle for convoys."

"So our best bet is to go to one of those buildings and climb up and into the fort?"

"They have mines, booby traps, and people watching," Thomas said.

"If people were watching, they'd know we were here," Miles pointed out. "There's no one in there. Or if there are, they're nae outside."

"Can you find out what happened?" Thomas asked. "I'll keep an eye on things out here."

Miles returned to Amelia and Church. "Church, keep Amelia safe. No, you can't come, either of you. I'm going around to the side of this fort, climbing in, and opening the door. I'll be ten minutes at the most."

Neither of them looked happy about it, but he set off at a run before they could complain. He was at the border of the wall when he smelled blood. Relatively fresh blood coming from inside the fort. A few days old, maybe. He stopped by a red-brick building that used to be, according to the sign, a video rental place. The outer wall was covered in shards of glass and nails. It wouldn't stop the desolate from climbing, but it would make it harder for them, and it would give vampires a second thought.

Someone had dug a four-foot-deep ditch all along the outside of the buildings and left the elements to turn it to mud. Anyone wanting to get up that side of the fort would need to jump over the moat, right onto the glass and nails.

Miles took a few more steps back, until he was at the highest point of the ground outside of the fort, and saw the machine gun emplacements that sat atop several of the buildings. "They did nae want any visitors," he said to himself.

Miles was grateful that after what had happened in Portland, he'd changed into a pair of old jogging bottoms and a T-shirt that was several sizes too big, the latter of which had the sides cut free. While his clothes made him look like he was about to take part in a 1980s music video, he was long since fed up with having to replace his clothes every time he used his beast form. Also, the being stark naked when he turned back to a more human shape was something he really could do without.

He slipped off his shoes, standing barefoot on the soggy ground, and out of the view of anyone on the bus, he turned into his vampire beast form.

Miles had gotten used to the transformation over the last few years, and what had once been agony that felt never-ending was now a white-hot pain that flashed through his body for only a moment.

In his beast form, Miles's arms were longer, his hands and fingers elongating even further than in his vampire form. Fur grew over his body and two black wings tore out of his back. Each wing was longer than he was tall.

Miles's face, while still vampiric in appearance, also changed. His jaw jutted out, his ears grew long and pointy, and his eyes became blazing red pools with black centres, with hardened ridges of bone over each eye. His cheeks sank into his face, and his fangs became accompanied by razor-sharp, sharklike teeth, along with two more fangs on the bottom row.

He beat his wings once and took to the sky, soaring over the top of the fort and looking down on it. There was nothing to see, no bodies, no people milling around, and thankfully no one looking up and trying to shoot him out of the sky.

Miles landed just inside the fort, his beast form fading away, his clothes thankfully not torn to tatters. He looked around the empty courtyard. He sensed no heartbeats close by, but there was a scent of blood. He considered searching the fort before letting anyone in, but keeping the pilgrims outside where an attack could come from any direction seemed less safe than getting everyone into the fort.

He found a lever at the far end of the courtyard, walked over, and pulled it with a loud clank. After a short pause, the main gates of the fort slowly opened inward.

Amelia and Church jogged into the fort. "There's no one here?"

"Nope," Miles said. "Nae a soul."

A short time later, all of the convoy sat in the middle of the fort, which was, as Thomas had said, two repurposed city blocks, one on either side of the street which ran through the centre.

"Any idea what happened?" Thomas asked Miles from the steps of his Winnebago as one of the Blood Guard went to close the fort gates.

"Stay here," Miles said, looking around the dark fort. "I'm going to find out."

Chapter Fifteen

Seeing how Amelia was determined to keep up with Miles wherever he went, he stayed back with her, and let Church use her exceptional nose to hopefully find out what had happened in the fort. The rest of the pilgrimage stayed back at the convoy, on their vehicles as it was safer, as they moved through the fort toward the exit that was identical to the entrance they'd just opened.

Church stopped by a four-story building with boarded-over windows, and pawed at the metal doors. Like most of the buildings in the fort, they'd been made of red brick, and had been repurposed after Maine had fallen to be part of their new defence in protecting valuable convoys that brought supplies to those settlements and towns that had stayed behind.

Miles pulled the door open, and immediately wished he hadn't. However bad the smell of blood was throughout the fort, the stench inside the building was overwhelming, even for a vampire who was used to it. Amelia physically recoiled from the reek.

"What is this place?" Miles asked as Thomas and one of the Blood Guard arrived.

"It's the main hall for the fort," Thomas said, frowning at the scent. "The staff came here to eat after a shift. Bottom floor is a dining hall, the other floors are all storage areas. And I guess this is the reason no one is here."

"I'd guess right," Miles said, stepping into the dark entrance hallway of the building followed by Thomas, who stepped in with his Blood Guard, Church and Amelia bringing up the rear.

The hallway had a set of stairs leading up right next to the door, and a pair of double doors at either side of the wall in front. Miles chose one set of wooden double doors, and pushed them open, walking into a scene from a horror film.

Blood adorned every wall, every surface. The four long wooden tables were overturned, chairs thrown around the room. The windows at the end of the room were all smashed, glass littering the floor, with trails of blood leading outside.

"There are no bodies," Amelia whispered.

"You noticed that, too," Thomas said, stepping over a large mound of blood-covered dirt. More dirt adorned the walls and floor. Between the dirt and blood, there wasn't much of the room untouched.

Miles walked over to the smashed windows and looked out at the small gap between the building and the external fort wall. Blood was smeared on the stone of the wall. "The bodies were dragged up and out."

"To where?" Thomas asked.

Miles quickly scaled the wall and crouched on the walkway, looking out into the forest beside them. Nothing moved in the darkness. Miles dropped back to the ground and stepped over the broken glass, back into the building. "How long has it been since you last had contact?" he asked Thomas.

"A few days, maybe a week," Thomas said. "That's not unusual, by the way."

"How many humans and vampires worked here?" Miles asked.

"Twenty-seven humans, eight vampires," Thomas said. "They swapped out with another group of thirty-five every three weeks."

Miles pointed to the bloodstains. "This is human. Blood is a few days old, but not everyone would be in here at once. There might be other scenes of attack, or hopefully some survivors in hiding. We go building to building, clear it all out. We don't leave until it's finished."

"Are you expecting survivors?" Thomas asked.

"No," Miles said.

"How can you be sure?" Amelia asked, she looked a little ill. "Sorry, I just . . ."

"Church, go with her," Miles said as Amelia turned and ran out of the room.

"I'll ask her question," Thomas said. "How can you be sure?"

"You think that any desolate who did this left survivors?" Miles asked him. "But we check anyway."

They both left the building, with Miles finding Amelia crouched at the end of the row of the fort, next to a collection of shrubs. Church sat a short distance away, keeping an eye on her.

"You okay?" he asked her.

"Nope," Amelia said without looking back. "How many people died in there?"

"I have no idea," Miles said, feeling as if he didn't know anywhere near enough about what was going on, and being unhappy about it. "There's a lot of blood in there, but a person has a lot of blood in them. You see something like that and think it must be dozens, but it might only be two or three. Don't know yet."

She looked back up at Miles, her eyes red, her complexion pallid. "How are you so calm?"

"Seen worse," Miles said. "Much worse. Doesn't mean it doesn't affect me. I'll probably nae sleep too well for a while, but I just learned to push it all aside when confronted with it. It's nae a person anymore, it's just bits of matter. I know that sounds callous, but any other way used to make me feel a lot like how you feel right now."

Amelia got to her feet, with Miles holding out his hands to catch her if she fell.

"I'm okay," she said. "You said we need to go help check the fort."

"This might nae get much better over the next few hours," Miles told her. "Chances are the opposite."

"Gotta find out," Amelia said, looking back at the bus. "And I don't really want to spend time with the pilgrims, so I guess I'll help search."

The search took an hour in total, the weather becoming increasingly unpleasant the longer the night continued. It was nearly three AM when they were done. Amelia, Church, and Miles had taken a quarter of the fort, with Thomas and his three Blood Guard, the military-trained driver, and the guard of the two supply trucks taking up the rest.

They all reconvened near the exit to the fort, with no one looking as though they were all that happy about what they'd found.

"Lots of blood, no bodies," Thomas said when everyone had shared their findings. "They took vampires and humans alike."

"It looks like the attacks took place in the canteen, the two barracks— one vampire, one human—and the last one in a storeroom which sat under the office of the vampire in charge," one of the Blood Guards said. "Still don't know how they managed to clear out this whole place without some- one noticing something and raising the alarm."

"We found blood all across the walkways on both entrances," one of the drivers said.

"They cleaned out the inside and went for the gunners and staff watching the gates," Miles said. "That's pretty goddamned advanced for a species who usually can't figure out much more than which hole to put their food into."

"Desolate Royalty?" Thomas asked.

"Possible," Miles said, not wanting to suggest it without more proof. "Where did the desolate come from? Where did they take the bodies to?"

"We need to scan the local forest," Thomas said. "Maybe we can follow the blood trail."

Miles looked over at Church. "You up for a hunt?"

Church barked once.

"We'll head out, follow the blood trails," Miles said.

"I'll come with you," Thomas said. "I'll leave two of my Blood Guard here and take the other with us. Just in case."

"Me too," Amelia told him. "Don't argue."

"If there's a lot of activity, we might not have the personnel to deal with them properly," Miles said. "May have to call in more people from the nearby towns to deal with it. But at least we'll know what's going on."

"You still think there's no chance of survivors?" Amelia asked.

"None," Miles said. "Desolate don't keep people alive. Desolate also don't usually attack in such an organised way either, so I guess we might find something really weird out there."

A short while later, with Miles and Church taking lead and Amelia back with Thomas and his Blood Guard, the five of them left the fort and followed Church's nose into the forest. It took five minutes before they came across their first body part—an arm—and another three to find the weird thing that Miles was expecting.

"What is that?" Thomas asked as he caught up to Miles and Church, who were standing a few feet back from a large hole in the soft muddy ground that was littered with drag marks and footprints.

The hole itself was about ten feet in diameter. It was streaked with blood and gore, which Miles tried his best to ignore as he peered down into the darkness below. The stink that emanated from the hole told Miles that this was where the desolate had come out, and had returned with their prey.

"What the actual fuck?" Amelia asked.

"The desolate drilled a hole," Thomas said, looking back at her. "There's no way this is man-made, or desolate-made, without machinery. It's an actual circle, for a start."

"Desolate aren't much for operating machinery," Miles said. "But you're right, this hole does not look like it was dug by hand. It does look a lot like the one in the garage we saw earlier. I think it's a bit too much of a coincidence for them to be unconnected."

"What do we do about it?" the Blood Guard asked.

"You got explosives?" Miles replied.

"What?" Thomas asked.

"Grenades?" Miles clarified. "Do you have any grenades? If not, I'd bet the fort has some. Need to find them, need to drop them down this hole, close it up. Or at least partially collapse it."

"There might be more of them," Amelia said.

"We don't have all day to search for holes in the forest," Thomas said.

Miles nodded. "Yeah, but we can close up the ones we find. If we find more. I want to know how they made it. If there are tunnels down here and the desolate start digging up, how'd they get here without the whole bloody thing collapsing on top of them?"

"Wait, you're going to drop down there, aren't you?" Amelia asked.

"Miles, no offence, but that sounds insane," Thomas said.

"I'll drop down, hopefully find out what's going on, and fly back up," Miles said. "There's been enough time since I used my beast form, so it shouldn't be an issue. And if I land down there and it's all dead people and desolate as far as the eye can see, I get out quickly."

No one spoke for several seconds and Miles wondered if it was because they were all trying to figure out different ways to call him an idiot.

"We need to be gone when you do it," Thomas said. "You drop down there and disturb a bunch of desolate, we could have trouble up here."

"I know," Miles said. "You're off to Brunswick next, yes?"

Thomas nodded. "It's a straight shot up there, no need to stop. Everything should be safe."

"Get everyone to Brunswick. I'll meet you there tomorrow night."

"You've lost your mind," Amelia said angrily. "You have no way of knowing what's down there."

"I know," Miles told her. "But if we just blow it all and leave, we run the risk of a much bigger problem. What if there's something down there creating these tunnels? What if they happen into Bangor? Then you're talking about potentially tens of thousands of people, nae just thirty-five."

"You need anything?" Thomas asked.

"Explosives to blow the hole when I get down there," Miles said.

"There's a quartermaster's station back in the fort," Thomas said. "We'll head back, gear up, we'll get everyone in place. Once you're ready, we open the gate and get going. Miles, if you find anything down there that—"

"I'll get out, don't worry," Miles said. "Just get everything ready."

They all returned to the fort, with Miles entering a boarded-up building that Thomas pointed to when they arrived. Miles walked off with Church and Amelia, entering the shop he'd been pointed to and going through the massive amount of clothing and weaponry that was inside.

"You know this is insane, right?" Amelia asked from the front of the shop.

"Which part?" Miles asked.

"Church, tell him he's insane," Amelia pleaded.

Church barked in agreement.

"We need information," Miles said as he picked up a pair of military-style black boots and a pair of matching combat trousers. "I can get in and out without too much risk. I would rather not. In fact, I'd rather do pretty much anything else, but we can't leave the hole there and bury our heads in the sand. We can't just *hope* they don't happen in bigger towns. Or, and this is the worst-case scenario, outside of Maine."

The silence that filled the room was uncomfortable.

"I still don't like it," Amelia said eventually.

"Noted," Miles replied, grabbing a stab vest and incendiary combat knife, pressing the button on the side of the handle, and watching the blade turn super-heated in moments. He released the button and the blade quickly cooled before he placed it in the sheath at his hip.

"You taking a gun?" Amelia asked him, pointing to an array of weaponry.

Miles picked up a shotgun and a box of incendiary shells. They were an effective weapon against the desolate, and he'd known a point-blank shot to kill one of them more than once. He grabbed a belt designed to hold a dozen shells and loaded the rest into the gun itself. He was almost done when he decided to pick up a second set of shells, and took a moment to slot each of them into a bandolier, which he put on. He looked as if he was going to war.

Amelia stood before Miles and sighed. "Please don't get hurt. I know we've only spent a few days together, but I've come to enjoy your company."

"I wouldn't dream of depriving you of my company," Miles said with a smile.

Amelia sighed again. "You're a pain." She kissed him on the cheek. "Just stay safe."

Miles blinked.

"Go on," Amelia said. "Before I do something stupid." She picked up a shotgun and box of shells.

"Is that the something stupid?" Miles asked.

"No, this is a chance to get some weaponry if this trip is about to become more complicated," Amelia told him, grabbing her own bandoleer before following Miles out of the store.

"You plan on killing them all yourself?" Thomas asked as Miles strode across the road, aware that the pilgrims in the bus were watching him, and trying not to glance their way.

Miles walked between the Winnebago that Thomas was using and one of the military trucks, when he found himself face to face with Jenny.

"What's going on?" Jenny asked Miles.

Miles looked over at Thomas. "You want to explain?"

"Everyone is dead," Thomas said. "Slaughtered by the desolate. Miles is going to figure out where they're coming from and stop them."

Jenny continued to stare at Miles, before nodding and walking away.

"She's a weird one," Thomas said when Jenny had reentered the bus, the door closing behind her.

"You're nae kidding," Miles agreed.

The group continued on back through the woods to the hole, where one of the Blood Guard and the drivers of the military trucks stood. They were all several feet back from the hole, and each of them glanced over on a regular basis, as if something might suddenly appear. Which, Miles figured, had already happened once, so it was a fair fear to have.

The Blood Guard passed Miles a detonator. "The explosives are planted about five feet down the well. Had to lower one of the other guards down there via rope. Apparently, it's not a fun job."

"How far is the range?"

"No idea underground," the Blood Guard said. "Probably two or three kilometers above ground, so I wouldn't try it much farther than that below ground."

"Taken under advisement," Miles said. He walked over to the hole, crouched, and peered down into the darkness. "Any chance someone has a fluorescent light tube? Forgot to check in the store."

The Blood Guard removed one from a pocket and passed it to him.

Miles cracked the stick, waving it about until it glowed bright yellow before dropping it down into the hole. It bounced off the side and landed with something approximating a *splat*, showing little more than a tunnel at the bottom of the well. A tunnel that to Miles's keen eye revealed a lot more blood and gore.

"You can land down there okay?" Amelia asked.

Miles did a quick judgment call in his head, before slipping the detonator into his jacket pocket. "It's maybe a hundred feet down. I can land that without issues."

"How did no one hear them make this?" Thomas asked. "I mean, it must have made a huge amount of noise."

Miles looked back at him. "Something I hope to answer at the bottom."

"You're going to get to us at Brunswick, right?" Thomas asked.

Miles nodded as Church nuzzled against his face. "I'll be fine. Just a little exploration before I leave here. Everyone get going. Once you're out, I'll drop down."

Everyone started to walk away, leaving Miles and Amelia alone. "I'm coming with you," she said.

"You are not," Miles said.

Amelia held out her hand and roots burst out of the hole, making a ladder that looked surprisingly sturdy. "I am. I'm probably safer with you than anyone else. And you might need the help."

"Amelia!" Thomas shouted, with Church beside him.

"Church, keep Thomas safe," Miles said. "Amelia is coming with me."

Church barked and followed Thomas to the pilgrimage, the latter shaking his head but offering no argument.

"You sure about this?" Miles asked.

"Yes," Amelia said.

Miles looked up at the sky as the rain continued to fall—at least he was going somewhere hopefully a little drier. He stared down into a place he would have given an awful lot not to go. Bit late now. He offered Amelia his hand, which she took. "This is going to be bad. The ladder isn't necessary, though."

The roots crawled back into the muddy side of the wall. "Good thing I'm there to help then," Amelia said. "I go where my bodyguard goes. It's the only way to keep me safe."

Miles smiled, turned into his vampire side, and stepped out into the unknown with Amelia holding on tight.

Chapter Sixteen

Miles's long talon-like claws on his hands were perfect to use to slow his descent as they scraped down the side of the hole. He had to ignore the occasional thing that didn't feel like dirt, and really hoped they weren't about to land in a large cavern of desolate. Or worse.

Instead, they landed in a dark tunnel, the only light coming from the illuminated glow stick, which had started to fade, casting eerie shadows about an already creepy location. Amelia let go of him and stepped to the side as Miles scanned their surroundings.

The hole was directly above his head. It was eight feet off the ground of the tunnel beneath it, and while the ground was slick with the remains of the desolates' victims, he wondered how on earth they'd managed to get the hole bored. There were no piles of dirt in the tunnel, no evidence that the desolate had been here with pickaxe and shovel. Miles wasn't even sure it would have been physically possible to have done such a thing without collapsing the tunnel he stood in.

Amelia lifted her shotgun and attached a torch to the barrel, shining the light around the dark tunnel. "Wish I hadn't done that," she said after seeing the state of their new surroundings.

To the left of where they'd landed was the end of the tunnel. Miles placed a hand against the rock, which felt cool and wet to his touch. To the right of the hole, the tunnel continued on for farther than Miles could see.

"Let's go find some monsters," Miles said.

They set off toward the end of the tunnel, where Miles knocked over what he thought was a large rock with his boot, but when he looked down, he discovered it was a metal cog. He bent down and picked the cog up, turning it over in his hand. He was about to put it in his pocket for later when he noticed the tracks.

Amelia shone her light on the tracks, as Miles moved the worst of the gore and debris to the side with his booted feet, revealing more of them. Two parallel tracks that resembled what you might find on a snowmobile. He searched for the name and wondered if caterpillar tracks were right. Something had been driven, or pushed, into the tunnel, and sat under what would become a large hole going up into the canteen.

"Huh," Miles said, his voice loud in the quiet of the tunnel.

"What is it?" Amelia asked.

"I don't know yet," Miles said. "Stay close."

They set off at a steady walking pace down along the rest of the tunnel. After a hundred meters, they came out at a crossroads, with four more tunnels. There were tracks on the ground leading to and from each tunnel. Miles motioned for Amelia to stay where she was, tried the first one, and discovered it was blocked only a short distance in. The second one was the same. Only one of the tunnels wasn't blocked, so he decided that was the one to go down.

"How do we get out again if you blow that tunnel?" Amelia asked.

Miles removed the detonator from his pocket and stared at it. "Good point. Let's wait for now."

They continued on down the only unblocked tunnel for several minutes, following the tracks that were still visible in the bloody ground. The smell of so much blood in such a small space made Miles need to occasionally stop walking and regain his composure. He should have had a blood pouch before he'd dropped down.

It was a few minutes more when the tunnel opened out into a large cavern with stalactites and stalagmites in abundance, and a clear path through the middle. The tracks continued on, several sets overlapping one another as they'd done since the crossroads. If the desolate were behind all of this, they were a lot more organised than any he'd ever met before.

On the opposite side of the cavern, there were two tunnels, one going northeast and one northwest. There were caterpillar tracks going down each tunnel, which didn't help in his choice one bit. Eventually, he picked the northeast one for no other reason than that it aimed toward the coast, and thus would put them closer to Brunswick should he ever figure out how to get out of this place.

"You smell anything?" Amelia whispered.

Miles shook his head. "Only blood, death, and the usual where the desolate are involved. Your magic sense anything?"

Amelia was quiet for a moment before she said, "No. Magic doesn't really work like that. I can sense magic users, but there's none nearby."

"Good to know."

They walked a few hundred meters further down the tunnel when they found a small room adjacent to the main tunnel itself. Miles stepped into the room, where a large machine waited.

Amelia joined him a second later, pointing to the machine. "Caterpillar treads."

The machine was five meters long and two high, and consisted of a large metal container sitting on top of the aforementioned treads. In the centre of the metal container was a tunnel boring drill that was about ten feet wide. At the far end of the room, behind the drill, were two large containers full of soil.

"I assume you'd like to know how it's done," a voice from the tunnel said.

"That would be nice," Miles replied, cursing the fact that he hadn't picked up any scent or heartbeat. The huge amount of blood and gore was messing with his scent of smell.

A man stepped into the mouth of the room. He was tall, broad, with a large beard and shaved head. He carried no obvious weapon, and appeared to offer no obvious threat, but having recognized him from the dossier Amelia had on him, Miles knew that looks could be deceptive.

"Liam," he said.

"Lower the weapon, Miss Roberts," Liam said without looking her way.

Amelia glanced over at Miles, who nodded slightly, and only then did Amelia lower the shotgun, although the expression on her face suggested she wanted to do anything but.

Liam carried a lamp from his belt, which illuminated the area without being overpowering.

Miles stepped to the side and motioned to the machine. "Please, by all means."

"The drill cuts up into the rock," Liam said. "It's been designed to be quiet. Not so quiet we can use it where people congregate, but quiet enough to be used in the forest away from prying ears and eyes. We designed it at Templar International. I assume you've heard of us."

Miles nodded. "Little bit," he said. "So . . . what . . . it slowly cuts up through the soil and rock, and then the dirt falls down and is collected in containers like those?"

The man nodded. "It took about four hours to do one hole close to that fort. Had to time the attack so that the humans were all at their tables eating. Shock and awe, I think it's called."

"I call it murdering people," Miles said.

"Yeah, well, you'd know all about that," Liam said. "You're the Arbiter, yes?"

Miles nodded. "You've heard of me."

"I heard about what you did to Sara Bakos. I liked her. Shame she drank from a desolate and turned herself into a monster."

"Talking of monsters, you murdered Heather," Amelia snapped. "She was my friend."

"I didn't kill anyone," Liam told her.

"Okay, fine, you had someone kill Heather," Miles said. "Let's not quibble with semantics."

"She wasn't meant to die," Liam said. "We warned her what would happen should she keep on the path she'd decided upon, but unfortunately things escalated."

"They killed her by accident?" Amelia asked.

"No," Liam said, his tone hard and full of anger. "Patrick and two of his Magistrate friends were responsible. He was meant to scare her, not meant to drown her and hang the fucking body from a fucking tree. They thought that leaving no evidence behind proved how good they were. They bragged about it. They didn't follow my orders. Patrick was the last of the three. They are now all dead. Apparently, the Magistrate's hatred of all things nonhuman extended to witches."

"One of your buddies killed Patrick?" Miles asked him.

"Almost killed me too?" Amelia asked.

"Yes," Liam said. "Had to send someone who could actually follow orders to go shut Patrick up, the stupid, hate-filled moron. The Magistrate have their uses, but they really don't know when to stop talking."

"To be fair," Miles said, "Patrick's not going to be doing a lot of talking anymore."

"How's your friend's head after I bounced it off the car door?" Amelia asked.

Liam turned to Amelia and nodded. "He wasn't meant to attack you, Miss Roberts. I guess I should apologise for that. Although the discovery that you are a witch of some power was useful."

"Fuck you," Amelia snapped.

Liam smiled.

"Why are you working with the Magistrate then?" Miles asked. "Aren't they all just more hate-filled arseholes?"

"Means to an end," Liam said. "I'm pretty sure you know how it is."

"So what do you want?" Miles asked.

Liam stared at Miles for several seconds before he said, "I expected it to be harder to creep up on an Arbiter."

"Aye," Miles agreed. "Nae my finest hour. All this blood isn't great for a vampire's senses. Should have heard you, though—you move quietly, didn't expect that."

"A benefit werewolves and vampires share," Liam said.

"True," Miles agreed. "Although I was also a little preoccupied with trying to figure out why you'd wipe out a fort."

"A few reasons," Liam said. "We needed to test out the desolate here, to make sure that we could use them in an effective way. I don't really think we need to discuss that further right now. Any more questions?"

"Oh, how kind of you to ask," Miles said thoughtfully. "How long have you been a werewolf?"

"A few years now," Liam said. "At first it was amazing. Just the best feeling ever, but over time, you can't quite get the taste of flesh and blood out of your mouth. You know what I mean?"

"I don't eat people," Miles said. "I quite like blood. Your tastebuds change after you become a vampire. And, while I drink blood from people, I would never feast on them."

"That's what I thought," Liam said. "Humans tasted . . . wrong. At least at first."

"You got a liking for it," Miles said. "I always thought that werewolves stayed away from feasting on humans."

"At first, it was horrific," Liam admitted. "I was hurt, dying, needed food. I saw an old man walking through the forest. I decided my need was greater. I was so sick afterwards when I turned back to my human form, but the *rush* I felt of taking a life to feed upon . . . it was exquisite. I still try not to feed upon human flesh, I don't want to have that feeling to come out at the wrong time, but we hunt as a pack, feed as a pack. Sometimes we find someone who might offer us some sport beforehand."

"You chase after humans and eat them," Amelia said.

"It sounds sordid when you put it like that," Liam said.

"Your friend, Stuart, is sick," Miles said, wanting answers rather than letting Liam's need to feed on people become the focus. "You brought him here for a cure, didn't you? You feel like telling me what that cure is? He's a witch, so he can't become a vampire, no matter how many times he tries to get one to turn him."

Liam bristled. "My friend needs help. The vampires were sought out in desperation. It was an error on his part. I aim to help him."

"Ah, so some questions are off limits," Miles said. "Stuart still setting people on fire?"

"People who deserve it," Liam said.

Miles rolled his eyes but kept his comment to himself. Instead, he said, "How are you getting the desolate to do as they're told?"

The change in topic clearly threw Liam for a moment. "You'll see."

"So you're nae going to kill us?" Miles asked, genuinely surprised.

"Oh no, someone wants to see you," Liam said. "It was just Miles they wanted to see, but seeing how you brought Amelia here, I guess I'll take you both."

"How'd they know I was even here?" Miles asked, disliking the way the conversation was going.

"Ask them yourself."

"You want to give me a name?"

Liam shook his head. "No more answers." He removed a gun from a holster on his hip. "Move."

Miles stared at the gun.

"It won't kill you, obviously, but I'm guessing it's not much fun either." Liam removed a UV grenade from his pocket, as he aimed the gun at Amelia. "I think this might cause you more problems. Don't make me use more unpleasant means." A low growl left his throat, the echo of it bouncing around the room.

Miles wondered if he could take Liam before the werewolf hurt Amelia. Could they both take Liam together?

"I know what you're thinking," Liam said. "I'll kill the girl before you kill me."

"Try," Amelia said.

"No one needs to die here," Miles said. "Let's just go see this *someone* who is apparently desperate to see me."

"Shotgun on the floor," Liam said to Amelia. "Slowly. You too, Miles."

"Can I keep the torch?" Amelia asked. "I don't have your eyesight."

"Sure," Liam said.

Amelia detached the torch from the shotgun and took a step back.

Liam motioned for Miles and Amelia to continue, which they did as Miles tried to figure out a way to get away from someone who was not only holding a gun and a UV grenade, but was also a werewolf. He could fight the werewolf, but in the close quarters of the tunnels, he wasn't certain he'd come off particularly well, especially if Liam used the grenade first. He didn't want to be walking through what was almost certainly an enemy landscape while needing time to heal up. And that didn't even account for what might happen to Amelia.

"You see okay?" Liam asked after a short distance.

"Yes," Amelia said tersely.

"Aye, it's good," Miles told him. "These tunnels always been here?"

"For centuries," Liam said.

"Is it a long walk?"

"No," Liam said. "We're going to get on what is basically a . . . tram or mine cart and go for a little ride."

"A mine cart?" Miles asked. "Like in *Indiana Jones*?"

"Not a literal mine cart," Liam said, a little annoyance creeping into his voice. "You'll see."

It didn't take long for Miles and Amelia to see exactly what Liam had been talking about. They exited the tunnel into a large underground hollow and stood next to a set of wooden stairs, with a ramp that led down to a large platform, where a modified car sat atop a set of train tracks. There were tracks set onto the stone which disappeared off into the distance. Behind the car were three more of the machines that had been used to drill holes underground, each one now on a flat bed with train-like wheels.

"You move them around underground," Amelia said.

"How quaint," Miles said.

"Get in," Liam told them both.

Miles descended the stairs to the platform and looked over the edge at the drop into the darkness below. "How far up are we?" Miles asked, as

Amelia climbed into the front of the car, sitting where the passenger seat had once been, although the front and rear seats were now three-person benches. Miles followed, taking a seat next to Amelia.

"About two hundred feet," Liam said, getting into the car, starting the engine, removing the parking brake, and letting the car roll forward.

It wasn't long before they were moving at a decent pace across the tracks, leaving the drilling machines behind them. Miles continued to look down at the darkness below, and tried to figure out how they were both meant to get out of the situation they found themselves in. At least without making things worse.

The journey lasted only a few minutes before they arrived at another platform, identical to the one before. There was a large hut a short distance away, joined to the platform by wooden steps that looked a lot less safe than the vehicle he'd just ridden in.

Liam got out first, waving the gun in Amelia's direction. "Out."

"I'm coming," Miles said, exiting the car. "I'm wondering if the shotguns you had us discard would have actually hurt you."

"Incendiary shells in a shotgun are going to do fuck all against me," Liam said with a growling chuckle. "And that little dagger is pointless; it's why I let you keep it. We both know you're not going to try to bite me, so I'm feeling pretty safe."

"I'm glad for you," Miles said as he walked up the ramp in the direction Liam had shown.

Atop the ramp was a large tunnel entrance, with several desolate sitting at the edges, watching Miles with barely concealed hunger.

"What are they doing?" Miles asked as they entered the tunnel and lights flickered on all around them, bathing them in a low-level warm light.

"Don't know," Liam said. "They just sit around places and do nothing. We leave them alone, they leave us alone."

At the end of the tunnel, Liam ordered Miles and Amelia to stop and take a seat on a nearby bench, which they did without complaint. Miles took the opportunity to look around, finding that they were in yet another large cavern. This one also had a drilling machine in it, and another man whom Liam walked off to talk to.

"You're going with him," Liam said, pointing to his colleague after returning to Miles and Amelia. "Don't be stupid, and you might just get to live to see another nightfall."

Liam walked back down the tunnel they'd just left from.

"He's nice," Miles said to the second man, who was a touch taller than Liam had been, but not quite as broad. He wore military fatigues and had a tattoo of a scythe on his bicep.

"You talk, I hurt you," the man said, showing the shock baton in his hand.

"That's a little—" Miles started.

The man jabbed him in the ribs with the baton, and pain coursed through his body, forcing him to one knee. "Understand now?"

Miles nodded as Amelia helped him back to his feet.

"On your feet, let's go," the soldier said.

Miles stood, stretched a little, and set off in the direction the soldier had pointed. No one said anything as they walked along tunnels that appeared to be identical to the ones that Miles and Amelia had just travelled, complete with more train tracks on the ground.

After a few minutes, Miles was hit by the overwhelming smell of blood, and a short while later, they walked by a large barrel that stank of blood both fresh and old. He glanced at it.

"Have to ship the blood where it needs to go somehow," the soldier said.

Miles looked back at him.

"Go on, ask," the soldier said.

"The people from the fort. You killed them, brought them here? We're a long way from the fort, though."

"We did," the soldier said. "And we are."

"You're putting the blood in barrels and transporting it . . . somewhere," Miles said. "You're draining the bodies into barrels. But where are the bodies? And why are you doing it?"

"You'll see why later. Keep walking."

Miles and Amelia walked by two more barrels, both also smelling strongly of blood and death, and stopped by a large section of wall that had been cut out. Bloodstains covered the outside of it, and there were several inches of it on the floor. Miles looked over at the containers and realised they all had a lever to let them tip up, spilling their contents into the hole.

"I said move," the soldier started, about to jab Miles with the shock baton.

It never connected.

Miles darted to the side and slammed his palm up into the outstretched elbow of the soldier, his strength breaking the joint, werewolf or not. He smashed his own elbow into the soldier's eye, feeling the socket break, before forcing the soldier headfirst into the side of the container.

"Down, go," Miles told Amelia, pointing to the tunnel beside them.

Someone shouted something farther down the tunnel, but Miles had no intention of finding out who it was and launched himself toward the tunnel after Amelia, certain of the fact that wherever it was going to take him would probably be better than with a bunch of desolates and werewolves.

The soldier intercepted Miles, a low growl in his throat. Miles let himself be pushed to the side, next to a second tunnel beside the one Amelia had used. He hoped he'd be able to find her again.

Miles headbutted the still growling soldier, breaking his nose with a loud crack, before catching him in the throat with an elbow that should have crushed the man's windpipe, but only managed to stun his assailant long enough for Miles to throw himself down the tunnel behind him.

After several seconds of sliding down something that he really hoped was water, Miles came out in a large room with lights all around it, illuminating the area. He hit the liquid below, causing a huge splash, and felt something bump into him as he was submerged.

It took him a few seconds to figure out where he was and what was going on. The first thing was that the water had long since been anything you'd want to swim in or drink from, considering the number of decaying bodies floating in the pool, too. Whatever had once been water was now a sort of soup.

He went under the soup and swam, as best he could, to the bottom, which he figured was about six feet deep. He reemerged, pushing aside the body parts of some unfortunate soul, and took a moment to figure out whether he'd just thrown himself out of the pan and into the fire.

As he floated in a pool of decaying corpses, Miles realised how much he'd underestimated just how bad it was going to be in the tunnels under Maine. He needed to find a way out. He needed to find Amelia. Preferably before the werewolves discovered them.

CHAPTER SEVENTEEN

The stench was overwhelming. The combination of fetid water and decay spliced in among the overall aroma of death meant Miles needed a few seconds to adjust. The bodies of dozens of people floated in the pool with Miles, not all of them whole. He imagined that those who had made the pit of blood weren't too fussed about the state of the bodies that went in it.

Miles slowly made his way across the pool, moving the bodies of the freshly deceased out of the way. He reached the edge and looked back at the death he'd just swum through. The deceased were all still clothed, but their throats had been cut, or in some cases their heads removed altogether. They were all newly dead, and all wore military fatigues. The victims from the fort. They had been bled out and their bodies dumped.

He was about to pull himself up out of the pool when he heard a voice ahead. "He jumped into the body pool."

Miles dropped back into the pool of death and swam over to the middle, using the bodies of the deceased as cover when the soldier he'd hurt ran into the room, along with two desolates.

"He's in there!" the soldier shouted at the shambling desolates.

Miles noticed the man's arm was no longer pointing the wrong way. Werewolves did heal fast.

Each of the two desolates held a long pole with hooks on the end. The desolates themselves looked as if they might fall apart at any moment. Each had greying skin which was sunken around the bones of their face and bare arms. Miles wondered how old they were. He wasn't sure how long desolate could live for, maybe forever, but he was pretty sure that those two were well beyond their sell-by date.

Miles slowly moved under the surface of what was best not thought about, as the first hook slammed into a body a few feet from him. He turned into his vampire form as he sank, looking up through the murk all around him as he reached the bottom. He couldn't see through the huge quantity of muck, but he heard the werewolf's heartbeat, a thunderstorm of sound and activity next to the empty shells that were the desolate.

Miles moved along the bottom to the edge of the pool behind the largest mass of bodies, and surfaced, moving as slowly as possible.

"He has to be in there," the werewolf shouted, snatching one of the poles from a desolate and immediately starting to thrash at the surface, trying to hook the bodies out of the way. The two desolates stood and stared at the werewolf, each with an expression on their face that, had they been alive, would have been suggesting that the werewolf was a moron.

"Fucking hell," the werewolf said, snatching one of the desolate up and throwing them headfirst into the bodies. "Fucking find him." He kicked the second desolate into the pool and stormed out of the room.

Miles sank back beneath the surface and drew his dagger. The heat activation was going to make everything smell horrendous, but everything already smelled horrendous, so it wasn't as if Miles was exchanging flowers for shite.

The two desolates were above him, floating without any effort, when Miles grabbed the legs of one, dragged it down, and slammed the heated blade into its head. Miles twisted the blade and pulled it free, kicking away from the now deceased desolate, and moving up toward the second one.

The second desolate looked down just as Miles slammed into it, grabbing it around the throat with one taloned hand and tearing it out. He punched the blade through the back of the desolate's skull, killing it, but frying the dagger's heating element at the same time.

With both desolates disposed of, Miles moved to the edge of the pool and pulled himself up and out. He removed the shotgun from its holster on his back and checked it, but it was full of gore, so he tossed it into the pool, along with the incendiary shells.

Miles was pretty sure he looked and smelled like something out of a nightmare, with globs of nothing good dropping off him with every step, but seeing how there didn't seem to be shower facilities in the room, he would just have to get used to it.

He paused at the room's only doorway and peered around the corner into a hallway beyond. The hallway was made of black stone and smeared, much like everything else, with muck and gore. There were four more door-ways along the hallway, three on his left, and one on his right, with another at the far left end. He crossed the hallway and moved into the room oppo-site, and found it to be identical to the one he'd just been in. A large pool full of water, also containing multiple decaying bodies. Miles left that room and tried the next, finding only pools of water in the others.

"Miles," Amelia whispered from the doorway as she exited one of the rooms and spotted him on the opposite side of the hallway.

"Hey, you okay?" Miles asked.

Amelia's eyes went wide with shock. "What happened to you?"

Where Amelia looked as if she'd been for a pleasant swim, albeit fully clothed, Miles looked as though he'd bathed in the remains of his enemies. The result, Miles had to admit, was a little gruesome.

"Pool of decaying bodies," Miles said. "Where'd you end up?"

"Big pool of water," Amelia said. "No gore, no bodies."

Miles stared at Amelia for a moment before exhaling sharply. "We should get out of here."

"Couldn't agree more," Amelia said. "I checked that room; it's an empty pool, too."

"Apparently whoever is doing this is making sure they have room for whatever they have planned."

"Let's not stay around and find out what that is," Amelia said.

As they reached the door at the end of the hallway, Miles heard someone approaching. He motioned for Amelia to go into the room beside them, the room with one of the pools of bodies.

"Have you found him yet?" the werewolf soldier that Miles had just hurt shouted from beyond the final doorway. "Can't smell anything down here; everything just stinks of rotting bodies."

Miles and Amelia remained inside the closest room with the full pool of water, pushing their bodies up against the darkness offered by the walls on either side of the hallway beyond.

"Goddamn desolate are so goddamned fucking weird," the werewolf said as he walked by the doorway. "It won't be soon enough to be done with this bullshit."

Miles heard the muffled shout from the werewolf somewhere outside.

Miles pointed to the pool and put his finger to his lips. Amelia looked over at the pool of death and rolled her eyes, before walking over and slowly lowering herself into the mess, her expression one of wishing she was quite literally anywhere else.

"You're here," the werewolf said with a menacing growl, making a show of sniffing the air. He opened the door to the room Amelia and Miles were hiding in and stepped into the hallway, closing the door behind him with a loud click. "You can't hide. I thought vampires were braver than this, not just cowering in the shadows like pathetic little cowards."

Miles placed a finger to his lips again and Amelia nodded as the werewolf continued to sniff the air in the hallway. They couldn't stay here forever—sooner or later backup would arrive, and then they were going to be back where they'd been before their escape. Miles doubted the werewolves would be as kind with either of them the next time. He glanced down at his feet and saw a small piece of rock, which he kicked across the room until it impacted with the far wall, making a small cracking noise.

The werewolf soldier rushed into the room, sniffing the air as he stood over the edge of the pool. Miles steadied him and slammed a telekinetic blast into the werewolf's back, sending him sprawling into the pool.

Miles ran over to the pool, grabbed Amelia's outstretched hand, and pulled her up out of the mess. Together, they turned and ran out of the room, along the hallway, and continued on down the tunnel beyond. Miles had no way of knowing where they were going, or how they were going to actually get out of this ant maze of tunnels, but they did not want to be dragged before whoever the werewolves were working for.

Miles carried Amelia on his back, her arms around his shoulders, so he could run at full speed. He dodged the occasional desolate, most of whom didn't even look their way as he ran by, leaping over any obstacles in his path. He ran for what felt like an age, before he eventually came out at a large room where there were cages hung from the ceiling. Several of the cages were empty, but a few of them had the remains of people inside, long since dead and decaying.

Somewhere behind him in the darkness he'd just run through came the livid roar of a very angry werewolf. Miles thought for a moment to consider his options. If they were outside, or if Miles knew the terrain better, he wouldn't even think twice about standing his ground. He'd just kill the werewolf and be done with it, but his beast form would be more of a liability in such a confined area.

Amelia dropped down from Miles's back, as he closed his eyes and sniffed at the air. His nose was nowhere near as powerful as that of a werewolf, but it was good enough to get the slightest morsel of scent from somewhere down in the tunnels. It was almost blocked through the smells of blood, decay, sweat, and shit, but it was there. The scent of salt water.

"That way," Miles said, pointing in the direction. "You want back up?"

Amelia allowed herself to be picked up again. "We never mention this to anyone."

"Got it," Miles said, and ran down the tunnel the seawater scent had come from, passing several more desolates who did nothing to stop him. Whatever had happened to them to make them so docile or controllable was something to look into once he was out of his current predicament.

Miles ran for several minutes until reaching a large room with a roaring fire in the centre and old-style cell doors built into the walls. A prison. Five desolates sat against the walls of the room, and sprang to life when Miles entered. Apparently, not all of their kind were subservient and docile.

Amelia immediately dropped from Miles's shoulder as the first desolate charged at Miles with no weapons in hand, just a roar of rage and hate. Miles used his telekinesis to blast it into the fire, where its roars were quickly swallowed up by the flames.

"I've got this," Miles said, not looking back. "Just keep an eye out for any newcomers."

"On it," Amelia said.

Miles was already moving to the next desolate, ducking under a swipe of its clawed hands, and using his talons to sever the creature's Achilles tendon as he moved by. The desolate fell to the ground and started to crawl toward Miles, who was already moving toward the third and fourth desolate, both of whom jumped toward him.

A blast of telekinesis sent the fourth desolate careering into the fifth, who had remained at the far wall, and the third flying off into one of the metal cage doors, where something inside grabbed hold of it by the head, repeatedly smashing it into the bars until it was nothing but pulp. Miles made a mental note to stay away from the cages.

The fourth and fifth desolate were in the process of disentangling themselves from each other when Miles smashed his talons through the one's skull, before another telekinesis blast sent his accomplice into the same fire as his ally. When silence fell again, Miles picked up the remaining desolate number and threw them into the fire, too.

"Miles," Amelia called out as she stood by one of the cells. "You need to see this."

Miles walked over, and a voice asked from inside the darkness of the cell, "Can you help me?"

A roar from nearby brought Miles back to a very real and immediate problem. "We've got a werewolf after us," he said.

"I know the way out," the voice said.

"Who are you?" Amelia asked.

The person from the cell stepped closer to the edge, the light from the fire illuminating him. He wore military fatigues, and apart from the blood and grime that covered him, and his emaciated appearance, he looked to be in relatively good condition. "Major Alan Parker of the Maine First vampire militia."

"The what?" Miles asked, waving the question away as he spoke it. "Don't care, you're from the fort, yes?"

The Major nodded.

"You the only survivor?"

The Major nodded again, this time sadly.

Another roar from somewhere in the dark, getting closer.

"Fuck," Miles said. "I guess there's no point in continuing to run."

"What does that mean?" the Major asked.

"It means if I let you out, that werewolf will hunt us down," Miles explained. "You don't look like you're in any condition to run, or to fight much. You need blood. How long since you last fed?"

"Two weeks," the Major said.

"Which House?"

"House Phalanx," he said. "Before the fall. Here when it happened. After, I stayed here to help."

"Why can't you get out of that cage alone?"

The Major shook the bars. "I don't have the strength to remove them. Bashing that desolate's head in used everything I had. Worth it, though."

Miles sniffed the air; the smell of wet dog was closer than ever. He probably had thirty seconds before a very mad werewolf came rushing into the room. He moved over to the bars, grabbed them, and pulled. There was a groaning noise as they started to shift, but the rock on either side of the cell held the cell door fast.

He was about to try again when the werewolf stepped into the room. Werewolves looked a bit like someone had crossed a human with a wolf but had no idea what they were doing and so cranked everything up to eleven to compensate. The werewolf in the room with Miles was seven feet tall with dark grey fur covering its massive frame. It had dark leathery hands which looked almost human except for how long the fingers were, and the black claws that sat on the end of each finger. The legs were wolf-like, although stood upright, the creature looked unbalanced and ungainly. Despite this, they were deceptively fast.

The head and face of the werewolf looked like a wolf, but it was larger, with bright amber eyes and teeth that might have belonged to a wolf if they were twice the size. The creature looked as if it was made to hunt prey and rend flesh from bone.

"I assume we won't be discussing this like gentlemen," Miles said with a shrug.

The werewolf charged at him, all rage and instinct, swiping with its claws a little too fast for Miles's liking. One swipe missed and punched through the rock next to the cell door holding the Major, raining pieces of dust and rock around as it let out a howl of irritation.

Blood dripped down from the wound on the back of the werewolf's hand, landing on the dirt-covered ground. Miles tried to push the idea of drinking it out of his mind, but the smell of such power, even in tiny drops, was something he had to fight against, considering he hadn't fed for a while.

Miles moved back gracefully, putting distance between himself and the brute force of the creature before him. He felt the heat of the fire behind him and moved to the side, edging around it as the werewolf followed, its eyes devoid of anything close to humanity. While werewolves retained some semblance of their intelligence and personality while in their monster forms, it was impossible to reason with one once it had decided you were its next prey.

The werewolf looked over at Amelia, whose eyes had turned a sparkling green as her magic ignited. "You," it growled, the one word full of anger.

Miles used the opening and kicked a piece of hot wood from the fire toward the werewolf, spraying little embers of flame around as the wolf batted it away.

"I don't want to kill you," Miles said. "I want answers. Dead wolves don't tend to be very conversational."

The werewolf roared in response and moved toward Miles faster than anything that size had any right to. But Miles was quicker. He darted to the side, around the rear of the fire, easily avoiding the werewolf's long, powerful arms, and blasted hot coal and wood at the creature, which roared in pain as it was peppered with bits of flame.

Miles stopped on the opposite side of the fire to the werewolf as the two of them locked eyes for a moment. Miles hoped it wasn't going to end the way he was pretty sure it was. He desperately wanted answers about what was going on, but he wasn't going to get them from the soldier across from him.

"Come on then, you fucking shitehawk," Miles said softly. "Let's get this done."

The werewolf leapt over the fire, his claws out in front, ready to tear into Miles's flesh, but the vampire was already moving to the side. He blasted the werewolf in the chest with his telekinesis, and as the werewolf flew back across the room into the wall, Miles followed, pinning the creature to the wall by its throat and jabbing his talons into the ribcage.

Miles stabbed into the side of the werewolf over and over in quick succession, until he was forced to move back to avoid the defensive swipe. As the werewolf's arm moved by Miles, the vampire darted back in, bringing his talons up into the elbow joint, tearing into the flesh and muscle. With a twist of his hand, Miles's talons rent the werewolf's elbow joint free. Miles tore the forearm off the monster, throwing it onto the fire as he skirted away.

Blood gushed from the wounded werewolf, but the fight remained in his eyes as he managed to stay upright, pushing himself off the rock wall and kicking out at Miles. Miles moved to its side, where it was missing an arm, and slashed through its ribs again. He moved behind the werewolf, leapt up, and sank his teeth into the creature's neck, feeling the warm blood geyser down his throat as he drank deeply.

Miles drank for only a few seconds, but it was enough to link his mind to that of the soldier beneath the wolf. The soldier who had killed Patrick in Boston. Who had killed so many and revelled in their deaths, in their blood. Who had attacked Amelia, thinking her easy prey. Who had learned very quickly that she was anything but.

The flickers of memories lasted only a few seconds, before Miles was left with something else, something more important: power.

The werewolf tried to backhand Miles with his only hand, but Miles caught it at the wrist, snapping the bone, and driving his talons back into werewolf's throat, ripping it open from ear to ear, and allowing the torrent of blood that cascaded forth to cover him.

The soldier dropped to his knees, looking up at Miles with surprise.

"You just weren't good enough," Miles told him, before punching his talons back into the side of the werewolf's neck, driving them in deep on either side, then tearing them out, decapitating the monster. Miles picked up the creature's head and tossed it onto the flames, before stepping over the remains and walking over to the cage. Vines retracted back into the ground, having torn the cage door free.

"You killed a werewolf," Amelia said with shock as she helped the frail Major out of the cell.

The Major looked over at the headless body of the werewolf.

"Feed," Miles said, emotionless as more and more of the soldier's memories flicked through his mind. He felt the power and strength of the werewolf flow through him. It was a heady amount of power. "You won't need much, but you need to heal. Body is fresh, so there's no issues with drinking dead blood. There's an exit this way."

Miles watched the Major dip his hands into the rapidly increasing pool of blood around the werewolf and drink deep, before gasping.

"There's so much power here," the Major said to Miles after he'd returned to his feet, his face no longer looking sunken.

Miles nodded, unwilling to speak as the rage and hate that the werewolf had felt flooded his body. "He killed the Detective," he said.

"You sure?" Amelia asked.

"I can see him tearing into flesh—I can see you," Miles said softly. "I feel his surprise that you defended yourself. He was hoping to get another chance to kill you."

"He died hard," the Major said, mistaking Miles's expression for one of regret or sadness for the way it had gone.

"Not hard enough," Amelia assured him.

CHAPTER EIGHTEEN

The map of the network of tunnels that had been placed in Miles's head from his drinking of the werewolf wasn't complete. There were large parts of the system that the werewolf had never been to, or at least hadn't been to enough that those memories were important to him. It was always a crapshoot about what memories you might get when a vampire drank from someone. Miles was just lucky it wasn't something useless like his first kiss or the first time he'd been deployed in a combat zone.

Miles wondered which of his memories the werewolf had gotten in return. It didn't much matter now considering the creature was dead and no longer an issue, but he was always curious for the moments after he'd killed while drinking from someone.

"You know the way?" the Major asked after they'd been walking for several minutes down dimly lit tunnels, warily passing by more desolate who didn't even look up from their seated positions.

"Why are they like that?" Miles asked him as they stopped by one desolate who seemed only interested in pushing the dirt around by his fingers.

"Never known a desolate not to try to rip your face off," the Major said quietly. "The ones that came for the fort, they were . . . they were not like that."

"How did you survive?" Miles asked, looking up at him.

"I don't know," the Major said. "I was in my office when I heard a scream from one of the soldiers, followed by the desolate, hundreds of them, all pouring over the walls into the fort. They killed everyone, attacked before we could stop them. They dragged me back through the forest to a hole there, brought me down here, and made me kneel in front of a werewolf. A large man."

"Liam," Amelia suggested.

"I didn't know his name," the Major said. "He brought me to the were-wolf you killed, and they put me in the cage. Told me to behave and that I might live to see another day. They wanted me to meet someone, I think their boss. I don't know why."

Miles got back to his feet, ignoring the desolate as he continued on down the tunnel with Amelia and the Major behind him. "To answer your earlier question, there's a tunnel ahead that leads out into the bay near Brunswick. The dead werewolf spoke about it with Liam, his boss. They didn't like the tunnel because it led down into water, but so long as you can swim, you'll be fine."

"How long is the tunnel?" the Major asked.

"Few hundred feet," Miles said.

"Are there sharks?"

Miles stopped walking and looked back. "Does it matter?"

"I don't like sharks," the Major said. "That never felt like it was an issue before Maine fell, but I guess the number of bodies that ended up in the water around the state has made it a bit of a feeding ground."

"Bodies?" Amelia asked.

"The desolate," the Major said. "A bunch of people ended up on the islands around Brunswick, trying to escape what was happening. The desolate arrived, and now you have a lot of desolate. And then the desolate swim back to shore, or float that way looking for food. Sharks come along and have a bite."

"What happens to the sharks?"

"They usually don't bite twice," the Major said. "I watched a great white bite a desolate in half once, but it didn't even eat it. Just swam away."

"Would that make the shark a desolate?" Amelia asked, a slight panic to her voice. "Are there desolate sharks? Because that doesn't sound like something I want to be near."

Miles considered it. "I don't think so. I've never seen any animals become desolate."

"What about normal sharks?" the Major asked Amelia. "How are you with those?"

"I'm not too bothered about them," she admitted with a shrug.

"Hopefully no sharks," Miles said, discovering he had a whole new concern to think about.

They continued on for a short distance as a rumbling noise could be heard up ahead. "What is that?" the Major asked as Miles motioned for the man to stay low behind him.

The pair moved slowly up the tunnel, which ended with a ten-foot drop to a large open cavern with two tunnels leading away from it. The cavern itself had dozens of the containers that Miles had seen earlier to move earth, all full of black stone.

"It's that one," Miles said, pointing to the most northerly of the two tunnels.

The pair dropped into the cavern and Miles ran over to the first container.

"What is it?" the Major asked, clearly unhappy about having to take a moment longer than necessary.

"What is this?" Miles asked him, picking up a large piece of black stone that must have weighed fifty kilos. It was completely smooth, and Miles wondered why they were excavating it. He let the rock drop to the ground.

"Rock," the Major said and picked up a smaller piece, turning it over in his hands. "It looks like the stone from under Augusta. When we were pushing the desolate back under the town, there were a lot of pillars that were this colour. Walls, too. But we blew the entrance and buried them all down there."

"You sure?" Miles asked. "It was forty years ago."

"Yes, I'm sure," the Major said. "They have some of it in Bangor; it's used in the fortifications of the main wall. I've never seen stone like it before or since, except in Bangor. There's a doctor in Bangor, a Joseph Davies. Someone brought some in a few months back, and he went mental. Started talking about making the walls bigger, and needing to go to Augusta to check. It was just before I was deployed to Falmouth. He's probably still in Bangor if you want to talk to him."

"Nothing more?"

"No one knew what he was talking about, and all he said was that it needed to be investigated."

The rumbling started once again, and Miles motioned for the Major and Amelia to duck down just as two twelve-foot-tall desolates marched out of the tunnel next to the one that was Miles's exit. They each pushed a large container of more black stone.

"What the fuck?" the Major whispered.

"Desolate," Miles explained. "They've been cocooned for some time, must have eaten a lot of their brethren to get that big. Makes them bigger, stronger, much meaner."

The desolates marched to the centre of the cavern, left their containers there, and returned down the tunnel.

"Someone is controlling them," Miles said. "Otherwise I have no idea why the desolate aren't just trying to get out of here and feed on everyone above."

"You ever seen someone control a desolate?" Amelia asked.

Miles thought back to not long ago when a human by the name of Henryk Greger had created a helmet that managed to let him control the desolate. It hadn't ended well for Henryk.

"That's what the vampires experimenting on the desolate before the fall were doing," Miles said. "Trying to control them."

"You think it worked?" the Major asked.

Miles shrugged. "I don't really want to find out who is controlling them. I want to get out of here and let Bangor and Brunswick know that they have a really big problem on their doorstep."

"You think those monster desolates will be back?" the Major asked.

"Let's not wait around to find out," Miles said, getting to his feet and starting to run the fifty feet of open ground to the mouth of the tunnel they were going to use.

They were almost there when a container of rock sailed out of the adjacent tunnel, slamming into the ground next to the Major, who was forced to throw himself to the side to avoid the impact.

The two huge desolates charged out of their tunnel like two exceptionally angry gorillas wanting to deal with an interloper. The Major rolled back to his feet and tried to get away, but one of the desolate backhanded him, sending him flying across the cavern into the far wall. The impact made a sickening noise, and the Major dropped to the ground unmoving.

Amelia ran back toward the stricken vampire, who was dazed and had a broken arm, but was otherwise not seriously hurt. At least not outwardly.

Miles covered the distance between him and his allies just as the Major got back to his feet. Miles pushed the Major and Amelia aside, throwing himself to the floor to roll under a swipe from one of the desolate that would have sent him flying. Miles rolled between the creature's massive legs, raking his talons down the back of its calf, cleaving into the Achilles tendon.

Unlike the desolate from earlier, the monstrosity barely seemed to register the blow, and tried to kick out at Miles, who was thankfully already several dozen feet back from imminent danger. The Major didn't have the same fortune, and was busy trying to scramble away from the second desolate, who was in the process of attempting to grab the smaller vampire. All the while, Amelia used her magic to shoot vines and roots out of the ground, entangling the legs of the desolate, although it seemed to barely slow the creature.

Miles looked up at the ceiling, which was at least sixty feet high, enough room to use his beast, although he wasn't sure how much help it would be considering the power and strength of the desolate. Instead, he grabbed a piece of rock from one of the containers and threw it at the head of the desolate, which roared in anger in response.

A second piece of rock bounced off the desolate's nose, making it even angrier, and it charged at Miles, who easily avoided it, slicing through the Achilles on the other leg of the monster. Blood was beginning to saturate the ground around where the desolate stood, and despite the initial lack of response to it, the desolate was starting to slow, and was looking wobbly on its feet.

The strength of the werewolf was still inside of Miles, but he knew he couldn't play dodge for long, especially with the Major and Amelia only just managing to evade the desolate chasing.

"Goddamn it," Miles shouted, his attention momentarily lapsed, and his attacker managed to connect with a backhand that Miles only just brought his arms up to block in time. The powerful strike lifted Miles off his feet and dumped him on the ground a dozen feet back, but at least he hadn't impacted with a wall.

"You know, I always wanted to try something," Miles said, effortlessly getting to his feet as the desolate charged.

Miles moved to the side of the creature, leapt up, his talons catching on the flank of the monster, and swung up onto its back. He slammed his hand into the back of the head of the desolate, unleashing his bloodline gift.

Used on a vampire, it separated the vampire and human sides, rendering the vampire fragile and much easier to deal with. He'd never used it on anything else, but had tried it on Sara Bakos, which had removed the desolate and vampire sides of her body, giving her clarity for a few precious moments. It had made him wonder what would happen should he use it on a desolate.

The answer was screaming. A lot of screaming.

Miles dropped down next to the desolate, who bellowed in raw pain, its hands grasping its head in agony. Miles paused for a moment, trying to figure out what he was meant to do next, when the desolate crushed its own head between gargantuan hands.

Whatever Miles had been feeling about a second earlier was replaced with complete and total shock. He'd never seen a desolate do anything of the sort. He'd seen them tear their own limbs off to try and get to prey, but to crush their own heads to deal with pain was a new one.

The Major and Amelia sprinted out of one tunnel a second later, immediately taking the tunnel Miles pointed at them to go down. Miles followed to the tunnel as the second desolate charged out of the first, just behind the Major and Amelia. The creature tried to change direction to get Miles, but it was an uncoordinated effort, and it landed face first on the floor instead.

Miles didn't wait and ran on, catching up with the Major and Amelia a few seconds later. None of them spoke as the roars of anger bounced around the inside of the tunnel.

"Down there," Miles said, pointing to another tunnel farther in as the ground started to shake when the desolate giant ran after them.

They'd made it only a few dozen feet when a container of stone bounced off the ground beside them, so they picked up the pace. Unfortunately, they didn't see the slipperiness of the ground they were about to tread on, and they were soon sliding down a steep incline at speed.

A few moments later, they hit the bottom of the tunnel and were all submerged in ice cold, clear salt water.

"Which way?" the Major asked after they resurfaced.

Miles pointed down. "This is the swimming part, you ready?"

"How far?" Amelia asked. "Human lungs."

"Hundred feet, I think," Miles said. "Memories aren't always exactly accurate. You hold onto me. Don't let go. I'm going at speed here."

Amelia moved around to grab hold of Miles around the neck, her mouth next to his ear.

"Ready?" he asked.

The Major nodded and Amelia took a deep breath.

Miles dove down into the water. He wasn't concerned about holding his breath—he was a vampire; the days of needing to hold his breath were long gone—but he knew he needed to be quick for Amelia. Unfortunately, the farther down he went, the murkier the water became, and he didn't want to get the wrong tunnel.

The werewolf had been here. He'd gone down the tunnel, and he'd swum out to the bay beyond. The fact that Miles didn't get the memory of sliding down the tunnel said as much about the randomness of memories as it did about the fact that the werewolf hadn't enjoyed the experience.

Miles remembered a pocket of air and swam up, letting Amelia exhale and catch her breath.

"You okay?" Miles asked.

"This sucks," Amelia said.

The Major's head came up into the air pocket, making the small area cramped.

"Ready?" Miles asked.

"Do it," Amelia said, taking another deep breath.

Miles descended back into the water, found the tunnel right where his memory told him it would be, and took hold of the Major's arm, pointing to it. The Major gave a thumbs-up, and Miles went first into the tunnel, swimming for several seconds at full speed before it opened up into the bay.

He swam up to the surface and looked around as the Major joined him, and Amelia disengaged from his back.

"You okay?" Miles asked, holding onto Amelia's arm as she tread water beside him.

"Never doing that again," Amelia said, gasping from the cold.

"Sun soon," Miles said, pointing to the start of dawn over the horizon. "I don't want to be tracking through the state during the day, if possible."

"There are caves around there," the Major said. "It's a few hours' walk to Brunswick from here, and there's no way they're letting anyone in this close to dawn. Besides, with the sun coming up, we have no way of telling what the UV will be without walking out into it, and I'd rather not do that. And if we can't go out, the desolate can't either—so there's some time."

Miles hated the fact that he was right—he wanted to get to Brunswick, he wanted to make sure that those on the pilgrimage were safe, but bursting into flames on the way there wasn't going to aid anyone.

The three of them set off at a steady swim toward the shore.

CHAPTER NINETEEN

The cave had been nice, as far as caves went. They'd set a fire and hunkered down to rest for the day, far enough in the cave itself to be unconcerned about local wildlife becoming an issue.

Miles hoped that the pilgrimage had gotten to Brunswick okay. It had been a long time since he'd had to run from something, but he didn't cherish the idea of fighting those large desolate again, and he hoped that they weren't a sign of a more common type within the state. The fort's entrance would not have been quite as secure against such monsters.

He'd seen desolate born from cocoons before, but never like that. It made him wonder if there was more to their creation than just cocooning desolates.

Despite the concern about being out in the open, the Major fell asleep within moments of dawn fully rising.

"I'll take the first shift," Miles told Amelia. "Gives me time to calm."

"You sure?" Amelia asked while stifling a yawn.

"Go sleep, see you in a few hours."

Amelia was asleep soon after, and once he'd extinguished the fire and Amelia had woken for her shift, Miles finally got some rest. Although it felt nowhere near enough, as Miles was already awake when the Major woke. He started the fire up again and waited for dusk to become night.

"I have to talk to the families of my people," Major Alan Parker said, the first words he'd spoken since waking.

"We will find them justice," Miles assured him. The swim had removed a large portion of the blood and grime he'd picked up running through the tunnels under Maine, but he could still smell it on him. An unpleasant reminder of what he'd been through.

The Major poked at the fire with a stick, the time-honoured tradition of men poking a nearby fire when they didn't know what else to do. Eventually, the Major said, "So, why are you in Maine, and how the hell can you fight like that?"

"The werewolf?"

"All of it," the Major said. "I've never seen a vampire take out a werewolf before. I once saw a werewolf kill three vampires before it was finally stopped. These things aren't puppies."

Miles felt Amelia's gaze on him, possibly wondering similar things.

"I've always been good at killing things," Miles said. "I'm an Arbiter."

"You here on official business?"

Miles shook his head. "Meant to be here helping a pain in the arse journalist do a story about the pilgrimage of House Idolator."

"That would be me," Amelia said with a wry grin.

"Those kooks?"

"Kooks?" Amelia asked.

The Major nodded. "They're nice enough people and all, and they do help out in a lot of ways, but have you ever spoken to the First Priest?"

Miles shook his head.

"Ah, well, he's up in Bangor," the Major said. "He's . . . intense. Thinks the vampire gods are going to return and be unhappy about how we've treated the place. The pilgrimage is all fine, until they start trying to get you to join their cause to worship some long-dead assholes, if they ever existed in the first place."

"The Dusk," Miles said.

"That's them," the Major said.

"They're vampire myths," Miles continued. "Nae sure I'd call them gods, though. In fact, I'm pretty sure they're the opposite. Never really understood why anyone would worship a bunch of creatures who did as they pleased until they just all vanished."

"Killed?"

Miles shrugged. "No clue. The stories just say that one by one they disappeared, and no one knows how or why. Or if they do know, they're not telling anyone. It's a fairy story."

"House Idolator believes otherwise," the Major said.

"So, House Idolator worships a bunch of people who weren't gods, but they just *really* wish they were?" Amelia asked.

Miles nodded. "That actually sums it up pretty well. Are they quite pushy in Maine, then?"

"The First Priest can be," the Major said. "He would turn up at the fort and lead everyone there in prayer. At least the vampires. Started off with only one or two joining in, but by the end it was anyone who was a vampire, and a few who weren't. Nothing was said, but there were glances your way if you didn't join in."

"So, you joined in then," Miles said. "Not judging."

The Major nodded. "It was advised to me that I should. Apparently, the First Priest has some friends in places that look favourably on participation."

"Bangor?"

"Yeah."

Miles considered his next words carefully. "Bangor got a lot of people there who look favourably on the Dusk?"

"A few, I guess," the Major said. "I think most of them just go along with it, but it's gone from being a fair and equal town to one that favours House Idolator above all others. They're not even a Great House."

"They're trying to make a comeback," Miles said. "I think Maine is a pretty big part of that plan."

"Like I said," the Major started, "they do some good work here, but they're very much keeping an eye on those who do and don't stand with them and their beliefs. You'll see the more time you spend with them."

Miles glanced out of the mouth of the cave to the darkness just beyond. There was a heavy patter of rain.

"And me without my raincoat," Amelia said.

"I just want to say thank you," the Major said. "Both of you. I didn't after we got out, but honestly, you two saved my life. I'll never forget that."

Miles looked down at the offered hand and shook it, followed by Amelia, who also nodded a thank-you. "Let's not get caught by anything that wants to take us back down there," she said.

"Agreed," the Major said.

Miles covered the fire with dirt, making sure it was completely extinguished before they left the cave. Standing in the mouth of the cave beneath a slight overhang meant they were kept dry from the increasingly hostile wind and rain.

"Do you get a lot of storms here?" Miles asked.

"More and more," the Major said, shaking his head. "No idea why. The weather changed after the fall—it was less predictable, more prone to unseasonal changes that happened day to day, but these days it feels like it happens with more ferocity. You know what can cause that?"

A lot of powerful magic, Miles wanted to say, but instead he said, "Nothing good."

Magic, Amelia mouthed, sharing Miles's thought.

The trio left the cave and ran north toward the woodlands that surrounded the area. They continued on for several miles, passing by the occasional partially collapsed house, and having to stop to kill the desolate that emerged from them.

It took a few hours of travel over rough terrain before the lights of what remained of the town of Brunswick were visible in the distance. Like the fort, there was a moat around it and razor wire topped fifty-foot-high walls just beyond that. There were guards on the towers and roofs that overlooked the area, and the road up to the two was brightly lit.

The Major took the time of the journey to tell his new companions all about Brunswick. Like the fort, there was one entrance and one exit. I-295, which would have taken travellers north to Augusta, had been all but destroyed, and the half of Brunswick on the northern side of the Androscoggin River was a no-go area, the bridges all either collapsed, mined, or guarded with enough firepower to make anyone with a functioning sense of self-preservation pause for thought. Shame the desolate didn't have a functioning sense of anything.

"You can hear the machine gun encampments all night during the winter," the Major said as they walked up the brightly lit road formally known as Pleasant Street.

"How much of Brunswick actually remains?" Amelia asked.

"The last time I was here, they were hoping to reclaim some of it," Miles said.

"The wall goes all along Maine Street, which is why it's called the Maine Wall by anyone who lives here," the Major said. "Starts at the Frank J. Wood Bridge, goes all the way south until Pleasant Hill Road, goes down Middle Bay Road, and then all the way east, by the airport, which I don't mind telling you isn't somewhere I'd want to land a plane these days, seeing how it's now mostly a large vegetable garden."

"So, there's a lot of land to watch," Miles said.

The Major nodded. "Lot of people there to watch it. Everyone works. Bit like Bangor, although on a smaller scale."

"How many people inside?" Amelia asked, her hand twitching as if she were writing with an imaginary pen.

"Ten, fifteen thousand," the Major said. "We keep meaning to do a census, but people come and go, and not all of them come back."

"Vampires and humans?" Miles asked.

"Yes, sir," the Major said.

"Stop," came a booming voice over a loudspeaker as Miles and the Major reached the edge of the hundred-foot-long bridge that had been built over the moat.

Miles, Amelia, and the Major stopped.

"Raise your hands and turn around," the voice commanded.

Miles, Amelia, and the Major did as they were told. "They do this every time?" Miles asked.

"Nope," the Major said.

"I'm sure that's not terrible news or anything," Amelia said.

The huge gates to the city slowly moved open, and a jeep drove out over the wooden bridge. A machine gun had been fixed to the rear of the vehicle, and there were two soldiers standing beside it, with a third aiming the gun at Miles, Amelia, and the Major. A fourth soldier drove the jeep.

The jeep stopped ten feet away, the engine still running.

"State your names and purpose for coming here," one of the soldiers on the rear of the jeep said.

"For fuck's sake, Billy," the Major snapped. "It's me."

"With all due respect," the voice belonging to Billy said. "We have to do this. Heard the fort was wiped out. Can't risk letting just anyone in."

"I was there when you were born, son," the Major said, his voice suddenly ice cold. "You and your human friends need to drive back into that town and get your commanding officer out here. Now."

"I'm afraid—" Billy said.

"I didn't ask your emotional state, boy," the Major snapped. "We have information regarding the well-being of Brunswick, and we are not to be held here by a bunch of fools who think they know what they're doing. Get your commanding officer out here, *now.*"

The driver of the jeep spoke to someone on a radio, using hushed tones.

"Commander Bailey is coming to see you," Billy said, with a lot less certainty in his tone.

"Good," the Major said. "Now it's raining, so I'm going to go stand over there under that tree. If you shoot at me, I'm going to be mighty irritated."

The Major headed for shelter, and Miles and Amelia followed.

"Friends of yours?" Miles asked.

"Billy's a fucking idiot," the Major said. "He keeps asking to join the fort, but I keep turning him down. He's more interested in looking good than actually being a soldier."

"You turning him down probably saved his life," Miles said.

The Major nodded. "His dad is a teacher in the town. Good man. Mom died a few years ago, cancer. Billy has the makings of a decent human being if he ever stops trying to act like he's tougher than everyone else."

"And his friends?" Amelia asked.

"All about the same," the Major said. "Little brains, too much testosterone. They're not bad kids, bad kids don't tend to live in the bigger towns, but they are stupid kids. Probably should have left the state and found their way elsewhere, but I think no matter where they ended up, they'd still be dumbasses."

"You never thought about leaving?" Miles asked, watching the large truck roll out of the town. The truck stopped, and a gentleman of at least sixty got out and started shouting at the soldiers who remained on the bridge.

"Not giving my state over to the desolate and their ilk," the Major said, pushing himself off the tree. "I'll die first."

Almost did, Miles thought as he followed the Major down to the bridge once again.

"Major," the man said.

"Commander Bailey," the Major said with a salute.

"And this is?" the Commander asked after returning the salute.

"Miles Watson," he said. "And Amelia Roberts."

"And you are?" the Commander asked, a slight edge to his tone.

"I'm an Arbiter," Miles told him, raising his wrist to show the torc which he'd replaced on his wrist after waking up in the cave. He got the feeling it was going to come in handy, and any pretence of hiding his profession was well and truly over. Besides, the attitude from the

Commander indicated that only power would garner any respect—Miles could play that game.

"And I'm a journalist working with the *Independent*," Amelia said.

"They saved my life, David," the Major said. "He killed a werewolf with his bare hands to do it, too."

"So not a normal Arbiter," the Commander said, never taking his gaze off Miles.

"It's raining, it's cold, I've had a long few days, and I'm pretty sure a convoy of people came through here and could tell you a lot more about me," Miles said. "We'd like to get into Brunswick and tell you about what we found."

"How bad is it?" the Commander asked the Major, ignoring Miles.

"It's really bad," the Major said grimly. "We need to talk."

"Let's go," the Commander said, before turning to Miles. "You behave, or you die."

Miles bristled at the threat; he wasn't used to having humans tell him what to do, let alone threaten to kill him. "Aye. You happen to have seen my dog?"

"Dog?" the Commander asked him.

"Church," Miles said.

"Big fucking thing?" the Commander asked.

"Aye," Miles said slowly, his irritation threatening to bubble over. "You'll get to see it soon enough."

"Her," Miles corrected.

The Commander visibly stiffened at being corrected, but climbed back into the truck, which had been turned around, and drove back into Brunswick, the smaller jeep with Billy and his friends following behind like a scolded child.

"He's an absolute dick," Miles said as they walked over the bridge, their footsteps echoing around them after the sound of the vehicle engines faded away.

"Yes he is," the Major said. "But I wouldn't cross him. He's run this city for a decade and doesn't really like newcomers. Especially vampires."

"Probably shouldn't be in Maine then," Miles said. "How does he deal with the pilgrimage?"

"He tolerates them because they bring supplies," the Major said. "I tolerate him because he kept his nose out of fort business. I guess that's over now."

"You going to leave?"

"Probably go back up to Bangor," the Major said. "They're a bit more tolerant than the Commander here. I think his dislike of vampires leaks out into the populous a little. At best guess, ten thousand people live in Brunswick on a permanent basis, and about forty of them are vampires. And all of those live close to the eastern edge, near the airport, or south, near the beach. Out of sight, out of mind."

"Any chance he's friendly with the Magistrate?" Miles asked as they reached the metal gate.

"I wouldn't be surprised if he has a lifetime membership," the Major said as they walked into Brunswick.

They all stood in a courtyard that was seventy-five feet long by fifty feet wide. A second gate sat directly in front, and armed soldiers stood atop the ramparts surrounding the courtyard, aiming rifles down at them. Miles turned and watched the metal gates slowly close, as the impression of hatred and loathing pressed down onto him from those armed soldiers above. He wasn't sure if it was him as a person, his job as an Arbiter, or his species as a whole, but he definitely wasn't welcome in Brunswick.

"He wants us afraid," Miles said.

The Major nodded.

"He wants us gone, too," Miles continued.

"Something to hide?" Amelia suggested.

Before Miles or the Major could reply, there were several loud clanks as the metal doors locked shut, followed by silence which lasted just a little too long until the second set of doors slowly opened. Commander Bailey stood framed in the exit as the gate opened.

Miles, Amelia, and the Major walked through the courtyard, pointedly trying to ignore the number of soldiers watching them.

"Let's go talk," the Commander said to the Major and turned on his heel, walking down the road beyond into the city.

The Major walked off without a word, and Amelia followed soon after, looking to stay close enough to overhear their conversation. Miles sighed and followed down the cracked road, walking by several buildings which had gun emplacements atop them, and more soldiers looking out of their broken windows.

The Commander reached a checkpoint a hundred meters along the road, where several soldiers saluted. He turned and watched with an irritated expression on his face as the Major and Miles caught up with him. "In here," he said, pointing to the single-storey building beside the checkpoint with two guards standing outside of it, each holding a rifle and wearing navy blue military fatigues.

Once inside the building, Miles, Amelia, and the Major followed the Commander through the large front room, and through the only door, which led to a hallway with two more doors on either side. The Commander selected the first door on the right, and stepped inside, shrugging off his soaking wet jacket and hanging it on a coatrack as he walked around the old, ornate looking wooden desk in the middle of the room, and sat in a chair that Miles immediately noticed was raised slightly higher than the two on the other side.

Miles took a seat without asking, because sometimes it's the little things you can do to piss someone off that warms your heart, and looked around the office. There was a bookshelf to the left of the entrance, with titles about running countries, about world history, and quite a few books on Julius Caesar and ancient Rome. The Commander had specific tastes.

The large desk, which Miles guessed must have taken ages to move into the office, was polished to a near mirror shine, with a glass top. There was a green lamp on it, two fountain pens, placed just so against a notebook, and a radio, which the Commander had just removed from his pocket. There was a photo frame on the desk too, the photo of which showed seven people in either military fatigues or medical scrubs. All were smiling for the camera.

Behind the desk was a painting of a forest, and one of American President Ronald Reagan, for reasons Miles was genuinely baffled by. The Commander would have been in his late teens when Reagan was in power, maybe early twenties, but quite why he would have a picture up forty years later was odd to Miles.

The Commander saw Miles's gaze and turned to the painting. "That is how Maine used to look," he said, pointing to the idyllic forest painting. "Or how it should look. Peaceful. Beautiful. Without the corruption that plagues it. And President Reagan was the last great man to sit in office before all hell broke loose."

"Okay," Miles said, unsure what else he was meant to say. He looked back at the photo.

The Commander turned the photo away from Miles. "Some things are not for discussion. You will tell me what you found under those tunnels."

"Who told you I was in tunnels?" Miles asked, paying attention to the level of dislike in the Commander's tone.

"Your House Idolator friends said you dropped down into them," the Commander replied with a slight smile as if he'd managed to get one over on Miles.

Miles told the Commander everything he'd found and seen, and the Commander, to his credit, didn't interrupt or give any indication that he would rather be elsewhere.

When Miles was done, the Commander said, "And you believe that these tunnel-boring devices could be used against my city?"

"Against *any* city," Miles said. "I don't know how many they have, at least one, but they require tracks to run along, and I don't think they attacked the fort without a lot of prep time."

"You believe it was a test?" the Commander asked.

Miles nodded. "I don't know why it was a test, and I have no idea what they used Falmouth as the test centre for, but yes, I think it was a test."

"To use on Brunswick?" the Commander asked.

"I do not know," Miles repeated. "I do know that there's a lot of desolate down there, and some werewolves, and that those tunnels must stretch for miles. We only saw a small portion before we found Alan here, and we only just managed to get out of there in one piece."

"Would it be safe to send in troops to clear them out?"

Miles shook his head. "Not unless you want a lot of dead people on your hands. They know the area, you don't. I don't know how to stop them, but we need to get to Bangor and warn them, too. If you have a radio that works, that might expedite things."

"We can contact Bangor," the Commander said. "Right now, you're going to be reunited with your friends and leave. And I'm going to spend the next few hours sending people to monitor the situation."

Miles was fine with that, anything to get out of the close proximity of a man whose disdain for him came off in waves.

"Patrol the surrounding lands," Amelia suggested. "They came out of the forest and attacked the fort that way."

From the expression on his face, Miles judged that the Commander did not like being told how to do his job, but he nodded curtly anyway.

Miles smiled. "Excellent. Where are my friends?"

"The old airport," the Commander said. "I'll have someone take you. Are you joining him, Alan? The Maine Militia was your baby, and there are many families and surviving members who will still be at Bangor."

"I aim to go with him, yes," the Major said.

"Good," the Commander said with an enthusiastic clap of his hands.

"By the way, there are giant desolate the likes of which I've never seen down there," Miles said.

"Giant desolate?" the Commander asked, a slight bit of recognition in his voice.

"You've heard of them before?" Amelia asked.

"No," Commander Bailey snapped.

"Any chance you've encountered a witch by the name of Stuart Murphy, or a werewolf pack, led by one Liam White?"

"I don't know what you're talking about," the Commander said.

As far as liars went, Commander Bailey was a bad one, but Miles let it drop for now. "You had any issues with the Magistrate in town?"

"Why?" Commander Bailey asked, his eyes narrowing.

"Heard they have a foothold here," Miles said dismissively. "Want to know if I'm going to run into any of those arseholes before we continue on. A place like Maine can breed the worst in humanity. The lowlifes, the bottom feeders. You know, Commander—criminals, scum. The Magistrate."

For a second, Commander Bailey's eyes lit up with anger, before he controlled them, but it was too late. Miles had felt the Commander's heart rate increase, caught the physical reactions to his besmirching the Magistrate, things a human couldn't easily mask, and Miles knew that the Commander was allied with the Magistrate.

"You need to get your town ready," Miles said, trying to impress just how dangerous these desolate would be, while changing the subject. Now was not the time to start a fight, physical or otherwise.

"You have no idea how ready our town is. If you're done telling me how to do my job, you can all leave."

Miles didn't need telling twice, and he was soon back out in the rain where a jeep awaited them. Miles and the Major climbed into the back, where two soldiers eyed them nervously, but Miles ignored them both as the jeep set off through the city as one thought raced through Miles's mind—just how long had Brunswick been home to an enemy of the vampires?

CHAPTER TWENTY

They'd driven through Brunswick for several minutes at fairly low speeds, giving Miles a good view of the surrounding city. There were the occasional gunshots from somewhere out of sight that betrayed the fact that not everywhere was as quiet and peaceful as the road they travelled down.

Considering the time of night, there were a lot of people out and about. All humans, if what the Major had said about the vampire population was accurate. A lot of them watched the jeep drive down the road.

The two soldiers stared across at each other, never deviating in their gaze toward either the Major, Amelia, or Miles, the latter of whom decided he wasn't going to stay quiet anymore. "This town looks to be in good condition," he said.

The soldier opposite Miles, and next to the Major, looked over at him. "We've kept everything working," she said softly.

"We're not to talk to him," the male soldier opposite her said.

"We've got twenty minutes to go," the female soldier replied. "It's weird that we can't talk."

"I don't bite," Miles said. "Mostly, anyway."

"It true you killed a werewolf with your bare hands?" the male soldier asked after a few seconds of silence.

"He did," the Major said.

"You're militia, yes?" the female soldier asked.

"I am," the Major replied. "Since the fall now. We have six stations all across the state, help to keep the desolate at bay."

"The fort at Falmouth is a great loss to us all," the female soldier said. "I'm sorry for your people."

"As am I," the Major said. "What are your names?"

"I'm Louisa and this is Clint," the female soldier said.

"How old are you?" Miles asked them.

"Twenty-four," Clint said.

"Twenty-seven," Louisa replied.

"You were both born after the fall," Miles said. "Why not leave?"

"My dad is a soldier," Clint said. "Sort of the family business. I decided I'd rather stay and defend our country."

"I did actually leave, went to university, got a degree in applied mathematics," Louisa said with a shrug. "Was going to get a job working at a big-time video game company and . . . something told me to come home. To help here."

"Something *told you*?" Amelia asked.

"Not like that," Louisa said, quickly. "Just, something felt right about coming home. I wanted to be here, to help. It's hard to explain. That was two years ago."

"Your Commander always hated vampires?" Miles asked; he didn't have the time or inclination to tiptoe around the subject.

The soldiers shared an uneasy look.

"You're both safe here," the Major said. "No one will hold your words against you, there's no one here to worry you."

"He's always been a bit odd," Clint said. "He was never outwardly anti-vampire, but my dad said he was always a little unnerved by them. The Commander was stationed in Maine when it fell. Was part of the US Army for thirty years before retiring and coming back, and he's gotten angrier in the last few years."

"How?" Miles asked.

"Blames the vampires for a lot of things that weren't their fault," Louisa said. "I mean, I know that the fall was partially their fault, but humans were working with them. No one is alone in shouldering that blame. Luckily his dislike of vampires isn't felt by everyone else who lives and works here."

"He fixated on the eighties?" Miles asked. "I was in his office. He has two paintings, the President at the time, and one of how Maine used to look. Or should look."

"So?" Clint asked.

"He just seemed fixated on it," Miles lied. "Like it was something deeply important to him."

"A lot of us try to stay out of his way," Louisa said. "We do the runs up to Bangor, so we're out of the city a lot. It's quieter up there, people are friendlier."

Miles noticed several diggers driving along the road a short way off. "You building something?"

"Putting defences around the bay," Clint said. "The Commander wants everything to be locked down. He's big on safety. We've been going down into the sewers beneath the town, clearing it out of any desolate. He's got security all over it now, doesn't want anyone down there until the defences are finished."

"The desolate we found were in tunnels much deeper underground than the sewers," Miles said. "Might be something to keep an eye on. If they manage to breach through, there could be problems."

"We'll look into it," Louisa said.

"You heard about anything happening at Blue Hill?" Amelia asked. "Or Ellsworth?"

The two soldiers were quiet for a moment. "Should we?" Clint asked.

"Just curious," Amelia said. "Parts of the pilgrimage go to Blue Hill, and I wanted to check there weren't going to be a horde of desolate waiting there."

"You're the reporter?" Clint asked. "Doing a story on the pilgrimage?"

"I am," Amelia said.

"The pilgrims came through not long ago. I heard someone talk about you, said he hoped you were safe."

Amelia looked between the soldiers. "Either of you ever met anyone by the name of Liam White or Stuart Murphy?"

Both shook their heads. "Who are they?"

"People who left Maine," Amelia said. "One of them is wanted for murder."

"We heard about them at Portsmouth before we started on the pilgrimage," Miles said, hoping that Amelia caught on to him not wanting to divulge too much about her quarry.

"Someone said they might be on the way to Blue Hill," Amelia said.

"Ah," Louisa said. "Blue Hill is always quiet. The vampires make sure of it for the pilgrims. If some humans have gone there to start trouble, they won't last long."

"What about Augusta?" Miles continued.

"You don't go to Augusta," Louisa said with a shudder. "Not if you value living."

"I hear that there's a lot of desolate there," Miles said. "That they keep coming up into the town from tunnels beneath it."

Louisa and Clint nodded in unison. "People who go there don't come back," Louisa said.

"And the Commander hasn't sent anyone to go check it out?" Miles asked. "Or consider what it would cost to retake the city?"

"He did," Clint said. "He sent several units a few months back, but none of them returned. It's completely off limits now. Like Louisa said, people who go there don't come back."

"You know anyone who went there?" Miles asked.

"Personally?" Louisa asked. "No."

"Me neither," Clint said. "But there are always soldiers who do know, always soldiers who are happy to tell people about what's happening up there. We've heard the tales. You step foot in Augusta, you don't return. The place is overrun with desolate, and things that we don't need to start poking with a stick to know they're dangerous."

The jeep started to brake, and eventually stopped all together. The driver got out, and with a smug smile on his face said, "This is where you get out."

Miles looked around. "This is the middle of nowhere."

"Commander's orders to drop you here," the driver said. "You can walk the rest. It's north, about a kilometer."

Miles and the Major got down from the rear of the vehicle onto the soft ground. "Thanks for your help," Miles said to Louisa and Clint. "Take care of yourselves."

"You too," Louisa said.

"Safe journey," Clint said as the driver climbed back into the vehicle cab, and the jeep's engine started up again.

"Driver's a dick," Miles said, watching the jeep perform a turn in the road before heading back the way it had gone.

"Following orders," the Major said.

Miles shrugged. "Still a dick."

"What was with the chat about the paintings in the Commander's office?" Amelia asked as the rear lights of the jeep disappeared from view.

Miles looked around the large, overgrown field, and the muddy road heading up the hill, where they set off to. "It was just a hunch at the moment."

"Enlighten me," Amelia said.

"Before we came here, Sam mentioned that he'd heard from people who were here when it fell that they felt compelled to return to Maine. That they were fixated on the eighties. Sometimes, when people have had their minds messed with, they become fixated on one point. A point in time where something important happened to them. Doesn't have to be a day, or a month, or anything like that, just an overall desire to make things like they were. The Commander's point in time is the eighties, or specifically the eighties when Maine fell. He was only a young man when it happened, already in the military, but he left this state, stayed in the army, and returned after he retired. His dislike of vampires has turned to hate over the last few years."

"You think that someone is making him think that way?" the Major asked.

"No, I think that maybe this whole place has a hold over people who were either here when it fell, or born here after," Miles said. "The Commander is an extremist arsehole, who is working with the Magistrate, considering his reaction to my mentioning them in a less than pleasant way."

"I caught that, too," the Major said. "No proof, though."

"I've done this job long enough to know when a human is lying," Miles said.

"So, Bailey has finally let his hate win out over doing the right thing."

"Stands to reason he's also met with Stuart and Liam, so whatever they're doing here, he's either helping them or at least knows about it."

"Brunswick is no longer safe for vampires," the Major said sadly. "I figured it was going to happen with Bailey in charge eventually. What did you mean about having a hold on him?"

"It felt like Bailey is fixated on the past, and it's possible that's not his choice," Miles said. "The hate is, a hundred percent, just not the rest of it. Sam said that those who are compelled to return, who were here before, have a fixation on that point in time."

"So it presents the same way that someone who has had their brain messed with does?" the Major asked.

Miles nodded. "Because technically, they *have* had their brain messed with."

"What about Louisa?" Amelia asked. "She left and came back—was she compelled, too?"

Miles nodded. "Judging from what I've seen and heard, there's something about this place that makes people want to stay here. Those who have links to the place, those who lived here when it happened, were born here, grew up here."

"What can do that?" the Major asked.

"Good question," Miles said, wishing he had a better answer. "You ever worked with someone who was like that? Could have left, but never did, or left to better themselves, and then came back for no reason?"

"A few, yeah," the Major said. "Hell you could be describing me. I could have left at any time. I just chose not to."

"You weren't born here?"

The Major shook his head. "Born in New England," he said. "Back when New England was a forest and people in red coats walked around. I was in Maine when it fell. I wasn't in the military or anything, I was just a vampire trying to find his way. I fought here, spilled blood here. And after that, I just . . ."

"Didn't want to leave," Miles said with a nod. "I remember you saying when we were in the tunnels."

"Yeah," the Major said slowly. "I spoke to my First Lord, who agreed that it was fine for me to stay. House Phalanx is probably the one Great House I could have been brought into and have them be accepting of my decision to remain in Maine."

"How do you feel about the eighties?" Amelia asked.

"I don't have a picture of President Reagan, if that's what you're asking," the Major said. "Although I will admit I've a fondness for the decade as a whole. More so than any other I can think of."

"You ever tried to leave?" Amelia asked.

The Major considered the question. "A few times. Never been away for more than a year or two—it starts to tug at my soul. It's like a homesickness you can't ignore. I'll see a TV show from the period, or a song that was around then, and suddenly feel the need to come back. The second I returned here, when I stepped on Maine soil, it was like a relief flooded through my body. Holy shit, what happened to me? To all of us?"

"An excellent question," Miles said. "Let's hope the good people of Bangor have some answers."

"You think that's where the answers are?" The Major asked, a little bit of hope in his voice.

"I think it's as good a place as any to start."

"You're not telling us something," Amelia said, giving Miles a sidelong glance.

"Louisa and Clint both said Augusta is a no-go area," Miles said.

The Major nodded. "Sure, we all know that."

"Said they have soldiers who will tell them that it's dangerous there," Miles continued. "But that personally, they don't know anyone who went. They just know that everyone who goes dies. That it's overrun with desolate and monsters."

"Like I said, we all know that."

"How does anyone know that, if everyone who goes there dies?"

The Major opened his mouth, closed it. Looked confused.

"Augusta *was* swarmed with desolate during the fall," Miles said, "but they were mostly eliminated, the last I heard. Those who remained underground still come out, but they're not huge in number. The problem with Augusta is the *potential* number of desolate underground. No one knows, because no one is stupid enough to go wandering about in the tunnels to find out. So, either my info is wrong and Augusta is still swarmed, or it's right, and it's actually pretty quiet. Either way, everyone who goes to Augusta disappears."

"So it's either the desolate or . . . something else," Amelia said.

Miles nodded.

"What else could it be?" the Major asked.

"We ran into werewolves yesterday," Miles said. "I'm not saying it's not desolate, I'm just saying that for a place that has everyone terrified to go there, no one has ever shown proof that the desolate are killing everyone who turns up. I'm thinking Maine is a lot weirder than it was the last time I was here. And Brunswick is even weirder than that."

"Brunswick is aligned with the Magistrate," Amelia said. "We found a few people in that town who were willing to talk to us about it. Bailey has contact with Magistrate members."

"That sounds about right," Miles said. "Because I'm almost certain he lied about seeing the witch and werewolves when I asked. Why would he risk his town, though?"

"Maybe he figured he could create a little human oasis in the middle of Maine," Amelia said. "Or maybe he wants out, and they're the best way. Either way, he's just a hate-filled arsehole."

Miles stopped walking when they reached the crest of a hill, looking down over what used to be the airport below. "He's definitely a hate-filled arsehole."

"Not everyone in Brunswick is a Magistrate supporter," the Major said.

"Probably not," Miles said. "But enough of them will be. Enough to make sure that they have a foothold here. I wonder if maybe those who were sent to Augusta were people the Commander didn't think would be loyal to the Magistrate."

"You're thinking he had his own people killed?" the Major asked. "He's a dick of the highest order, but I can't imagine he'd put his own people in jeopardy."

"What if he was given orders by those above him in the Magistrate?" Amelia asked. "He strikes me as a *following orders* kind of person."

The Major considered it. "I just . . . I don't know."

The airport, or what remained of it, had long since been given over to the more useful endeavour of growing crops. The runways had been destroyed, almost to the point where you'd have never known they'd existed at all.

"They made it into a lot of farmland," Miles said as they started down the steep hill toward the terminal, which was still mostly intact from what he could see. "Where are the vampires you mentioned?"

"They live out to the east of here," the Major said. "We'll be bypassing their small part of the city."

They were halfway down to the terminal when Miles spotted the convoy, complete with Thomas standing outside, waving at them.

"I think they missed you," the Major said.

"I get that a lot," Miles told him.

The Major stifled a laugh. "Yeah, I'm sure you're just the life of the party."

They reached the group, with some of the members—Jenny for one—not even bothering to hide that they were less than thrilled about Miles's return. Church sat outside the Winnebago, and she ran over to Miles the second he called her name.

"*That's* your dog?" the Major asked.

"Church, Alan," Miles said.

"Amelia, Miles, I'm glad you're both well," Thomas said after walking over to them.

"It was not a fun time," Amelia said. "I need several dozen showers."

"I'd be interested in hearing all about it once you're cleaned up," Thomas said, as Amelia entered the Winnebago.

"Where are the supply trucks?" Miles asked, noticing that they were both missing.

"One was for Brunswick," Thomas said. "The other went ahead. They wanted to get to Bangor before there were any more issues. We tried to radio Bangor, but the reception is shit here. They wanted to make sure they knew what we'd found at Falmouth. Can't blame them. So, I assume you have a lot to tell."

"I'll let you tell them everything," Miles said to the Major. "First, I'd like to change out of clothes that stopped smelling good about a day ago."

The Major offered Miles his hand, which the latter shook. "You saved my life, and I will repay that one day."

"No need," Miles assured him. "You're coming with us to Bangor, so it's already repaid. I doubt it'll be a quiet journey considering what we've gone through so far."

Miles watched the Major walk off with Thomas into his Winnebago. He set off for his own Winnebago and waited outside for ten minutes before knocking.

"Come on in," Amelia said.

Miles opened the door and stepped inside, where Amelia was waiting, a large peach-coloured towel wrapped around her. She stood barefoot on a second identical towel she'd placed on the floor. She'd already removed her jeans, top, and underwear, placing them, along with her shoes and socks, on a third, much smaller towel, beside her. Her hair and bare shoulders were still wet from the shower.

"Did I miss anything interesting?" Amelia asked once he'd closed the door.

"Nothing of note," Miles said. "I'm going to shower. Then we can share war stories."

"You need a hand?" Amelia asked.

Miles raised an eyebrow and smiled.

"With the armour, smart guy," Amelia said.

"Actually, that would be good, I think getting this stuff drenched with blood, grime, shite, and water, and then having it dry, may have done irreparable damage to it. It's beginning to sound like it creaks when I lift my arms. I could just tear it apart, but I would rather that be plan B, as I'm nae sure what's going to fall out when I take it off."

Amelia followed Miles into the small bathroom, and managed to get the latter out of his upper body armour, complete with quite a lot of dried blood, and some small bits that neither Amelia nor Miles wanted to identify. Once he was topless, Miles assured Amelia he could do the rest, and stripped out of his clothes, before turning on the shower and watching as the water at his feet went from pink to clear.

As Miles washed himself, he felt a wound on the back of his neck and tried to get a look in the mirror, but it was steamed up from the hot water. He opened the door slightly. "If I put a towel on, can you come look at something on my neck?"

"That's your line?" Amelia asked. "Can you look at my neck? Does that work with all the maidens?"

"Very funny," Miles said. "Truly you are a wit. I think the werewolf caught me on the back of the neck, just want to check it's healing okay. I can feel the wound, but don't have eyes in the back of my head."

"Sure," Amelia said.

Miles wrapped a towel around his waist and stepped out of the shower, turning around so that Amelia could get a look.

Miles paused. Amelia was still wearing her towel.

"The light is terrible," she said, pushing him forward into the bedroom, and turning him to face the light as she knelt on the bed. "Ouch, that looks sore."

"Doesn't hurt," Miles said. "Wounds from werewolves take longer to heal, but considering what I had to swim through, I'd rather make sure it was clean." He turned back to Amelia.

"It's fine," she said. "Just a small bit of scar tissue. I imagine your vampire healing will have it back to normal skin soon."

Miles nodded. "Thanks."

"Anything else you'd like me to check while I'm here?" Amelia asked.

Miles smiled. "I mean, I may have many wounds. It's been quite the day."

Amelia nodded, her expression worried. "You know, I think I may have injuries that need looking at, too."

"Oh, no, did you get hurt?"

Amelia nodded. "Banged my elbow pretty hard on the cupboard earlier."

"Are you mocking me?" Miles asked her.

Amelia moved closer to Miles, dropped her towel to the floor, and whispered, "What do you think about checking each other for injuries? Need to be thorough. Might take some time."

Miles let his own towel drop to the floor. "It's the responsible thing to do," he said.

"Gotta be responsible," Amelia said, as she pulled Miles down to the bed.

CHAPTER TWENTY-ONE

So, was that the stupid thing you didn't want to do before we flung ourselves into those tunnels?" Miles asked. He was naked from the waist up, lying back on the bed.

Amelia sat up, her back against the window next to the bed. "Yes it was," she admitted. "I know it's probably not professional to sleep with your bodyguard, but it's been on my mind for a while now."

"Since?"

"Since Scotland," Amelia said. "You do realise that you're an exceptional powerful, confident, broody vampire, yes? And you have that accent. Makes me go all aquiver."

Miles laughed. "Nae sure anyone has ever said that about me before, but I'll take it."

"There it is again," Amelia said with a playful smile. "Now, we can't be running off to do this all the time. This was a one-time thing, because I figured we could both use a bit of a diversion."

"And you were horny."

"Yeah, basically," Amelia said. "But even so, one-time thing. At least until we're done in Maine. Neither of us can afford the distraction." She leaned over to him and ran a finger from his chest down to his stomach before moving back. "And while you are *very* distracting at this exact moment, it would probably be better for us to concentrate on why we're here."

"You know you're naked, right?" Miles asked. "That's pretty distracting."

"Well, you are a vampire and should be over such base things," Amelia said, shifting in the bed.

"Base things?" Miles asked her, moving toward her with a smile. "You want me to show you the base things I'm meant to be over?"

Amelia leaned in and kissed Miles with passion. "God, yes," she whispered when she pulled away.

"Someone's at the door," Miles told her as he slowly ran his index finger over the inside of her thigh.

"Can we pretend we're out?" Amelia asked.

There was a knock on the door.

"Not really," Miles whispered into her ear.

"Motherfucker," Amelia said. "We will take this up at the soonest opportunity."

Miles got to his feet and pulled up his jeans without fastening them, as he willed parts of his body to cooperate. "Be right there," he called out as there was another knock.

Amelia stared at Miles's predicament and smiled. "Oh, yeah, right there," she said in a voice full of need.

"You are not helping," Miles told her.

"I can definitely help," Amelia told him in the same voice.

"Still not helping," Miles said, going into the bathroom and splashing cold water on his face as Amelia got dressed and went to the door first.

"Thomas," Amelia said. "Come in. Miles is in the bathroom. He had to shower all the . . . I don't even want to think about it."

Miles left the bathroom having fastened his jeans, and went back to the bedroom to grab a black long-sleeved jumper from his bag, putting it on. He grabbed a pair of socks and exited the bedroom. Amelia was sitting on the sofa wearing a T-shirt and jeans, without anything covering her feet. She smiled at him, and he wondered how quickly he could get rid of Thomas again.

Thomas sat opposite Amelia as the kettle boiled and the latter got up to make a drink. "Coffee?" she asked Miles.

"Please," he said, taking her seat. "So, Thomas. I assume the Major has gone through everything with you."

"You swam in a lake of gore," Thomas said.

"Pool of gore," Miles corrected, the memory of it finally extinguishing the thoughts he was having about Amelia. "Or a pool of bodies, if you'd prefer. Either way, there were lots of dead bits."

"Any idea what it's for?" Thomas asked.

"My guess?" Miles replied. "To feed the desolate. They took everyone from the fort. Killed them all, bar the Major, and dumped them in a pit.

There are a lot of desolate down there, and desolate need feeding. Although they appear to be mostly controlled, as they didn't try to kill me, Amelia, or the werewolves, until we tried to escape. They bled the bodies first, though, which makes me think the blood is for something else. No idea what, though.

"On top of that, we found a lot of black stone. They have equipment for moving a lot of rock and soil down there, I don't think they're just making holes above to attack people. I think they're actually drilling in the tunnels."

"Why?" Thomas asked.

"Feels like they're looking for something," Miles said.

"That was the impression I got, too," Amelia agreed.

"Liam wanted me to meet his boss," Miles said. "I assume he knows what they're looking for, but no one said anything to me."

"Liam has one less werewolf on his side," Thomas said. "That's good fortune."

Miles nodded.

"But you think whatever they've got planned, it's still to come?" Thomas asked.

Miles nodded again. "We're not shot of them. I am curious about what they're doing, and who they wanted to take me to. I assumed they're working for Stuart Murphy, but I saw no evidence of that. Nor of magic, for that matter. We can't just leave it all down there, though; it'll need to be dealt with."

"That's going to be dangerous," Thomas said. "We'll need to talk to the rulers of Bangor. Maybe they'll have some insight into what's happening."

"The quicker we get there, the better," Miles said, royally done with everything Maine had to offer so far.

Thomas stood. "We'll leave within the hour. Brunswick is considerably less hospitable than I remember it, and I don't like the idea of leaving Bangor without the knowledge of what happened in Falmouth. The second truck has already headed off that way, but I'll feel better knowing everyone is safe."

"What's your thought on Commander Bailey?" Amelia asked. "Good guy?"

"Honestly, not even slightly," Thomas said. "I never liked the man, but he's gone from tersely impolite to outright hostile towards us in the last few years.

"Good, because he's definitely working with the Magistrate," Miles said.

Thomas nodded sadly.

"I'm surprised that Brunswick doesn't have a satellite phone," Miles said.

"They do, but it's broken," Thomas said. "Apparently. We have one too, for emergencies, but it's spotty at best."

"You kept that secret," Amelia said.

"We don't like to make it known we have one," Thomas said. "Like I said, it's for emergencies. Which I see this might be. But there's no response. The hills and forest around here make it a very expensive brick."

"Okay, so we get to Bangor quickly, leaving tonight," Miles said. "We've got a few hours of night left, so we should get there by daybreak. No more stops if we can manage it. I know you're on your pilgrimage, but this has all become a lot more involved than just House Idolator."

"Agreed," Thomas said. "I'll go arrange everything. The Major will ride with me; I think the man needs sleep and a meal more than anything. The stuff he told me about, the things he saw. Even vampires have their limits to the brutality we can endure or witness. I assume you're both okay?"

"Had better days," Amelia said.

"I'm grand," Miles said.

Thomas stared at Miles for a moment.

"Okay, not *grand*," Miles admitted. "It was a shite few hours, and frankly I'd rather never have to go through it again. But no long-term harm was done to me, and I've seen worse, which is a depressing indictment of humanity and vampires alike."

Thomas moved toward the door and paused, looking back at Miles. "You killed a werewolf," he said, as he opened the door and Church bounded into the Winnebago, jumping up onto the sofa next to Miles for him to give her some attention.

"I did," Miles said as he scratched Church behind the ears. "Amelia was there."

"I did fuck all," Amelia said. "I was only going to step in if it looked like Miles was in trouble, but . . . well, he didn't look like he needed assistance. I just broke the Major out."

"Alone," Thomas said. "You killed a werewolf alone."

"There's a lot of emphasis on one word," Miles said, glancing Thomas's way. "You got a point to make?"

"I don't think I know of many vampires who can take out a werewolf one-on-one," Thomas said. "You got anything you're hiding from the class?"

"I'm just an Arbiter," Miles said with a laugh. "We've been pretty highly trained. And I was First Librarian of House Venator for a long time. I'm not a slouch when it comes to power, Thomas. I'm just *really* good at killing things."

"We all have our crosses to bear, I guess," Thomas said. "Be careful, Miles. You killed a member of a group of highly trained soldiers, I imagine some of his companions will want retribution for his death."

Miles shrugged. "There's always someone who wants retribution for someone I killed, or stopped, or hurt. The need for retribution only ever gets someone so far, Thomas. It's a lot more likely to get someone dead."

"Just be careful, Miles. I would hate to think you've come all this way only to have some werewolf *pack* try to end your life."

"You know, it's weird. Werewolves don't normally hunt in packs, they don't live in packs, there's no alpha or beta, they're solitary creatures. They're fiercely territorial, and they fight to the death with any other werewolf who dares enter their territory. Apart from when I was handed over to the werewolf I killed, I never saw them interact, never saw the other members of their group."

"These werewolves aren't behaving like the usual," Thomas said. "That what you're saying?"

"I don't know what I'm saying," Miles said. "I'm just—there's a lot of stuff I don't understand. Maybe if this group comes after me together, I can ask them about it."

"Don't even joke, Miles," Thomas said. "You killed one werewolf alone, but I wouldn't want anyone to go up against four or five of them at a time."

"You and me both," Miles said.

Thomas left the Winnebago, closing the door behind him.

"You really think they'll come for you?" Amelia asked, taking a drink of her coffee.

Miles nodded. "At some point, probably. Not because they're werewolves, but because I killed one of their mates. Unless whoever they're working for forbids it, then maybe they'll slink off to wherever they're hiding and stay there. We can all hope for that, I guess."

Arvid Holmlund climbed into the Winnebago cab and started the engine, setting off a few minutes later after the remains of the convoy.

Miles watched out of the window as they slowly left the city of Brunswick, and felt more than a little bit of happiness about it. They drove over the bridge, stopping for the inevitable checks on both sides, before being allowed to continue on north, up toward Bangor.

"It's not a long drive to Bangor," Arvid said without looking back after being on the road for a few minutes. "The road isn't great, though, so it might get a little bumpy even at low speeds. If you need to get rest, I'd do it now. By the time we get to Bangor, there's going to be a lot happening."

"We're up now," Amelia said, looking over at Miles. "If I go back to bed, I'm going to be no use to anyone by the time I'm done."

"Probably not sensible to sleep in case there's an emergency," Miles said, keeping Amelia's gaze.

"Yes, emergency," Amelia agreed. "Gotta keep alert for those."

Church looked between Amelia and Miles and let out a snort of derision, before moving to the floor as Miles and Amelia moved to the bedroom.

Forty-five minutes later, Miles left Amelia to rest, and rejoined Arvid, sitting beside him in the passenger seat. "Heard you found some nasty stuff under Falmouth," Arvid said.

"All of it," Miles said. "There's no good bits under that fort."

"Glad you managed to save the Major," he said. "He's a good man. Good vampire. Helps out a lot in the state. He's . . . that's weird."

Miles glanced beyond Arvid out of the front window. All he saw were the vehicles in front, illuminated by the headlights of the Winnebago, as the weather began to take a turn for the worse.

"What's up?" Miles asked.

"Probably nothing," Arvid said. "Thought I saw a light in the distance."

"Didn't there used to be a lighthouse near here?" Miles asked.

"Rockland Breakwater Lighthouse," Arvid said. "Hasn't been used in years . . . wait, look again."

This time, Miles saw the light in the distance. "The lighthouse?"

"Maybe," Arvid said. "It looks like it. But it's derelict."

"Can you radio the front vehicle?" Miles asked.

Arvid lifted the radio receiver and pressed the button to connect with the front vehicle.

"What's up, Arvid?" a female voice asked.

"You see the lighthouse?" Arvid asked.

"Yeah, weird," the voice on the other end said. "I've driven this way a thousand times since the fall, never seen it working."

"Put your foot down," Miles said. "Go as fast as is possible to stay safe."

"You think there's trouble?" Thomas asked through the radio.

"I think after what we saw in Falmouth, I'm not opposed to the idea of someone using the lighthouse as a signal," Miles said. "What's Rockland like?"

"It's gone," Thomas said. "One of many of the smaller towns that were evacuated and then firebombed. Nothing left but some stubborn buildings that wouldn't fall down, and a lot of ashes."

"Dangerous to drive through?" Miles asked.

"Not really," Arvid said. "The roads are all fucked, but never had a problem here."

"What's the next town ahead like?" Miles asked.

"Belfast has a small population," Thomas said. "It's a fort, like Falmouth was. Few hundred people live there, maybe four hundred in total. About ten percent are vampires who work for Bangor and travel back and forth, keeping the roads open."

"Anything between there and Bangor?" Miles asked.

"No," Thomas said. "Any villages or towns are abandoned or destroyed. It's not a great drive, but there's nowhere to stop that's populated. We go up by Swan Lake, never even had desolate to worry about. You think there's an attack about to happen in Rockland?"

"Can't say for certain," Miles said. "I think someone is signalling that we're on the way. If Rockland is all but flattened, there's no point in attacking here, they're just as exposed as we'll be. Belfast maybe, but they'll hopefully already be warned by the truck who went ahead. My guess is it'll be beyond there, lots of open forest and hills. Lots of places to stage an ambush."

"Liam's people?" Thomas asked.

Miles thought for a moment. "Not his people, but whoever he's working with will know the land. Once we leave Belfast, be prepared for trouble."

The radio conversation ended, and Miles went to wake Amelia, explaining that they might be expecting trouble.

The convoy full of pilgrims slowly moved into Rockland. The town was almost exactly how Miles had expected it to be, and pretty much how Thomas had described it. It was a barren wasteland, devoid of anything close to liveable. While it took nearly forty minutes to drive through it because of the state of the roads, Miles felt a little relief when they were beyond it, heading up toward Belfast.

The fort of Belfast resembled Falmouth so much that they might well have been twins, although the Falmouth fort was several times smaller than the Belfast incarnation.

Everyone waited in their vehicles as they drove into the fort, with fifty pairs of eyes all looking down on them from the buildings on either side.

Miles watched Thomas and his Blood Guard get down from their vehicle and speak to the man in charge, who saluted to the Major when he joined them. The conversation was brief, and Miles noticed that the soldiers or guards in the fort who weren't watching them were all searching the buildings in small groups. Miles hoped that, should the worst happen and the desolate attack, Belfast would at least be prepared for it. The desolate would find it a considerably harder target than the unprepared soldiers at Falmouth.

Amelia stood next to Miles and watched the conversation play out in front of them. "It feels like the closer we are to Bangor, the more danger we're in."

"That's about right," Miles said. "That lighthouse was used for a reason. Maybe it's just some enterprising soul who decided to make it their home and activate it, but right now, I'm not taking any chances."

"Is this how you work all the time?" Amelia asked. "Seeing the worst-case scenario?"

Miles nodded as he kept his eyes on the fort. "It's always the little things that end up being the biggest problems. You can't live your life expecting the unexpected, because that's frankly exhausting and you'd be living in a state of perpetual fear. You *can* keep an eye out for something that's not right, or just out of place. Somewhere you need to go that would make for an advantageous place for your enemies to just show up."

"Like the vast amount of wilderness beyond Belfast?" Amelia asked.

"Aye, just like that."

"You think they'll attack us?" Arvid asked.

"Would you do it?" Amelia asked Miles.

"Maybe," Miles said. "You eliminate the first vehicle. Cause confusion and panic. You force everyone to stop, make sure that the attack is fast, brutal. No time for anyone to take a breath. You'd need more than five werewolves to do it with this many people in the convoy."

"Unleash the desolate," Arvid said.

"They could, but they'd lose a lot of them," Miles said. "No matter what the campsite talk is about them being unkillable, the desolate aren't regenerating themselves. They're a finite resource. Even if some of them have been bigger and tougher than I'm used to seeing in their kind."

"Why do they keep coming back, then?" Arvid asked.

"That is a question I can't answer right now," Miles said as Thomas shook the Commander of the fort's hand and entered his vehicle, along with the Major and Blood Guard.

Miles grabbed the radio and switched on Thomas's frequency.

"They were told about Falmouth," Thomas said as he picked up the receiver on his end. "They're searching the fort and putting countermeasures in place. Everyone is on edge. They said they've done sweeps of the road ahead and seen nothing out of the ordinary. It looks like we're clear to go."

Miles considered what Thomas had said.

"You still there?" Thomas asked.

"They have underground mine carts that they used to get about in the tunnels," Miles said. "They could stretch all around the state and we know nothing about it. It's possible they've gotten ahead of us and are waiting. Hiding from patrols until the time to strike."

"Well, we can't stay here indefinitely," Thomas said.

"I know," Miles said. "Let's go, just keep your eyes open. They think they have the element of surprise. Let's use that against them."

The pilgrimage was off only a few minutes later, and Miles watched the guard all around the fort as they continued.

"Miles," Thomas radioed through. "Whatever happens between here and Bangor, I just want to say thank you for being a part of this pilgrimage. I appreciate it. You've helped keep my people and my charges safe, Miles."

"Thomas, thank you, but we're not done yet," Miles said. "When we get to Bangor, and I mean when, not if, you can buy me a drink. Until then, keep your eyes open, and if you see *anything* out of the ordinary, you let me know."

He ended the call and said to Arvid, "Drop back a little from the bus. I want to see more of the area."

"We should have gone first," Arvid said.

"No one is going to attack from up front," Miles said. "It'll be from one of the sides. Maybe the rear."

"I'll go look through the windows at the back," Amelia said.

"Church, keep Amelia safe," Miles said.

Church barked and followed her through to the rear bedroom.

Miles switched off all the lights inside the Winnebago and went from window to window in the living area, looking out into the darkness, wondering if there were people out there just waiting to attack.

They drove slowly along the road, as Miles felt the concern growing around him as if it were a living thing, smothering those who were unlucky enough to be close to it.

The moon was hidden behind thick cloud, the rain pummelling the vehicles and road they drove on, making it little more than slippery mud, with the occasional stretch of tarmac. Miles continued to look out of the windows, moving from place to place in the hope he didn't miss something.

After twenty minutes, the radio went off. Arvid answered it immediately, before passing the receiver to Miles.

"We've found something," Thomas said as the convoy stopped moving. "Can you see it?"

Miles looked out of the front windscreen and some ways in the distance, to the left, down what looked like an embankment, something was on fire. The flames leapt up at the sky, as if in defiance at the rain.

"What is it?" Miles asked.

"No clue," Thomas said.

"Wait there," Miles told him and hung up.

"There a problem?" Amelia asked.

Miles shrugged as he picked up his rain jacket from the coat hook next to the door. "Something is on fire ahead. I'm going to check."

"Alone?" Amelia asked.

"I'll be fine," Miles assured her. "Church, stay with Amelia. No matter what happens, you protect her."

Church barked once, before walking up to Miles and letting out a slight whine.

"I'll be fine," Miles repeated, giving her a stroke under the chin. "Be back shortly."

Miles opened the door and took a few seconds to get used to the downpour happening outside. He dropped down to the ground, which squelched as he walked along the broken road, by the bus, receiving a few more glares from those who had decided their hatred for him. He stopped by Thomas's vehicle and knocked.

"This is my Blood Guard," Thomas said as one of the guards stepped out into the rain. "His name is Valter Casio. He will go with you to check the fire. You think we should stop here?"

"I'll figure that out in a few minutes, I guess," Miles said. "You ready to get really wet and muddy, Valter?"

"It's a dirty job, my lord," the Blood Guard said, his voice muffled from behind the mask, just like the others. "But needs must."

"Miles is fine," he said. "I stopped being anything like a lord a long time ago."

The Blood Guard bowed his head.

"Be prepared to move fast," Miles told Thomas.

"Be safe," Thomas told him.

Miles and the Blood Guard moved through the rain to the top of the embankment. It was maybe a hundred feet down to the on-fire vehicle, which from this distance Miles could see was the truck that had gone off to deliver the supplies.

"They were one of ours," the Blood Guard said.

"Let's go take a look," Miles said, looking over at the broken road which had fallen to the side of the embankment, forming a makeshift path. "You see anything, you shout."

"Yes, my . . . yes, Miles."

Miles ran over to the broken part of the road, and used his speed and agility to make it down to the bottom of the embankment without either having to become covered in mud, or turn into his beast form. The heat from the vehicle was intense enough that it made Miles skirt around the trees close to the impact site, to avoid it.

Miles looked up at the road above, and back to the truck. It appeared to have come off the road and smashed into the trees at the bottom, bouncing farther down the bottom of the embankment, where it eventually came to a stop. The front end was all but sheared off, and the contents of the truck covered the muddy landscape.

Miles sniffed the air as the Blood Guard joined him. No burned bodies. No blood. Where did the driver and passenger go?

"You see any bodies?" the Blood Guard asked.

"You got a radio?" Miles asked as he stared into the forest, the hairs on the back of his neck standing at attention.

The Blood Guard nodded and passed it to Miles, who activated it. "Get going," he said to Thomas. "We'll catch up to you."

"You sure?" Thomas asked.

"Go. Now," Miles said, passing the radio back as a low growl left the darkness of the forest, followed by the smell of fresh meat. And blood.

"An ambush," the Blood Guard said, drawing his broadsword.

"Get back to the trucks," Miles told him. "I'll lead it away. They want me to meet their leader." Hopefully that was still the case.

"It?" the Blood Guard asked.

"Just go," Miles said.

"Come with me," the Blood Guard said.

"If I come, it'll follow," Miles said. "We'll either be caught or this thing will end up at Bangor. Neither are acceptable."

"My lord," the Blood Guard started.

Miles turned to his vampire form, making out the shape of the massive desolate a hundred feet inside the trees. The desolate howled in rage and charged at them, the need to do violence easy to see. Miles was wrong—they did not want to take him to their leader. They wanted him dead.

"Run!" Miles shouted at the Blood Guard.

Chapter Twenty-Two

Miles sprinted along the bottom of the embankment, back toward the fort of Belfast, although he'd have been lucky to make it before the desolate giant caught up with him. But he wasn't trying to get away from the desolate, he was trying to get the desolate away from everyone else.

The sound of engines roared behind him as the convoy moved away. He hoped the Blood Guard had done as he'd been told and run back to rejoin the pilgrims. Miles didn't need to worry about someone else while doing something stupid. And whatever his plan would be, he was sure he was going to regret it later.

Miles had run a few hundred meters when he stopped and looked behind at the lumbering form of the desolate, who was still screaming in rage. He prepared for the fight, when he caught the scent of the werewolf. He threw himself back as the werewolf sailed by him, crashing into the wall of dirt and muck that the road drove along.

The desolate giant was still coming after him as the werewolf disengaged itself from the situation it had found itself in. Miles blasted the werewolf with a shot of telekinesis, slamming it back into the wall with enough force that it buckled part of the wall itself, and the werewolf suddenly found itself being partially buried by several tonnes of muck and rubble from the road above.

The desolate was at Miles a heartbeat later, and the vampire only narrowly avoided the massive crushing hands of the creature as it tried to grab at him. If that had happened, it would have surely ended with Miles's death.

The giant was twelve feet tall, at least, and tore the remains of a tree from out of the ground, launching it at Miles, who easily avoided it as he ran into the woodland, hoping there weren't more desolate waiting inside.

Miles wondered just how many of these giant desolate there were in Maine as he scaled one of the larger trees, hiding out amid the dense foliage higher up as the desolate stomped and crashed around the area, smashing its fists into trees and tearing them apart.

The desolate let out a roar which vibrated through Miles's body, making part of him want to run and keep running. He watched the desolate slope around some more and tried to come up with a plan of attack. Miles had used his bloodline gift on the desolate giant in the tunnels, and it had worked, but with a werewolf to worry about too, he wasn't sure it would be a great idea to do the same again.

Miles leapt from branch to branch, moving around to the side of the desolate in an effort to get behind it. The werewolf was roaring in rage at having half of its body covered by dirt and mud, even more so that it was face down and couldn't get purchase to cut its way free. And if it turned back to its human form, the weight of the debris would almost certainly crush it.

Miles dropped down to the ground and stepped out toward the werewolf, who roared at him, trying to swipe him with its claws. He was about to use his bloodline gift to turn it human when the Blood Guard dropped down from the road above, burying his broadsword into the skull of the werewolf. The blade went down through the top of the werewolf's mouth and came out the bottom, pinning the creature's maw to the soft ground.

"I told you to leave," Miles said.

"My First Lord would disapprove," the Blood Guard said, twisting the blade, and making a crunching sound, before he pulled it free, bringing it down again in one smooth motion to decapitate the werewolf a second later.

The desolate charged toward Miles and the Blood Guard, smashing its fist down where the Blood Guard had stood, and meeting nothing but the remains of the werewolf, which was turned to a bloody smear on the wet ground.

The Blood Guard darted forward, trying to get a good hit with the blade, but the desolate was faster than it looked, and hit the Blood Guard with the back of its hand, sending the vampire flying back fifty feet. The Blood Guard used his bloodline power, wrapping himself in a crimson shield of energy, which exploded in a burst of light as he slammed into a large tree, a huge branch punching through the back of his armour and out the front. The branch cracked from the added weight, and the Blood Guard slid down along it, until he fell from the branch, letting out a gasp before hitting the ground hard, where he remained unmoving.

Miles picked up the discarded sword and tested it in his hands as the desolate giant stood to its full height and bellowed at him. "Let's do this," he said.

The giant moved quickly, but Miles was faster, easily avoiding the swipe of the creature's hands. Miles drove the sword through the back of the desolate's hand, out through its palm, and using all of his strength to force the hand back, drove the tip of the blade into the desolate's opposite knee as the creature tried in vain to stop Miles's brute strength.

Miles blasted the leg nearest him with telekinesis, which momentarily wobbled the desolate, allowing him to thrust the sword into the leg as planned. The desolate bellowed in pain, and Miles used a second telekinesis blast on the now injured leg of the giant, sending it toppling over onto the remains of the werewolf. Miles grabbed the sword hilt, pulling it free, stepping around to the side of the giant, and driving it into the neck of the desolate, wrenching it up and out, before bringing the blade back down onto the wound, decapitating the creature.

With both threats dead, Miles ran back over to the Blood Guard, who was on his knees, his mask cracked down the middle, his armour dented badly enough that blood streamed out of the new hole in the breastplate.

Miles used his telekinesis to pull the breastplate back, causing the Blood Guard to gasp in pain. Eventually he managed to make the breastplate look like something approximating its original shape, and he helped the Blood Guard to remove it, along with his mask. The Blood Guard gritted his teeth as it was removed, and fell back to the ground when it was done.

Blood covered the torso and face of the vampire, who looked exhausted. Miles examined the gaping wound in the guard's chest and back; there was nothing good about how large the wound was. Even as a vampire possibly capable of healing such wounds, the Blood Guard wasn't going anywhere for a while, and would need blood to feed on as soon as possible. Vampires were hardy, but even a vampire would need time to heal from a fist-sized hole in its chest.

"You're going nowhere until that heals," Miles said, folding the tunic back across the chest, after making sure the large wound had started to close.

"It is dead?" the Blood Guard asked.

Miles looked back to the desolate and werewolf, the former of which was beginning to dissolve. "Aye, they're not getting up from that."

"Killed a werewolf," the Blood Guard said, before coughing up more blood.

"You did, I'm very proud," Miles said. "If you like, when we get back to Thomas, I can have them write a sonnet about you."

"I'd like that," the Blood Guard said with a smile. "Never had a sonnet."

"It can start something like, *There once was a dickhead from House Idolator*," Miles told him.

The Blood Guard laughed, started to cough up more blood, and made an awful wheezing noise. "This really fucking hurts," he said.

"Good," Miles told him. "Next time don't get hit."

"Next time?"

"No matter how stupid or bad you think something is, there's always something more stupid, or more horrible just waiting down the road for you to stumble across."

"Don't get hit," the Blood Guard said. "Good advice."

"Glad you think so," Miles said, getting back to his feet. "It's a good job it was just those two shites, or we'd be fucked, what with you having a wee lie down."

"My sword came in handy," the Blood Guard said.

Miles wiped the sword with the back of his jacket sleeve and placed it back in its scabbard. "Don't go getting a big head now."

"I can safely say that I have no intention of getting a big head. I can barely breathe without it hurting."

"Once saw a vampire get hit with a cannonball," Miles said. "He just walked right into it. At least you didn't have that happen."

"It's the little things that make life worth living," the Blood Guard said with a smile.

"Hello," a voice said from back toward where the giant was now all but done and the werewolf's corpse remained.

Miles turned to see the newcomer as he walked along the muddy ground, using a walking stick for aid. He wore a black raincoat, with a large rimmed matching hat.

"And who the fucking hell are you?" Miles asked, getting the feeling that he and the Blood Guard might well be a lot more fucked than he'd previously considered.

The man looked up, and Miles recognised him from his photos in Amelia's notes.

"You know me," the man said, having stopped walking with fifty feet between him and Miles. A silver pendant hung from a chain around his neck. He touched the pendant and let out a little sigh.

"Stuart Murphy," Miles spat. "Priest killer and neighbour cooker."

Stuart laughed. "I did do that. Both deserved it."

"And the people just going to church?" Miles asked, putting himself between the witch and the still seriously injured Blood Guard.

"Collateral damage," Stuart said. "You killed two werewolves."

"Technically, I only killed one," Miles said. "My friend here killed the other."

"They were *very* keen to kill you," Stuart said. "You were meant to be brought without harm, but you saw an end to that when you killed the werewolf and desolate giant in the tunnels. These two wanted vengeance."

"How'd you get here so fast?" Miles asked. "It's those little mine cart things, isn't it? You take one here, hide in some hole for the day, wait for us, and pop out."

Stuart smiled. "Something like that."

"It's funny, you say the desolate wanted revenge, but desolate don't want anything except food," Miles said. "I also don't recognise that desolate. It looks more scarred than the two I met in the tunnels."

"The larger desolates have a . . . bond," Stuart said. "Almost a hive mind. Some of the smaller, too. I think you'll find a lot of them know what you did. They're not happy about it."

"Can I assume you've given up on taking me to meet your boss?"

"Oh no, these two went against orders," Stuart said. "I'm your last chance. You won't get another. If it helps, I would have killed these two had they completed their need for vengeance. It'll be a shame if I have to kill you now, my . . . boss so badly wanted you to come see the person who has made all of this possible."

"All of what?" Miles asked.

Stuart waved his arms around. "This."

"Maine?" Miles asked. "The person responsible for what happened to Maine is your boss? He cured your cancer yet?"

Stuart's expression darkened.

"Yeah, I read about that," Miles said. "Your wife and kids did a runner to the other side of the country, too. Turns out you're not a barrel of laughs to live with."

"You are quite irritating," Stuart said.

"And you, Stuart Murphy, are a murderous gobshite."

"You're going to come with me quietly, or I'm going to have to hurt you."

Miles stared at the witch for a moment. "And you can fuck yourself, ya little shitehawk."

"I want you to remember that I gave you a chance," Stuart said.

"I'm going to rip your head off now," Miles said, and took a step toward Stuart as the witch's pendant started to glow. A second later, a rock the size of Miles's torso that had been sitting on the ground smashed into his ribs, spinning him around to face a second similarly sized rock, which hit him in the chest.

Miles had tried to use his telekinesis as a way to slow down the speed of the rock, but it had moved through his ability as though he hadn't even tried. He landed on the ground, the rock atop his chest, pushing down on him, forcing his body to sink into the mud.

Miles roared in anger as he tried to lift the rock off his body, while more and more rocks piled up onto his chest. Each one pushed him down further into the mud, as if they weighed dozens of times more than their size suggested.

"This is what happens when you don't behave," Stuart said, as he stood over a helpless Miles. "I'll come and find you shortly."

Stuart, the pendant still glowing blood red, brought his walking stick back across his body as if he were about to hit a baseball, and quickly snapped it back the other way, toward the woods. Miles flew back into the woods, colliding with a large tree and bouncing off onto the ground as flames encircled him.

Miles looked around him and saw that more and more of the trees were dying, the remaining grass withering away to nothing as it powered Stuart's chaos magic.

"Don't you fucking dare!" Miles shouted at Stuart, who stopped walking as he reached the Blood Guard and slammed the bottom tip of his walking stick into the Blood Guard's head, right between his eyes. The Blood Guard reacted as if he'd been shot, his body quickly going prone and unmoving as blood poured out of his open eyes.

The fire intensified, burning Miles's arm as he attempted to walk through it. Miles yelled out in pain as the burn felt more like a UV light than normal fire.

"I'll come with you!" Miles shouted.

Stuart placed the tip of his walking stick against the Blood Guard's head and turned to Miles. "Like you ever had a choice." He pressed down with the tip of his cane, drawing life energy from the trees around him and forcing it through the front of the Blood Guard's skull, burning away the man's head until it was nothing but ash.

"No," Miles said, screaming in rage as he turned into his beast form. He launched himself forward, through the fire, beat his wings once, and flew at Stuart, whose face was a picture of shock for just a second until Miles's taloned hands grabbed hold of where the witch's skull should have been.

Miles landed and flexed his talons as he looked over at Stuart, who had vanished and was now back where he'd started, fifty feet away.

Fear was now etched across the witch's face. "How did you get through the fire?"

"You didn't need to kill him," Miles said, stalking toward his prey, ready to rend flesh from bone.

"How?" Stuart shouted.

Miles beat his wings again and launched himself forward at incredible speed, only just missing Stuart as he opened a portal and stepped inside. The portal snapped shut behind him, leaving nothing but the smell of burning flesh and hair in the air, mixed with the scent of decaying and dead vegetation.

Pain racked through Miles's body, and he looked at the burns that covered his upper torso and wings. He'd flown through that fire at speed, but it hadn't stopped the unnatural flames from doing their job. He beat his wings, taking to the sky, feeling the pouring rain soothe his skin, his wings. The cool air blew across his body as he tried to figure out where Stuart had gone. He looked back along the road the convoy had travelled down, but he saw only darkness and dirt. He'd never heard of any witch, no matter their designation, being able to teleport. And that staff appeared to give him greater control over his magic, another thing he hadn't known existed.

Miles landed close to the quickly dissipating pile of ash that used to be the Blood Guard. He moved the breastplate aside and picked up the necklace that lay in the mud. A steel chain with a smooth grey stone attached to it. The stone was flat and about two inches in diameter. It had the badge of House Idolator on one side, and a bloody slash across the back. A Blood Guard mark. Miles, still in his beast form, pocketed the necklace and picked up the still-sheathed broadsword, holding it in one hand as he looked down where the Blood Guard had lain.

"I'm sorry," Miles said softly, the words catching in his throat. "I'll make sure everyone knows what you did here today. I promise."

Miles looked up at the rain as it continued to pelt down. He looked back at where Stuart had been and sniffed the air. No scent apart from the blood of the Blood Guard and the dead body of the werewolf. He walked over to the werewolf, grabbed it by the arms, and with a blast of telekinesis, and a lot of strength, pulled the remains out from under the rubble that covered it.

Miles had hoped the werewolf might have worn something that gave away any clue as to what was going on, but it wore no clothing, no jewellery. Miles let the body drop back to the dirt, beat his wings once, and took to the sky. He needed to catch up to the convoy; he needed to tell Thomas what had happened. He gripped the broadsword tightly in his hand and set off as fast as he could toward Bangor.

$\backsim$ CHAPTER TWENTY-THREE $\backsim$

Miles spotted the pilgrim convoy when they were about halfway between where he'd fought the werewolf, desolate, and witch and their destination of Bangor. He'd only been flying for about ten minutes, but with his injuries, his body was beginning to scream at him to stop, to land and rest.

After another thirty seconds, his body made it clear that he either rested or he fell. He chose to land, and returned to his human form, grateful for clothing that had been large enough to accommodate his beast form. They were ripped, and he was basically topless, but at least he wasn't running through the state of Maine naked.

The weather had intensified since the fight, and Miles was soaked to the bone, although he welcomed the cold wind, and hadn't been concerned about catching a chill for about four centuries. He was, however, exhausted. The fight, the elongated time he'd spent in his beast form, the fact that his skin was still scarred from where he'd flown through the witch's magical fire circle—everything combined to make sure that he just wanted to feed and sleep, not necessarily in that order.

The taillights of the vehicles were easy to keep in his vision as he trundled along the broken road. They were probably only moving at about fifteen to twenty miles per hour; any more than that and even a vampire's enhanced reaction speed probably wouldn't save you from an accident should the road no longer be where it was meant to be.

Miles looked down at his bare feet. He wished he could figure out a way to save the shoes. The hard, jagged rocks on the road cut open the soles of his feet, which immediately healed the tiny wound, but the constant irritation of it happening over and over again was beginning to grate.

As Miles continued on, his thoughts went back to the desolate. To what Stuart had said about how they'd changed in Maine. The desolate giant had wanted vengeance. That some of the desolate had a bond. He'd never heard of anything like that, but then he'd never known any desolate to want or feel anything. Except the need to feed. The idea that it had wanted vengeance, even over its own self-preservation, was a new one. He wondered if those people in Maine who had been experimenting on the desolate for all those decades before the state fell had managed to do something to their brains.

Miles wasn't entirely sure he was comfortable with the idea of giving desolate thoughts and feelings. Would they know who they were before they became desolate? Would they be able to deal with such information? Would they even understand it? He didn't have answers, but he let his brain ponder the questions as he walked, anything to drown out the need to rest.

Finally catching up to the paused convey at the gates of Bangor, he reached the Winnebago at the back of the trail and walked by the side of the vehicle, running his hand along it to the door. The interior was dark, and the engine stopped, so he continued on to the bus, which like the Winnebago was empty and dark. Thomas's vehicle was similarly empty and dark, so Miles continued on for the fifty feet toward the towering walls of the city of Bangor. It was at that exact moment that he reached the first floodlight, which bathed him in light so bright he had to blink.

"Who goes there?" a voice shouted from somewhere beyond Miles's now hazy vision.

"A blind man, apparently," Miles shouted. "Could you lower the fucking lights? It's been a shite night."

"Answer the question," the voice shouted back.

Miles took a deep breath. He wasn't in the mood to be questioned, but he also knew now was not the time for him to be a dick. "Miles Watson," he called out. "Arbiter, vampire, ex-House Venator First Librarian. Bodyguard to Amelia Roberts, owner of a large dog by the name of Church. Although I guess *owner* isn't really the right term, as she pretty much owns herself."

"Are you done?" the voice asked.

Miles noticed that he'd been rambling. "Aye, I guess so. You want to know anything else?"

The floodlights extinguished, and Miles had to blink a few times to get the floating white orbs out of his vision. "Ta, very much," he called out.

"Why are you partially naked?" the voice shouted as the doors slowly began to open.

"Are ya taking the fucking piss, lad?" Miles called back. "I've just walked several fucking miles, through the pouring fucking rain, after having fought a fucking werewolf, and a desolate giant, and a massive twat by the name of Stuart Murphy. Witch extraordinaire, apparently. Look, please just get First Authority Thomas Reed. I have something I need to give back to him."

Miles raised the broadsword in the air, swayed slightly, and dropped to the ground with a sigh. He stayed there as several guards from inside the town arrived, all aiming spears at him.

"Stand down," a voice boomed, and the six guards immediately stepped to the side. They remained at attention as a human woman with long grey hair wearing an old navy blue sweatshirt and jeans walked by them and offered Miles her hand. "Carol Walters."

Miles took her hand, and allowed himself to be pulled up to his feet. "Thank you."

"Let's get you inside," Carol said. "You have some people who are waiting for you. And I'd like a debrief about what you encountered out there tonight."

Miles walked by the guards, none of whom looked up from the ground they'd been staring at.

"If possible, I'd very much like a blood pouch and some clothes," Miles said as they passed beneath the portcullis into a large courtyard, which looked a lot like the ones in the forts Miles had been to. "Has Thomas, or anyone else, told you about everything we've found at Falmouth?"

"Yes," Carol said. "We have additional security on standby within the city. If they try something like that here, they're going to find out why Bangor has managed to stay in one piece all these years."

"Good," Miles said. "So am I okay to feed and change before the debrief? I'd like to see Dr. Joseph Davies, too, First Lord Drest told me to speak to him."

Carol nodded. "We can do the food and shower, and even a change of clothes, but Joseph Davies is missing."

Miles stopped walking in the middle of the courtyard. "He's what?"

"We'll explain everything," Carol said, motioning for Miles to continue through to the opposite end of the courtyard, where a second set of large doors had already been opened. "We'll get you somewhere, and bring in those vehicles your friends arrived in. We need to check them over first, make sure they don't have any passengers they shouldn't."

"*Passengers?*" Miles asked.

"You'd be surprised," Carol said grimly.

Just beyond the second gate was a large open area that looked as if it had once been a car park. It had dozens of vehicles, both civilian and military, parked there, and a large building sat off to one side, where several armed people entered and left on a regular basis.

Beyond that were six small single-storey buildings set in a line, each with a turreted machine gun outside of it. Miles looked up at the towers that sat at several points as the walls stretched around the city, and noticed dozens of personnel and more weaponry.

There was street lighting all around the place, and several small generators that hummed as cables ran from them into the buildings.

"This place has changed a lot since I was last here," Miles said as they stopped by a golf cart, and Carol motioned for him to get in.

"The buildings here used to be a residential district in the town," Carol said as the golf buggy set off. "We had to demolish them, repurpose as much as we could. Large parts of what used to be the town are now outside of the protection zone we put in place. They're safe, for the most part, but we don't advise people go out there alone. The city is divided into parts now, with the residential area being what used to be the Broadway District and Whitney Park. What was Fairmount is now where you just came through, and is mostly our military area. One of four. We kept the Union and State Street Bridges, and on the other side of the river is where I'm taking you. We use it as a guest area, and it's where most of the council members live and work. There's another military encampment close to what was I-395. You know, before big parts of it were blown all to hell."

Carol drove through the alleyway that separated the six buildings, and out onto what Miles thought might have been the main square for the city. There was a large green area in the centre, with buildings all around it, and three roads leading off. Carol took one of the roads, and continued down, driving by shops and a diner, all of which looked to be in use. There were dozens of people out and about, too, all seemingly going about their lives.

"How many people live here?" Miles asked as they continued on toward one of the bridges.

"About twenty-two thousand," Carol said. "It's approximately seventy-five percent human, but we all get along."

They crossed one of the bridges and went down a hill, as fewer and fewer buildings populated the area, until it was fields, although the large walls were still visible in the distance. The rain had stopped, thankfully, and visibility had improved, but the roads were so slick with rain that Miles wasn't sure driving a golf cart at speed was the safest way to get around.

"There used to be an airport here," Carol said. "Or back there. We repurposed it for training. In fact everyone who lives here has to have been a part of the guard to defend the city. We have electricity, and internal phone lines, although don't ask about using your cell phone, and definitely don't ask about Wi-Fi. Sometimes I wonder why those who leave for the outside world ever come back. A simpler life, I guess."

"Yeah, that must be it," Miles said. "You have a lot of people leave?"

"No," Carol said. "And about ninety percent return if they do."

"You like the eighties, by any chance?" Miles asked, trying to sound conversational.

Carol looked at him confused. "We do movie nights here. Eighties films are always the most popular. Why, are you a fan?"

"Of some of it," Miles said. "Maine seems to have consolidated a bit of a fanbase for the decade."

They'd been driving for about ten minutes when Carol pulled over to a large motel. There were shutters attached to the outside of every window, and whatever the sign out front had once said, it now read *Vampire Inn*.

"We converted this place to let vampires stay here when they arrive," Carol said. "Your friends are inside. The governing body is over there."

Miles followed Carol's gesture to a large single-storey building on the opposite side of the road, next to what had been another parking area, and was now clearly a staging zone for the city guard. The building was all glass and wood, and looked a lot more inviting that the large number of armed personnel would have suggested. There were dozens of people, along with tanks, APVs, jeeps, and a lot of other tech that looked to Miles to be a lot newer than fifty years.

Carol nodded as if she knew what Miles was thinking. "We get shipments of weaponry every few years," she said. "Mostly military stuff. They just keep sending it on in here, and we use it to keep the desolate population as low as possible. They tried to send us helicopters a while back, but they don't work. No one seems to know why. You can get about a hundred feet up, and they just stop. No one wanted to figure it out after the first two crashes. Anyway, we'll be over in that building. Your room is 109." She passed Miles a key.

"Thank you," he said.

"There's a fridge inside, stocked with blood pouches," Carol continued. "You'll have to see your friends about a change of clothing. We had them cart everything out of their vehicles, so hopefully your clothes are here."

Miles climbed out of the golf buggy and looked north up the empty road. "The wall go that far north?"

"All the way up to Veazie," Carol said. "Where the wall can't be built, we had permanent encampments put there. Moats, razor wire, machine gun batteries. The whole thing. The northwest is the worst for it. Lot of woods, grasslands, and the like. The US military sent in a few thousand troops a year to train here, you know that?"

Miles shook his head. "The Assembly, too?"

Carol nodded. "Yeah, we get a lot of vampire assault teams up here. They go out, remove a lot of desolate."

"Any go to Augusta?"

"No one goes to Augusta," Carol said. "It's a dangerous place, even for vampires."

"So people keep telling me," Miles replied. "Someone mentioned that Dr. Davies was shown some black rocks. You know anything about that?"

Carol nodded. "He was obsessed with it."

"Any idea why?"

Carol shook her head.

"Thanks very much," Miles said. "I'll go get changed and see you shortly."

Carol left with a wave of her hand, and Miles stood in the parking area of an old motel for several moments. He needed to see Thomas. He made a lap of the building, and found that it had an old basketball court at the rear of it, although with the amount of plant life growing through the concrete, it was probably the triffids' basketball court now.

Miles returned to the front of the motel to find Thomas and his two Blood Guard standing outside. "I saw you come in," Thomas said, eyeing the sword in Miles's hand.

"I'm sorry," Miles said, passing Thomas the necklace.

Thomas stared at the necklace for several seconds, before encasing it in his fist. "What happened?"

"A lot," Miles said. "I need a blood pouch before I fall down."

Thomas blinked as if seeing Miles's state for the first time. "Oh shit, Miles, you look like you were set on fire. Get up to your room. We've had your things brought there. Go feed; we'll be waiting for you in the . . . common room. It's just beyond the reception there."

Miles walked up to the two Blood Guard, who both stared at him from behind their masks. He passed one of them the sword. "Your comrade was a brave man. He killed a werewolf with this sword. Took its head."

The Blood Guard whom Miles had passed the sword to took it in hand, staring at it. "Thank you," they said eventually.

Miles nodded and took the stairs up to the room on the key, opened the door, and stepped inside. He dropped the key on the queen-sized bed and tore off the remains of his clothing, letting them fall into a pile in front of an old battered chest of drawers. He opened the door to a small bathroom and stepped inside, turning on the shower before leaving and opening the mini-fridge in the room. After removing one of three blood pouches inside, he tore it open and sniffed the contents—synthetic blood. Probably a few weeks old. Not a problem with synthetic blood, although it was probably mass-produced stuff that tasted like nothing.

He took a sip—he was right about the taste, but his body didn't care, and he drank the blood pouch down in one go, closing his eyes and feeling the aches that filled his body leave. His body healed quickly, and when he was done, he practically crawled into the bathroom, dragging himself up and into the old bathtub to let the cool water flow over him.

He remained lying down for a few seconds before getting to his feet, noticing the dirty colour of the water that was coming off him. When the water was clear, he washed himself with the nearby soap, and when he finally felt . . . normal again, he climbed out of the shower and dried himself in a towel that was big enough for three people.

Miles found his clothing bag and removed a pair of jeans—one of the few he had left—a plain blood-red T-shirt, and a black hoodie. After he was dressed, he sat on the edge of the bed for a minute and let out a long sigh.

Deciding that staying in his room wasn't going to get anything done, Miles left and easily found his way to the common room, where Church practically knocked him over the second he stepped inside. Most people said their hellos, with only those he'd expected to be unhappy at his return staying silent.

"Are you okay?" Amelia asked as Miles scratched Church's chin.

Miles nodded and Amelia hugged him tightly.

"So," Thomas said. "I think we need to talk."

Miles nodded. "Yeah, we do, I'm sorry about your Blood Guard. He was a good man, Thomas."

Thomas nodded. "He will be missed."

Church followed Thomas and his two Blood Guard as he left the common room with Miles, stepping out into the clear and cold early Maine morning. Amelia strolled out after them.

"Is there any point in telling you to go back inside?" Thomas asked Amelia.

"If this has anything to do with werewolves, I want to know," Amelia said. "I heard the Blood Guard talk about how you fought another one."

"It wasn't much of a fight," Miles said. "I'm going to go across to that building and tell this tale to everyone at once. There's nothing in it that is specific to House Idolator, I promise you. But if you want to know it now instead, I can tell it twice."

"You sure there's nothing?" Thomas asked.

"Werewolf, giant desolate, witch who had a staff and pendant or talisman which allowed him to do things I'd never seen a witch do before," Miles said. "You ever heard of a teleporting witch?"

Amelia shook her head, worry written across her face.

"No," Thomas told him. "Let's just all go see Carol and her people together. We can figure out where to go from there."

They all crossed the road, nodding a thank-you to the guards who were outside the building as they opened the doors to let them in.

Chapter Twenty-Four

The single-storey building had a large open lobby with three doors lead-ing off it, two on the right and one on the left. There were two more doors directly in front of the main entrance, both with the word *bathroom* written on them.

A fire door sat next to the bathrooms, outside of which stood Carol, leaning against the wall, smoking a cigarette.

"You're allowed to smoke in here?" Thomas asked.

"*Allowed* isn't a word I'd throw about," Carol told him, stubbing the cigarette out on an ashtray she held in her other hand. "It's more of a *who's going to tell me to stop* situation. Besides, some days you just *really* need a cigarette. You ready to debrief us?"

Miles nodded.

"The journalist is coming?" Carol asked. "Not sure how I feel about that."

"She's writing a story about a group of murderers who fled from Boston into Maine," Miles said, twisting the truth enough that it wasn't a complete lie. "Seeing how I just bumped into one of them, I think she's probably earned the right to be told what I saw. Besides, it's not like she can publish it out here, so anything she learns that might not be great for Maine, you have time to fix the problem."

"By problem, you mean murderers running around," Carol said, push-ing open the fire door to reveal a hallway beyond. "Fine, let's go."

Everyone followed Carol down the hallway, by the glass windows on either side, overlooking more of the military personnel outside.

"You gearing up for a conflict?" Miles asked.

Carol said nothing, taking a left at the end of the hallway and opening another fire door into a large meeting room. Heavy blackout blinds had been pulled down, covering the windows within the room, and the lighting inside was warm and pleasant. There were refreshments along one wall, with paper cups and bottles of water, along with a coffee percolator and several mugs.

Miles took a seat at the long table in the centre of the room, which, considering the fourteen chairs around it, was clearly designed for a lot more than who were going to be at the meeting. Unless Bangor was going to be bringing a lot of its own people.

Carol poured a mug of black coffee and took a seat opposite Miles. Amelia sat beside him, while Thomas walked to the end of the table, a Blood Guard on either side. Church slunk under the table, eventually lying down by Miles's feet when she finally found a comfortable position.

"This it?" Miles asked.

"We're waiting on some of the other council members," Carol said. "It's early, and not everyone is used to being up at three in the morning."

"So, you said the doctor is missing," Miles said. "You want to fill us in on that? While we wait?"

"We'll wait," Carol said. "I think there's a lot going on here that you need to hear about."

Ten minutes of uncomfortable silence followed Carol's last words, and Miles let out a slight sigh of relief when the doors opened and eight people walked in one after the other. They were all either in smart suits or wearing scrubs, with no middle ground.

"You didn't need to dress up," Miles said as the five wearing suits took their seats next to Carol.

"These are the leaders of the Bangor council," Carol said. "From right to left, we have Xander Mills, Eric Dunlap, Graham Chen, Toby Richardson, and Rosie Ford. Xander and Rosie are the vampire members of the council."

Miles looked along the line of people and nodded a hello. He looked over to the three in scrubs, who had taken seats on the opposite side of Carol. A man and two women. "And you three?"

"My name is Bethany Parker," the woman next to Carol said. "These are my associates, Madison Delaney and Theo Gallagher."

"And you're all here for?" Thomas asked.

"We have a lot to get through," Carol said, removing a tape recorder from her pocket and placing it in the middle of the table. "It would help if you walked through everything that you've encountered since arriving in Maine?"

"Didn't they already tell you?" Miles asked.

"They did," Carol said, pressing record. "Now I'm asking you to."

Miles walked through his time in Maine; he left out not liking the Commander in Brunswick, and the fact that he thought Maine was weird, but did add about the desolate hole they'd found before arriving in Falmouth.

"Why do you think there was a hole in the shop?" Bethany asked when Miles was finished.

"Testing out the equipment, I imagine," Miles replied. "You'll probably find a few holes in out-of-the-way places they could get to."

Bethany made a note on a pad of paper in front of her. She was the only one making notes on that side of the table, and for some reason Miles found it unnerving.

"Any more questions?" Miles asked.

"You said this Stuart Murphy could use his staff to channel magic," Rosie asked. "And he teleported. Have you ever seen anything like that before?"

"No," Miles said. "You?"

Rosie shook her head.

"Anyone here seen anything like that before?" Miles asked, looking around the table.

No one moved or spoke, but several people shook their heads, including Amelia, who continued to look unnerved by the news.

"Anyone here ever seen a desolate behave oddly?" Miles asked, and noticed the slight twinge in Bethany's eye. He pointed at her. "You have."

"I don't know what you mean," Bethany said.

"You know, I've come a long way to help Thomas over there bring his pilgrims to your city," Miles said. "I've killed some desolates and a werewolf, and I've been covered in gore more times than I think is healthy. That desolate giant wanted revenge on me because I killed its friend. I assume its friend, maybe it was its mum, who knows. And you have seen something like that before. So, you've asked me to be open and honest, and now you are going to repay that kindness with an open and honest discourse of your own."

"And where is Dr. Davies?" Thomas asked.

"Missing," Bethany said after sharing a glance with her colleagues.

"How?" Miles asked. "Where?"

"That's not something I can discuss at this time," Bethany said, immediately looking back at her notes.

"Come on, ladies and gentlemen," Miles said. "Stop making this weird."

"We have had an unusual amount of desolate activity," Carol said.

"Define *unusual*," Miles replied.

"We were aware of House Idolator's plan to make a safer and quicker route from Kittery to here," one of the men beside Carol said. It took Miles a moment to remember he was called Eric. "Waterville is no longer there. It was destroyed after the fall. But we've been clearing it out in an effort to make it into a fort, or a base closer to Augusta."

"But you haven't been in Augusta," Miles said.

"No one goes to Augusta," several of the people said at once.

"People who go there don't come back," Carol and Eric said. Carol continued, "We've all heard the stories about it. Brunswick told us that it's not safe there."

"No one?" Amelia asked.

"No one," Carol repeated.

"We've been told that by a few people now," Miles said. "You believe Brunswick?"

"We have no choice but to trust one another," Carol said. "They say they've sent people who have not returned. Vampires. Told us it's unsafe to go there."

"How long ago did they say this?"

"Few months," Eric said.

"You were saying about Waterville?" Miles said.

"We went to clear it out and found some ruins beneath it," Carol said.

"Ruins?" Miles asked.

"Old tunnels and the like," Bethany said. "Really old, but also strange. The tunnels were made out of this black stone."

Miles remembered the same stone being in containers back under the tunnels beneath Falmouth. There was a possibility that black stone was in abundance all over the state, but to find old ruins made from the stuff did have Miles wondering what the werewolves and Stuart were looking for.

"Anything else?" Amelia asked.

Several of the people opposite Miles shared glances with one another. "We found steps that went down into a cavern," Bethany said eventually.

"We sent a team down to see what was down there; the team included Madison, Theo, and Dr. Davies. All returned without problems that first time, but after that Dr. Davies started to become obsessed with getting back down there, with mapping out the tunnels, of finding artefacts. He's not an archaeologist."

"What's he a doctor of, then?" Miles asked. "Drest said he's an expert in magical energy, but that's about it."

"He's a cardiologist," Rosie said.

"A vampire cardiologist?" Miles asked. "Seriously?"

"It's not as funny as you think," Bethany said, sourly.

"You'd think it was pretty funny if you'd just had the last few days I've had," Miles assured her. "So, Dr. Davies is missing at that site? That about sum it up?"

Everyone nodded again.

"What actually happened to the doctor?" Miles asked.

"When we first arrived there, at the ruins, the desolate weren't there," Rosie said. "We were mapping out the top floor of the ruins when they arrived. A horde of them. We managed to get out, but Dr. Davies was left behind. We only just escaped with our lives; we didn't even know he was still down there until we were outside of the city. We've been working on trying to figure out how to get back inside, but there are too many desolate."

"How long ago?"

"It's been three days," Rosie said.

"A horde?" Thomas asked.

"A literal horde," Bethany said, removing ten photos from the rear of her notebook and passing them over to Miles, who picked them up. He started to flick through them one at a time.

The desolate were indeed milling around a collapsed hole in what looked to be the basement of an old building. "What was the building?"

"It was just an old house," Bethany said. "Legend says it was haunted."

"So, under the haunted house was an old set of ruins," Miles said. "When was the last photo taken?"

Rosie slid over a larger photo. "This was taken twelve hours ago."

Miles and Amelia looked down at the photos showing a literal horde of desolate standing around the hole. When he was done, Miles slid the photo down to Thomas.

"Damn," Thomas said. "These are hundreds and hundreds of desolate. Possibly well over a thousand."

"Since the doctor went missing, more and more desolate have moved into Waterville," Carol said. "We've tried to get a rescue team together, but we don't know where the desolate are coming from, and we don't know how many there are. These desolate are different from the others—they're more durable, stronger. Almost smarter. We don't know why."

"Any giants?" Miles asked.

The inhabitants of Bangor traded horrified glances.

"Guess not," Miles said.

"There are giants?" Carol asked.

"Aye," Miles said. "Two less of them now, thankfully."

"So, Dr. Davies could be trapped underground in old ruins, with no way to get out because the desolate have made Waterville their new home," Amelia said. "Have the desolate gone into the ruins?"

"We don't know. I personally sat in a foxhole watching the desolate for eight hours," Bethany said. "I took the photos from there. Not one of them entered the ruins, but that doesn't mean they haven't."

"How do you know he's still alive?" Amelia asked.

"We can't leave someone behind," Carol said. "Can't leave them to the desolate. The last anyone saw of him, he was alive. And the Doc is smart and capable, and we need to keep the faith that he is fine."

"That's why you've got people outside of here gearing up," Miles said. "You're going to go to Waterville and try to forcefully get your doctor back."

"That's the plan, yes," Bethany said.

"Are you all high?" Miles asked, looking around the room. "The more people you send in, the more likely you're not all coming back."

"There's a second entrance," Bethany said.

"Where?" Miles asked her.

"It's along Sebasticook River," Bethany explained. "You'd need to be able to swim down and under the tunnel for about five hundred meters in pitch black conditions. We considered having a diver go in there, but there's a lot of jagged edges, and with almost zero visibility, it's just not safe."

"And you know this how?" Miles asked.

"We sent a remote toy submarine down there with a camera on it," Bethany said. "Before the doctor went down, we managed to map out a big chunk of the upper levels of the ruins. There's a part that's submerged; the tunnel comes up there."

"What did the submarine find in the ruins?"

"We don't know," Bethany said. "The submarine stopped working a few seconds after it made it through. The feed just went dark. We were going to be put an expedition together but there are too many desolate outside of there now."

"So you were going to swim in there?" Miles asked. "That sounds problematic."

"We can't just leave him," Bethany repeated, raising her voice slightly before apologising.

"Okay, let's say he is alive," Miles said. "Best-case scenario."

"We have no way of knowing where he is," Rosie said softly, placing her hand on Bethany's and squeezing slightly. "No way of knowing how many desolate are in there, if any. We were going to send a small team into the water to get in and try to find out, but we don't even know *if* they could get out again."

"If they can get in, they can probably get out," Miles said. "Somehow. Any chance this doctor has made it deeper into the ruins and found another exit?"

"It's possible, but we've had no contact," Carol said.

"What are you thinking?" Thomas asked, as Miles studied the photos.

"I'm thinking I'm going for a swim," Miles told him. "You need help, we need help, and the longer the doctor stays in there, the bigger the chance he becomes lunch. If I do this, we need help finding a group of deeply unpleasant murderers. I don't want to have to search all of Maine for them—the more eyes, the better."

"If you do this for us, whether the doctor is alive or not," Carol said, her voice wavering slightly, "we'll help you however we can."

"Can't very well refuse that," Miles said.

"Anything else?" Rosie asked.

"Yeah," Amelia told her. "Also, Commander Bailey is working with the Magistrate. He may have fabricated how dangerous Augusta is to keep people away."

"Seriously?" Xavier asked. "He's never been the most pleasant of people to deal with, but what could they possibly be keeping secret?"

"No idea," Miles said. "After I've got your doctor back, we'll figure it out."

"House Idolator wants to reclaim it," Thomas said. "And I can't imagine that the Commander would be thrilled about that if he's using Augusta for his own ends."

"His behaviour has worsened over the last few years," Xavier said thoughtfully.

"His hate for vampires?" Thomas asked.

"He has made it known that he dislikes our influence in the state," Rosie said.

"Maine is weird," Miles said. "It's gotten considerably weirder since I was last here, and frankly, the people are the weirdest of the lot."

"Something is off here," Bethany agreed sadly. "And none of us know what it is. Bangor is mostly a safe town, but . . . we're worried it won't stay that way."

"You had any dealings with the werewolves?" Amelia asked.

Everyone shook their heads. "We didn't even know they were a thing in this state until you told us."

"Okay, one problem at a time," Miles said, feeling the conversation lose focus. "Rescue the doctor first, then we can deal with anything else."

"What equipment do you need?" Carol asked.

Miles considered it for a moment. "He can't get out the top way without having to go through a horde of desolate, so why hasn't the doctor swum out the way you get in? And if he's not affected by Maine's weirdness, how far into the ruins has he gone?"

"We don't know," Bethany said.

"I know, I'm just thinking out loud," Miles told her. "I need a way to get him out of there, through that water tunnel if he's in no state to get out himself. He's a vampire, so I'm not concerned about him drowning, so worst-case scenario, I can just drag him through the tunnel."

"You'd have to made sure he didn't snag on the detritus under there," Carol said.

Miles considered the problem. "Might have to use telekinesis to push him along. You got a collapsible stretcher, something I can drag or push, that folds up small and doesn't leave a big footprint?"

"We can arrange something," Carol said.

"Any reason the doctor didn't use the tunnel to get out?"

"He probably didn't know about it," Eric said. "We only found it after when we were searching for ways in."

"I assume the fact that he hasn't waited for morning, when the desolate would all go into hiding, and just left is a problem."

"They might go into the ruins to hide," Bethany said. "We're not entirely sure. It's possible he just doesn't want to risk it, if he isn't aware what the UV level is."

"This is getting better and better," Miles replied.

"Anything else?" Carol asked.

"Heat blade," Miles said. "A shotgun with incendiary rounds, specifically one that won't fuck up when it gets wet. The last one I used ended up in a pool of blood, and it wasn't so useful after that."

"We can arrange that, too," Carol said.

"Stab vest," Miles said. "Some clothes that should I need to tear apart to turn to my beast form won't leave me naked. Blood pouch, two or three, in case the Doc hasn't eaten and is weak. Three days isn't long to be missing in some ruins, but if he's hurt, he might need the blood."

"All of that can be done," Carol said, as Bethany made more notes.

"The pilgrims can help should any desolate attack," Thomas said. "We'd like to be able to do that, if you'd let us."

"We'd be happy for the extra hands," Carol said. "Though hopefully it won't come to that."

"Church will stay here," Miles said.

Church banged under the table, and several of the council members looked under, as Church extricated herself and stood next to Miles.

"That's a . . ." Bethany said.

"Big dog," Miles said. "Aye, I know. This is Church. She's a genetically enhanced Doberman, and she's about as smart as everyone in this room. She's also staying here, and will be protecting Amelia. Who is definitely not joining me on this incursion."

Amelia held up her hands. "This one is all yours."

"I would advise people don't try to poke the large dog," Miles said.

"You're looking my way," Bethany said.

"Whenever I see a doctor's eyes light up when Church is involved, just as yours did, I like to put the warning out there," Miles told her.

"Warning received," Bethany told him, a shade icily.

Miles wasn't overly concerned; he'd met people who liked to prod and poke things they didn't understand, and Bethany looked like a prodder.

Better to get it out of the way now than come back and find several people with fewer limbs than when he'd left.

"Glad we all understand one another," Miles said. "How long before you can get everything together? How long is the drive to Waterville?"

"About two hours usually," Carol said. "The roads aren't great, but we have some all-terrain vehicles that make it in good time."

"Get one of them prepared," Miles said. "Thomas's familiar will be my driver. He going to be okay with that, Thomas?"

"Arvid will be fine," Thomas assured him.

"Excellent," Miles said, clapping his hands. "I'm going to sleep for a few hours, and have something else to eat, and then I'll be good to go rescue your doctor."

CHAPTER TWENTY-FIVE

Miles woke when it was still sunny outside. Church was already up, sitting in front of the door, watching him. He checked the UV levels, which said *zero*. Considering the time of year, that was another odd thing to add to the ever-growing list.

"What?" Miles asked.

Church let out a slow whine.

"I know you want to come, but you can't," Miles said. "I wish you could, I do."

Church pawed at her nose.

Miles got to his feet and walked over to Church, kneeling before her as she rested her head on his shoulder. Miles stroked Church and they sat like that for a few minutes before Church sat back.

"You'll be with Amelia," Miles said. "And when we're done, we'll go back to Scotland, and I'll get you a nice steak."

Church pawed Miles in the chest slightly.

"I promise," Miles assured her.

Church let out a slight whine, and Miles kissed her on the top of the head.

"I'll be safe," he whispered. "I'm just going for a swim and a little light exploration."

Church snorted as there was a slight knock on the door.

Miles opened the door after Church moved to the side, and Amelia stepped into the room. She held a large rucksack. "Just wanted to come say bye before you left," she said, before looking down at Church. "You ready to be roomies for a day or two?"

Church let out an enthusiastic bark and walked out of the still-open door, leaving Miles and Amelia alone.

"I think they're all good to go," Amelia said, passing Miles the bag. "They got some stuff for you."

"You okay?" Miles asked her as he walked back to his bed, dropping the bag onto it, and removing the clothing he'd asked for, as well as the heat dagger and a flare gun. No shotgun, though.

"The gun will be in the vehicle," Amelia said. "They told me to tell you that."

Miles looked back at Amelia. "You are not okay."

"I am not," Amelia said, heaving a sigh. "I am slightly less than okay, and I don't know why. I feel like I came here to find some semblance of justice for my friend, and it's just spiralling out of control. We now have ruins, and more monsters, and people dying, that Blood Guard died, and Jenny and her mates, they just shrugged it off, and having spent the last few days on the pilgrimage, I'm very much in the not liking Jenny camp."

"That was a lot of words in a long stream," Miles said, happily already on board the disliking Jenny train. "Have you slept?"

"No," Amelia said. "I haven't slept since we arrived here. I close my eyes and drift off okay, and then I just see death. Everywhere. The dead and dying and desolate. I see the dead in those tunnels, I hear screaming, I just . . . the nightmares are a lot. And then I was worried about you, and the combination has meant not much in the sleeping department."

Miles crossed the room and took Amelia in his arms, hugging her tightly. "I think Maine does weird stuff to people's heads."

"The only time I rested was after we spent the night, or day, together, and I have to ask something . . ." she said, holding Miles's eye contact.

"What?" Miles asked.

"You didn't bite me," Amelia said. "When we had sex, you didn't bite me. I thought vampires did that."

Miles laughed. "Ah, okay. Look, if both people agree to it beforehand, sure. It's a little intense, for both people. There's a connection that happens, it's like we tune into each other's senses. It can be overwhelming the first time. And when a vampire has sex and drinks the blood of the person they're with, it can be a lot of emotion for the vampire to take on. It's an all-around intense experience."

"I didn't know," Amelia said. "I think, for future reference, should we do that again, I would not be against it."

Miles nodded. "Noted. Amelia, why don't you get into my bed here, I'll have Church come and lay in the room, and you can rest?" Miles asked. "She has an oddly calming effect on people when they sleep. And you'll be safe. Probably the safest person in Maine."

Amelia kissed Miles softly on the lips. "You be safe."

"I'll be back by tomorrow, I hope," Miles said. "Rest, relax, have a bath, get some food."

He called Church and told her that Amelia was going to rest in his room, and asked that Church keep an eye on her. Church responded by licking Amelia's hand and resting her head against Amelia's hip.

Miles kissed Amelia. "I'll be back soon. Be safe."

Amelia nodded.

Miles crouched down and gave Church a hug. "You too. Keep each other safe."

Church licked his face, and Miles got back up, grabbed his bag, and left the room. He closed the door behind him and stood on the gangway outside. What was he doing? A nearly four-hundred-and-fifty-year-old vampire, and a thirty-six-year-old human woman. People wrote trashy romance books about this kind of thing.

He pushed the thought aside and looked over at the parking area below where a large SUV was parked. Arvid stood outside the front of it, smoking something that, judging from the smell, was definitely not a cigarette.

Arvid waved Miles over, and Miles leapt over the handrail, landing softly on the floor below. He walked over to Arvid, who extinguished his smoke.

"You going to be okay to drive?" Miles asked.

"I will be," Arvid said. "Don't touch the stuff when driving for the pilgrimage, but after being told where we're going, I figured I could use it to calm my nerves."

"You're a vampire familiar," Miles said, slapping him on the shoulder. "I think you'll be just fine."

"Everything about this trip was meant to be just fine," Arvid said. "Then the fort happened, and people have been dying. Blood Guards aren't meant to die."

"Everyone dies," Miles said. "Even Blood Guards."

"Yeah," Arvid said. "Doesn't help that Jenny and her group keep talking about the coming of our saviour. I'm proud to be a House Idolator familiar, but they're a lot."

Miles opened the rear passenger door and tossed in the rucksack, finding the shotgun wrapped in a waterproof bag, along with a bandolier of incendiary shells. He closed the door and looked up at the sky. The sun was nowhere to be seen, and for the briefest of moments he could have sworn the low-level clouds *shimmered*.

"You ready?" Carol asked as she stepped out of the motel reception, along with Bethany and the vampire Xavier.

"I am," Miles told them.

"You know the car can't wait around for you," Carol said. "Arvid will return here and go back the following afternoon, UV allowing. Otherwise it'll be night."

"Aren't you lucky," Miles said to Arvid, who managed a forced smile.

"The area you're going to is devoid of desolate," Bethany said. "At least it was when me and my team went there. We've sent a small contingent of soldiers to the area; they'll be waiting for you, just to scout ahead. If there's trouble, they'll meet you on the way."

"Hopefully the desolate haven't declared squatters' rights in the area," Miles said, and turned to Arvid. "Right, shall we go?"

"Good luck," Carol said, shaking Miles's hand.

When everyone was gone, Miles opened the rear passenger door and was about to get in when someone behind him cleared their throat. He turned as the Major walked toward him.

"You good?" Miles asked.

"I'm coming with you," the Major said. "Not into the tunnels. Just to the drop-off. If there's trouble, Arvid can concentrate on driving, and I can concentrate on killing stuff."

No one had any issues with the idea, and they were soon off, driving through the open land of Bangor, toward an opening at the west gate of the city. Once beyond that, which was just as packed with soldiers and weapons as the main gate had been, they were out in the countryside.

The journey was slow going, and more than once, Arvid had to drop the speed down to single digits to get through a partially tricky section, but by the time they reached Waterville, it was dark outside. Miles looked out of the window, having gotten changed into a wetsuit that went over his clothing and packed everything he needed into the lightweight waterproof bag that held the shotgun. He also found some goggles, which he figured would come in handy. While he could see underwater just fine, if the water was full of dirt and grime, he didn't want to have to start trying to clean out his eyes the moment he exited the water.

Arvid stopped the vehicle a short while later next to a black 4X4, and everyone exited. A group of three soldiers stood atop a hill that overlooked the eastern side of Waterville. In the dark, Miles saw figures move in the distance, scrambling over the remains of buildings, the moonlight doing its best to show up the danger.

"We were sent by Bangor," one of the soldiers said. They all wore military fatigues, with a stab vest and mask that covered their faces and necks.

"Any trouble?" Miles asked.

The soldier shook their head. "Only a lot of desolate. None seem to be concerned with the river, so you should have a straight shot. However, you need to see this."

The soldier passed Miles a set of night vision binoculars, and he used them to look across the remains of the city. "Holy shit," he whispered, passing the binoculars to the Major, who had a similar expression upon seeing the hundreds, if not thousands, of desolate roaming the wastes of Waterville.

"What's bringing them here?" Arvid asked. "The ruins?"

"Maybe," Miles said. "Where's my entry point?"

Arvid pointed farther down the hill. "I'll drop you off as close as possible."

"Can you go farther down, beyond where you're dropping me?" Miles asked, wanting to check out a theory.

Arvid nodded, and everyone walked back to the car.

Miles stopped by the soldiers. "You can head on back. I'm only getting dropped off and leaving."

"We'll stay here, just in case," the soldier said.

Miles shook the soldier's hand. "Thanks for your help."

"Be careful down there."

Miles got into the car, and Arvid drove for another twenty minutes before Miles told him to stop and pull over.

"That's the Kennebec River," the Major said.

"How far back is the drop-off?" Miles asked, looking out of the window at the barren wasteland of nothing that stretched for miles in all directions.

"The tunnel is about a five-minute drive back there," Arvid said. "This whole area used to be forests and buildings, but it was bombed to shit as the desolate started to congregate here during the fall. There's quite literally nothing here."

Miles removed the binoculars and passed them to the Major. "Look down beyond the city limits, the roads into Augusta, you see anything on any of them?" Miles asked.

The Major turned his head slightly and adjusted the magnification. "Oh, fuck me."

Miles took the binoculars off the Major and looked through them at the hundreds of desolate milling around the road toward Augusta. They were of all shapes and sizes, and in all states of decay, with the vast majority no longer looking anything close to human, their bodies taking a more ghoulish appearance, their jaws permanently slack, their eyes dark holes with nothing close to emotion inside of them.

"They're not in a hurry," Arvid said after taking a look.

"Let's go drop me off," Miles said.

Arvid turned the car around and moved slowly back to the drop-off point, where Miles immediately jumped out. "Get going, just in case the engine brings all the desolate to come look."

"We'll be back in a day," the Major said.

Miles looked over at the dark water beside him. "Park up by the hill—if I'm out, with or without the doc, we'll go up there. Put a little distance between us and the gathering of the desolate."

"Good luck," Arvid said.

The Major saluted Miles, who nodded in response. He watched the SUV drive away, and crouched down by the bank of the river. The water was fast flowing, and the stillness put in Miles's mind a sheet of dark glass. He placed the goggles over his eyes, and stepped off the bank into the water.

The cold was a shock, and Miles's mind flared at the sudden temperature drop. Vampires liked the cold, but too cold and they went into a hyper hungry state, and no amount of feeding would satiate that hunger. Continuing on in that cold would eventually shut down a vampire's body, sending it into a sort of hibernation mode. Any human waking up a hibernating vampire was going to become food, no matter if they were friend or foe. Miles had never had to go through that state himself, and he hoped that he never would, but as he submerged in the icy cold river, the need for blood flared inside him.

He swam across the river, and dove down in the area he'd been told to go. It didn't take long to find the tunnel entrance on the riverbed as it was covered in the same black stone as he'd seen earlier on the trip into Maine. The stone littered the riverbed around the tunnel entrance, as if something had smashed its way out of the tunnel. He didn't want to find out what.

Miles entered the tunnel and swam slowly for a few dozen feet. It was, as he'd been told, just about big enough for someone to swim down, and there was a lot of build-up of old stone and pieces of debris. He'd attached the bag to his ankle via a strap, and he felt it tugging at his leg occasionally, but it didn't snag, thankfully, and he was able to move through the tunnel with relative ease.

The tunnel itself moved straight down for fifty feet, before veering off to the left, moving in a relatively straight line for several hundred feet, then moving up, this time diagonally. At the end of the tunnel was a large area which Miles swam out into.

Miles emerged at the bottom of the area, kicked up off the stone floor, and swam up to the surface a hundred feet above him. In no time at all, he softly broke the water above. He looked up at the columns far above his head, and judged the roof of the ruin he was now in to be over a hundred feet high.

He turned in a slow motion, getting a view of everything around him, but there was little to view. There were no lights in the ruin, and the only way out of what was clearly a pool was via the ladder that was attached to a wall at the side.

Miles swam over, pulling the bag up from his leg and removing the strap before he hooked it around his shoulder. He climbed up the ladder, which was made of the same black stone as everything else.

Pausing at the top of the ladder, Miles waited for a moment, listening out for anything that might signify someone, or something, was waiting for him. Upon hearing nothing, he pulled up onto the platform above and surveyed the ruins around him.

Considering they were *ruins*, they were in pretty good condition. He was standing at the apex of a set of black stone steps, which led down to an archway below. Behind him was a partially open large wooden door, revealing eight black steps beyond. He took the steps, going up until they ended at a platform, where a staircase started up. He looked up the centre of the staircase at the roof fifty feet above his head. He knew the doctor was probably farther inside, but he wanted to know what was above. He took the stairs quickly and quietly, until he reached the top, and immediately stopped when he saw the desolate crowding the entrance. Several of them looked his way, but they made no effort to attack or even come through the door.

Miles dropped down the centre of the stairs, landing on the ground below. He removed his wetsuit and folded it up, placing it at the top of the stairs, next to the ladder; he didn't want to be wearing it the whole time he was in the ruins. He left everything else in the bag except for his heat blade, which he removed, along with its sheath, and attached the latter to his belt. Once ready, he moved on at pace down the stairs through the ruin until he reached a set of twelve-foot-tall black stone doors, which were slightly ajar, although not enough to squeeze through, or even to be able to see what was beyond them. He paused, looking at the shimmering light that covered the surface of the stone.

Miles placed his hand on the shimmering surface of the doors and pushed. Even with Miles's vampiric strength, the doors moved slowly, but they made no noise, and when they were finally open, torches beyond flared to life, bathing everything in blue light.

He paused, his mouth agape at the sight before him. There were more steps that led down to a large open space, which stretched for hundreds of feet before him. Six more sets of stairs, three on either side of the open area, led up to platforms a hundred feet above, on which stood stone huts of various sizes. Miles noticed that everything was made from the same black stone he'd seen throughout the ruin.

In the centre of the open space was an ornate white bridge, which appeared to be made of wood. Turquoise water flowed gently beneath it.

There were patches of greenery across the area, with several containing colourful flowers in bloom. Light cascaded from the ceiling hundreds of feet above Miles's head, bouncing off crystals that had been placed all around the cavernous wonder.

At the far end of the open area was another set of black stone doors, each one a hundred feet high. The blue light came from flaming torches set in sconces beside them. The doors were closed, and had a mural carved into their surface depicting the setting of the sun and rising of the moon.

Miles descended the stairs and walked across the open area toward the bridge. He stopped by it and looked down at the water, realising that the colour was from the illuminated crystals along the bottom of the stream.

He crossed the bridge, paying attention to the carvings in the wood, all of them depicting the coming of the moon, of night.

He made his way across the bridge and continued on toward the gargantuan doors, finding that one of them was helpfully ajar, just enough for someone to step between them.

Miles walked between the two doors and paused at the sight before him. There were six two-hundred-foot-tall towers, all made of black stone, with walkways connecting them at various places above. They sat in an area that was easily a thousand feet wide and double that in length.

Water ran around the outside of the massive space, crisscrossing through the massive area at several points. There were more of the ornate bridges allowing people to cross over the streams, and a second set of doors identical to the ones he'd just walked through at the far end of the monstrously large underground . . . well, for want of a better word, a city.

Miles had never seen or heard of anything like it. None of the books in Drest's library had ever mentioned that such a place sat beneath Maine, at least none of the books he'd read. He wondered how long it had existed for, how long it had been closed away from everyone above.

Between where Miles stood and the second set of doors were hundreds of crystals lighting up the area. Miles looked around and wondered where the good doctor might be. It was like looking for a needle in a large vampire city haystack.

He crossed the bridge and walked over to the first tower, the large wooden doors of which were open. Miles stepped into the dark hallway beyond and continued onto a spiral staircase which, judging from the look of it, went all the way to the top of the tower. Light cascaded down every floor from the ceiling to where he stood.

"We sure he went this way?" a voice asked from somewhere above.

Miles shrank back into the shadows.

"No," a second, gruffer voice said. "Can't you get his scent?"

"No," the first voice said. "I catch little bits of it, and then it goes again. It's like trying to catch smoke."

"Right, so we take those little bits of scent, and we follow them," the second voice said. "The doctor *has* to be here somewhere. We've gone through four fucking towers now, and this is the first one we've gotten anything like a sniff of him. He's this way."

"We've been here for, what, two days?" the first voice asked. "Maybe he's dead."

"If he were dead, we'd have smelled him by now," the second voice said, its owner clearly reaching the end of their patience. "Stuart and Liam want this asshole found, so we find him."

One of the two above sniffed the air. "I got something else," the first voice said, followed by a low growl. "Something . . . new."

Werewolves, Miles thought as he moved back, farther away from the bottom of the stairs.

Another sniff.

"Fresh meat," one of the two werewolves above growled.

Miles retraced his steps back outside, where a middle-aged man, who looked a little worse for wear, stepped out from behind a pillar. "You're not with them," he whispered.

He had light brown skin and short dark hair, and he wore a long black trench coat over charcoal trousers, and a white shirt that was now more grime and muck than shirt.

"Dr. Davies?" Miles asked. "Drest sent me to find you."

The doctor nodded, leaned behind Miles, and tossed a glass vial into the bottom of the tower, which shattered on impact, covering the whole area in a floral scent.

The doctor looked back at Miles. "Come with me if you want to live."

Chapter Twenty-Six

M iles followed the doctor across the open area on which the towers sat, to the next tower along. The doctor pushed open the door and bid Miles inside, closing the door behind him and dropping a thick wooden block behind the doors to lock them in place. Miles wasn't convinced it was going to give two werewolves an awful lot of trouble, but it was better than nothing.

"Where are we?" Miles asked.

"Talk soon," the doctor said and exhaled. "I'm very tired."

"I've got extra blood pouches," Miles told him.

"We'll get somewhere safe, we have time," the doctor said with the confidence of a man who didn't believe a word of it. "Those two idiots will run right into that scent bomb—screws up a werewolf's sense of smell for a few hours. I've been trying to use one since they started hunting me."

"Umm, you didn't use one before?" Miles asked as he followed the doctor down the hallway to the staircase, which was identical to the one he'd just seen in the other tower.

"No, but it definitely works," the doctor said, starting up the stairs.

"You know this how?" Miles called after him.

"Explain in a minute," the doctor said. "Each tower has four doors, four sets of stairs, and links to the other towers by those walkways. We need to get across the walkway to the tower adjacent to this one. We'll lose the werewolves well before then."

"Lead on, Doc," Miles said.

They ran up the stairs, although the doctor started to slow once they'd reached floor fifteen, and after floor twenty needed to take a minute.

"Doc, an exhausted vampire is not going to be an awful lot of good at getting away quickly," Miles said. "Take a drink, get your energy back."

"I'll drink after we've gone across the walkway," the doctor assured Miles. "Not far now."

They entered a hallway where several torches adorned the walls, more blue fire flickering. "They're magic, aren't they?" Miles asked. "I can feel power coming from them."

The doc nodded.

Miles spotted that the hallways crossed over one another, making a sort of spiderweb of them. They continued on by a dozen rooms, all with open doors, revealing old furniture and little else.

"Why'd those werewolves want you?" Miles asked, desperate for some answers.

"You're an impatient one," the doctor said without stopping.

"Yes, it's kept me alive," Miles told him.

The doctor stopped walking, sighed, and turned back to Miles, leaning up against a wall. "Fine, those werewolves want to find me and take me to their boss. Or Stuart Murphy. Neither is a good idea. In answer to your other question, I knew the scent bomb would work because I found a book detailing it. I'd never actually used one before, but I am now eternally grateful for learning Latin when I was a boy. I was waiting down here, hoping Bangor would send someone to help. I figured that was you, seeing how you're wearing an Arbiter's torc. I watched you walk through this place, and made myself known when I was sure you weren't with those wolves."

The doctor set off again, opening the door and dropping to a crouch as he started off across the hundreds of feet of walkway.

Miles followed in the same manner, keeping low and listening out for anything that might suggest the werewolves had figured out what was going on, despite the earlier perfume grenade.

They made it to the opposite side of the walkway and through into the tower without anyone noticing them.

"So who's their boss?" Miles asked.

"Let's go to my hideaway, and then all the answers you can stomach," the doctor said.

"Hideaway?" Miles asked. "You've only been here a few days."

"Technically, it wasn't *my* hideaway, I'll explain shortly."

Miles let it drop and followed the doctor through the tower, passing by dozens of identically sized and empty rooms, until they reached a room with black wooden double doors and bronze carvings all over it. Like everything else he'd seen, they depicted the coming of the moon.

"Some answers now?" Miles asked.

"You got that blood pouch?" the doctor asked as he retrieved a brass key from his pocket and unlocked the doors, pushing them open and closing them behind him after Miles had entered the room.

Miles removed a blood pouch from the bag as he looked around one of the most impressive libraries he'd ever seen. The room was a hundred feet long, with fifty-foot-high ceilings, and the entire wall was covered in floor to ceiling books, parchments, scrolls. They were stuffed into whatever small gap would take them, the bookshelves almost overflowing in places.

Miles left the doctor to his meal and walked over to the nearest bookshelf, removing a limestone tablet. "This is in a language I don't know," Miles said, turning back to the doctor, who was sat on the floor drinking his blood pouch desperately.

"It's Sumerian," the doctor said.

Miles stared at the pictures carved into the stone. "What does it mean?"

The doctor shrugged. "No clue, I don't read Sumerian. I don't know anyone who does."

Miles carefully placed the tablet back and set off down the long but thin room, picking up the occasional book or scroll to see if he could read it. He walked by dozens of piles of books on the floor, some over six feet high, and wondered if this was the doctor's doing, or if they'd been here a long time. He was almost at the end when he got to languages that actually looked familiar.

"Latin," the doc said as Miles replaced a scroll on the shelf.

"It talks about the Dusk," Miles said.

"You read Latin?"

"My father taught me when I was little more than a bairn," Miles explained. "After they died, my grandparents had tutors who taught me more. When I started working for Drest, he expanded my knowledge of a few languages by having me drink blood from people who could already speak them. Took a lot of blood."

"You learned a language by drinking the blood of someone who knew it?" the doctor asked, seemingly puzzled.

Miles nodded. "Drest taught me how to. It was a long few months."

The doctor chuckled. "I always knew Drest had some serious power, but you are definitely his child."

"Child?"

"Oh, you know, he turned you, you're his child," the doctor said. "It's what the Dusk used to call their first turned. He's one of the Dark. So he's a first descendant of the Dusk. I think the power lessens after about the third or fourth descendant, but you were lucky, you got a lot of extra power and none of the side effects."

"What side effects?" Miles asked.

"You didn't have to be turned by one of the originals," the doctor explained. "The Dusk were not known for their gentle and caring approach to turning people. You should ask Drest."

"I always got the impression the Dusk and Dark were just myths," Miles said, offhandedly. "I've certainly never heard Drest call himself one of the Dark."

"Hmmm," the doctor said. "Is that what you think? The Dusk were very real. The Dark, too."

"How can you be so sure?" Miles asked. "Aren't you a cardiologist?"

"I've been a vampire for three hundred years," the doctor said. "A doctor of various medicines for about two hundred and eighty of those, and a cardiologist for about fifty. I learned to help people. That's the thing with being a doctor who can live for centuries—there's always a new way to help people. I'm a doctor, not a fighter."

"Doesn't explain your knowledge about the Dusk and the Dark."

"You'll see," the doctor said. "It's better to show than tell."

"Before we go further, how old is all of this?" Miles said.

"The towers or books?"

"Both," Miles said.

The doctor looked around. "The towers are about seven or eight hundred years old, give or take a century," the doctor said. "But the books and scrolls and the like are, in some cases, thousands of years old. They must have been brought down here when this whole place was built."

"What I don't understand is how I've never even heard of this place," Miles said. "I was First Librarian of my house. You'd have thought a giant mysterious library holding a wealth of vampire lore might have been mentioned somewhere? And how is everything in such good condition?"

"I think it's something to do with the magic in the stone," the doctor said, placing his hand against a bare patch of stone as if for emphasis.

"I hear you got pretty excited about the stones," Miles said. "This black stone is all under the state, isn't it? What is it?"

"It absorbs magical energy," the doctor said.

Miles nodded. "Do you know why or how?"

"No. That's what I've been trying to figure out. Maybe Drest will know more if I ever get to speak to him."

"You're House Venator?"

"No," the doctor said. "I was House Umbra."

Miles stiffened slightly.

"Let me guess, you have had a few interactions with the people from my house?"

"A few," Miles said.

"The kind that ended with one survivor, you?"

Miles nodded. "That's a very diplomatic way of putting it."

"My House courted me to work for them, and when I discovered that they valued control and power over actually helping people, I left. Took a lot of work, and more than a little help from a few friends in other Houses, but eventually I broke free."

"Drest said you could help me find Stuart Murphy? That you're an expert in magical energy."

"That's mostly right," the doctor said. "My secondary ability allows me to track magical energy would be a more accurate statement."

Miles stared at the doctor for a second before saying, "What?"

The doctor smiled. "I can track magical energy signatures. Which usually means magic used by witches. I came to Maine in the early 1980s when I felt a build-up of magical power. It was everywhere, but I had no idea how to get to it. Like the whole state was flooded with the stuff. A few years later, it all went to shit. No more magical energy to sense. Up until a few weeks ago, when I started to get little tastes of it in the air. I wanted to search for its location, but Bangor needs me, and when we found the ruins above, I went with them. The magic is in the rocks. The black rocks. I don't know why. Anyway, yes I can help you, if we get out of here alive."

"Quick question, how can a witch teleport and use their staff to amplify their magic?"

"Stuart Murphy, I assume?" the doctor asked. "You sure it was his staff?"

Miles nodded, although he wasn't sure. "He had a pendant that glowed. He kept stroking it. I've never seen anything like it, but I also saw him cook a vampire with his staff, and he vanished when I tried to grab him.

I assumed it's one or the other items that let him do it. Considering he's dying, he's quite the spritely little fucker."

"The talisman of Dusk," the doctor said, walking off and returning with a book, which he opened to show twenty talismans, all of different shapes, sizes, and colours.

"These talismans are all from Dusks. Each Dusk wore one, it's part of them, the gems contain their blood. It amplifies the wearer's power. If a vampire wore one, their bloodline gift would be stronger, possibly, but if a witch wore one and they had something to channel that power through that wasn't their own body, say, a staff, they could use that amplified power to do all manner of things. Teleporting, however, would take a lot out of them. A lot. That's something that's only powered by the body using it. It's why *no one* uses it. You're more likely to turn yourself inside out than actually end up where you're wanting to go. It's a last-case scenario kind of thing."

"He was avoiding me tearing his head off," Miles said. "He did it twice, second time farther away than I could see."

"He probably needed rest after that," the doctor said. "He almost certainly won't be doing that again in a hurry. If he has a talisman of Dusk, he will be incredibly powerful. More so than a normal witch, even a normal chaos one. I do wonder where he could have picked up the talisman from. It's not like they're just handed out to people."

"He's working with a werewolf by the name of Liam White," Miles said. "His werewolf buddies you've already met."

"Liam White?" The doctor said, with a curious thought. "That name rings a bell. Why does that name ring a bell?"

Miles was pretty sure the question was rhetorical, so he just waited for the doctor to figure it out on his own.

"Liam White," the doctor said as he started to pace around the room. After a minute, he stopped and turned back to Miles. "Oh, no. I've met him. About two years ago, he was in Maine, at Ellsworth. He was looking for an old burial mound. I told him that I didn't know of any such thing, but he asked if he could look around. I said it was fine, and told him that he might be better off looking in Blue Hill as it was where House Idolator went on their pilgrimages, so they might know more. I told him that the House Idolator First Priest was there, and he should speak to him."

"First Priest Pedro de Moxica," Miles said.

"That's the one," the doctor said, with no love lost at the mention of the priest's name. "He's in Blue Hill right now, has been for months. Refuses to talk to anyone outside of House Idolator, refuses to engage with anyone except that wretched Commander from Brunswick for some reason."

"So, Liam White and First Priest Pedro de Moxica had a little conversation, and now Liam and his goon squad are killing people in Maine, with help from a chaos witch. And the Commander of the second largest city in Maine is working with the Magistrate. None of that is good news."

"It gets worse," the doctor said, picking up a scroll and opening it on a partially empty table nearby. "This is a map of the ruins we're now in."

Miles walked over to the table and studied the map. It showed the ruins they were in now, with the towers and cavern and the doors in and out. It also showed a vast network of tunnels.

Dr. Davies picked up a leather satchel and removed a map of Maine and New Brunswick, placing it over the map of the ruins. Someone had already drawn the ruins map atop the modern-day portion. The tunnels of the ruins stretched down to Augusta and across from Waterville, under Bangor, Blue Hill, and Ellsworth, all the way into Saint John, New Brunswick.

"Wait a second," Miles said, his brain finally catching up with everything. "So who else knows that the Dusk and Dark are actually real?"

"No one knows," the doctor said. "Or no one is meant to know. The Dusk are not creatures we want back among us."

"Why?"

"Their blood unlocks a power inside humans," the doctor said.

"What?" Miles asked slowly, thinking that his brain might just catch fire.

"The Dusk created the first vampires," the doctor said. "But unlike what House Idolator want you to think, not all Dusk were vampires. Some were the first werewolves, some the first witches, etc. At least as far as we know, they were the first. Their blood started the whole line of nonhumans who came after them. It's different for each of them. A werewolf only has to bite a human, a vampire has to do a bit more than that, a witch needs a grimoire to link to, but all of them can trace their powers back to the Dusks."

"And desolate?" Miles asked, almost afraid of the answer.

"Yes," the doctor said. "The vampire Dusks are also the first creators of the desolate."

"There's no werewolf or witch alternative," Miles said.

"Aren't we the lucky ones," the doctor said. "The original desolate—those turned by the Dusk—are different from what we would call desolate today. Smarter, stronger."

"Larger?" Miles asked.

"Some would be, yes."

"I've met some desolate that could be labelled that way," Miles said.

The doctor nodded.

"Does all of House Idolator know this stuff?"

The doctor shook his head. "I doubt it. I've spoken to First Lord Fuller about it before, and while he's happy to let his flock believe that the Dusk were real and were wondrous, he definitely doesn't want anyone knowing the truth."

"What does that have to do with Stuart and Liam being in Maine?" Miles asked. "And how did Stuart get a powerful relic from the Dusk?"

"Good questions," the doctor said. "I don't have answers."

"Did those who worked here before the fall know about these ruins?"

"Some certainly did," the doctor said. "I've found evidence of excavation in the tunnels farther inside. The people who worked here before the fall had been conducting experiments on the desolate for decades. Some of those experiments used magic. It's why Drest asked me to come here, to figure out what was going on, but it was too late. I found evidence that they opened the tunnels beneath Augusta, finding thousands of desolate down there. All in some form of stasis. Although strangely, they had no food source, and they weren't cocooned. Just thousands of desolate with no obvious way of telling where they'd come from. Instead of firebombing the whole place, they built a laboratory on top of it."

A pit of dread grew in Miles's chest. "They knew what would happen if those desolate got free, and they just kept on experimenting?"

The doctor nodded. "There are tens of thousands of desolate under Augusta." His voice was full of fear for the first time. "All of them just trapped down there waiting for centuries for their time. And no one doing the experiments on desolate thought there was an issue, or they didn't care. But someone definitely cared."

"Who?" Miles asked.

"The person who made them all."

"I think you're going to have to explain a lot more than that," Miles said.

"The disaster in Maine wasn't what people think, it wasn't the hubris of vampire and human scientists getting them in over their heads." The doctor paused. "Well, it was, but not in the way that it's taught. It was a long-term plan set into motion centuries before the United States was even a thing. And almost every single person involved died during the fall."

"Doc, do we have time for a full history lesson?" Miles asked, looking out of the window at the ground below. He scanned the walkways above. He couldn't see the werewolves, but it was almost certain that they were still out there. And probably a lot angrier than they'd been before the doctor had destroyed their sense of smell.

"Okay, I'm going to put the information in your head," the doctor said.

"You're going to do what?" Miles asked with a little more force than he'd anticipated.

"Look, at some point those werewolf idiots are going to actually figure out where I am. It was always a matter of time, and it's pretty clear that whatever is happening in Maine is escalating. People are dying, but you need to know what's going on. The whole backstory, everything. I can't think of a quicker way."

"How long will it take?" Miles asked.

"Seconds," the doctor said. "My bloodline power is a little different from most House Umbra. I can't actually change what anyone else is thinking, I can't push people to think certain things or start screwing around with their sense of reality, but I can add stuff to their brain. Information, memories. I have a lot."

"How long are you going to leave me a gibbering wreck for?"

"About ten minutes, depending on how fast you heal," the doctor said. "You got another blood pouch, that'll help."

Miles retrieved one from his backpack.

"Okay, sit down, get comfortable, and be prepared to learn some stuff you probably didn't want to learn," the doctor said.

Miles sat on the floor and crossed his legs. "This going to hurt?"

The doctor sat opposite him and nodded. "It's going to leave you with a headache for a few minutes, but nothing long-term. It may feel weird, though."

"Weird?" Miles asked.

"It's what people always say it feels like," the doctor said with a slight smile. "You ready?"

Miles sighed. "No, but do it anyway."

CHAPTER TWENTY-SEVEN

Miles opened his eyes to find himself sat on the deck of a boat. He could practically smell the aroma of seawater, the stench of sweat and blood. He looked around to see several dozen men who appeared to be Vikings, considering the ship in question was a longship. The men were hardy, determined, and fear came off them in waves. There was no land anywhere to be seen. He stood, wished he hadn't, and immediately sat back down.

Why were there Vikings? Why was he on a longship? What the actual fuck was going on?

"You okay?" the doctor asked from beside Miles.

"This is really weird," Miles said.

"Yes," the doctor admitted. "It never gets any less weird no matter how many times I do it."

"Vikings?" Miles asked.

"I don't know the exact year, but yes, Vikings."

Miles turned to look at the rear of the ship and saw one of the men had a shroud over his head. He was covered head to toe in black clothing, and power practically radiated off him. "Who is that?"

"His name is Ulfrik," the doctor said. "He is, at this time, approximately two thousand years old. He is one of the few remaining Dusk."

Miles glanced over to the doctor, and back at the hooded man, noticing the blood-red jewel that hung around his neck on a silver chain. "He's a Dusk?"

"Yes."

"That talisman is what Stuart was wearing."

The man looked up as if realising someone was there, and a coldness settled on Miles. "Can he see us?" he asked.

"No," the doctor said. "I wasn't actually there when he came to America; this is all my memory's way of dealing with the information I gathered in the tower. Snippets of the man, how he came to America. It might not be completely accurate."

"How do you know what he looks like?"

"There are paintings of him," the doctor said. "Quite a few in one of the other towers. The man really liked to look at himself. But also, from books."

"Books?" Miles asked.

"Journals from those who knew him, who met him," the doctor said. "They were collected and kept together, I presume for posterity. Maybe as a record of what happened. I don't know for sure."

"So what *do* you know for sure?" Miles asked.

"I got the fact that Ulfrik moved from Norway to Greenland, and then from Greenland to Maine. He was one of the earliest Vikings to move there. A few centuries later and the Viking colonies in North America would all be decimated. But those he turned, his trusted few, they remained. Until . . ."

Miles found himself standing atop a large rock, with waves crashing against it. In the distance were two huge galley ships, and people milled about on the nearby beach, next to the rowboats which had taken them from deeper water to the shore they would call home.

"Around about sixteen twenty-two-ish," the doctor said. "The Pilgrims come from Europe. I'm not sure if this particular group are called Pilgrims. You recognise that man?"

Miles followed off to where the doctor pointed, and the image around him changed. He was now on a beach, directly in front of a man wearing, he had to admit, very Pilgrim-looking clothing. He was one of five men, all similarly styled, although the one in front of Miles, he recognised immediately. "That's First Lord William Fuller. He's human."

"It is," the doctor said. "He was nearly thirty. Born in Denmark in fifteen ninety-three—or thereabouts—to a religious fanatic father and a young mother who wouldn't see his first winter. His father died six weeks before William left for better things."

"He killed his father?" Miles asked.

The doctor shrugged. "No clue. Probably. There's a book in here, an old book, written by Ulfrik. It details a lot of this, although obviously you have to take into account the possibility that it isn't the most credible of historical documents. Ulfrik likes to make himself sound impressive, and everyone else needy, whiny, and frankly deeply irritating."

The world shifted again. This time Ulfrik stood over a kneeling William, blood pouring from the latter's neck, as Ulfrik held his cut wrist to the human's waiting mouth.

"I'm going to leave out the parts in Ulfrik's writing where he spent a month turning people in the nearby town, and murdering everyone he felt wasn't worthy of his time and power. He murdered a lot of people. *A lot.* He wrote about every single kill. Hundreds and hundreds of them all across the east coast of America. Some you'll have heard of, like the Roanoke Colony, but many more were lost in time."

"And before then?" Miles asked.

"There are no writings about him before he comes here," the doctor said. "He even wrote in his book that he would not be talking about past events. They are no longer who he is. *He is reborn in a new land.* His words, not mine."

"So he turned William into a vampire," Miles said. "A first-generation vampire."

The doctor nodded. "Of those he turned, some were vampires, some desolate, and some Desolate Royalty. He unleashed them on unsuspecting towns that simply vanished off the map. Men, women, children, Ulfrik didn't much care. They were either someone who could help him with power of their own, someone who could help him by becoming a desolate, or food."

"A very singular way of living," Miles said.

"Ulfrik would laugh at you," the doctor said. "Anyway, we should move on."

The scene changed again to one of nighttime as Ulfrik, William, and hundreds of others stood atop a field next to a river. "Waterville," the doctor said. "This was two years later. This was the start of the ruins we now sit in."

"What are they for?" Miles asked.

"An underground city," the doctor said. "Dusk—all of them, not just the vampiric ones—have a weakness to the sun, not just UV like we do, but any sunlight. It's possibly their only weakness. Unless you're good enough to remove their head from their shoulders, burn everything into two separate piles of ash, and scatter them in different places. Even then, I couldn't say they wouldn't return."

"So he built himself an underground city to hide in?" Miles asked.

"No," the doctor said. "Ulfrik wanted an underground city that he could *rule*. It seems that most of the Dusk at this time are gone. He believes he's the last."

"Dead?"

The doctor shook his head. "Hibernating. Of some kind or another. Ulfrik thinks that once the Dusk have spread their gift, which he believes is their entire reason for existing, they go into a deep hibernation. They will awake when someone finds them, and needs them, or something like that. He romanticises it quite a bit. Anyway, he wants to build this city with his minions, so that he may rest here while they go about their lives protecting him until he needs to wake again. He seems like he knows this is going to happen, that with every person he turns, he takes a step closer to his hibernation. He is—and he never uses this word, but it's there for all to see—afraid."

"And this city stretches for miles and miles under Maine?"

The doctor nodded. "It is a massive undertaking. One that could never be completed by humans. Ulfrik mentions that it will be his legacy. A city built by the hands of the nonhuman. Greater than anything humans were capable of. A city where once the Dusk arise from their slumber, they can come to, live in. Ulfrik's last journal entry details his need for sleep. He states that he *allowed* his many of his minions to leave, that he wiped the minds of many more, to ensure they do not know where he is. I doubt he allowed anyone to do anything, I think most people he thinks of as allowing them to leave, fled before he could kill them. He did wipe the memories of his most trusted, although by this point he's paranoid that they'll try to bleed him, take his strength, use his mind, or just outright kill him and take his place. He wasn't exactly stable to begin with."

"And no one knows where he's buried?"

"They didn't at the time," the doctor said. "They knew he was in Maine. His power leaches out, has done for centuries, I don't think he can help it. I think it's the stone. Whoever Ulfrik used to create the ritual that allowed the stone to absorb or nullify magic, or whatever it was meant to do, they fucked up. It appears like it's meant to absorb magical properties, but if any of it is out of alignment, it starts to bleed magic instead. His power slowly seeped out into Maine. Maybe the ritual was done when Ulfrik didn't bury himself deep enough, or something, I don't really know. Before he took himself off to sleep, he gifted a piece of this place to the desolate who had helped him. He didn't bother to wipe their minds; they didn't have one. He killed any Desolate Royalty he'd created, taking control of the desolate himself. He'd built a large ruin for them to slumber in. A timeless prison, the black stone making sure that the magic stored in them ensured they knew nothing. That they would be fresh the day he woke up and needed his army."

"All of that is in the diary?" Miles asked.

"No," the doctor said. "That information came from another source. You'll see once we're done here."

"The army of desolate, then," Miles said. "That's under Augusta."

The doctor sighed and nodded. "When the doctors in Augusta found the first few desolate in stasis, they weren't the desolate ones created by the Dusk. They were normal, for want of a better word, but the discovery spurred the scientists on to see what else was down here. They broke more and more of the magical stone used to create the ruins, which was also what kept the desolate in stasis. Once it started to fail, those creatures created by the Dusk, and who were closest to the exit, started to wake. Eventually, they made their way topside. Where they'd be killed or, as became the norm, captured, taken to Bangor, or to Augusta and experimented on. After dozens of them had been found and experimented on, there was a surge of energy from somewhere in the Ellsworth area, which woke *all of them*."

"Hence the fall," Miles said.

The doctor nodded. "It didn't happen for a while. All of that magical energy I said I could sense all over Maine, well, it built up and up, and then there was a massive surge of it that exploded across the state, waking up anything that slumbered, but also blanketing the whole place with a miasma that meant no planes, electric appliances fried, phones wouldn't work. The miasma still sits there, about two hundred feet in the air, stopping signals, making tech stop working."

"What actually triggered the surge?" Miles asked. "Just the waking of desolate?"

The doctor sat back. "The stone. I think. Once enough of it was destroyed, it triggered the surge. And that led to the fall of Maine."

"So, this Ulfrik is in Ellsworth, buried nowhere near deep enough. And the destruction of so much of the stone triggered his power to explode and roll out across the land. That's a lot of power."

"From what I've extrapolated, the power was amplified by the same stone that was meant to keep it contained. Stone that had magical energy stored inside of it, more and more energy over centuries like a battery, until it reached its maximum capacity and was all released at once. A magical bomb, if you will."

"Why hasn't Ulfrik woken up?" Miles asked.

"Good question," the doctor said. "I don't know."

"I know this is a tangent, but Stuart has cancer," Miles said. "The witch. He's here for a cure. Could Ulfrik give him what he wants?"

"As I'm sure you know, the witch is a witch," Dr. Davies said sadly. "Can't make him a werewolf or vampire, or anything else. He's a witch now. There's nothing that can be done to save him. If he'd become a werewolf or vampire, or even Desolate Royalty, his body would have healed itself, but magic isn't like that. He became a monster for nothing."

"He was always a monster," Miles said. "Just figured out a way to make sure everyone else knew it, too. Turned a lot of people into monsters. What can you tell me about the desolate in Maine?"

"The desolate guard parts of this state. These desolate are old. You can tell because they don't really look anything like the humans they once were; they look more like ghouls or something. Greenish or grey skin is a good giveaway."

"There are giant desolate, too," Miles said. "They seem smarter."

"They could have been cocooned before the stasis," the Doctor said. "Once cocooned, they feed on whatever food source is put in with them. You get enough desolate in one cocoon, and you get . . . well, nothing good."

"I didn't even know they cocooned until a year or so ago," Miles said.

"It's rare," the doctor explained. "Most die when first turned by the hands of vampires, or humans, or the sun. Most don't live long enough to consider a cocoon, and when in a cocoon, they're susceptible to fire, the elements, any number of things. Few make it long enough to become . . ."

"Giants," Miles said.

"That's a good word for them," the doctor said, showing Miles a picture of an old stone temple. "This is where I think Ulfrik is buried."

"So where is that building?" Miles asked.

"I don't know," the doctor said. "It does look familiar, though."

"I think we need to get out of here and get back to Bangor," Miles said. "We need to find that building and put a stop to whatever nonsense Liam and Stuart are up to. Both have ties to the Magistrate. Oh, I forgot to mention, the Magistrate are almost certainly involved in Brunswick, too."

The doctor sighed. "I've had my suspicions for some time, yes. No actual proof, although Commander Bailey doesn't make his dislike of vampires a hidden thing. If the Magistrate sent Liam and Stuart here, and if they're looking for Ulfrik, which considering Stuart is wearing a talisman is a good assumption to make, we need to stop them. I can't imagine the Magistrate would want to wake up a Dusk for anything close to a good reason."

"You know, while we're talking about the Dusk, I dreamed about a man under a crypt," Miles said. "They told me to see Drest. There were skulls and a sarcophagus. He turned into a flock of bats. I spoke to Drest about it, who says he had no idea who it is. I haven't had any dreams while I've been here."

"Drest has his reasons for everything," the doctor said. "It's possible he doesn't remember. It's possible he believes whoever it is that's talking to you is dead, or that he's had his own memories tampered with. As for your lack of dreams, I imagine it's the miasma. That much uncontrolled magical energy can cause nightmares and mess around with a person's dreams, so it stands to reason it might not let someone from outside of Maine contact you while you sleep."

"Who could possibly tamper with Drest's memories?"

"Nothing good," the doctor said.

Miles filed all of the conversation away. If there was another Dusk out there communicating with him, it was a problem for another day.

"What happens if Ulfrik actually wakes up?" Miles asked.

"Well, it would be bad for everyone," the doctor said. "He's an exceptionally powerful individual. A warrior, a man who is capable of horrific violence on a whim. He would slaughter his way across this state, and any other he cared to move into. The Assembly would have to stop him, and there would be a lot of casualties, as people chose to side with the species a lot of vampires consider their gods. If he wakes up, he'll need to be stopped before he hurts a lot of people."

"How do you stop a Dusk, apart from sunlight?"

"An Abrams tank?" Dr. Davies suggested. "Lots of them. Maybe some attack helicopters, too."

The world went black, and all of a sudden Miles was back in the tower. He felt lightheaded for a moment before the worst headache he'd ever experienced exploded behind his eyes. He rolled onto his back as he clutched his head in his hands.

"It'll pass," the doctor said, trying to comfort Miles.

Miles couldn't speak, couldn't see, his blood pounded in his ears, and he felt something wet drip out of them, drip out of his nose too, more wetness trickle down his cheeks. And then it was gone.

Miles lay on the ground panting as the agony faded. His hands were covered in blood.

"Your face and hair are a mess," Dr. Davies said. "You might want to clean up and drink a blood pouch."

Miles rolled onto all fours and saw the pool of blood that had been expelled from his body. He was hungry. He snatched the offered blood pouch out of the doctor's hands and devoured it as if he had gone weeks without sustenance.

When he finally felt normal again, Miles got to his feet and walked to the window, looking down at the ground which held the towers. "We need to get out of here," he said. "There's an enormous number of desolate converging on Waterville, and judging by who those werewolves work for, there are very bad people who want to find you."

"The desolate sleep in the ruins during the day," the doctor said.

"Why do these werewolves want you anyway?" Miles asked. "Apart from to take you to Stuart or Liam, or someone else equally as bad."

"I don't know," the doctor said. "I haven't had time to ask."

"Any idea why they came here to begin with?" Miles asked, ignoring the obvious lie that the doctor had just said.

"No," the doctor said. "I wish I did."

Miles rubbed his temples, removing the idea he'd had to leave through the front door of the ruins during the daylight hours. "You really don't know what's going on, then."

"Not as much as I'd like to," the doctor said. "I have no idea."

"Any chance you've seen something you shouldn't have before you came here?" Miles asked.

"I think it would be difficult for me to know what I had and hadn't seen that might have been out of context," the doctor admitted.

"A valid point," Miles conceded. "Where's the First Priest in all this?"

"No idea," the doctor said. "I saw him a few days before we came here, he was talking about staying in Ellsworth. Apparently, there's a dig going on there."

Miles stared at the doctor for several seconds.

"You can't possibly think the First Priest is involved," the doctor said.

"Why not?" Miles asked.

"He's the First Priest," the doctor said, incredulous.

"People in positions of power are often unhappy with just how much power they have," Miles pointed out.

"I just can't see it," the doctor said. "He's such a nice man."

"Okay, any chance that the building in Ellsworth, where the First Priest said there was a dig, is Ulfrik's burial ground?"

The doctor considered it. "I would suggest that's a possibility."

"Which means the First Priest *might* be trying to raise Ulfrik?"

"I will admit that is also possible," the doctor said slowly. "I guess. Although I have no idea why he would want . . ."

Miles waited for the doctor to finish his thought.

"House Idolator," the doctor said. "If they could prove the Dusk were real, and then reveal the Dusk that helped create part of their House, that might help them get back into Major House territory."

"So we need to go to Ellsworth and see the First Priest," Miles said.

"It would be prudent to do so."

Miles considered his next words carefully before he spoke. "Stuart was looking for a vampire to help heal him. Any chance that a Dusk would be a much better proposition?"

"I don't honestly know," the doctor said. "We're getting into the realm of conjecture. We need to talk to the First Priest before we make any decisions."

"But it's possible that Stuart and Liam are here, in Maine, to help the First Priest in the hope of finding a cure for Stuart? Or to help the Magistrate somehow?"

"I have long since learned that almost anything is possible among those who seek power," the doctor said.

"What else could someone be getting out of waking up a Dusk?"

"If they could control Ulfrik, he would be a powerful weapon," the doctor said.

"I don't see that happening," Miles said.

"Me neither," the doctor agreed.

"If Liam and Stuart are working with the First Priest, and the Magistrate, I see only two possible ways for them all to work," Miles said. "Either

Liam and Stuart will betray the Magistrate, or they'll betray the First Priest. I'm not quite putting all of the pieces together. We need more information. We'd better go back to Bangor, maybe we'll get answers there."

"I think Bangor is in trouble. If you're trying to raise a long-dead vampiric god, and there's a bunch of people who might try and stop you should they discover your plan, and they're mostly in one place, and it's on the way," the doctor said, "wouldn't you send your forces to deal with the problem?"

"I-95 goes from Waterville to Bangor," Miles said. "That road still in one piece?"

"I-95 from Augusta back to the border is a mess, but no one wanted to destroy it from Augusta up. First Priest Pedro de Moxica had a chat with the council of Bangor, when First Lord Fuller was there a few years back. They floated the idea of rebuilding Augusta, clearing it out, making the journey safer. It was the Priest's idea originally, I believe. If he's working to bring back Ulfrik, it's been a plan a long time in the making."

"Would all of those desolate just milling around above decide they need to go to see their long-dead creator?" Miles asked.

"I think the desolate who are created by a Dusk have some level of control over those who aren't," the doctor said. "Like a sort of weakened Desolate Royalty."

Miles stared at the doctor. "I think Bangor might be in a lot of trouble."

"Those werewolves senses will be screwed up for a while yet, I hope," Dr. Davies said. "But if they do see or smell us, I don't think they'll fall for the perfume bomb trick more than once."

"We go across the walkways," Miles said. "Go back the way we came, out of these ruins. I hope you're okay with swimming. It'll take us to the arse end of Waterville, where we'll get a lift back to Bangor."

The doctor remained quiet.

"You know, there's something bothering me," Miles said. "Those images you showed me, they're so real."

"The paintings are quite lifelike," the doctor said, and for the first time, Miles saw the nervousness in his eyes.

Miles stared at the doctor as he became visibly uncomfortable. "I didn't see it when we were in the memory, but now that we're out, I'm pretty sure if you were human, you'd be sweating bullets. Where did you really get all of that information, Doctor?"

"I don't know what you're talking about," the doctor said.

"You're a terrible liar," Miles told him, getting to his feet. "Those werewolves down there want to find you a lot more than they want to go back to their boss and say they didn't do the job. Why are they really after you?"

The doctor looked out of the window.

"Doc, I genuinely don't have time to fuck around. So, you can tell me what you did, or I'm just going to leave you here to figure out those werewolves by yourself. No lies this time."

The doctor sighed. "Let me show you."

CHAPTER TWENTY-EIGHT

Miles followed the doctor out of the library and up several flights of stairs to the walkway high above where they'd both been. The doctor opened the door to the walkway, and Miles grabbed him before he could take a step forward.

The doctor looked afraid for a moment, before he noticed Miles pointing down.

"We can't fucking find him!" one of the werewolves shouted as they walked along the walkway directly beneath where Miles and Dr. Davies crouched.

One of the werewolves sniffed the air. "Still got that fucking perfume in my nostrils, but I think I smell something."

The doctor removed a small perfume grenade from his pocket, and Miles motioned for him to pass him the small sphere, which after a little trepidation, the doctor did.

Miles threw the sphere across the room as hard as he could, aiming for one of the towers across from where he stood. The sphere hit the middle walkway connecting the central tower of the three to the one adjacent to it, exploding upon impact and raining pieces of glass down over the side of the walkway.

"What was that?" one of the werewolves asked.

"Up there!" the second one shouted, followed by a low rumbling growl.

Miles looked through the gap in the walkway as two huge werewolves vaulted off the walkway below and landed on the ground after a fifty-foot drop, before running toward where the sound had been.

The doctor looked back at Miles, who held a finger to his lips and motioned for him to go to the door opposite.

When they were both in the tower opposite to the one they'd left, the doctor said, "I've been dodging them for maybe two days now. Going from place to place, never staying in one area for long. I was in here for a day before they turned up again. I thought I'd lost them in another cavern farther south."

"Surprised they didn't find you yet," Miles said. "What did you do? Because we both know they're not putting this effort into finding you because you opened the door to the ruins."

"You'll see," the doctor said a little sadly.

Whatever the doctor had done, Miles got the impression he wasn't all that proud of it. Which meant, considering the context, it was either something deeply embarrassing or horrific.

They continued down two flights of stairs, and the doctor stopped outside of a door that had the aroma of death seeping through the cracks. He removed a key that looked as if it was made of glass from his pocket, and unlocked the door.

Miles took a step to the side, just in case the doctor had arranged something unpleasant to happen, but when Dr. Davies opened the door and stepped inside, it was obvious that the contents of the room weren't meant to be anything more than a prison cell for its only occupant.

Miles stepped into the room and the doctor closed the door, locking it behind them.

"What the fuck, Doc?" Miles asked as he stared at the lone occupant of the room. A desolate sat cross-legged on the ground, his hands in thick metal manacles. Its skin was a sickly green, and its eyes were not like any desolate Miles had seen before. There was an intelligence to the creature.

"Hello," the desolate said, making Miles take a step back.

"A talking desolate?" Miles asked. "What the fuck are you?"

"Tired," the desolate said.

"The accent," Miles said, looking between the doctor and the desolate. "That's Scandinavian. You're a Viking, aren't you?"

"I am," the man said, smiling broadly, showing rotting teeth and a black tongue. "You're one of the Celtic tribes, I think."

"Scottish is fine," Miles told him.

"Scottish," the desolate repeated. "I remember that word. I think someone must have said it at some point. I've never been there, is it nice?"

"Aye," Miles said, unsure what he was meant to say. "This is all very fuckin' weird. You're a desolate?"

"I am, yes," the man confirmed cheerfully.

"And you're, what, a thousand years old?"

"A little more, but close," the man said.

"Do you have a name?" Miles asked.

"I did," the Viking said. "I don't remember it. I've been in a sort of . . . frozen . . . thing for a long time."

"Stasis?" Miles asked.

"Yes, that's what the doctor said it was," the Viking said. "It's not entirely true. We were in a deep slumber, connected to my king until he one day would wake up and our slumber would be over. Until I was woken up by another man, who wasn't my king Ulfrik. A lot of us woke at the same time, but it wasn't done properly, and our minds were jumbled. There was a man, he had a part of Ulfrik's power, and he used it to enslave my brethren before we could fully wake. He turned them into guards and builders. But I escaped, and the good doctor found me down here. I think he was going to kill me until I explained that I could tell him all about the great vampire city we find ourselves in."

"A talking desolate is like a talking horse," the doctor said. "You kind of have to see where it goes when you find one."

"You haven't tried to eat me," Miles pointed out to the desolate Viking.

"No," he said with genuine disgust. "I do eat people. Quite like it. But it would be considered rude to eat a friend of the doctor. The man who helped to clear my head. To remember who I was."

"There's a lot happening here," Miles said. "I'd quite like it explained to me. Use small words."

"I woke up," the Viking said. "I already said that, but I didn't remember anything. Actually, that's not true, I never really slept. I would see snatches of memories from people, from vampires within Maine. I saw them build the tunnels under the state, I saw them move the desolate from our place of slumber to under what the doctor tells me is called Augusta. I saw the . . . tram . . . ." The Viking looked over to the doctor, who nodded.

"Well done," the doctor said, as if he were congratulating a small child.

The desolate beamed. "Tram. The people moved the desolate from our slumber to Augusta. King Ulfrik's royal guard. All desolate. The desolate of the Dusk. We had our minds linked. We maintained our minds, to a degree, although we still require feeding. There are not many of us left."

"You saw them experiment on the desolate?" Miles asked.

The Viking nodded. "They took so many of us who were in . . . our slumber. Brought them to Augusta, performed experiments. They assumed we were just normal desolate who were found. But we were linked to our king, and the stones were wrong. He sleeps, but his power is not fully contained. When one of his children died, a part of the power contained within us would return to him, weakening those measures put in place to ensure he remained asleep. Until one day, the power that returned to him was too much for the defences that had been placed there, and the power inside them tore through the land."

"The miasma in the air," Miles said.

"Yes," the doctor agreed.

"So the scientists caused the fall of Maine by experimenting on a bunch of desolate who were linked to a Dusk," Miles said, wanting to get the details right. "And with every desolate they killed, they weakened the defences keeping the Dusk's power in check, until the dominoes all fell and unleashed horror upon the area. Including ten thousand desolate that were still hidden . . . in ruins like this one?"

"Not all of the desolate have my . . . intelligence. Not all were turned by the king himself."

"You came to America with him," Miles said. "I saw your memories. It was your memory, yes?"

"Yes," the doctor confirmed.

"So you didn't learn all of this from just books, Doctor," Miles said.

"A slight fabrication," the doctor replied. "I wasn't entirely sure how you'd handle this meeting."

Miles figured that was probably fair. "You stayed here with him for hundreds of years before the Pilgrims arrived," Miles said to the desolate. "You were building this whole time."

"A city for the children of Dusk," the desolate said. "It was to be King Ulfrik's crowning achievement before his sleep."

"You think a lot of him," Miles said.

"He is the greatest man I have ever known," the Viking said. "A man of vision, who wants to make this world better for all of us. Or was."

"Was?" Miles asked.

"Things changed," the Viking said, making it sound as if he was unwilling to go further on the matter.

"You said there was a man who had part of your king's power," Miles said, changing the subject. "You mean the talisman?"

The Viking nodded.

"Stuart Murphy?" Miles asked.

The desolate looked confused.

"A witch," the doctor said.

"Ah, the witch," the desolate said with no shortage of disdain. "No, it was another man. A vampire. He wore the talisman, and the desolate would wake for him, but he was angry that he couldn't do the same for Ulfrik."

"They found Ulfrik?" Miles asked, suddenly a great deal more concerned.

"His burial ground, yes," the Viking said. "But the vampire thankfully could not wake him. They were using the desolate they woke to dig out the burial ground. He was angry that our waking did nothing to help find our king."

"So the talisman acts like a Desolate Royal," Miles said. "It controls the desolate?"

The Viking nodded. "Although with one talisman and a lot of ground to cover, they were looking for a Desolate Royal to help them. The witch, he was given the talisman by the vampire, I remember them talking about it. The vampire said that there was a Desolate Queen coming, that they could use the talisman to control her to help them get more desolate. The talisman only works on desolate that my king created."

"But Desolate Royalty can only control the desolate they create, right?" Miles asked.

"No," the Viking said. "They can be taught to control other desolate. It's difficult and dangerous to do. The vampire told his allies that my king has been speaking to him in his dreams. That the Desolate Queen was going to be in Augusta. I was sent with them to wait for her arrival, and that was when I escaped. I blended in with the throng of desolate leaving Augusta, heading northeast."

"The same desolate that are hanging around outside this place?" Miles asked, concerned about the idea of a Desolate Royal being able to control *any* desolate they find.

The Viking nodded.

"Any idea why they're hanging around?" Miles asked. "Why they're not moving toward a populated town? There's a horde of them coming from Augusta, too."

"The desolate above, the ones that you say are hanging around, are not the creation of Ulfrik," the Viking said. "They will act like normal desolate. Those moving from Augusta will have numbers among them that will be my brethren; they will try to get back to Ulfrik. When those two groups meet and Ulfrik gives the order, they will all march as one toward their destination."

"So all of the desolate above, they're just waiting in Augusta until they get more orders?"

The desolate nodded.

"They're going to march on wherever Ulfrik is buried," Miles said.

The Viking nodded again.

"Can I assume that would be bad news for anyone in the way?"

"Yes, it would be . . . bad to be in their way," the Viking said.

"So, where is Ulfrik buried?" Miles asked, feeling a pit of horror in his gut. "And how long before he wakes up?"

"Ellsworth Falls is the place," the Viking said. "And while they have his resting place, he is not yet awake. I would feel it."

"Why hasn't Ulfrik been woken up?" Miles asked.

"They are having difficulty gaining entry to his sarcophagus," the Viking said. "It is made from the same black stone as all of this. Made to contain his power from being able to get out, but to allow his link to his desolate to remain. It kept him weak."

"If they know where Ulfrik is and just need to wake him up, why are they digging tunnels under another part of the state then?" Miles asked.

"They were trying to gain entry to this city," the Viking said. "Judging by the werewolves I've heard, I assume they've done just that."

"What do they want down here?" Miles asked.

"I do not know," the Viking said.

"Any chance Ulfrik has a library or something of the like down here?" Miles asked. "Stuart is looking for a cure."

"There are chambers filled with knowledge and wealth," the Viking said. "The city had a great library, and many of my desolate brethren were placed outside of it to guard such a treasure."

Miles looked over at the doctor, and back to the library. "Stuart is trying to find a cure for his cancer. Vampire blood does all kinds of wondrous stuff to humans when it comes to healing. The blood of a Dusk—"

"It might cure him," Dr. Davies finished, although he didn't sound partially hopeful.

"My king's blood can cure a great deal," the Viking said. "He used to use the promise of his blood as a healing tool to get the humans to work with him. He promised a lot."

"I thought he just killed everyone who stood in his way," Miles said, noticing the sadness and anger in the Viking's voice.

"At first, only if necessary," the Viking corrected. "Pointless human deaths serve no one. They are food, servants, workers, some even became advisers."

"So if, say, a human found information in that library about Ulfrik's blood and its properties for healing, that human might well align themselves with the vampires they're meant to hate in hope that they can get some of that blood for themselves."

"They will have been lied to," the Viking said. "You cannot change who you are. A witch who drinks the blood of a Dusk will not heal from their wounds; it might actually do the opposite."

"So this might actually get Stuart killed quicker?" Miles asked.

"It's possible—there would be more information in the library, but I do not think you have time to search for it."

"Is it the room with all the books that we came from?"

"That is a small number of books in comparison to the library itself," the desolate said. "The library is grand, and vast."

"Do you know where the library is?"

"From here? No," the Viking said sadly. "Although I believe the people who took me to Augusta, one of whom was a werewolf, said something about allies in Maine who are digging out part of a city near the ocean."

"Got to be Brunswick," Miles said. "The Commander there is working with the Magistrate, who in turn work with Stuart and Liam. So, he was digging around, found something interesting, and got his Magistrate friends to come in and do the dirty work. The question is what do the Magistrate get out of it?"

The Viking and Dr. Davies both had blank expressions.

"Rhetorical question," Miles said, and turned to the Viking. "What do you want for telling me all of this?"

The desolate stared at Miles for a moment. "Peace."

"Death?"

The desolate chuckled, which sounded like someone with a chest infection. "No. The city of Dusk, this city, needs to be resealed. The interlopers need to be removed."

"Why don't you want Ulfrik woken?" Miles asked.

"He broke his promise," the Viking said sadly.

"What do you mean?" Miles asked.

"He told us that all of his children were loved," the Viking said. "That we were *special*. He lied. He only trusted that which he could control. Dusk need to rest. Once they have used a lot of power in the creation of their children, they must rest for a long time. Ulfrik knew this; he knew his time was coming to an end, and that he would need to rest."

"What did he do?" the doctor asked.

"He killed everyone he couldn't control," the Viking said. "The vampires that he had created, he was afraid of them. He was afraid that they would try to take his power, that they were trying to take what he had done for himself. So he started to cull them."

"He murdered his own creations?" Miles asked.

The Viking nodded. "He hunted them down, slaughtered them. Those of us desolate whom he personally created saw what was happening and knew that our autonomy would be our death sentence. Many of the vampires had fled by this point, but those of us who remained—vampire and desolate—banded together and stopped him. It took many lives, and we were unable to kill him. All we could do was hurt him enough that he fled. We could not find him, although we searched for many days. Eventually, we found his tomb in the city, and knew that despite his injuries he would awaken with a rage the likes of which none of us had ever seen before. We moved the black stone sarcophagus, dragging it to a new place, away from his influence. Once he was entombed in his new burial site, we put the black stone pillars around the sarcophagus. We'd already taken his talisman, ensuring that his power would be weakened so long as the pillars remained. And then those of us who survived came to the city to rest. The vampires left."

"Why didn't you kill him when you had the chance?" Miles asked.

The Viking looked at Miles with nothing but sadness in his eyes. "He is our father. It was one thing to kill him on the field of battle, but to murder him in his burial ground defenceless and weak? None of us could do it, so we ensured that no one else could wake him. The black stone sarcophagus was made to contain his power, to afford him a good sleep. We added extra defences for it once he was entombed."

"Right up until the fall of Maine," Miles said. "When the defences you had put in place were weakened."

"Where was First Lord Fuller?" the doctor asked.

"He had left America some months before," the Viking said. "Only a handful of desolate such as myself survived the encounter; hundreds of normal desolate died in the battle. I do not remember how many vampires survived, but it was not many."

"If he wakes up, how do we put him back down?" Miles asked.

"You hurt him enough, and he will need to heal again," the Viking said. "He has not been asleep long enough to have healed fully. He will be weak and feeble. That will be your only chance, unless you wish to see many of your friends die."

"Even a weakened Dusk is a dangerous amount of power," Miles said.

"True," the Viking agreed.

"Will the other desolate like you side with us?" Miles asked.

"I do not know," the desolate said. "I think that those of us who fought against Ulfrik are small in number. They will be first-generation desolate like myself who will be on the side of the Dusks."

"How many of those ten thousand under Augusta are his children?" Miles asked.

"A few hundred," the Viking said. "The rest were turned by us from the human population. They're not quite the mindless creatures that their children became, but not far off either. They are weapons and slaves, little more."

Miles looked over to the doctor and back to the desolate. "How do we reseal the city?"

"I do not know," the desolate said. "I assume you'll figure that bit out."

"Okay," Miles said, rubbing his eyes with his fingers. "We need to get to Ellsworth and stop someone, possibly the First Priest of House Idolator, from raising a long-sleeping vampiric god of death and blood. That about sum it up?"

"Yes," the desolate said. "My king is not a god, although I do understand that you may see him as one. The death and blood part are accurate."

"Anything else?" Miles asked, feeling he needed to be away from the creepy desolate. "You mentioned the Desolate Royal you went to find. Do you know her name?"

"Lauren Gibson," the desolate said.

Miles shot to his feet. "Lauren is here?"

"Ellsworth," the desolate said. "Had I known you are aware of her, I would have said something sooner."

"Is she okay?" Miles asked.

The desolate shrugged. "I fled before they found her. But if they have her, she will be with Ulfrik. They wanted to use her to help keep the desolate in check."

"How can Desolate Royalty control desolate they didn't create?" Miles asked. "I didn't think it possible."

"Control is not the same as subdue," the desolate said. "She can keep them compliant, but she cannot *control* them. Is she your friend?"

"Yes," Miles said.

"You're friends with a Desolate Queen?" the doctor asked.

Miles turned toward him. "You kept a desolate chained up in a tower like hairless Rapunzel. I'm not entirely sure you're in a position to criticise."

"When you leave, please release me," the desolate said. "Promise me that you will find those trying to raise my king, and stop them. Should he rise, a lot of people will die."

"Will he be like a desolate?" Miles asked. "Mindless, savage, only looking for food?"

"It is in the nature of Dusk to be all things that they create," the desolate said. "Being a mindless monster is as much a part of him as his ability to care for those he creates. By modern standards, he would be considered evil, maybe. He might have been considered evil by the standards of our time, too, but he brought us all to this new land, and gave us purpose. At least in the beginning. Until he decided that his trust and love were conditional with his control."

The doctor bent down, removed a key, and unlocked the manacles from the desolate's wrist. Miles waited for the frenzied need to feed to begin.

"Thank you," the Viking desolate said, rubbing his wrists. He looked over at Miles. "This isn't new to you. The surprise at a desolate behaving oddly."

"Lauren is the first Desolate Royal I've ever met who was not interested in bathing in the blood of everyone around them." He paused and considered it. "Actually, she was, but they all deserved to die horribly, so I'm not too concerned."

The desolate got to his six-foot-four height and looked down at Miles. "You would kill me if I did something to concern you. It is not a question."

Miles didn't see the point in responding to the not question.

"Doctor, thank you for your help. You have been an interesting companion."

"Thank you for sharing your knowledge," the doctor said, offering his hand, and then reconsidering it when the desolate didn't bother to shake.

"How do we get out of here?" Miles asked.

"The large doors at the end will take you to the part of the city that had been joined to the tunnels used by those scientific rats who decided to kill and torture my friends," the desolate said. "They're all dead now. Anyway, go up through the hole they created, and there's a tram that will take you all around the state."

"That might actually be quicker than waiting for a ride," Miles said, checking his watch. "Which isn't due for several hours."

"I ask you only one favour," the desolate said solemnly.

"Sure," Miles said.

"Blow the hole up before you leave," the desolate said. "Reseal this city."

"What about the werewolves?" Miles asked.

The desolate's smile contained a hunger for the first time. "I will be dealing with those. They want to find me, but I will find them first. I will show them why they should never have come here."

Miles was going to ask if he needed help, but decided that if the desolate and the werewolves wanted to kill each other, he was perfectly fine with it.

"Will you be able to leave this place once we seal it?" the doctor asked.

The desolate shook his head. "I am going to go deeper into the city. When I'm done, I will make for the great library, where once my lord's rest is no longer disturbed, I will drop back to slumber. Go safely."

"You sure you can't help more with the location of the library?" Miles asked, he was sure it was Brunswick, but confirmation would be nice.

"Southwest of here," the Viking said. "I remember sitting outside of it and watching the ocean. It will be nice to walk within the halls of this city, to see the great library once again."

The desolate left the room a moment later, and Miles remained where he was, not entirely sure how he was meant to deal with what had just happened. He'd just allowed a talking, cognitive desolate to leave. A creature who, by all rights, wasn't meant to exist. It was another bit of proof, as if he needed any more, that those created by the Dusk were a different level of power from those not.

"We go across the walkways," the doctor said. "We go through the doors, across the cavern beyond to the hole. I don't know how we're going to blow it up to seal it after we're through."

Miles considered the problem for a moment. "Any chance there's something a bit more potent than the ingredients to make a perfume bomb in this place?"

"No, although the trams do use fuel to work," the doctor said. "We could use a tram as a bomb."

They left the room, returning to the top floor to take the opposite exit from the one they'd arrived in, using the walkway to move close to the two double doors that were identical in all aspects to the doors opposite.

There were screams and roars from somewhere inside the chamber. "I guess they found one another," Miles said, hurrying the doctor along.

"I will miss him," Dr. Davies said sadly.

"You want to stay?" Miles asked as they reached the door of the tower.

"Not even slightly," the doctor said.

Together, they descended the tower, leaving to more sounds of fighting—whatever was going on, it was not a short-lived contest. Miles wondered just how much stronger and faster a first-generation desolate might be, and pushed the idea aside. He did not want to find out. Ever.

The pair ran to the large doors, which were slightly ajar, and moved through into the cavern beyond. Before they went anywhere, Miles used his telekinesis to pull the open door closed, the noise of it closing reverberating through his chest.

The cavern beyond was exactly the same size and shape as the previous one, with six more towers. The only difference, apart from no other sets of doors to go through, was the car-sized hole in the side of the room, beyond which some kind of machinery could easily be seen.

The pair ran to the hole, clambering up inside to find one of the drill machines that had been used to help kill everyone at Falmouth. Miles walked around to the control panel, and after changing to his vampire side, tore out the panel and wiring, before pushing the machine off the tracks it sat upon and down into the hole, where it got stuck with a calamitous amount of noise.

The dark tunnel that both the doctor and Miles were inside had tram tracks and a tram, and nothing else now that Miles had removed the drill.

"Does it work?" Miles asked, going to the cab of the tram and finding the doctor already there.

"It does," the doctor said, tapping the dash. "It's a map of the whole system. It only goes one way. So it's north from here to Bangor, and then east, south, beyond Ellsworth, and back across down under several places, before heading over to Augusta. It takes several hours to do a whole loop, from what I figure."

"We should set off, then," Miles said.

"Need to blow the hole," the doctor said.

"What about the ruin entrance in Waterville?" Miles asked.

"We'll have to come back here and deal with that," the doctor said. "I don't think we have time. Do we even have any way to blow up this one?"

Miles removed his bag and opened it, showing the doctor the dozen incendiary shells. "You think this will do? That drill has fuel in it. Can't drill otherwise."

It took the pair of them ten minutes to rig the drill to blow, although without a timer, they had to load a single shell into the shotgun and climb back in the hole, and Miles had to aim at the cluster bomb they'd created. "Move the tram forward a little," Miles said. "This isn't going to be a little boom."

The tram started, the headlights revealing nothing but darkness in the tunnel ahead. It moved forward a hundred feet, the red rear light on the vehicle blinking as it moved. Miles held the shotgun steady, aimed it at the cluster of explosives they'd used on the drill, hoped like hell this was going to work, and pulled the trigger.

Miles was already running as fast as he could as the tunnel collapsed behind him. He leapt onto the already moving tram, the vibrations of the explosion rocking the vehicle.

"That was more exciting than I would have liked," the doctor said after the tunnel stopped shaking.

"Doc, where we're going, I think we're only just getting started with the excitement."

PART THREE

Church didn't really like being left behind. She'd gotten used to it, because there were some places that taking a dog, even one with her abilities, was a terrible idea, but she still didn't like it.

She enjoyed spending time with Amelia, though; she liked Amelia. She thought that she was kind and attentive, and understood that while, yes, Church was a dog, she was also a dog with the intelligence of a human. Church understood people perfectly in several languages, and disliked it when humans or vampires spoke to her as if she were a small child.

With Miles gone, and having been placed in charge of Amelia's security, Church had taken the job seriously. She had slept in the same bedroom as Amelia, and she had followed her everywhere she went in Bangor, although she drew the line at accompanying her in the bathroom. Some things a dog didn't need to be a part of.

Church thought that Amelia had a nice smell. It wasn't quite the same as a human scent, as there was something *earthy* about it. It reminded Church of a fresh-cut lawn, although the human scent was still there, lingering under it all. Church was certain it was the magic inside of Amelia that changed her scent.

She could tell a lot about a person from their smell, and usually that included whether or not they were trustworthy. Or at least whether or not they were happy lying to people. She'd met the Commander that everyone had been talking about, and was certain he was not on their side. He had the stink of distrust. She also didn't trust several of the councillors after being under the table the whole time, and thought that Bethany was lying about something. Although Church had to admit that when it came to scientists, she had a . . . Miles called it a negative opinion.

She missed Miles. He'd only been gone a day, at most, but she was always sad when he went somewhere without her. She liked to keep watch over him. That was her job, after all. He was in charge, and she was the one to ensure he stayed safe. Miles had trusted her with an important job, so she was going to continue doing it until he returned.

Being human, Amelia had a slightly odder way of living than Miles did. While Miles was awake all night usually, allowing Church to do what she needed under the comfort of darkness, Amelia's sleep schedule was a bit strange. Church had to admit that Amelia had tried to turn herself into a nocturnal creature for the duration of her stay in Bangor, but it was more difficult staying up all night and sleeping during the day than most humans thought.

Amelia appeared to operate on caffeine, and she wasn't all that concerned where the caffeine came from. Coffee, tea, horrific-smelling drinks that Church was pretty sure could dissolve metal. All were drunk while Church wondered if protecting Amelia extended to protecting her from her own terrible diet.

As Church followed Amelia through Bangor toward the main entrance, several people came over to talk to her. Word had apparently gotten out that she was doing a story on the pilgrimage, and wanted to know if she might like to do another story about the largest city in Maine and how it had stood the test of time. Church had no opinion on this, but Amelia appeared to be enthusiastic about it, which made Church happy.

Church stayed out of the way as Amelia arranged interviews with several Bangor inhabitants, all of which took place in a small room just off the main entrance. Church stayed outside, watching the people of the town go about their lives, occasionally yawning to scare off anyone who felt like coming over to check what she was doing, or who she belonged to. Church *belonged* to no one. She was her own dog, something Miles had told her several times. She *chose* to stay with Miles because she liked him, and without her he would inevitably end up hurt, and she was not having any of that.

The moon was high above them when the interviews ended, and Amelia came out, crouched beside Church, and started to stroke her. "You been okay out here?" Amelia asked.

Church licked her face, which made Amelia giggle. Church enjoyed the sound of laughter. There was a loud crunch a moment later, which Church did not enjoy. She stood, almost knocking Amelia over.

"What's up?" Amelia asked.

Church sniffed the air, getting the unmistakable scent of . . . death. It wasn't close enough to be an immediate danger, but the smell was something she had caught before. Desolate. Church barked several times, and sniffed the air again just as the ground shook, and something loud and unpleasant came up from beneath her feet. Amelia drew a gun from her hip and aimed it at the floor.

"Church!" Amelia shouted as the ground exploded all around them. Dirt, rock, and mud rained down over them, and screams found their home in Church's ears, as the scents of blood and decay assaulted her nose.

"We need to get away," Amelia said.

Church agreed. Amelia was human. Amelia was squishy. And Miles liked Amelia. Church liked Amelia. She took Amelia's hand in her mouth and started to lead her away from the shouting, the fighting, as desolate poured out of the holes all around them. This was what happened in Falmouth. But this would be different. Falmouth didn't have a Church.

When they were closer to the motel, after several minutes of Church running slower than she'd like so that Amelia could keep up, Church let go of Amelia's hand and let out a low growl, stepping in front of her human, as desolate poured out of an alleyway.

Church let out a howl and charged the desolate, leaping at the first, her jaws gripping the desolate's head for an instant until she crushed it like a grape. The taste was vile, but she would drink water later until it went away. She had no time to consider the bitter, disgusting aftertaste as she tore into five desolates, ripping flesh from bone with teeth and claw, and crushing the skulls of all five. When she was done, she turned to be congratulated by Amelia for her good work, but found that the human was gone.

A panic settled inside Church's body for a moment. Her human was gone. Where had she gone? Why had she gone? Had something taken her? She forced herself to be calm and sniffed the air. The human scent was steady, and led down toward the motel.

Church set off at a run, keeping the scent in her nostrils the whole time, until she saw Amelia getting bundled into the back of a vehicle . . . a car . . . no, a truck. A big truck. Like the ones that had been on the pilgrimage. A military truck. The two people throwing Amelia in the back looked over at Church and jumped into the vehicle before it took off. She recognised two of them, they were on the pilgrimage, and there was someone else on the back of the truck she couldn't see. A vampire—she smelled them, smelled the dead body of a Blood Guard on the ground. They were missing their head, while a second Blood Guard, who still lived but was badly injured, leaned up against the wall near the same desolate horde that congregated next to the truck. The still-living Blood Guard stank of his own blood, something that Church decided was almost certainly a bad thing. There was no time for that now, she had to get to Amelia. Had to rescue her.

Fucking hell, Church thought, barking several times to let everyone know exactly how she felt. She'd picked up swearing from Miles.

She ran at the horde of desolate just as the Blood Guard roared and charged into battle, swinging his sword around to cleave the heads from any desolate stupid enough to get in the way. It was Church's opinion that all desolate were stupid. She'd liked Lauren, but that wasn't the same.

She brought her thoughts back to the present and slammed into the first desolate at the legs, sending it spiralling back into the others like a bowling ball. She moved far too quickly for any of the desolate to get anywhere near her, but not quick enough to stop a group of them from killing the seriously injured vampire Blood Guard.

Before she could kill the rest, Carol Walters and a dozen guard members charged into the fray, all of them in their vampire forms. The resulting battle was bloody and quick, which was pretty much how Church liked all battles to go. When it was done, Church found Carol and barked twice.

"What is it?" Carol asked.

Church barked again, frustrated that this particular vampire didn't know that two barks was bad.

Church ran over to the tyre tracks of the van that had barrelled away. She pawed at the ground, looked back at Carol, and pawed again, willing the stupid vampire to understand her.

"We saw the truck," Carol said. "Who was in it?"

It was Amelia, you fucking cretin, Church thought, barking four times to get her point across.

"They took Amelia and Thomas," a young woman said as she left the nearby motel reception area. She was covered in blood, too, and Church wondered if it was as much fun for them to roll around in it as it was for her.

"Who took her?" Carol asked.

Church forced herself to concentrate on the new woman. She smelled familiar.

"Jenny, Travis, Jeremy," the woman said. "They knocked out Thomas, and killed Arvid."

Church remembered that her name was Maeve. She looked around to see if anyone was going to tell her she'd done great, decided now probably wasn't the time, and started to sniff the ground again. The truck was moving at speed, but she could catch up.

"Jenny was driving," Maeve said. "I don't think Thomas even knew what was happening."

"He's an administrator," Carol said.

"He's still a vampire," Maeve said. "He was helping me kill the desolate. They came up in the middle of the common room. There were humans in there."

"Go look," Carol said to one of the guards with her.

Church looked between the two women and willed them to say something useful. *Do you know where they are going?* she asked, barking several times so that someone might actually pay attention.

"You know where they're going?" Carol asked Church.

Church blinked. *How have you survived this long?* She barked a few times, and decided to paw at the tyre tracks of the military truck.

"You want to go after them?" Carol asked.

Church wondered if Miles was some sort of dog genius for actually understanding her when she did stuff. She barked once for yes. Surely these idiots understood once meant yes.

"Is one bark yes?" a newcomer asked.

Church barked once, relieved that they finally might be getting somewhere.

"Miles said she understood us," Maeve said, looking back at Church. "Do you know where they've taken Thomas and Amelia?"

Church turned back to Maeve. Two barks. Now we were getting somewhere.

"Can you follow them?"

Church rolled her eyes.

"She didn't bark," Carol said.

Church wondered how many barks it would take for Carol to not be stupid. She barked once and looked over at Maeve, who was clearly the more intelligent of the vampires she had to deal with. She wished Miles was here.

"If you go ahead, we'll send people with you," Carol said.

Church barked once.

"I'll come with you," Maeve said.

Church snorted before she could stop herself, decided the conversation was over, and turned on her heels, running off through the town, following the truck. She had a lot of ground to make up, but the scent was strong, and she wanted those in the truck to think she wasn't following. She wanted them to get complacent. She wanted to see the look on their face when she grabbed them by the throat and squeezed. Dog revenge was the best revenge.

She smelled Maeve before she caught up with her, quite impressed that the young vampire could actually keep up to begin with.

"We're going to get them back," Maeve said. "Thomas is a good man, and Amelia was nice to me."

Church let out a low growl of determination, and continued on without slowing. They soon reached another hole, and lots of dead desolate surrounding it, along with many vampires who had died protecting their home. Many more still lived, although the large gates to the city were wide open.

Church wanted to continue on through the gates, but there was a scent in the air that made her stop. Her ears twitched as she looked around, trying to place where the smell was coming from.

Maeve went over to talk to several of the guards, and Church continued to feel something she couldn't quite place. The scent was all desolate, although considering they were everywhere in town, that wasn't a surprise. But it was something else. A condensed, powerful scent, like someone opening a can of fish. A wave of smell that felt as if it was continuously crashing against her senses.

Church stepped outside of the gates as the horde of desolate tore through the hillside toward them. She barked over and over, until people came to see what the trouble was.

"Oh my god," Maeve said. "Church, you'll have to go on alone. I'll stay and help here."

Church looked up at Maeve and snorted.

"Be careful," Maeve told her.

Church barked once, hoping Maeve would understand that she was saying good luck, turned, and ran down the road as fast as her legs could carry her. The roar of desolate as they rushed toward the city gate threatened to overwhelm her sense of smell, but she pushed on, tracking the vehicle with her friend inside.

She'd run for several minutes when she stopped because the ground had shaken. She looked back at the city of Bangor in the distance. She hoped it would still be there when she found Amelia and Thomas. There were a few desolate who had broken off from the hundreds strong horde and had started toward her, but they were no threat, and were far enough away that they'd either find something easier to hunt, or they'd be unlucky enough to catch her. She was not in the mood to play with her prey.

Church continued along the road, which quickly turned into cold mud where the concrete had deteriorated or in some places been destroyed all together. She didn't care; she only cared about the task at hand.

She continued running for some time, never stopping to drink or eat, never deviating from the trail laid out before her. The vehicle she tracked took several detours. Church assumed it was done to see if they could stop her from following them. It wasn't going to work. The smell of diesel, the smell of Amelia, of the vampires. The fear that peppered it all. It was a cornucopia of scents that there would have been no way for Church to ignore, even if she'd wanted to. She occasionally came across a lone desolate, but they were worth neither the time nor the effort to deal with.

The landscape was sparse, with no lights except for the moon above, but that was fine; Church could see without artificial lighting. It made things easier for her, as her sense of smell was good enough to take her where she needed to go.

Eventually, she saw lights in the distance. Like all dogs, Church had red-green colour blindness. She could see other colours just fine, but she didn't need to see the colours of red and green to notice the van parked up along the side of the road.

Church moved into the trees that nestled on either side of her, and continued on toward the van. She moved quietly, but maintained her speed, and was soon at the van, sniffing around the back of it to make sure she had the right one. She did.

She sniffed the air and followed the scents of Thomas, Amelia, and several others, as they walked along a dirt road into thick woods close to the truck. Church followed, keeping low and quiet as she moved through the darkness of the forest.

The farther into the forest, the more intense the scents got, and they were soon followed up with the sounds of voices. Church knew that vampires had a good sense of smell, considerably better than a human's, but she also knew that beyond knowing something or someone was there, they still weren't good enough to pick out individuals, unless they were tracking their blood. Church knew they wouldn't have picked out her specific scent during their time in Bangor, and she doubted any of them could pick it out from the time they'd spent with her on the pilgrimage. Even so, she would need to be careful.

After a few minutes of walking, Church arrived at a large barn. There were several people outside, whose scents immediately gave them away as vampires. They were clearly the guard to the main barn entrance. Church stayed within the safety of the trees, and made a circuit of the barn, discovering it had multiple desolate sitting around it, looking out to nothing. *Waiting for what?* Church thought.

The light inside the barn spilled out over the surrounding area, illuminating a lot of machinery that looked to Church like something which would be used to dig. There were several military-style trucks too, and more than once, as she completed her circuit, she spotted motion detectors on trees, and trip wires, all easily avoidable.

She'd made her complete circuit when the barn doors opened, revealing a large number of people digging inside. Amelia and Thomas were sitting on chairs at the side of the barn, as a man she didn't recognise spoke to a second man in dark-coloured robes whom Church had also never seen before. Judging from the yelling, the second man was in charge.

Amelia was taken out of the barn, and Church moved back deeper into the woods, following from a distance as a large man with a stick pushed Amelia along. He took her up a path at the rear of the barn, to a second building, which was made of wood and brick and looked to Church like a house. The house was surrounded with a small lawn, and had flowers planted all around the border of it. The second the man and Amelia walked over the lawn, a powerful light came on, illuminating the entire area.

The door opened, and Amelia was shoved inside, the man with the stick retracing his steps back toward the barn, never knowing that Church was so close to him. Something about him smelled bad, not in an unwashed way, but in an unclean soul way. It was a scent that, like Amelia, masked his human smell, but it was . . . unpleasant. She knew, without ever needing to know anything else about him, that he was her enemy. *Magic*, she thought. *He's the witch.*

Church watched the witch walk back down the hill toward the barn, and when his scent had gone, she moved up to the house. There was a large open gap from the woods to the house itself, and despite the darkness, Church knew there would be no cover for her if she approached over the lit-up lawn. Instead, she walked around the perimeter of the house, listening out for anyone, or anything, and smelling only Amelia, and . . . Church paused, and got low to the ground. A werewolf. The smell was unmistakable.

The rear door of the house opened, and a large man stepped onto the decking, the light above the door illuminating him. "Who is out there?" he asked.

Church saw Amelia sitting inside the building, on a sofa. She looked up at the werewolf standing outside the house. Even in his human form, the werewolf could smell her; he just didn't know *who* she was. She could smell the confusion in him.

"Come here," the man said, going back inside, and dragging out another woman. "Get your desolate to comb this area."

Church recognised the woman immediately. It was Lauren from Seattle. A Desolate Queen, and someone whom Church had liked very much. Church's happiness at seeing a friend stopped when the werewolf went back inside the house, and Lauren walked down from the decking to the grass at the rear of the house.

A set of basement doors opened, and the desolate scrambled out of them, surrounding Lauren in a shield. "Who goes there?" she asked.

Church made up her mind and stepped out into the light, letting Lauren see her.

Lauren's hands went to her mouth, and she looked back at the door, before running over to Church, dropping to her knees and embracing her warmly. "Oh, Church," she said sadly. "I can't leave. I'm tethered here. I can't get away. They control me. You have to go get Miles. Do you understand?"

Church pawed at Lauren's hand once.

"Good girl," Lauren said. "Is Miles with you?"

Church pawed twice.

"Okay, you need to find him. If he rushes in here, Amelia will die."

Church pawed once.

"Can you get Miles, bring him here? We have to stop them before they raise a Dusk."

"Nice dog," Stuart said from the decking.

"She's just a dog," Lauren said, pushing Church slightly, and getting back to her feet. "Probably belongs to someone in the remains of Ellsworth."

"Big dog," Stuart said. "Doesn't that vampire Arbiter have a big dog?"

Lauren stepped in front of Church. "She's just a dog. Leave her be."

"Bring her here," Stuart said.

"No," Lauren snapped.

The talisman around his neck started to glow, and two men stepped out of the building nearby and began walking toward them.

Werewolves, Church thought, the smell coming off them easy to identify.

"Bring. Her. Here," Stuart commanded.

Lauren let out a scream of pain before shouting, "Run!"

Church let out a low growl. She wasn't afraid, but then she smelled the fear coming off Lauren in a crashing tsunami, and she stepped back. She needed to find Miles. He would know what to do. She turned and ran off into the darkness, followed by the howls of werewolves giving chase.

❧ CHAPTER THIRTY ❧

"Where is Church?" Miles asked.

The tram had taken Dr. Davies and himself to Bangor, ending at an underground station where the tunnel was partially collapsed, barring the tram from going further. The entrance of the station had been bricked up long ago, but a quick blast of telekinesis had seen it unbricked in short order. The number of armed people beyond who didn't look happy about it was somewhat of a surprise.

"Miles," Bethany said, motioning for the guards to lower their guns. "Dr. Davies."

"We have a lot of information," the doctor said. "Information I am happy to divulge. Why are these people here?"

Miles looked around the small park they were in. There were fires somewhere nearby; the smell of them would have been obvious even to a human. "What happened?" Miles asked.

"We had a desolate attack," Bethany said. "It's been resolved, and the desolate were stopped."

"Where are Church and Amelia?" Miles said, fear flooding his voice.

"Church was fine," Bethany said hurriedly.

"Was?" Miles asked, taking a step forward.

The guards raised their weapons once again, and Miles took a deep breath, calming himself.

"She took off after Amelia," Bethany said. "She was taken, along with Thomas. Thomas's Blood Guard were killed. Maeve said that Jenny and her friends kidnapped Thomas and Amelia. We're all cleaning up the town at the moment."

"How'd you know we'd be here?" the doctor asked.

"We didn't," Bethany said. "I've been doing a sweep of the area with my team, and we heard something underground. Thought it was another desolate attack."

"Which way did Church take off?" Miles asked.

"I'll take you," Bethany said. "Dr. Davies, please go with my people to the council offices. Carol and the other councillors will need to be told about what you found."

"Short answer," the doctor said, "a bunch of idiots are trying to raise a Dusk."

Bethany paused. "What? That can't be right, they don't exist."

"I'll explain on the way," Miles said. "Let's just get going. Doc, thanks for your help. Stay alive."

"I'll do my best," the doctor said.

Miles followed Bethany out of the park, and into an identical golf cart to the one he'd used when arriving in town. "Anyone else hurt?" he asked her.

"We've had several hundred people hurt, some seriously. About twenty deaths so far. We were prepared better for the attack than we would have been if you and the pilgrimage hadn't arrived."

Miles stayed quiet for the rest of the journey, until they reached the motel, where the Major stood, looking worse for wear. "You okay?" Miles asked him.

"Spent the last few hours killing desolate," the Major said. There were several deep gashes over his arms and face, and despite the fact that they were healing, he looked as if he'd been in a war.

"You going to heal up?"

The Major nodded. "It's been quite the few hours."

"What did you find out in Waterville?" Carol asked as she rushed out of the nearby building.

"The doctor will fill you in," Miles explained. "Just point me in the direction that Church went."

Carol pointed toward the eastern side of the city. "It's been hours."

"She'll be fine," Miles said, hoping that was the case. "You need to prepare for more desolate. There's a lot of them, and they're marching up the way from Augusta to Ellsworth Falls. Want to guess which town is in the way?"

"Those we saw?" the Major asked.

Miles nodded. "There's a lot more where they came from. I'm heading off now. If I'm not back by dawn, you need to prepare for the worst. Which is basically that the First Priest from House Idolator is possibly trying to resurrect a Dusk. Stuart and Liam are helping him, despite working with the Magistrate, because the blood of the Dusk might cure Stuart, although I think there's more to it than just a cure."

Carol and Bethany shared an expression that Miles took to mean *oh shit.*

"And you know all of this because?" Bethany asked.

"Partly because an old desolate who this Dusk created over a thousand years ago told me," Miles said. "And also because the First Priest is conducting a dig in Ellsworth, which is close to where the Dusk's burial ground is. I might be off, but he's either helping or he's dead. I doubt there's a third option here."

Bethany stared at Miles for a second before she said, "He's always talked about finding the burial ground of the Dusk. I figured it was just in an archaeological sense of the word. Not in an *actually bring them back from the dead* way."

"You believe this?" Carol asked Bethany, who nodded in reply.

"I need a car," Miles said. "I can start running, but I'd rather not."

"How do you know where they're going?" the Major asked.

"It's a longer story than I have time to tell, just trust me on this." Miles turned to Carol. "Vehicle please. Not a golf cart."

"We have some 4x4s we use for travelling around outside of the city," Carol said. "I'll get one sorted for you."

Miles took a moment and sighed.

"You okay?" the Major asked.

"Where's Maeve?" Miles asked him.

"Common room," the Major said, nodding toward the motel. "We turned it into a makeshift triage. She got pretty banged up during the fight. She'll be fine, but I don't think she's up for visitors."

"She mention Jenny?" Miles asked.

The Major nodded. "You know they killed the Blood Guards?"

"Aye," Miles said. "They'll get what's coming to them for it."

"Were they working for this Priest all along?" Bethany asked.

"I'll ask them that, too," Miles said.

"I assume nicely," Bethany asked.

Miles said nothing as Carol exited the council building at a run, throwing the keys to a Toyota to Miles. "It's around the back," she said. "All gassed up and ready for you."

"Be careful," the Major said. "These people are clearly not fussed about hurting folk."

Miles was already in a flat-out run to the side of the building, and used the key fob to find which of the four Toyota Land Cruisers was his. A short time later, he was in the driver's seat and speeding away. There were several triage stations all along the road, with a lot of people being seen to by clearly overworked doctors and nurses.

The gate at the end of the city limits was in the process of being fixed, and after stating his purpose, Miles was waved through. He drove as fast as the terrain would allow, and was constantly irritated at having to slow to a crawl in his pursuit of wherever Church had gone.

After thirty minutes of driving with all of the windows down in an effort to get even a hint of Church's scent, Miles was almost halfway toward Ellsworth Falls. Driving at such a crawl didn't do much to help Miles's need to find Thomas, Amelia, and Church, but the road was bad, and the trail went all over the place, not just a straight shot toward Ellsworth. Presumably, the driver of the escape vehicle was trying to evade Church. *Good luck with that,* he thought.

Miles pulled over to the side of what remained of the road, stopped the car, and got out. The moon was still high, and he had no idea where Church would have gone, but he was sure this was the direction she would have taken.

Miles walked for a few minutes along the soft ground until he heard a howl in the distance. Wolf howls had a strange effect at night in that you were never sure if they were a hundred feet in front of you or a mile away. All Miles knew for sure was that it was no normal wolf.

After placing his bag in the car, he turned into his beast form and took to the sky. He looked out over the trees and flew toward Ellsworth Falls, hoping to catch sight of movement below. His sense of smell in beast form was considerably better than in his human appearance, and his vision at night was good enough that it would let him see the movement of a mouse on a woodland floor.

Miles had been flying for only a few seconds when he saw movement out of the corner of his eye. He turned to see something move beneath the gaps in the tree canopy far below him. Something large darted along the floor of the forest, and as he tried to pick up what it was, he saw two more large somethings moving after the first. He caught a whiff of their scent. *Werewolves.*

With prey in his sights, he beat his wings once and took off after whatever was moving beneath the trees. He turned his wings slightly and flew down beneath the tree canopy, moving between huge tree trunks and branches with deft turns as he tried to keep his speed up to catch the fast-moving creatures in front of him.

Those on the forest floor moved with such speed and agility that Miles wasn't sure he could catch up to them, but then he caught a scent of the lead animal: Church.

Miles let out a roar and beat his wings, speeding up toward Church, who was slowing down. The two werewolves—which he could now smell easily—turned to look back at Miles as he dove down atop one of them, driving his talons into the werewolf's throat and tearing it out.

The werewolf dropped to the ground as Miles sprang off it, clipping the back leg of the werewolf in front and sending it sprawling to the ground with a sliced tendon across its foot. With both werewolves on the floor, Miles stood between them.

"Vampire," the closest werewolf said.

Miles moved quickly toward the werewolf with the damaged throat, taking it by the scruff of the neck and soaring up into the sky as he held it aloft.

The werewolf struggled, stopping when he realised they were several hundred feet above the ground. A werewolf could heal a lot, but that didn't mean they wanted to experience the impact of having their body broken.

Miles beat his wings, brought the werewolf close to him, and said, "How many left?"

"Liam," the werewolf said hoarsely, his body healing from the deep wound across his throat. "I'll tell you whatever you want to know."

"I don't want to know anything," Miles said, and let the werewolf drop the near thousand feet back to the ground.

Miles overtook the falling werewolf, slowing his descent just as he hit the top of the trees. Branches snapped from the impact as he flew toward the ground where the second werewolf was close to a snarling Church who had come back to finish the werewolf off.

The second werewolf hit the ground a moment later, the scream that accompanied the fall immediately silenced.

Miles smashed into the back of the werewolf at speed, breaking its spine in a dozen places, and sending it into the ground with such force that it threw up a crater of dirt around them. He placed one foot on the back of the werewolf's neck, grabbed its head in both hands, and tore it free, tossing it aside.

Miles turned back to his human form and dropped to his knees to hug Church, who buried her face in his neck. "It's good to see you, too," Miles said, scratching Church behind the ears. "You know where Amelia and Thomas are?"

Church barked once.

"Good girl," Miles said. "You show me in a moment. I'll go finish off the other werewolf."

Miles walked back toward the unconscious werewolf, who instead of hitting the trees had missed them and smashed into what remained of the road in front of the Toyota, making quite the mess in the process. Miles killed him in the same way he had the first, tossing the werewolf's head into a nearby bush. He was very much done with playing nice.

Church stood by Miles as he removed his bag from the Toyota. "How many bad guys?" Miles asked her.

Church pawed at the ground with both feet several times.

"A lot," Miles said.

Church nodded.

"Did you see Amelia or Thomas?" Miles asked her. "Maybe Stuart or Liam?"

Church wagged her tail and barked once.

"All of them?"

Church whined.

"Amelia?"

Church barked.

"Stuart?"

Church barked.

"Thomas?"

Church barked again.

"But not Liam?"

Church barked twice, before growling.

"You could smell him?"

Church barked.

"Are there other people there?" Miles asked.

Church barked again, before whining.

"You didn't see them, but there are?"

Church barked.

"Right," Miles said. "We need to get to this place. Can you take point on this? There's a witch there, right?"

Church barked.

"You did good," Miles said, scratching her behind the ear. "Let's go get people to safety."

Church took off with Miles following behind. He never let her out of his sight as they ran through the forest, easily avoiding branches as they moved at speed. Miles had missed running with her, with having someone beside him who he knew, with every ounce of his being, would have his back. The sense of relief he felt that she was okay was palpable. If either of those werewolves had hurt her, he would have done much worse to them than he had.

It took an hour before Church slowed to a trot, and another thirty minutes before she stopped. Maybe he'd find something useful while in Ellsworth.

Church sat still as Miles crouched beside her, looking at the house before him, and a barn farther away. The barn was old, made of wood, with parts of it looking rotten even from a distance. The house, however, appeared to be in good condition from the outside. As Miles looked at the front of the building, he closed his eyes and took a long sniff, recognising Amelia's perfume. It was subtle, but there was definitely a hint of it going up to the house. He wished he had Church's nose.

Miles followed Church around the perimeter of the house, letting him see the small garden, the basement shutters, and the spotlights over the front and back doors. He wondered if there were alarms on the doors and windows too. Probably a good idea to expect the unexpected.

Miles remained crouched looking at the back door with Church beside him. He needed to get inside. He didn't want to leave either Thomas or Amelia, nor anyone else for that matter, to the devices of the kinds of people that Liam and Stuart were.

He paused. The werewolves would probably be able to smell him if Church could smell them. He wondered just how good their noses were, and wished he'd taken some of the doc's grenades from down in the city.

Miles sighed; if they knew he was here, there was nothing he could do about it. He needed to hurry and hope for some luck.

He motioned for Church to stay where she was, and he moved around to the side of the building. There was no obvious entry point there, with the two windows both boarded up, just like every other window on the property. He could pull the boards free, but they would alert anyone inside, and that was the last thing he wanted to do.

He ran to the house wall and, using his talons, scaled the wall as quickly and quietly as possible, landing silently on the roof. Miles walked along the top of the roof to the attic skylight, which was also boarded up, but the lack of proximity to those inside the building meant he could use his telekinesis to slowly prise the nails free of the wooden boards. The glass window beneath it was another matter, and shattering the glass would alert everyone inside. He picked up the four wooden boards and tossed them over the side of the house, using his telekinesis to shatter the glass window the second they hit, catching the shards before they hit the floor of the attic. There was still noise, but he hoped it was muffled by the sounds of the boards.

Sure enough, he heard footsteps below and the front door slam open. There was no voice, and the door quickly slammed shut again, as Miles placed the broken glass on the floor and removed the telekinetic bubble around them. He crossed the attic floor slowly and remained crouched at the wooden hatch. It was attached to an old ladder, and Miles was pretty sure the second the hatch moved, the ladder would fall down, making a lot of noise.

Miles moved back under the skylight and waited until he heard footsteps coming up the stairs. He leapt up, back out of the skylight, landing softly on the roof, where he jumped off, onto the ground next to the back door. He opened the door and stepped into the empty kitchen, where Liam sat at the table, Amelia beside him. He was in his human form, his hand wrapped around her neck, his eyes the yellow of a werewolf.

"You really want to see her head pop off?" Liam asked.

"She dies, you die harder," Miles told him. "My advice would be to start running and never stop."

Liam pointed through the kitchen door beside him. Miles didn't move.

"You're going to want to see this," Liam said. "I'm not going to hurt her, just come look."

Miles walked toward Liam until he could see through the door. Thomas sat on a sofa with Jenny beside him, a shotgun pointed at the First Authority's head. A slight smile played on her lips.

"He'll live," Miles said.

"It's an explosive round," Liam said. "Templar International was working on them. At that distance, it will remove Thomas's head."

"So what's your plan here, Liam?" Miles asked.

"You should have just come to meet our boss," Liam said. "None of this would have been necessary."

"First Priest Pedro de Moxica?" Miles asked.

"You know?" Liam asked.

"His name popped up a few times over the last couple of days," Miles said. "Apparently, he's big into finding something near Ellsworth. When I found out that the Dusk's burial ground was around here somewhere, I figured he was involved. Nice to have it confirmed."

Liam bristled slightly; apparently he hadn't meant to confirm something Miles hadn't already known.

Miles smiled, enjoying the mild discomfort on the face of the werewolf. Because when you're about to be someone's captive, you get your enjoyment where you can. "What did he want with me?"

"Why don't we go talk to him and you can see for yourself," Liam said. "No one has to die here today."

"A lot of people have already died today," Miles said.

"No one else, then," Liam snapped. "We go for a little walk, everyone lives. Thomas will stay here with people I trust, and if you cause any trouble, I'll have them kill him, and I'll pop Amelia's head. Do we understand each other?"

Miles nodded. "Who went up the stairs to check on the attic?"

"You remember Travis, one of Jenny's friends," Liam said. "We've all been working to get this done for a long time."

"I don't get it," Miles said. "I already know that you're working with Commander Bailey because he sucks at lying. I know he works for the Magistrate, because he's a hateful prick. I know that you work for the Magistrate, because I had people look into your time in the CIA, and it popped up more than once. I also know that you're working to raise a Dusk from their grave. Not sure how those two things can work."

"Need a cure for Stuart," Liam said.

"There's no such thing as a cure," Miles told him. "The only cure for being a witch is death. He's a witch. Can't change that."

"A Dusk can," Liam said, letting a little anger out. "The First Priest told us all."

"First Priest lied to you," Miles said, feeling no need to say where that information came from. "He just wants to resurrect the Dusk, I assume because he's insane. Do you know what will happen once Ulfrik wakes up?"

"Not my problem," Liam said, motioning to the door with his free hand. "Move. And if that dog does anything, I'll make you watch as I kill her, too."

Miles kept his anger in check. There would be time for it later. "Where's Lauren?"

"Safe," Liam said. "You'll see her soon enough."

Miles stared at Liam, and looked over to Amelia. "You okay? Considering."

Amelia smiled slightly. "Not my best day."

"You two can chat amongst yourselves later," Liam said. "Move."

"Go fuck yourself," Miles said.

Liam let go of Amelia and pushed the table aside as he stood. He radiated anger and a need for violence. "When this is done, you'll be dead, and I'll hunt down everyone you care about," the werewolf said, his words low and gruff. "And if by some miracle you can keep a civil tongue in your head and you make it out of here alive, I'll happily make you watch as I kill your dog and hunt down your friends, bringing them back so you can watch as I take my time with them. You should be thanking your lucky stars if you die here, *boy.* It means you escaped my wrath."

Miles's smile was unpleasant and he thought he saw a glimmer of worry in Liam's expression. "It's a date," he said. "Now go take me to your boss, I think the grown-ups need to talk."

CHAPTER THIRTY-ONE

Miles was marched along the path toward the large barn he'd seen in the distance. He knew that Church was nearby, just out of sight, watching from the darkness of the woods that surrounded them.

"I can smell your dog," Liam hissed in Miles's ear. "You think I should go bring her, make you watch as I—"

Miles stopped walking and turned to face Liam. "Not on your best day could you take Church."

Liam's face contorted with anger.

"You let the werewolf control you," Miles said calmly. "You're just a ball of rage and hate."

Liam pushed Miles a little, who took a step back from the force. He looked over at Amelia, who remained on Liam's side, and back to Liam. "Do you remember when the werewolf started to take control?"

The snarl that left Liam's lips told Miles that he did.

Miles nodded sadly, turned, and recommenced walking toward the barn.

"Why aren't you angry?" Liam shouted after him, shoving him in the back when Miles didn't respond. "Why are you so fucking calm?"

Miles took a deep breath and let it out slowly before turning back to Liam again. "You want me to see your boss, so let's go. You want to fight, we'll do that instead. The vampire part of me doesn't control who I am, Liam. I control it. I don't think you'd enjoy seeing me lose control."

Liam stepped up toward Miles.

"You're like one of those people on a night out," Miles said softly. "You've had too much to drink, maybe a bit too much coke, too. You think you're invincible, you think you're the toughest man in the world, and you're so desperate for a fight that anything you perceive as a slight should be met with brute force. Someone says something innocuous, or they bump into you, and you meet that small act with a completely unnecessary level of violence.

"You ruin lives, you take lives, and all because you need to show the world how tough you are. Because inside you're a man who never lived up to whatever potential he believed he had. Or a man who thinks the world owes him something. Or someone who just bullies others to make himself feel better. Either way, you offer nothing good to this world. And when you're gone from it, the only people who mourn you will be those who never really knew you. Because anyone who knows you thinks you're little more than a piece of shit."

Liam stood still for a moment as Miles turned and continued on his path.

"Don't you walk away from me!" Liam shouted, the words coming out a growl. The werewolf inside of him was in control now. Probably had been for a long time.

Miles reached the barn, the main doors of which were wide open, showing a dig site inside. Black stone covered the floor. A dozen desolates stood guard, and moved aside as a man in long red and purple robes strolled toward Miles, who was still ignoring the furious growling from behind him.

"First Priest Pedro de Moxica," Miles said.

The First Priest clapped his hands together and bowed his head slightly. He was a slender man of about five and a half feet tall, with long dark hair streaked with grey that fell over his shoulders. He had a neatly groomed beard that was more salt than pepper and bright green eyes.

Miles recognised him immediately. "You were with the Pilgrims," he said, remembering the scene that Dr. Davies had placed in his head. "With First Lord Fuller."

The First Priest tried and failed to hide his surprise. "How do you know that?" he asked, looking behind Miles at Liam. "Is there a problem?"

"He offended me," Liam said.

The First Priest shrugged. "So? Go do your job. Leave the girl here with us—I brought her because she is going to tell the world what's really happening here. About the rebirth of a god. It's good that she wasn't killed during her stay here; I do so hate to lose valuable assets. The First Lord sent you here to cover the pilgrimage, but you're going to get a better story."

"I didn't come here for the story," Amelia said as she stood beside Miles, who watched Liam walk away. "I came to reclaim what is not Stuart's to own. I've come to see justice done for those he murdered."

The First Priest looked confused for a moment. "Oh, he didn't tell me that. He stole the grimoire? Is that it?"

Amelia said nothing.

"Oh, you'll like this next bit, then," the First Priest said, before looking back at Miles. "You appear to have angered my werewolf."

"I think he's your last one," Miles said. "I don't think he's too happy about that."

"You kill the rest?"

"Some," Miles said. "I think two of them are in the city that Ulfrik had his thousands of slaves build. Although I'm pretty sure they'll be dead by now, too."

The First Priest smiled. "You know about that? Good. It will save us all some time. Oh, I believe you know this lady, too." He snapped his fingers and Lauren Gibson walked out of the pit.

"Miles," Lauren said softly, her single word slurred.

Miles looked from Lauren to the First Priest, and desperately wanted to wipe the smile from his face. "If you've hurt her," he said softly. "We will definitely have a problem."

"She's not injured," the First Priest said. "We took her from Augusta. Ulfrik himself brought her there, spoke to her over the weeks and months beforehand, in preparation for her coming here. He told me to retrieve her, that she could help ensure the digging remained on schedule."

"He's awake?" Miles asked, thinking back to how the Viking hadn't wanted Ulfrik to be awakened because Ulfrik was essentially a powerful psychopath. It sounded like the First Priest either didn't know, or didn't care. His rush to raise his . . . *god* more urgent than his need for that same god to be in peak condition.

"Semiconscious," the First Priest said. "Have you ever spoken to a god while you slept? It's quite the experience."

Miles noticed that Lauren only looked ahead. "You're controlling her."

"Ulfrik is," the First Priest said. "We tried to do it nicely, but she wouldn't play along. And when Stuart is around, his talisman helps and allows Ulfrik to rest more."

"You sent him the talisman, yes?" Miles asked.

The First Priest nodded. "Gave it to Liam, told him to give it to Stuart. A chaos witch is hard to find, and I knew he would make a great ally. The talisman amplified his power, and it allows the wearer to control the desolate, even Desolate Royalty to a degree. Although we had to drug her first and bring her back here because we weren't sure just how much control he would have. Turns out, she's quite compliant, although we can't send her off to kill people; her will is quite extraordinary. And in the meantime, it helps keep Stuart alive. It'll be a shame when Ulfrik takes it back."

"And Ulfrik was okay with this?" Miles asked.

"Of course. He is uninterested in *how* he is resurrected, just that he is."

Miles stared at the First Priest. "I wonder, do you know that he's going to awaken underpowered? Maybe even vulnerable."

"Nonsense," the First Priest snapped.

"Oh, so you do know, you just don't care," Miles said. "You just want your daddy back."

The First Priest looked ready to launch himself at Miles. "Ulfrik will strengthen over time. He is ready to awaken. I have assured him that he will be glorious."

"I know Ulfrik is weakened," Miles said with a slight chuckle. "You were there when he first arrived. So, you're . . . you're one of the Dark. You're literally his child trying to claim his father's favour from someone else, in this case First Lord Fuller."

"You know *nothing*," the First Priest shouted.

"Where were you when he started murdering all of the vampires he created because he was afraid he couldn't control them?"

The First Priest reacted as if slapped across the face.

"You know," Miles continued, "he was murdering your fellow Dark because he couldn't control them. First Lord Fuller was already out of the country when it happened, I assume you didn't take part in the attack on the Dusk, otherwise he wouldn't be happy to talk to you. He certainly wouldn't be happy to see you. Which means you either heard about it happening later, because how could you not, or you knew it was happening and you ran away."

"You don't know what you're talking about," the First Priest repeated dismissively.

"You still letting Stuart think there's a cure?" Miles asked, needling the man as much as possible.

"He's a dangerous man," the First Priest said, rubbing his hands through his hair, seeming to calm himself in the process. "Dangerous men make good short-term allies, but only if you can control them."

Miles ignored the First Priest and looked to Lauren. "That true?" he asked.

She nodded, her eyes finally focusing on Miles after several seconds. "I have to control the desolate. Keep them calm. I can't stop."

"Release her," Miles said.

"I do that, and the control stops," the First Priest said. "There are *a lot* of desolate here. I don't think anyone wants them to wake up and find out they're hungry."

Miles bit back his reply and walked into the barn, the smell of blood causing him to pause for a beat.

"Oh, yes, sorry, I sometimes forget that not everyone is as used to the working conditions as we are," the First Priest said. "It'll pass."

"What did you do with the blood in the mines?" Miles asked.

"What?" the First Priest asked.

"There was a pool of bodies, but you collected the blood, why?"

The First Priest's smile was unpleasant. "The bodies were to feed the desolate. They do so love flesh, even if it's not fresh. The blood was to feed those desolate who were cocooned. You know about those, yes?"

Miles nodded. "So, you pumped blood into the cocoons. You're helping to create more giant desolate. It's going to take a long time for them to be ready."

"We have time," the First Priest said as he motioned toward the pit where a set of steps led down to a large wooden door, which was already open. All four of them descended the steps, with Miles wondering how he could get everyone out in one piece before all hell inevitably broke loose.

"What is this?" Amelia asked.

"Some might call it a burial chamber," the First Priest said. "But it's more of a dungeon. We've got a few minutes to walk until we reach our destination. The dungeon is safe, Lauren here has made sure any desolate inside are no longer an issue, and we've tidied it up, but do be careful where you step."

Just inside the dungeon entrance were more desolates lined up on either side, all with vacant stares as the First Priest and his "guests" walked by.

As they reached the end, two desolates, who were both huge, took up the front of the group and walked with them along the hallways and through large chambers for several minutes. Miles thought for a moment about killing the First Priest, but the idea of Amelia being caught in the crossfire was an unacceptable outcome, and Thomas being back at the house meant his death was almost assured should anyone outside of the tunnels become aware.

"This is amazing," Amelia whispered as they walked through a chamber which had hundreds of small crystals hanging from the ceiling. "I know we're in deep shit, but even so."

The First Priest laughed behind them. "No one else has to die here today. Liam wanted to kill you, but I decided that telling the story of my king would be preferable. You mentioned you saw me, Miles. How?"

"A desolate that Ulfrik created," Miles said, seeing little point in lying. "Don't know his name, because he doesn't know his name. He was one of the Vikings who arrived with Ulfrik originally. He was there when you came ashore. He was there when you met Ulfrik for the first time. I saw you in his memory, stood behind the man who would become First Lord to House Idolator. The Dusk responsible for the bloodline of your House is a Viking warlord. A murderer of the innocent. Is that the true story you want Amelia to tell the world?"

"The minor details of my king's history won't matter," the First Priest said with no hint of irritation at Miles's words. "My king was a Viking. But he's so much more than that now. He helped build us a city beneath Maine. A city for the vampires. Unfortunately, I didn't remember where it was built. Neither did First Lord Fuller. We knew it was in Maine, and he was content with that knowledge, but I *needed* to know more."

"You didn't know where it was built?" Miles asked. "But you were both Dark, both his first children. Unless . . ."

"Unless what?" the First Priest snapped, practically daring Miles to continue.

"You weren't part of his inner circle then?" Amelia asked.

"By the time my king was laid to rest, he had sent his vampire children away to tend to other things," the First Priest said. "Only the desolate were allowed with him. I believe it was safer if none of his children knew where he was buried."

"He didn't trust you," Miles said with a laugh. "He only trusted the desolate because he could control them, as I mentioned earlier about him murdering the vampires he created."

The First Priest looked between Miles and Amelia, radiating anger. "I would tread *very* carefully."

"You were here before it fell," Miles said. "You got out just before Maine fell. You were looking for the city back then, weren't you?"

"Guilty," the First Priest said. "I wasn't First Priest then, just a lowly member of House Idolator. I assume you're about to ask me if I'm guilty of causing the fall."

"Are you?"

"No," the First Priest said with a wave of his hand as if dismissing the very notion of the idea. "I wasn't a scientist; I was an archaeologist. I went around the state, and New Brunswick too, testing soil samples, trying to figure out where Ulfrik had built his great city. Assuming he had been buried inside its grandeur. By the time I found the truth, that the scientists had managed to find the city, it was too late. The desolate were released, and the fall happened. After that, no one alive knew exactly where the entrance to the city was, except that it was in Augusta. Took me a long time to actually find it."

"Why does Commander Bailey keep people away from Augusta?" Miles asked.

The First Priest smiled. "Liam has been working with me for a long time. Did you know that he's also part of the Magistrate?"

"It came up," Miles said.

"He got the Commander to agree to spread the rumour that Augusta was a death trap, so that Liam and his people could finish searching for the city in peace. Didn't want people finding out that actually the desolate there really are small in number."

"You're looking for the library," Miles said. "I know why Stuart and Liam are. They think there's information about a cure for Stuart there. To use the Dusk's blood. It won't work, you know that, right?"

The First Priest said nothing.

"And you thought that Ulfrik's tomb would be down there, too," Miles continued. "So you had them do your dirty work, but when you figured out the burial ground was here, you decided you'd just let your helpers continue as they were out of your way. Means you don't have to answer any awkward questions when Ulfrik wakes up. How'd you find the burial ground, anyway?"

"There's a great library under Brunswick," the First Priest said. "It has a great many wondrous things there. Including information about my king's burial, and those desolate he considered his closest to stand watch over him. It's where I found the talisman that Stuart wears. Finding that place is what led me to my king."

The level of pride in the voice of the First Priest reminded Miles that he was dealing with someone who *believed*.

"Ulfrik could have just told you where it was," Miles said.

"The attack that left him in this state has made his memories suffer," the First Priest said, sounding a lot more confident in his words than Miles did. "He knew roughly where it was, near the ocean, but we needed access to Brunswick to get to it. We'd already started digging in Augusta when I managed to get information out of Ulfrik. My king congratulated me on a job well done."

"Pride goeth before destruction," Miles said, aware that his comments were infuriating the First Priest, but not caring much about it.

The First Priest glared at him.

"What did Liam promise him?" Amelia asked.

"What the Magistrate always want," the First Priest said, happy to be back on a conversation that didn't ask him questions he didn't want to think about. "Power."

"How?" Miles asked.

"I may have fabricated a little bit of information about what the blood of a Dusk can do," the First Priest said.

"You know, it would be better if you didn't speak in riddles," Amelia said.

The First Priest readjusted his robes and let out a sigh. "It was Liam's idea. He told Bailey that he'd *found* a centuries old document detailing how the blood of a Dusk could be used to cure vampirism. Could be used as a weapon against vampires. The Magistrate ate it up. They think they're going to get a weapon that kills vampires, and that Liam and Stuart will kill me, capture Ulfrik, and take him to them. Bailey thinks that Liam and Stuart are going to double-cross me and get him the blood of my king."

"You told them that Dusk blood kills vampires?" Miles asked.

The First Priest nodded, clearly pleased with himself. "A weapon to put humans on equal footing with vampires. Commander Bailey jumped at the chance. Agreed to let Liam research down in the library, which allowed me to sneak in and continue my search. It didn't take long to find what I was looking for."

"Miles was right," Amelia said. "You're going through a lot to raise your long comatose dad."

"He's not my father," the First Priest snapped. "He is more important to me than my father ever was."

"If only more therapists could suggest that as a way to help people with parent issues," Amelia said.

"I don't need therapy," the First Priest snapped.

"You really do," Miles said. "A lot."

"Move," the First Priest said, and Miles noticed the power inside the First Priest.

"How'd you hide what you are?" Miles asked as they started walking again.

"You are right about William—sorry, First Lord Fuller—and I both being the first generation of true vampires," the First Priest said. "The *Dark*, they call us. It's a stupid label for an important people. I asked him to keep my origins secret. I didn't need the notoriety, I told him, but in truth, it was just easier to operate without the eye of House Idolator's people watching me. Expecting me to become something. People always expected William to become something. It took him to the death of the old First Lord to do it—I would have bumped off the old bastard long before."

"You don't like First Lord Fuller much, do you?" Amelia asked.

"He is a man of little vision," First Priest de Moxica said. "A man who is happy to bumble along with all the power and comforts his position affords him. I am a visionary. I see only how to better our people."

"By waking up a long-dead monster," Lauren said. They were the first words out of her mouth for several minutes.

First Priest de Moxica stopped walking and turned to Lauren, as Miles and Amelia looked back at them. "We must be too far from Stuart; his influence is waning. No matter, we'll be with Ulfrik soon enough."

Lauren shrugged, although it looked as if she might fall over after. She raised a middle finger in his direction.

First Priest de Moxica slapped Lauren across the cheek, but the Desolate Queen didn't flinch, just swayed slightly from side to side. She stared at the First Priest with an expression of defiance, which was quickly replaced with the glazed-over look from earlier.

"Keep fucking walking," First Priest de Moxica bellowed at Miles and Amelia.

The silence that followed was uncomfortable at best, although it only lasted a few minutes before Amelia said, "Did Thomas know you were working against the House?"

"No one knew," the First Priest said. "And I'm not working *against* my House, my House only exists because of Ulfrik. I am bringing my House into the next age. I am placing them back among the Great Houses where they deserve to be once again. For too long, we have suffered ill effective rule from people with no vision for the future. Bringing back our Dusk will solve that. I am giving back my House's legacy and our rightful place within the vampire world."

"And getting lots of people killed," Miles said. "You do know that, yes? Ulfrik killed or enslaved tens of thousands of people during his lifetime."

"The weak need to be removed anyway," First Priest de Moxica sneered.

Miles knew there was no point in trying to get through to the First Priest; he was convinced he was right and that Ulfrik would bring about a new era of prosperity for his House. Besides, the man clearly wanted something from someone he considered a father figure, and Miles was pretty sure that something was never going to be achieved. The First Priest was the same as the desolate who couldn't even remember his own name, so utterly convinced that the power Ulfrik had given them had come from something pure. That Ulfrik was worthy of the praise and love he received. Everything that Miles had heard since finding the doctor had suggested the opposite was true. Ulfrik had enslaved, murdered, and built himself a city for vampires with what appeared to be the aim of keeping his name alive as some sort of benevolent god among the Dusk. The desolate had come to realise the truth, but the First Priest was far from anything close to a realisation.

The fact that Ulfrik clearly didn't trust anyone he couldn't directly control meant that Miles wondered what the endgame for the Dusk was. He wondered if maybe the Priest and Dusk weren't exactly on the same page for what was going to happen when the latter woke.

They eventually reached a large chamber, complete with a small waterfall at the far end, making the kind of constant noise you might expect in a garden feature. The walls of the chamber were adorned with dozens of torches, which lit up the entire room in a sort of spooky candlelight effect. At either side of the entrance were several stacks of wooden crates, and what appeared to be ornamental ceramic jars, each with a faded motif of the moon or sunset painted on them. In the centre of the chamber was a sarcophagus that was larger than any Miles had seen before, and he'd seen more than was probably normal for a person. It was made of the same black stone, but it was suspended by thick chains between four black stone pillars, two of which were missing their tops and were slightly bent away from the sarcophagus, giving the whole thing a skewed look.

"That the cause of the fall?" Miles asked, pointing to the two broken pillars.

"Every time one of his disciples died at the hands of those scientists, the power flooded back to Ulfrik, damaging the structure of what kept him entombed," the First Priest said.

"So what's the plan here?" Miles asked. "To destroy the pillars?"

"You'll see," the First Priest told him.

Miles took another step and saw the hole in the floor off to the side of the sarcophagus, the light inside bouncing off the steps. "What's down there?" he asked.

"The rest of the dungeon we stand in," the First Priest said. "It's a bit of a labyrinth down there. Never really managed to map all of it, although we're certainly trying."

"Why?" Amelia asked.

Stuart Murphy stepped out of the hole and dusted himself off. His talisman glowed a faint red colour, and Lauren stood a little straighter, staring ahead with no emotion on her face. Miles was going to have to do something about that.

Stuart looked over to Miles and frowned. "I see you survived."

"You too," Miles replied. "Can't have everything."

"Things would have been easier if you'd just come with us," Stuart said.

"Why?" Miles asked, looking back at the First Priest. "Why did you want to see me to begin with?"

"You are the son of Drest," the First Priest said.

"Not exactly," Miles told him.

"Okay, fine, you are the first generation of vampire after the Dark," the First Priest corrected. "Drest and I are children of the Dusk. We are the Dark. You are a child of the darkness."

"So?" Miles asked. "Stop lying and just tell me the truth. You do know how to do that, right?"

"You are from House Venator," the First Priest said. "You are a powerful vampire with a powerful *gift*."

"You want me as an insurance plan," Miles said. "If this goes wrong, my bloodline gift might be able to short-circuit Ulfrik. That's why you wanted my help?"

"Yes," the First Priest admitted. "You are exceptionally powerful. You killed Vedran. I wanted a House Venator vampire to come and aid me, but Drest would never have allowed it. When I heard about First Lord Fuller sending a . . . witch into Maine with a bodyguard who was from House Venator, I knew my prayers had been answered. And then you killed my people."

"I'm not going to kill your Dusk if he decides you're a disappointment," Miles snapped.

The First Priest laughed. "You couldn't kill him."

Miles stared at the First Priest for a moment. "No, just make him easier for you to kill."

"Never!" the First Priest shouted with far too much enthusiasm for someone trying to deny his plan. "He is our way forward. He is our light. He agrees with my plan for a better future."

"What plan?" Amelia asked.

The First Priest took a moment to compose himself once again.

"You want the vampires to be the main species," Miles guessed.

The First Priest laughed. "Humans aren't meant to *be*. They each possess the ability to be something else. Something *better*. We can help deliver that. We could make the world one where humans never have to fear us, because they *are* us."

Miles stared at the First Priest for a moment trying to figure out if he was insane, evil, or both. "You know that would kill a lot of people."

"The weak mean nothing," the First Priest said with a dismissive wave of his hand. "Three billion children of the Dark would make a far better world than seven billion humans."

"So you think half the world's population might die?" Amelia asked. "That's the plan?"

"A long-term goal starts with the first step," the First Priest said. "And that first step was to show someone close to a First Lord what we can achieve. We tried with Thomas, but he's a simpleton, and would never agree to such a thing."

"You're fucking mad," Miles said. "Actually fucking mad."

"Those with no vision always confuse the line of genius for madness," the First Priest said calmly.

"And you've decided to goose-step all over that fucker," Miles snapped, before looking back at Stuart. "You got your cure yet?"

Stuart's face clouded.

"Guess not," Miles said. "You do know you're not getting one, yes? The First Priest all but admitted that the talisman you're wearing is keeping you alive. Once his dad wakes up, he's going to find out that someone has his talisman hanging around their neck and take it back. Want to guess what happens to you?"

The First Priest moved to slap Miles, who caught his wrist an inch from his face, pushing the hand away.

"Don't embarrass yourself." Miles turned back to the sarcophagus and Stuart, the latter of whom was walking around the structure, pushing at the pillars as if testing them.

"You know, it's a shame," the First Priest said. "I'd hoped that you might have understood what we're trying to achieve here."

"You're waking up a Dusk so that people can die," Miles said. "They're asleep, or dead, or missing, for a reason. They're not meant to be running around anymore."

"We need them more than ever," the First Priest said as he moved Lauren over to the sarcophagus. "Now, stand there and behave."

Lauren did as she was told, turning to look back at the First Priest.

"Is it ready?" the First Priest asked Stuart, who nodded, raised his staff, and blasted Lauren in the chest with a plume of energy, splattering her blood over the sarcophagus and sending her sprawling down the open hole in the floor.

Miles darted forward toward the Priest, but was hit from behind by one of the two desolates, sending him sprawling to the floor by the sarcophagus. He tried to turn into his vampire form, but couldn't—it simply wouldn't happen.

The First Priest crouched down by Miles as Stuart grabbed at Amelia, but vines exploded out of the ground, pushing the chaos witch back.

The First Priest leaned over Miles and drove the dagger into his side over and over again, spilling Miles's blood over the sarcophagus.

Miles collapsed to the floor as his blood poured freely onto the ground, while the First Lord buried the bloody knife into a small hole on the lid of the black stone sarcophagus.

"Your blood will wake our king," the First Priest said. "It has so much power in it, Ulfrik won't be able to resist. He's almost woken right now. I can feel him on the edge of consciousness. He just needs a little more power to wake."

"No!" Amelia shouted, and turned and headbutted Stuart, who, considering how much magical power he had, was still a frail, deathly ill human. She tore the staff from Stuart's hand, the light of the talisman dimming to nothing in the process. She smashed the staff on the head of the First Priest, spilling his blood over the sarcophagus, too.

"You fucking bitch!" Stuart shouted, his face pouring with blood, magic sparking from his fingers.

"Hole!" Miles shouted, his voice now coarse and pained.

One of the desolates picked up Miles and threw him across the room at the hole in the floor. He hit the wall next to the hole and fell down into it, only to be caught by Lauren as he reached the bottom.

"Amelia!" Lauren shouted, dropping Miles to the ground. "Jump!"

Amelia didn't need to be told twice and was soon falling through the hole, where she too was caught by Lauren.

"We need to leave *now*," Lauren said.

Miles nodded as he got to his feet, wobbled, and fell face first to the cold, wet ground.

CHAPTER THIRTY-TWO

What's wrong with him?" Amelia asked as Lauren carried a semi-conscious Miles through a maze of tunnels that led down through more of the tomb of Ulfrik.

"Don't know," Lauren said. "Need to get some distance between us and the people who would like us dead, though."

Miles listened to the whole conversation, although he wasn't really paying attention. He hurt. His entire body felt as if someone had cut it open, put hot coals inside him, and sewn him back together. He wondered which nursery rhyme that was a part of. Probably something inappropriate for children. His brain tried to remind him of where he was, and his current situation, but the pain would occasionally lance through his body, with no further reminding needed.

After an unknown amount of time, but what Miles considered to be at least a year, he stopped being jiggled around like a bag of oranges and was still. Mercifully still. Oh, stillness is underrated. He felt cool liquid on his face. *Coolness.* Oh, coolness is even more underrated. The liquid touched his lips, and he let out a soft moan.

"Is he dying?" Amelia asked.

"I don't know," Lauren said, a might tersely in Miles's opinion.

Miles opened his eyes as it felt as though someone was stabbing him with a hot poker in the ribs. "What the actual fuckery!" he screamed, not really caring who he was screaming at. The pain subsided, and he went back to the blissfulness of being still. He only then realised he was naked from the waist up.

"He's bleeding a lot," Lauren said. "The wound is closing, but I think that bastard used a black stone dagger."

"A what?"

"He has a dagger on him," Lauren said. "It's made of black stone. I think it's actually made from part of the sarcophagus. The black stone absorbs energy, so you stab a vampire with it and . . ."

"I really fucking hate that prick," Miles said, feeling a little lucid. "Body is healing, but I'm fucked without blood."

"You're okay?" Amelia asked as she crouched beside him.

Miles opened his eyes. He was atop a desk, with hundreds of scrolls all around him. "Where are we?"

"Not a clue," Lauren said. "You need blood."

"You got some?" Miles asked as he tried to ignore the continuous agony that was playing the xylophone on his ribcage.

"None you want," Lauren said grimly.

"Yeah, I'd rather not go down that route," Miles told her, remembering what had happened to the last person who had drunk desolate blood. Eventually, the pain in his side subsided a little. "I really want to hurt that Priest."

There was a crash from somewhere inside the tomb, the echo of the noise bouncing all around them. "Nothing good is coming our way," Amelia said. "I'll give you my blood."

"That's not a great idea," Lauren said.

"It's a terrible idea," Miles said, closing his eyes. "Badly wounded vampires do not take blood from people they want to see alive."

"It'll kill me?" Amelia asked.

Miles shook his head. "Not on purpose. I might not be able to stop, and you definitely won't be able to stop me. But also, you'll see my memories, and I'll see yours. Neither of us has any control over it."

"We can't stay here long," Lauren said. "If I move you, you're going to pour blood everywhere. We've been running an age without stopping. I think we've got distance between us, but sooner or later, they're going to send people down to track us."

"How big is this tomb?"

"It's huge," Lauren told him. "They've been excavating it for years and managed to crack into where Ulfrik's attackers dragged his sarcophagus, but the Priest and his followers uncovered a lot more in the meantime. This was meant to be where Ulfrik's servants would be buried, but Ulfrik himself was never meant to be here. His attackers buried him in what is essentially the poor bit."

"Oh, he's got to be mad about that," Amelia said.

"There's another exit near Lakewood, about two kilometers north of here," Lauren continued. "About two kilometers back is the way we came. There are stairs that lead up from this level to the one above; they wind around until you get back to the sarcophagus. They found it and just dug straight up, blew out the roof."

"Lakehouse safe?" Miles asked.

"The desolate found it when they were excavating, but the First Priest wanted it closed up. There are desolate guarding it. I can get us there and out."

"You headbutted Stuart," Miles said to Amelia, feeling a little lightheaded.

"Deserved it," Amelia said with a forced smile.

"Never been more attracted to someone in my life," Miles told her.

Lauren stifled a laugh. "I'm not sure this is the time to be horny."

"Point, right, Lauren, give me sixty seconds," Miles said. "After which if I haven't stopped drinking, you need to make me."

"And how do I do that?" Lauren asked.

"Punch me very hard in the face," Miles said. "Should do the trick."

"So what you're saying is, today has a silver lining?" Lauren said with a grin.

"This is only going to take sixty seconds?" Amelia asked with a smirk as she sat down beside Miles, who lifted himself up onto his elbows.

"Out here, aye," Miles said and tapped his head. "In here, it might feel somewhat different."

"I was being coy," Amelia said.

"Ah," Miles replied. "I am not healthy enough for coy."

"Get on with it," Lauren said, leaving the room to stand guard outside.

"You ready?" Miles asked.

"Be gentle," Amelia joked, moving her hair out of the way of her neck.

Miles said nothing as he pulled Amelia toward him, smelling her perfume, hearing the beat of her heart. He felt the need course through his body as he turned into his vampire side, and sank his fangs into her neck.

Images of Amelia's adult life flashed through Miles's mind. He saw glimpses of her at work, with friends, times when she was happy, when she cried. He saw her with Heather, her reporter friend, saw the day she'd been told about Heather's murder. Felt the determination at finding where

Heather's killers had fled to, and why. Felt the need to get Heather's story out there. The rage at having lost a friend to monsters like Liam and Stuart. Every emotion crashed against Miles's will as he tried to keep his need for blood in check, as he tried to make sure he only took what he needed.

"Let it go," the imaginary Amelia said, as she bent down and whispered in Miles's ear. "Just let go."

"No," Miles said, feeling a raw power flood his body until pain erupted from the side of his head. He was thrown back, the image of Amelia fading to one under the tomb. He looked around in a panic, trying to figure out what had happened.

"It's okay," Lauren said, from beside Miles.

Miles looked down at his chest, where nails had been racked across his torso, leaving red marks in their wake. "Amelia," he said, his voice low, gravelly.

"She's okay," Lauren said.

Miles sat up and saw Amelia lying on the ground, up against the wall, her breathing shallow. Long spindly roots had torn out of the ground beneath them and wrapped around Miles and Amelia, keeping them together until the bite had been stopped. She stared at Miles with an unrelenting hunger.

"That's some powerful shit," Lauren said. "Both your vampire stuff and her magic."

Miles nodded and rolled off the table as Amelia's expression softened, her lips parting and a low exhale leaving her body. "That was a lot," she whispered as the roots moved back under the cracks in the floor once more.

Miles checked her neck. The wound had already closed. "Fucking hell," he said. "That was a little intense."

"There are people heading this way," Lauren said.

"You both need to get out of here," Miles told her. "Amelia needs something to eat, and rest. Go up to Lakehouse, get out and to Bangor."

"What are you going to do?" Lauren asked.

"Ulfrik is dangerous," Miles said. "Of that I don't need convincing."

"If they manage to wake him, he'll need to be forced back to sleep," Lauren said. "I had Ulfrik in my head for weeks. Talking to me about coming to Augusta, about helping him become free. He didn't go down willingly the first time; he was betrayed by some of his own. A mob. They couldn't kill him, but they hurt him, forced him into the sarcophagus he'd built, dragged him here. They put up the pillars to trap him down here."

Miles nodded. "The Viking desolate told me all about it. Ulfrik was not a good father figure. He's going to be *really* mad when he gets up."

"Yes, he is," Lauren said. "He's angry at everything."

"How do you force a Dusk to go back to bed?" Miles asked.

"With great difficulty," Lauren said. "The First Priest is dangerous, more so than the witch. He's been lying to the First Lord of House Idolator for decades, while he searched for Ulfrik. He's a true believer, Miles."

"Believers are always dangerous," Miles said.

"He's also one of the Dark," Lauren said. "He doesn't seem it, but he's not a pushover."

"Are Stuart and Liam working for or against the Priest?"

"Both, I think," Lauren said. "Liam works for the Magistrate, but he's convinced them he needs to pretend to work for the First Priest. He really does want a cure for Stuart, that's why he's here. Liam is losing control, though; you can hear him growling to himself."

"He's letting the wolf take over," Miles said.

"You killed his people," Lauren said. "I think the werewolf in him wants to hunt, and the human in him wants revenge. You won't be getting Thomas out of here without dealing with Liam first."

"I'll meet you at Bangor," Miles said. "We need to get Amelia to safety and rescue Thomas. You okay with that?"

"I'm fine," Amelia said, trying to stand up, before deciding better and sitting down. "I may be a little drowsy. First time having the blood of a witch?"

Miles nodded. "You have an incredible power, but you still need rest."

"I'll get her out," Lauren said. "You sure you can deal with all of these assholes by yourself?"

"I'm not by myself," Miles said. "Church is up there. I won't be long. I'm not leaving Church anywhere near these bastards, and if I go with you, she won't know where I am and she'll wait. Not going to do that."

"Be careful, Miles," Lauren said. "I'd hate to meet up after all this time only for you to go and die on me. And I have some retribution I'd like to dish out on those people who decided to wake up a monster. Stuart in particular. He's a nasty little worm of a man. Thinks that the magic he wields makes him someone to respect, but he's only really interested in making people afraid."

"He wants a cure for his cancer," Miles said. "But there isn't one."

"He won't accept that," Lauren said.

The room shook, with various items on the shelves falling off, smashing on the ground. Lauren waited for it to stop shaking before gingerly picking up Amelia. "Any idea what that was?" she asked Miles as he opened the door.

"Nothing good," he said, looking up the passageway outside the room. "I think it's safe. Which way is your exit?"

Lauren nodded to the left.

"Any chance you can control the desolate here to attack everyone?" Miles asked.

Lauren shook her head. "Not while that talisman is up there. The talisman controlled me, I controlled the desolate, but as it's a part of Ulfrik's power, the desolate are submissive whenever it's around them. I'm able to control some desolates I didn't create, but not the larger ones. I can make a whole bunch of desolates docile near me, but any under the control of that talisman are going to be free to do whatever they want when no longer in proximity to it."

"Damn it, well, I'll go make sure that Thomas is safe and meet you back at Bangor," Miles said. "Keep both of yourselves in one piece."

"I'll do my best," Lauren said. "It's good to see you, Miles."

"Don't die," Amelia said. "I mean it."

"Good to see you too, Lauren," Miles said with a slight nod, before turning to Amelia with a smile. "I don't plan on it."

CHAPTER THIRTY-THREE

Miles made his way back toward the hole he'd fallen down, with only a loose plan in his head. He needed to get to Church, make sure she was okay, get to Thomas, get him out, and if there was time, kill everyone trying to raise a monster. That last part was probably not going to happen, considering he was outnumbered, but if he could cause them some problems on the way, he'd be happy. Worst-case scenario, get to Bangor, come up with a plan, and bring their entire army of people back to Ellsworth.

Getting to Church was first and foremost, though. Everything else was a secondary objective.

Miles stopped jogging through the dark corridors when he heard someone shout, "You can't hide forever!"

The voice had belonged to Travis, the friend of Jenny's who, along with Jeremy, had betrayed the people of Bangor and thrown their lot in with the First Priest. He'd known they would be trouble since the incident with the desolate.

"I want to see them flayed," a man said. Jeremy. He sounded angry.

"We will find him," Travis said.

"Yes, and then we will show them the wrath of our true god," Jeremy said, sounding more than a little bit happy with that idea.

"Searching through this tomb will be worth it when that Arbiter learns his place," Travis said.

Miles stepped into the darkness of the shadows of one badly lit corridor and crouched low, behind several large wooden barrels. Two vampires, both young, both supremely stupid and/or arrogant enough to think that they could take him out.

His ribs still felt tender to the touch, but he was pretty sure he was capable of taking out these idiots without further damaging himself.

"You think Jenny is okay above guarding Thomas?" Jeremy asked, as the warm glow of torchlight illuminated the end of the corridor.

"She's fine," Travis said. "She'll be the first to meet our new god. The First Priest ordained it. She's quite special, you know. She wanted to be in the room with the sarcophagus, but the First Priest said it was too dangerous until our king awakens. I wish this old Arbiter would just die, though; it's taking the sheen off what is meant to be an auspicious day."

"We're still doing our god's work," Jeremy said. "Those who do not bow before him, who dare to show anything but the respect he's due, deserve what comes to them."

"Amen," Travis said.

Miles remained motionless and silent as they passed by at the end of the passageway. Travis, holding the torch, continued on without even glancing toward where Miles hid. Jeremy walked just behind him.

With them both gone, Miles followed to the end of the passageway and watched them walk away. He picked up a rock from the ground and threw it at the barrels he'd been hiding behind. He moved quickly back up along the way the two vampires had arrived from, using his telekinesis to extinguish a lantern on a nearby wall.

Miles watched as Jeremy entered the passageway, and remained where he was until he left the passageway a moment later.

"Some old barrels," Jeremy shouted off into the distance. "Probably a rat."

The moment Jeremy turned his back, Miles sprang forward, turning into his vampire self and covering the distance between him and his target in seconds. He stepped up close to Jeremy, who must have felt the presence behind him and turned, only to have Miles drive his talons into the younger man's throat, ripping it out.

Jeremy's eyes went wide as blood poured down his chest, but it was only for a moment before Miles punched his other hand through the side of Jeremy's neck, ripping his head off and tossing it to the side, letting the rest of the body collapse to the ground.

He removed a heat dagger from Jeremy's belt and stepped over the man's head as he set off in pursuit of Travis. He caught up to him in moments, as Travis was looking around a crossroads of passages.

"Jeremy," Travis said, bellowing before turning back to spot Miles as he walked toward them. Travis's eyes went wide from surprise. "Shit."

Miles threw the heated dagger into Travis's shirt-covered chest, causing the vampire to gasp in pain and step back, as Miles continued on without skipping a beat. He reached Travis, removed the dagger, plunged it back into his skull, and ignited the heat, leaving the vampire to scream in the darkness as the inside of his skull was turned to ash.

Miles ran through the catacombs, following the obvious trail of footprints that Travis and Jeremy had left in the dirt. Eventually, he reached a set of stairs that led up to a single wooden door.

Miles ascended the staircase, pushing the door open to reveal a basement beyond. It was a fairly normal looking basement as far as they went, with a water heater and several benches full of tools, all of which appeared to be rusty and unused.

He crouched behind the door and listened for anything beyond. When there was no sound, he tried the door, pushing it open a fraction, and stepping out into the kitchen beyond.

The kitchen had seen better days, with parts of the floor rotten through to the wooden beams beneath. Miles stepped over them and moved through the kitchen quietly, pushing open the door beyond after listening out once more, this time picking up a single heartbeat in the room beyond. It was slow and steady, someone not expecting trouble.

Miles pushed the door open into the living room, which was where he'd been when last inside the house. Jenny remained on the sofa, and looked over at Miles a fraction of a second too late.

Miles closed the ten feet between the two of them, grabbing the shotgun from the coffee table and smashing the butt into Jenny's face, sending her sprawling back onto the sofa.

"Don't," Miles said as Jenny moved to get up. Instead, she looked up at Miles with hate-filled eyes. "I'd hate to give you more than that broken nose."

Jenny let out a breath of air and moved her nose from side to side between her thumb and forefinger. She chuckled to herself. "You know that you can't kill me, right?"

"Really?" Miles said, checking the pump-action shotgun and emptying it of its shells, making sure the last one remained in his hand. When the gun was completely empty, he took a step back from Jenny and studied the shell, keeping the vampire in his field of vision. "Explosive."

"Remove a vampire's head," Jenny said with a shrug. "But, like I said, you can't kill me."

"Oh," Miles repeated. "I'm pretty sure I can. I mean, if I load this shell in here and aim it at your head, and pull the trigger. Well, that would kill you. You're a vampire, and like you said, this would remove the head of a vampire. Decapitation will *definitely* kill you."

"I can help you get back to the sarcophagus," Jenny said. "The First Priest trusts me; who do you think turned me?"

Miles stepped back. He had thought Jenny a *believer* in the idea of the Dusk, but she was more than that. Her hard eyes and stern expression spoke of something deeper than just belief. She was a fanatic "We both know you're not going to betray the First Priest."

Jenny's gaze hardened. "You will be sacrificed to our god."

"You're a wee weirdo," Miles said.

"Your insults just show me how far beneath my level you are," Jenny said with an eerie smile across her lips. "The Dusk will rise. He will feast on your bones, and the bones of all the unbelievers. My death won't stop that. Go ahead and do whatever you need to. I'll tell you nothing."

"I'll tell you what, you tell me where Thomas is, no tricks, you get to live."

Jenny laughed. "I don't need your deals. I have Ulfrik's blessing, and that means more to me than anything you can offer."

Miles sighed. Religious extremists were exhausting. "Last chance," Miles said, taking a step toward Jenny.

The ground beneath Miles's feet shook violently, and Jenny took less than a second to use the distraction to her advantage, diving toward Miles, drawing a pair of daggers as she moved.

Miles dodged the blades and moved until he was back in the kitchen, and then outside where he'd first entered the house several hours previously.

Jenny jumped through one of the windows, narrowly missing Miles, who hadn't expected such an attack strategy from the relatively young vampire.

Miles continued to jump back, dodging and avoiding the blades until he heard the low, familiar growl coming from the side. He used his telekinesis to blast Jenny mid-leap back into a large tree, the sound of the slam both satisfying and, Miles hoped, painful.

After running over to Jenny, picking up one of his sharp curved blades, and dragging the vampire away from the house, into the woods, Miles heard shouting coming from the house itself. Time to put a little distance between him and whoever came to investigate.

"Where is Thomas?" Miles asked as Jenny used her bloodline gift to create a shield of red energy, which slammed into Miles, knocking him away from her. He rolled several times over the rough forest floor, catching sight of Jenny who sprinted away, paying very little attention to the number of branches that hit her across the face.

Miles ran after her, catching up just as Jenny reached the edge of the forest. She turned back to him, her red shield in place, but a quick blast of telekinesis to her legs sent her tumbling back.

Jenny got up and ran at Miles, who easily avoided her talons using his telekinesis to throw her back across the grassy area toward a fast-flowing portion of the river nearby. "Where is Thomas?" Miles said. "Don't make me ask again."

"In the crypt," Jenny said, hoarsely. "Everyone is in the crypt."

"Why aren't you?"

"Waiting for those two idiots who were looking for you to come back," Jenny said, as Miles let go of her, placing a foot on her chest to pin her to the ground.

Church came out of the undergrowth like a nightmare, snarling as she moved toward Jenny, who looked genuinely scared for the first time.

Jenny looked over at Church, whose teeth were bared. "What do you want to know?"

"Church, go make a nuisance for whoever came to check on Jenny here," Miles said.

Miles walked toward Jenny, who now held her head up high, showing no fear.

"You will die screaming!" Jenny shouted at him, before turning and jumping into the river, where the rapid current took her.

Miles blinked in surprise. "Didnae expect that," he said as Jenny's shouting form was dragged under the water.

Chapter Thirty-Four

Church ran up to keep Miles company as he watched the river for a few minutes to make sure Jenny didn't make a triumphant, if short-lived, return. She was a vampire, so she wasn't about to die in the river, but the current and cold water might make her life miserable for a while. He'd pick up her trail once it was all over and make sure she tasted justice for her crimes.

Miles kept to the woods as he moved by the house, which now had several desolate outside of it, milling around as if in a daze.

With Church beside him, they continued on down toward the barn, which they saw was devoid of anything guarding it. Miles wondered if the desolate up by the house had originally been the guards.

"Once inside the barn," Miles said, "we both go down into the crypt, but you need to stay back and out of sight when we get to the burial chamber."

Church huffed.

"Let me finish. You'll be able to see anyone just inside the chamber itself, so when you get the chance, move inside, be quiet, and don't get spotted. I'll try to take the attention of everyone in the chamber. That okay with you?"

Church licked Miles's hand.

Miles scratched Church behind the ear. "Be safe, don't go getting your-self in trouble or doing anything silly."

Church rolled her eyes.

"I don't plan on doing anything silly."

Church rolled her eyes again.

"Point taken," Miles said. "Just stay safe, Church."

Church bumped Miles's arm with her head.

"I will," Miles promised.

The pair moved quickly across the open ground to the barn, only slowing down once inside. They both moved around to the side of the hole in the ground, behind a stack of crates that gave a good view between them down into the crypt. The door at the bottom of the steps was open, and the torches in the hallway beyond showed no desolate anywhere. That was either really good or really bad, depending on where the desolate had gone.

Miles moved around the crates, with Church following close by, and together they descended the stairs, moving beyond the doors and into the lengthy tunnel beyond. However creepy the place had been with the desolate lining up along the walls, it was oddly even more so with nothing but lit torches and the shadows they cast. More than once, Miles rubbed the back of his neck as the thoughts of being watched ran through his mind.

They reached the room at the end and moved through, retracing the steps that Miles had taken when he'd been the guest of the First Priest. After a few minutes, and a few more rooms, he started to hear voices. He motioned for Church to keep quiet, and they continued on at a slower pace.

"I can't stay down here any longer," a voice that Miles recognised as Liam shouted. "Why isn't this Dusk of yours woken up yet?"

"Liam, calm yourself," Stuart said.

Miles slipped in through the ajar door into the burial chamber and motioned for Church to move behind the crates opposite to where he was.

"Whatever you're doing, it's fucking up my senses," Liam shouted. "I can't smell anything. Do you know what that's like for a wolf?"

"Annoying," Thomas suggested.

He was sat against one of the pillars, next to the sarcophagus. One of the pillars was completely missing, the chain attaching it to the sarcophagus trailing across the floor. Of the other three, the two which had already been cracked when Miles had last been in the chamber were now split down the middle, and the last one had chips missing from it.

Stuart stood beside the last pillar, pouring magical energy into it. He looked tired and sick. Miles figured that was why he'd been given the Talisman by the First Priest, so he wouldn't die before he'd done what the First Priest needed.

Liam went to hit Thomas, drawing Miles's attention.

"Stop," the First Priest said. "We are not barbarians, Liam. If you can't keep it together, leave."

If Liam had left, he would have walked right by Miles, and he wanted a few more seconds to figure out what everyone was doing.

"We need to wake Ulfrik up," the First Priest said, "And we need to do it now."

"First Lord Fuller will execute you all for this," Thomas said.

"First Lord Fuller sent you here to spy on me because he didn't trust me," the First Priest snapped.

Thomas waved his arms about. "Rightly, it turned out."

"If he'd only had more vision," the First Priest said, "we could have worked together to bring House Idolator back to the greatness it once held. Instead, he sent a worm to look in on me. I just happened to get to you before you could get to me."

"And that's all worked out for you so well," Thomas said sarcastically.

The First Priest stood before Thomas, glaring at him.

"You don't actually have a plan beyond *raise the Dusk*, do you?" Thomas asked, looking around the room, a slight concern to his voice. "That's it, that's your whole plan."

"I have a plan," the First Priest bellowed.

"Okay," Thomas said. "I just think I'd like to hear it."

"Do you know why you're here, Thomas?" the First Priest snapped. "I let people think you were the first meal for our risen king, but actually, you're here because with you in our grasp, First Lord Fuller will come for you. We both know he'll come for you, so don't try to deny it. Once Fuller is gone, I will be put in his stead, while Ulfrik continues his plan to create a great vampire city beneath this state. Together, we will change humanity for the better. And anyone not of his bloodline will be culled."

"You're going to declare war against the other Houses?" Thomas asked. "Are you all insane?"

There was another tremor, this one much larger than the last, and Miles became concerned that Church would be revealed when the crates fell. He motioned for her to stay and stood himself. "Hey, everyone. Having a nice time being weird?"

Liam turned to Miles and snarled at him.

"You didn't die," the First Priest said as the tremors came back stronger once again. A second pillar exploded, raining pieces of sharp stone across the chamber.

Miles used his telekinesis to move the worst of them, and caught Liam still staring at him. "He good?" Miles asked the First Priest with a thumb in Liam's direction. "He seems tense."

"His werewolf side is corrupting his mind," Thomas said. "It's a side effect of not keeping yourself calm. Doesn't help that this place is screwing around with his senses, so he's a bit . . . well, mad."

"You know nothing," Liam roared.

"Liam!" the First Priest shouted.

"I got it," Stuart said through gritted teeth, as more tremors started, and the other two pillars exploded just as Thomas rolled out of the way, toward Miles.

"We should not be here," Thomas said to Miles.

The tremors got worse and worse until parts of the ceiling began to rain down over the sarcophagus, forcing Stuart to move away, wincing with every step.

"We should leave," Miles said, backing away.

The door to the crypt burst open and the desolate who had been outside only moments earlier charged into the room. Liam stepped into the path of one giant desolate who'd almost had to crawl through the door and was backhanded by it, sending the werewolf flying across the room and into the far wall next to the waterfall.

Miles and Thomas moved back against the wall as the desolate surrounded the sarcophagus and began to slam their fists on the lid, cracking it with every blow.

"Church, get Thomas out of here!" Miles shouted, shoving Thomas toward the exit. "I'll be right behind you."

Thomas didn't need telling twice, and was out through the door with Church behind him, as Miles tried to figure out how to bring everything down from atop the burial chamber, removing anyone as a threat. He quickly decided that being inside the burial chamber was a terrible idea and ran to the door.

A blast of fire cut Miles off from the exit. It incinerated the crates and pots there, forcing Miles back. The fire tracked him, and Miles jumped back several feet, blasting Stuart in the chest with his telekinesis as he moved.

Stuart hit the ground hard but continued to hold on to his staff. He brought it around in an arc of flame, turning several desolates to charcoal, which none of the others appeared to notice.

The First Priest dived behind the cover of a large rock near the waterfall, and Liam ran through the throng of desolate to the exit, looking back at Miles and deciding he had a better plan. He pounced in Miles's direction, but a quick flick of telekinesis sent him slamming into Stuart, and they both went down again.

The fire had all but consumed the entrance to the burial chamber, and as pieces of the ceiling continued to fall down due to the tremors, it was beginning to look more and more to Miles as if diving back down into the dungeon below was the best bet.

He'd taken two steps when a blast of air hit him mid-stride, sending him careering into the waterfall, where he narrowly avoided smashing his head on a rock, but in doing so smashed the rest of him. He fell into the almost freezing water and felt a little better, but First Priest de Moxica took the opportunity of Miles's momentary daze to try to stab the black stone dagger into his side again, opening up a wound Miles had already healed once.

Miles stopped the First Priest from driving the dagger all the way into his side, but he still yelled out in pain when the edge sliced against his skin. Miles headbutted the First Priest, who staggered back a little, and Miles pulled him off balance into the water, smashing his head on the rock as he did.

Bleeding from the side, and with pain racking his body, he looked across the burial chamber at the werewolf and the witch, who both appeared to be eager to continue their attack. Miles climbed up out of the pool of water as the sarcophagus exploded.

The power of the blast threw Miles back into the waterfall once again, where his body met the same rocks he'd been acquainted with only a short time ago.

The First Priest scrambled out of the water, his robes saturated, his face badly bleeding, as a massive hand grabbed the side of the sarcophagus and pulled itself out.

The images that Miles had seen of Dusk Ulfrik had shown him to be a large man, but a man. What crawled out of that sarcophagus as the desolate all dropped to their knees, was nothing even close to human looking. It had dark grey skin covering its overly muscular body. Its fingers were long and had sharp talons in place of nails. To Miles's eye, the creature looked like a cross between a desolate and a vampire's beast form.

The creature stood to its full eight-foot height and bellowed so loudly that Miles thought his eardrums might burst.

"Ah, to be awake again!" the thing shouted.

How does it know English? was probably not the most pressing matter at the moment, but it's what Miles thought.

"My lord," the First Priest said, bowing as he walked. "My lord Ulfrik."

"Finally, I am free," Ulfrik said, turning toward the grovelling First Priest and revealing a face with an overly wide smile with sharklike teeth inside. Ulfrik's eyes burned crimson, and Miles instinctively knew this creature was more dangerous than the idiots who had raised him from his sleep could possibly have imagined.

"This world is in need of your guidance, my lord," the First Priest said.

Ulfrik stepped out of the sarcophagus, kneeing a desolate out of the way as he moved. He towered over Liam, who looked back at Stuart. "The First Priest said you could cure him."

"Cure him?" Ulfrik asked, amused.

"I have cancer," Stuart said. "I brought you back to heal me."

Ulfrik's mocking laughter bounced around inside Miles's chest. "A cure for your sickness, is it?" Ulfrik asked.

Stuart nodded, keeping himself upright on his walking stick.

"I see you have my talisman," Ulfrik said, his tone suddenly full of menace.

"I found it in the city beneath the state," the First Priest said. "It's how I managed to find you, my lord."

Stuart removed the talisman and held it out to the Dusk, who seemingly ignored him.

Liam let out a roar and turned into his werewolf form. "You help him first. We want what's owed to us or I will take your blood myself."

Ulfrik punched his hand through the werewolf's chest, removing it, and tearing the werewolf in half, letting the sides drop to the ground as if what he'd done was nothing. "Here's what you're owed!" Ulfrik shouted. "You petty impurity."

He turned to the witch. "The talisman," he said, taking Stuart's hand and ripping the arm off from the elbow.

Stuart screamed as Ulfrik gingerly removed the talisman. "This let me see through your eyes. Silly little traitor." The chaos witch started to use a spell, his hand glowing red hot, before Ulfrik crushed the man's remaining hand, snapping off each finger in turn and eating them.

Miles tried not to pay attention to the horrific levels of violence he'd just seen, although Stuart's screams were cut short a moment later when Ulfrik grabbed the witch by the head and bit down on his neck, the Dusk's jaw opening wider than a vampire's was able to. The Dusk drank deeply from the chaos witch, the blood spilling all around until Ulfrik was done a few seconds later. He tossed the broken and dying body of Stuart against the far wall, which he hit with a sickening crunch. A paperback-sized book, bound in red leather, tumbled out of the inside pocket of Stuart's coat and landed on the ground beside him. The grimoire.

"There is another," the First Priest said, pointing over to Miles.

"You little fucker," Miles whispered.

"A vampire," Ulfrik said thoughtfully. "But not of my blood. Despite his strength."

Miles stepped out of the pool, wishing he wasn't about to have a battle with a creature several times more powerful than him, while utterly drenched.

"Which House are you?" Ulfrik asked.

"Venator," Miles said.

"Drest's House," Ulfrik said with a frown. "One of my brother's ilk. Drest was a great warrior in his day. One of the few bloodlines worth a damn. Have you earned any of his talents? For even one of impure blood, there could be exceptions made for those who are strong."

Miles shrugged. "I don't grovel."

Ulfrik looked around him at the still-prone desolate and continuously bowing First Priest. "Yes, well, some people should know their place."

"How do you know modern English?" Miles asked. "It's been bothering me. I expected something more archaic."

"When my power exploded out of me, it rushed back. I've been asleep, but my mind has sought out others over the years, learning, talking to those who would be of assistance."

"Like Lauren."

"You are friends with the Desolate Queen?" Ulfrik said. "She had no knowledge of her true power. I had hoped that the vampire world would have realised just how much the Desolate Royalty are like the Dusk. They are the closest to my kind. The true successors to the Dusk. Although most of my brothers and sisters disagree."

"She's gone," Miles said. "She had enough of feeling like she was being drugged."

Ulfrik took a step toward Miles. "She was desolate. She *belonged* to me."

"The desolate do not belong to you," Miles said.

Ulfrik laughed again.

"I met one of your desolate in the city you built, one of the original Vikings who came over here," Miles said. "He did not like you one bit."

"The betrayers are in *my* city?" Ulfrik roared. "I will hunt them down and flay their skin from their bones for what they did to me. I will ensure their punishment is swift."

Miles wondered if he'd just signed the Viking desolate's death warrant.

"My kin will not give me much time to do what must be done," Ulfrik said, as if he'd totally forgotten about his swearing of punishment and torture only a moment ago.

"You are the only Dusk awake," the First Priest said.

Ulfrik looked over at the cowering vampire. "No, I am not. But that is a problem for later. Now, I will bring this place under my will. I will ensure that the people of this . . . Maine . . . are punished for what they did."

"The people who experimented on the desolate you created are all dead," Miles said.

Ulfrik stared at Miles for a moment. "I will find their ancestors, those who have come to this place and think that they are in charge, and I will give them a choice. Bend their knee and become my people, or die. And when I'm done with Maine, I will move on. I hear that the number of humanity has grown increasingly large in this country in the centuries since I was here. It is time for them to understand their true place in this world."

"I won't let you," Miles said. "You're a threat to everyone you don't deem good enough."

Ulfrik's laugh was deep and long. "You are a little vampire. I am a Dusk. You are nothing to me, but I admire your courage. And because you are friends with Lauren, I will give you a chance. You will find her and bring her to me, and I will let you serve a new master."

Miles laughed. "Go fuck yourself."

Ulfrik moved so fast that Miles barely had time to react to him as his strong hand wrapped around the Arbiter's throat, lifting him off the ground with one hand. "I will kill you here."

Miles wrapped telekinesis around Ulfrik's thumb, and with every bit of strength he had, snapped the digit.

Ulfrik roared in a mixture of pain and anger, dropping Miles, who channelled his bloodline gift and slammed it into Ulfrik's chest.

Ulfrik staggered back several feet, dropping the talisman onto the ground as he wobbled, helped up by the First Priest, who used his own bloodline power to turn his energy into a physical manifestation, putting up a shield of crimson power around Ulfrik. The shield had stopped Miles's bloodline gift from fully connecting with the Dusk.

The Dusk charged forward, through the First Priest's power, which made him wobble again, and Miles took the opening, moving under the flailing arms, and leaping up onto Ulfrik's back. Miles sank his fangs into the Dusk's throat, drinking down the warm, powerful blood in an effort to weaken the creature.

Miles used his talons to hold on to Ulfrik, but the Dusk grabbed hold of Miles's neck, ripping him free, and throwing him across the chamber. As Miles had still been fang-deep in Ulfrik's neck, the resulting wound was a huge hole in the side of the Dusk's throat, which pulsed blood all over the floor.

"I will not die," Ulfrik said, running through the door and wall, collapsing a large part of it as the First Priest followed close by, with the desolate shambling after.

Miles knelt on the ground, the blood of the Dusk covering him as a feeling of overwhelming power racked his body. He screamed in pain as the sounds of heartbeats from outside the crypt flooded into his mind. He could smell the desolate who had left; he could hear their footsteps as they shambled up the ground. He felt his body repair itself, felt the bumps and bruises heal, the cut on his side stitch itself back together. It was all so overwhelming, and in the distance, high above him, he heard the bark of a dog.

Miles forced himself back to his feet, his body practically pulsating with power. He walked by Stuart, who was surprisingly still alive, although even his magic couldn't heal him from having his arm and hand torn off.

"It wasn't meant to be like this," Stuart said softly. "I don't deserve this."

Miles stopped beside the murderous witch and looked down at him, picking up the book and flicking through the blank pages, which started to be filled before his eyes.

"This wasn't yours," Miles said.

Miles heard Stuart's heartbeat as it slowed and tasted the particles of blood in the air. He looked over at the two halves of what had been Liam. Apparently they could add *torn in two* to the ways that werewolves could die. He looked back at Stuart, who stared up with a mixture of fear and pleading.

"Help me," Stuart said.

Miles crouched down beside the witch and whispered, "You deserve a lot worse than what you got. Enjoy your tomb." He spotted the talisman on the ground and picked it up. He stood and walked up out of the burial chamber. He was done with Stuart and Liam, but he wasn't finished with Ulfrik.

CHAPTER THIRTY-FIVE

Church!" Miles bellowed as he left the barn. The sounds of every living thing for a kilometer all around him burned into his mind; he heard their heartbeats, felt their fear, and it overwhelmed him. He crashed to his knees but refused to give up, practically pulling himself out of the barn and into the mud outside.

It wasn't until he was some distance from the barn that he saw Church, who ran toward him and buried her face against his neck.

"Good to see you, too," Miles told her and looked around. "Thomas."

Church turned and looked off to the distance.

"Ulfrik took him?" Miles asked.

Church barked.

Miles sighed. "He came back to help, didn't he?"

Church barked again. Followed by a low whine.

"Damn it," Miles said. "How'd they get away so fast?"

Church ran a few feet away and sniffed the ground before running back.

"There was a vehicle here," Miles said.

Church barked.

As the power inside his body began to calm itself, Miles managed to use a nearby fence post to pull himself upright. "I can feel the heartbeats of so many things. Where are the desolate who were here?"

Church barked and pointed to the ground.

Miles followed the multitude of scuffed footprints in the soft mud to a set of tyre tracks. "They followed the car."

Church barked.

Miles looked up toward where he had flown in an effort to get to Ellsworth. "We need to follow these tracks," he said.

Church whined, turned to the side, and barked as something approached them.

Miles readied himself for a fight as Lauren and Amelia exited the trees at a jogging pace. "I'm fine," Amelia said as she reached Miles and Church. "Witch constitution is better than a human's."

"She wouldn't take no for an answer," Lauren said. "Also, we found your car and brought it here; it's just beyond those trees."

"Good," Miles said.

"So, he's free," Lauren said, looking over at the barn.

"And very angry," Miles said.

Lauren shook her head. "He's afraid."

Church let out a snort.

"No, really," Lauren said. "I was in his head for days. He would talk to me, make me feel like I wanted to be there. Now that I'm away from that influence, I can remember stuff he said. He *hates* what happened in Augusta, but he's also scared of what happened there. He felt the deaths of the desolate he'd created. They were first-generation desolate. They spoke, they were closer in kind to what I am. These soldiers, these scientists didn't just kill mindless desolate who were killing people—they killed desolate who tried to tell them what they were."

"Those responsible are all dead," Miles said. "There's no one left."

Church whined.

"We need to follow Ulfrik," Miles said. "Wherever he's going, we need to stop him."

"Just the four of us?" Amelia asked. "Is that possible?"

Miles and Lauren both shook their heads. "They have Thomas."

"Why?" Lauren asked.

"Thomas is a trap to get First Lord Fuller here, so Ulfrik can kill him."

"Why?" Lauren asked.

"Ulfrik doesn't trust anyone he can't control," Miles said. "He wanted to kill all of the vampires he made, but Fuller and the First Priest weren't here. I think the First Priest has made it very clear he's happy to be controlled. Fuller much less so."

"Anything else insane?"

"I was there because if Ulfrik had turned on the First Priest, he wanted me to use my bloodline power so that he could kill the Dusk himself,"

Miles said. "The First Priest is power hungry, and he's not fussed how he gets that power."

No one spoke for several seconds.

"On the plus side, Ulfrik killed Stuart." Miles passed the grimoire to Amelia. "This is yours."

Amelia took the small book and smiled. "Thank you," she said, flicking through the pages. "This means a lot."

Miles removed the talisman from his pocket. "This belongs to Ulfrik. It has part of his power inside it. The First Priest said that he found this under Brunswick, in a library there. That he found how to locate what was meant to be Ulfrik's tomb there, too. Any chance they're the same thing?"

"You think the talisman is a way to find Ulfrik?" Lauren asked.

"I think we're running out of options," Miles said. "Maybe my drinking from him will help, too. I don't know, millennia-old vampire gods being real was not on the list of stops for the pilgrimage."

Lauren blinked. "You did what? Are you okay?"

Miles considered it and nodded. "Feel fine. Feel better than fine. I feel like I could fly all the way across this state without stopping, but I'm nae sure if I actually can, or if the power of Ulfrik's blood inside of me just makes me overestimate my strength. Either way, we've got somewhere to head to before he makes things much worse."

"So that talisman is linked to Ulfrik, yes?" Lauren asked. "And you drank from him. Any chance you can put it on and see where he is?"

"Let's see if we can find out," Miles said, putting the talisman over his head and letting it fall across his neck.

The talisman glowed red, and Miles took two steps before a wave of memories hit him, doubling him over. He crashed to his knees, his mouth open in a wordless scream, as the memories of Ulfrik crashed into his brain like a runaway truck. He saw Lauren rush to him, talk to him, but he couldn't hear anything, not even Church's barking as her concern took voice.

Miles blinked, and collapsed to the ground as memories that were never his swirled inside his brain.

He recalled being picked up by Lauren, being carried back to the car that he'd abandoned. He knew he was being placed inside the back seats, and that Lauren had started the car, driving off at speed. He knew all of it was happening, but it was as if he was watching something that was happening to someone else.

Instead, Miles's brain only wanted him to concentrate on seeing Ulfrik. He saw similar memories to that of the talkative desolate down in the city beneath the state. He watched as Ulfrik fled Norway, narrowly avoiding a large number of vampires who wanted him dead. He feared them. Miles felt it in his chest.

Miles watched Ulfrik arriving in America, watching as he enslaved so many people to his *cause*. He watched it fail, he saw the Pilgrims arrive, saw so many who were eager to give away their humanity for a taste of power. Saw the regret of so many when they realised that they were now under the control of a much more powerful creature.

Ulfrik's life flickered before Miles's eyes, jumping years or even centuries with every blink, seeing the betrayal of his creations as they realised that he would kill them one by one. The sense of betrayal tore through his soul, the multitude of dead at his feet as they forced him into his sarcophagus. Until there was only darkness. A deep slumber that was anything but. He could *feel* those desolate who still lived, the ones who hadn't betrayed him. He knew they were out there, like a comfort blanket. He cared for them, in a way, more so than anything else he'd ever cared for. He considered them his personal property.

Miles saw that Ulfrik felt the death of every single one of the desolate he'd created. He saw Ulfrik talk to the First Priest in a dream, tell him about a group of men and women who had *desecrated* those he had created. They had worked in a laboratory under Augusta. That Augusta was to never be sullied with their kind again. That he wanted them dead. He reached out to coach the First Priest, to swear that he would never have killed him, that he knew that the First Priest had been loyal. The First Priest told him that First Lord Fuller had known the betrayal was going to happen, and that's why he fled. Ulfrik hadn't been sure if it was true or not, but it *felt* true, so he accepted it as so.

He spent years telling the First Priest where to look for his tomb, trying to find any of the desolate who might be able to offer a glimpse at where he was buried. His black sarcophagus was meant to be under the city, and he was enraged that those who had forced him into his sleep had moved it. The rage and hate filled Miles's mind, flooding it until Miles couldn't think of anything but the need for vengeance, the *need* to inflict suffering on those who had wronged him. But more than anything, he wanted his throne back. He wanted his *city* back.

Miles sat up and screamed. He looked around at the five people who were all staring at him with a mixture of shock and horror.

"Hey," Miles said as Church jumped up onto the bed beside him. "How's Amelia?"

"She's good," Lauren said. "Getting ready to head out when we know where we're going."

Miles looked around the faces of the Bangor council members who had come to his room. His head still swam as the huge amount of memories swirled around his head. He had never felt anything quite like it. He still saw flickers of memory. A library. A huge expanse of knowledge and power. A crypt. And desolate guards, a lot of desolate guards.

Miles lay back on the bed and let everyone else talk as he tried to figure out the images and information that had been dumped in his head.

Lauren nodded. "Also, the First Priest is a seriously bad person, and they have Thomas."

"This is sounding worse and worse," someone said.

"So, where is Ulfrik going?" someone else asked. "Augusta?"

"He's not going to Augusta," Miles said, sitting up. "That's not the feeling I got when I drank from him."

"You *drank* from him?" Bethany asked.

"Little bit," Miles said, removing the talisman and dropping it to the bed beside him. "I have a memory of Ulfrik talking to the First Priest, telling him to find that talisman, to give it to someone who can be controlled. It increases your power exponentially, but it also links you to Ulfrik. It lets him know where you are, lets him see through your eyes. He was in contact with the First Priest throughout. He's been watching everything through Stuart's eyes. He knew that Stuart and Liam had made a deal with the Magistrate to get them some of his blood."

"So can he see you?" Carol asked.

"It's why I removed it," Miles said.

"Why would they make a deal with the Magistrate?" Bethany asked.

"They found something in the library that suggested the blood of a Dusk can be used to kill vampires," Miles said. "The Magistrate have scientists who think that they can use it to create a weapon, although I don't know if they really can or not. Ulfrik saw it all. Thought it was pretty funny, considering that he was just going to kill them all anyway."

"They were just going to betray one another," Lauren said.

"That's what happens when you get a bunch of egotistic arseholes together and ask them to cooperate," Miles said, tapping his head. "I also have a lot of shitty memories of Ulfrik now living in my head. Ulfrik wants what's his. Those who betrayed him took away his city, moved him away from it. He wants it back. He has a connection with those he turned; he knows that some of those who betrayed him are still in the city. He wants vengeance first before he continues his plan."

"And that was?" Bethany asked.

"The subjugation of humanity," Miles said. "He wants to destroy anyone who is of a bloodline he decrees to be lesser than his. And he thinks *all* bloodlines are lesser than his. And his throne sits directly under a human city. A human city that would give him a lot of people to subjugate."

"Ulfrik is heading to Brunswick," Lauren said.

Miles nodded. "That horde of desolate we saw outside of Waterville is going to Brunswick. They're following their master. Or their master's master. Either way, Ulfrik is the pied piper where the desolate are concerned. Thousands of desolate are making their way through the Maine countryside toward Brunswick."

"You sure?" Carol asked.

Miles nodded. "Yeah, he's like a gigantic beacon for desolate. Every single one of their number in this state is linked to him, even if it's by generations removed."

"If we kill him, will that kill everyone he turned?" Bethany asked.

"No," Lauren said.

"It will weaken those he turned," Miles said. "But it will be temporary. Killing him shouldn't be our goal. I don't even know *how* we'd kill him."

"Brunswick," Amelia said from the doorway. "We need to get a warning to them."

Miles stood and stretched. "Yes we do. They're about to fight tens of thousands of desolate. By the time they're done, no one is going to survive. Ulfrik is probably the most dangerous thing I've ever seen. He's not fully powered up, and he's not altogether there in a mental sense. He's also very not human. He looks like some kind of monstrous amalgamation of vampire beast, and a desolate. It's not good. He's stronger than me, faster, definitely more resilient, and honestly I'd like to not have to fight him alone. So, anyone who wants to can come with us and try to stop a vampiric god-like creature from, I presume, murdering a lot of people."

"This is going to be a hell of a day," Lauren said.

"Aye," Miles said. "So, now everyone is caught up. Let's get to that tram, let's get back to Brunswick and stop him. Because I don't think any of us is prepared to fight a Dusk if that same Dusk ever actually recovers all of his power. Also, does anyone have a satellite phone? I have friends at the border, and we might actually need help."

"Friends?" Carol asked.

"The FBI," Miles said. "Or a part of them. Anyway, we need to stop Ulfrik, and the more the merrier at the moment."

"We haven't been able to use it for a few weeks," Bethany said.

"Oh, fucking hell," Miles exclaimed, before he thought for a second. "Okay, where's the Major?"

"Outside," Bethany said.

Miles exited the room with everyone following him as he descended the stairs outside, crossing the parking area at the front of the motel toward the car he'd abandoned a while ago. Where the Major and Maeve stood talking.

"Hey, I need a hand," Miles said. "You up for a very dangerous job?"

"Glad you're awake," the Major said. "What do you have in mind?"

"I need you to get to Kittery," Miles said. "Move fast, don't stop. Take whatever you need. We need Samuel Austin—he's an FBI agent, and hopefully he'll be able to get some people to help stop Ulfrik if we can't. When you get outside of this miasma bullshit, get in contact with Drest, First Lord of House Venator. Let him know what's going on. If we can't stop Ulfrik, you're going to need every bit of help to take down a Dusk."

"You think you can kill a Dusk?" Maeve asked.

Miles shrugged, thought for a second, and shook his head. "I tore his throat open, and he still managed to get away without much trouble, so no. But if we can hurt him enough, he'll be forced to go back into hibernation."

"So, we just have to hurt a Dusk?" the Major said. "Not sounding a whole lot better."

"At this point, I'll take forcing him away from the town with thousands of people living there."

"We're not exactly brimming with good odds here," Lauren said.

"What happens when you get into the city and Ulfrik takes control of your mind?" Miles asked. "Between him and this talisman, they had you for a while."

"The talisman interferes with his ability to communicate or control me," Lauren said. "He could never talk to me if Stuart was nearby, it was like having them both together shorted out that power. I won't be able to fight Ulfrik, but so long as that talisman is near, I won't worry about being controlled."

"The last time I wore it, my brain broke," Miles said. "And he'll be able to see what I see."

"So don't put it on until we're close enough that the latter doesn't matter," Lauren said. "And maybe try it on now that the blood you drank has dissipated."

Miles reluctantly put the talisman on, bracing himself for . . . whatever might happen. When nothing did, he looked over at Lauren. "I don't feel anything."

"Maybe you shorted it out," Lauren said.

Vampire. A familiar voice boomed in Miles's head.

Miles removed the talisman. "He can see me," he said. "If it stops him controlling you, I'll keep it with me. Maybe it'll be useful."

"I'd like the chance to give some payback," Lauren said.

"I guess I'm your shield, then," Miles said, not exactly thrilled about wearing the talisman again, but hoping by the time it was necessary any advantage that Ulfrik might have when Miles put it on would be useless.

"Anything else?" the Major asked.

"We need to rescue Thomas," Miles said. "I'm not leaving him in the hands of the First Priest. Also, I'd very much like to kill the First Priest. Definitely sure he can die."

"I think it would be better to keep him alive," the Major said. "He needs to answer for his actions. I think First Lord Fuller would like to have a conversation."

"I'm not promising anything," Miles said. "But I'll do my best. How long to get us to Brunswick? And I mean without stopping like the pilgrimage."

"Few hours," Carol said. "But I can't leave Bangor undefended."

"What about Commander Bailey?" Amelia asked. "He won't be happy to see us again."

"The Commander knows where the library is," Miles said. "He let Simon and Liam use it to find out more about using Dusk blood as a weapon, so we find him, he tells us where it is."

"And if he doesn't?" Amelia asked.

"We'll ask him *nicely*," Lauren said.

"If Simon and Liam found something that lets the blood of a Dusk get turned into a weapon against vampires, we need to know exactly how much they told Bailey, and how much the Magistrate knows," Miles said. "One way or another, Bailey has a reckoning coming his way, but let's get to the library and intercept Ulfrik first. Who knows what else that mad bastard has squirreled away in there."

"This is going to be a long day," Lauren said.

Miles looked around at the determined faces before him. "Okay, let's go stop a Dusk from burning a city to the ground."

CHAPTER THIRTY-SIX

You could see Brunswick burn from miles away.

The second Miles smelled the unfortunately familiar scent of burning, he climbed out of the back of the truck, where Lauren, Amelia, and Church sat, and onto the top of the truck cab. The wall around the city was broken in several places, and a lot of the larger buildings spewed dark smoke and fire into the night sky.

The truck pulled to a stop several hundred meters from what had once been one of the fort-like entrances into the city, and was now little more than a heap of burning brick and stone. Gunfire sounded from inside the town, populated by the screams of people who had been unfortunate enough to encounter the huge number of desolate that Miles expected inside.

"There are thousands of them in there," Lauren said as she joined Miles on the soft dirt road. "Tens of thousands. I can feel them like a pressure on my mind. So many desolate."

Miles grabbed Lauren's hand as she stumbled back, catching her before she fell.

"Thank you," Lauren said. "I'm okay. It's just . . . a lot."

"Are you going to be okay in there?"

Lauren shrugged. "I have to try."

Miles watched as the second truck took a different turn behind where they stood and set off along a firmer road. He touched the talisman that was inside his pocket. He couldn't risk putting it on and having Ulfrik see where he was, but at the same time, it was something that might come in handy.

Five soldiers climbed out the back of the truck, along with Xander the vampire councillor from Brunswick, and Bethany, who Miles wasn't sure had ever seen actual combat before. Bethany climbed down from the truck cab and leaned up against it, lighting a cigarette and taking a long drag, before blowing smoke rings into the air.

"Right," Miles said. "We get inside, and all head toward wherever Commander Bailey is. After that, Church, Lauren, Amelia, and I will find Thomas. Bethany, I want you and the soldiers here to help the Commander's people. That means killing a lot of desolate. Do not engage Ulfrik, just try to help the people here."

"Yes, sir," the soldiers all said in unison.

Bethany flicked her cigarette onto the floor, stamping on it with a world-weary sigh. "Let's go."

They moved up toward the town as quickly as possible, with Church taking the lead until they reached the hole in the wall, and the smell of the dead made everyone pause.

Miles looked around the wall and saw the uniformed bodies that littered the ground, most missing large parts of them, which certainly explained the stench. He wished they could've gotten the trucks into the city, but it would have meant clearing out a lot of debris, and they didn't have time.

"Church, check out the inside, and remove any targets that might be a problem," Miles said. "Stay low. Stay hidden."

Church licked Miles's hand and bounded off into the remains of the fort-like structure. Miles, Lauren, Amelia, and the others followed shortly after, with Miles motioning for the soldiers to head off to the right toward a two-storey building that looked like an old repurposed office block.

The inner courtyard was a mess of blood and bodies—both human and desolate—but the controls to the gates were still functional, and Miles was grateful that they opened without any problems. Although that feeling quickly went away when the scale of what had happened to Brunswick was visible.

"Holy shit," Amelia said.

The street beyond the fort was awash with more bodies, both desolate and human. A large apartment block sat at the end of the street, flames flickering out of the smashed windows as the desolate crawled over the outside. Some desolate were sitting on the front lawn of the apartment block, feasting on those people unlucky enough to get caught.

"Clear," one of the soldiers said as they exited the old office block to the side of the courtyard. They stared at the carnage a few hundred meters in front of them. "We have to help."

Everyone set off at a wordless run toward the apartments, when a Humvee pulled up outside of it, a machine gun sitting atop, which opened fire on the desolate, turning them to chunks of meat in seconds. An APC rolled in behind, the doors opening and troops in full tactical gear exiting, quickly making their way into the block.

The machine gunner atop the Humvee noticed Miles and the others, and swivelled the gun in their direction.

"On your side!" Miles bellowed, raising his hands in the air. "Not desolate."

The door to the Humvee opened and a young man got out. "Miles!" he shouted.

"Clint?" Miles called back. The group hadn't stopped walking the entire time, but every single one of them kept an eye on the machine gunner hoping they didn't have a nervous disposition or a twitchy trigger finger.

"It's okay," Clint said. "He's on our side."

"He's a vampire," the gunner said. He was loud enough that even without his exceptional hearing, Miles would have heard.

"Stand down, soldier," Clint snapped.

That did the trick, and the machine gunner visibly relaxed.

Miles reached Clint and they shook hands. "Where's Louisa?"

"She's farther in the city," Clint said. He had spots of blood on his face and armour, along with several scratches along the armour itself. He'd been in a hell of a fight.

Gunfire sounded out from inside the apartment block.

"You need any help?" the soldier asked.

Clint shook his head. "We've got this."

"Where's Commander Bailey?" Miles asked.

Clint looked a little confused.

"We need to coordinate," Amelia said. "Otherwise we're all running off doing our own thing."

"The Commander is fighting inside the city," the machine gunner said and chuckled. "He's killing a lot of desolate; we can take whatever is thrown at us."

"I assure you," Lauren said, "you can't."

"She's right," Miles said. "This isn't something your people can do alone."

"He went over toward the bay to look at the defences there," Clint said. "He was there when the attack happened. I imagine he's still there."

"What's the quickest way to get there?" Miles asked.

Clint motioned off down the road to the left of where they stood. "Straight down here for a few miles, until you reach a sign pointing to the right. It says *Bay Area* on it in red writing. Turn down there, and follow it until you reach a bridge. Over the bridge, turn first right, first left, and continue on. It's signposted after that. You can't miss it."

"Any chance of a vehicle?" Amelia asked.

"About a kilometer in that direction is an old garage," Clint said. "We use it to take our transport to get fixed. Should still be a bunch of vehicles there, although I can't vouch for their condition."

"That'll do," Miles said. "Take care, Clint. We're going to go stop this mess before anyone else gets hurt."

"You too, sir," Clint said, shaking Miles's hand, before nodding to Lauren and Amelia. "I'm glad you're on our side."

"Me too," Miles told him.

The group set off at a run along the road, the sounds of fighting getting more intense the farther into the city they went.

"This is bad," Lauren said. "I can smell so much blood."

"Can you ignore it?" Miles said.

"It's not easy," Lauren said. "It's . . . a lot."

Miles continued on until they reached the garage that Clint had told them about. The garage was open, tools thrown onto the floor, presumably in the haste for everyone to get away from the impending desolate attack.

There were two converted Toyota Land Cruisers that had been adapted to include several bulletproof panels around the doors and wheel bases. Each vehicle also had a roll cage inside, and most of the extraneous parts of the interior that had once been there for comfort or storage replaced with bare floors and seats, which looked as if they would keep you strapped in should the car flip but not actually provide anything close to a comfortable riding experience.

They found the keys easily enough as they were on a rack at the rear of the workshop, and Miles was happy to discover that they were both fuelled and ready to go. With the soldiers in one vehicle and everyone else in another, they set off through the streets of Brunswick.

Miles considered flying the distance to where the Commander had last been seen, but he didn't want to arrive tired and be forced to turn back into his more human vampiric self, removing a large weapon from his arsenal when he had to go up against a Dusk. He knew he was going to have to at some point, and he didn't want to fall at the finish line.

The two cars stopped a short distance from a burning two-storey wooden building, as pieces of fiery paper fluttered out of the smashed windows and rained down onto the ground. The building was beyond saving, and Miles was pretty sure it would collapse under its own weight at some point. The bridge that Clint had mentioned was off in the distance, and there was a lot of fighting between him and their destination.

Miles grabbed the radio from the car, which he'd already made sure was set up to talk to the soldiers in the other vehicle, and activated it. "We've got a rough run ahead of us. After that is a lot of open ground, and almost certainly a lot more fighting. Be prepared for some shit to hit the fan."

"We're with you," one of the soldiers said.

Miles replaced the radio and turned to Church. "You ready?"

Church barked.

"And you?" Miles asked Lauren and Amelia.

Lauren nodded, her expression stern. "Let's go."

"No time like the present," Amelia said.

"Lauren, the second you can start taking control of these desolate, let me know," Miles said.

"They're too far away now," Lauren said. "I can feel them, though."

Miles drove the vehicle through the town at high speed, hitting which-ever desolate were stupid enough to stay in the way. They made it through the pockets of fighting and over the bridge, where dozens of desolate waited to climb up from the sides of the bridge and leap onto the car.

"I can't reach them," Lauren said. "I can't get into their minds. Ulfrik has taken complete control."

"I guess we're doing this the hard way then," Amelia replied.

"Little help," Miles said as he grabbed the arm of one desolate who tried to reach him through the window, snapping the bone and hitting the desolate hard enough to dislodge, sending it back into the desolates behind with a noise that implied it wasn't a fun trip.

They cleared the bridge and found themselves narrowly avoiding open warfare between the desolate and citizens of Brunswick.

Miles continued on, following the directions that Clint had given him, until they were past the built-up part of the town and were hurtling along a dirt road that led to the bay, and hopefully Commander Bailey.

As they rounded a corner next to a sign that pointed toward the bay, Miles lost traction for a second, and their wheel hit a large chunk of rock. The car appeared to be okay, but it quickly lost power in the steering. Miles slammed on the brakes, forcing the car to a skidding stop. He got out of the Toyota as the second car arrived.

"I guess they were in the workshop for a reason," Lauren said as Miles popped the bonnet of the car and looked inside. "You know what you're looking for?"

"Nope," Miles said. He'd always meant to learn more about automobiles, but it had always seemed like the thing to do later. Apparently, now was much too late.

"You got room?" Amelia asked the second vehicle.

Everyone piled into the second Toyota, which made a bit of a squeeze, as Church had to sit in what had once been the boot of the car before its refurbishment. Once everyone was in, the driver set off at high speed, driving across the bumpy dirt road with Miles hoping the suspension didn't snap from the continuous assault it was under.

As they drove by a patch of dense woodland, the facility in the bay came into view. It was a sprawling mass of fifty-foot-high concrete walls, which encircled a long building that, to Miles, looked a bit like a hangar for an airplane. Although it was big enough that it would have easily housed a 747.

"The fencing is electric," Lauren said. "There's a sign there."

"Stop here," Miles said. "Just by those trees."

"Yes, sir," the driver said.

The car pulled off the road and stopped where Miles had indicated. Miles got out, letting Church out of the boot. "We're going to head to the side," Miles told everyone.

"There's a lot of desolate in there," Lauren told him as she exited the Toyota, too. "I can feel them, but I can't break through into their minds. Maybe if we're *really* close I could."

"Do you want to get *really* close to them?" Amelia asked.

"I'd rather not," Lauren admitted.

Everyone else exited the car and started to check their gear as Miles checked out the facility from a distance. "What do they do here?" Miles asked no one in particular.

"From what we heard, the Commander was putting in defensive capabilities in the bay," one of the soldiers said.

"Capabilities for what?" Lauren asked.

"No one knows," the soldier said. "Or it's way above my pay grade. One of those two."

They set off toward the facility, with Church in front until they reached the edge of the entrance, and Church dropped to the ground, her ears flat against her head. Miles crouched beside her, a hand on the back of Church's neck for reassurance. He looked back at the others and motioned for them to stay, before heading alone into the facility.

There were multiple dead desolate lying on the ground between the entrance and the hangar-like building, and several military vehicles sat up against the interior of the wall, with dead soldiers lying around them. They'd tried to get out, or get to weapons, and had been caught too quickly.

Miles motioned for everyone to enter the facility, which they did wordlessly.

At the far end of the facility were several more buildings, all of which looked like the kind of red-brick houses and offices that had populated Brunswick. Miles pointed to the soldier in charge, and over to the buildings. The soldier nodded, motioned for his people to follow, and they set off along the side of the hangar.

"You ready to go inside?" Miles asked.

Church made a huffing noise and both Amelia and Lauren nodded.

Miles made it to the door first, which was slightly ajar, and pushed it all the way open, revealing a large helicopter inside. "What the fuck?" he said as he stepped into what really was a hangar. There were dead soldiers and desolate all over the floor, with blood splashed across the white-and-blue helicopter.

"They built a hangar for a plane that can't take off," Lauren said. "What's the point?"

Miles looked around. "Yeah, bit odd, isn't it?"

"How did they even get it here?" Amelia asked.

"That's a Bell Huey UH, something or other," Miles said. "I know because I was on one that crashed in the seventies. Long story for a different time. This thing must have been here for nearly fifty years."

Amelia walked under the helicopter. "You think it will fly?"

"I think they can't get a plane or helicopter here from outside," Miles said. "So they kept an old one ready to go. Although I wouldn't get in that damn thing if you paid me."

"Because of the crash?" Lauren asked.

"No, because in helicopter terms, it has to be ancient by this point." Miles walked to the end of the hangar and opened the door there, revealing a dirt runway at the end that went to the far end of the wall next to where the buildings he'd seen earlier were. There was a red helicopter tug just outside the hangar, which explained how they planned to get the Huey outside. To the far side of the grounds outside of the hangar were fuel stations. A huge amount of it to fuel one helicopter that wasn't going anywhere.

He was about to go back inside when the top floor of the building farthest to the left exploded. Miles set off at a sprint across the facility toward the buildings, when more explosions were triggered throughout the buildings there.

Two soldiers threw themselves out of windows onto the dirt ground and started rolling around in an effort to put out the flames which had caught their clothes.

Amelia used her magic to summon roots out of the ground, creating large holes which threw a lot of dirt over the soldiers, smothering the flames. Both soldiers lay on their backs, their faces singed, but otherwise looking okay.

"The rest of you?" Miles asked.

"Inside," one of the soldiers said through gritted teeth. "Stairs went down into a basement. Smaller building. Booby-trapped."

Lauren joined them and set about helping the second soldier, who appeared to be in more shock than anything.

Miles moved toward the buildings, the largest of which was now an inferno, and used his telekinesis to blast away the debris from the doorway of a less damaged building. He quickly found the stairs that led down, and crouched by the hole in the floor. He spotted the remaining explosives and incendiary device that were on the walls of the basement next to the stairs. The booby trap hadn't gone off properly, as this part of the building was meant to be just as much of a fireball as the rest of it.

He dropped down into the basement, the metal staircase warped from the explosion that did actually set off. He found one soldier on the ground, next to a large hole in the floor.

"You okay?" Miles asked, touching the young vampire on the shoulder. His face was a mass of melted skin and burns. The booby traps hadn't gone off properly, but they had still worked enough.

The soldier let out a strained reply.

Miles looked down the hole and spotted two soldiers lying on the ground. "You two okay?" he shouted.

"We'll be fine," one said.

"There are stone steps here," one of the soldiers said. "They lead down toward some kind of large black stone door."

"Do not go through the doorway," Miles said, making sure there was no ambiguity to his tone. "Can you get back up here?"

"Yeah, it's fine," a soldier said. "We'll meet you back up top."

Miles picked up the young soldier and leapt up through the hole in the ceiling, back up to the ruined building above. He carried the seriously injured vampire outside and laid him down next to the soldiers. "He'll be fine," Miles said. "He needs blood, though, so when you're both able to, move him into that hangar and see if you can find any. There's a lot of places in there we didn't have time to search. I'm going back for your . . ."

The floor beneath their feet shook, and dirt exploded up from the ground close to the hangar, as dozens of desolate poured out, all hungry for flesh and blood.

Lauren walked toward them and shouted, "Stop!"

They stopped.

Miles blinked as Church, who had been growling and ready to fight a second ago, sat back, a look of bemusement on the dog's face.

"Me too," Miles told her.

The thirty-eight desolates, some of which were *huge* in size, all stood around as if they weren't entirely sure what they were meant to do next.

"You got them?" Miles asked Lauren.

Lauren shook her head. "They're a lot bigger than the ones I'm used to. I can control the smaller ones no problem, but the larger, they're outside of my power."

Miles removed the talisman out of his pocket. "How about if you wear this?"

Lauren stared at the talisman for a moment. "It can be used to control me."

"Not if you're wearing it," Miles told her.

Lauren tentatively reached out and took the talisman, dropping the chain over her neck. Her mouth opened wordlessly, her eyes turning to pools of darkness.

Miles watched her for the short period of time that she reacted to the talisman, before she looked back at him. "I can feel Ulfrik watching what I do."

Miles stuck two fingers up at Lauren, who laughed. "Want to try those desolates again?" he asked.

Lauren nodded, and reached out with her power. The desolates all turned toward her as one. "It's done," she said. "I have them. But Ulfrik knows."

"Good," Miles said. "He can be aware of how close we are to finding him."

"I would not want to meet one of the Desolate Royalty who aren't on our side," Amelia said.

"I don't advise it," Miles told her before calling to Lauren, "Any chance they know where Ulfrik, the Priest, or Commander Bailey are? Or Thomas?"

Lauren pointed a long finger at one of the desolate. A large creature that reminded Miles of the Viking he'd met. Maybe not a first-generation desolate, but only one removed from them. There was an intelligence in the creature's eyes that Miles found unnerving.

"Where is Ulfrik?" Lauren commanded.

No one spoke, but the desolate turned toward the hole.

"He's down there," Lauren said, pointing to the same hole.

Miles walked over to the hole and looked down the hundred-foot shaft, beyond the drill that sat halfway up. Part of the drill had snapped off and was lodged in the side of the hole, giving a large gap with which to get down to the bottom. "That's the vampire city," he said, recognising the black stone that almost shimmered at the bottom. "Is Thomas down there?"

"Answer him," Lauren commanded.

The desolate opened its thin, ruined mouth, and no words came out. It looked to the desolate beside it, but it was in considerably worse shape.

"Ulfrik down there?" Miles asked, pointing down.

The desolate nodded.

"Okay, I'm going after Thomas," Miles said. "Church you want to join me?"

Church barked.

"I'm coming, too," Amelia said.

"The desolates will climb down okay," Lauren said. "They'll follow us. I'll stay back from Ulfrik, though. I can't risk it."

Miles looked over at the soldiers, who were all still seriously injured. The two soldiers he'd spotted earlier made their way out of the ruined building, with one dropping a bag next to the soldier that Miles had rescued and removing a blood pouch.

"Let's go hunt," Lauren said, and stepped into the hole.

Miles waited for the desolates to scramble back down the hole, before picking up Church in his arms. "You ready?" he asked.

Church barked.

"You want to go down the same way as that hole at the fort?" Miles asked.

Amelia wrapped her arms around Miles and whispered, "This is a lot less fun than vampire romance books had me believe."

Miles chucked and stepped out into the hole, turned into his vampire self, and used the talons on one hand to ensure his descent was slow enough to give Church the easiest time possible. He landed beside Lauren, and Amelia let go of him, moving away so that Church had more room to jump to the floor.

They were all soon running through the tunnels, the desolates in the front, leading the way as Lauren's control over them was absolute. Eventually, they arrived at a set of stairs that led to a large black stone door, much like the ones Miles had seen several times since arriving in Maine.

"This the door you told them not to go through?" Amelia asked.

Miles nodded.

"I assume we're going to break that rule."

"Unfortunately, yes," Miles said, as the desolate pushed open the door with the sound of stone scraping on stone.

They continued on through the archway into a large empty chamber with three exits. Miles checked them quickly and found two pools, like the ones he'd found himself in under Falmouth, although thankfully these weren't full of blood and body parts, just dust and cobwebs. Someone used this place to feed desolate, and by someone Miles was pretty sure it was Ulfrik and his followers from back when he first roamed these lands.

They all continued through the third and final exit, eventually reaching a massive door like the one Miles had seen earlier. The desolates pushed the door open, revealing more of the city. More towers, more walkways connecting them.

In the centre of the room was a kneeling Commander Bailey. Blood drenched his arm, dripping steadily into an ever-growing puddle beside his knees.

Lauren stopped the desolates and Miles continued on, smelling the fresh blood on the Commander. His face was a mass of bruises and blood. He was missing one ear, and his nose had been badly broken, leaving him with a whistling noise as he tried to breathe. His arm was pointing in a direction a human arm wasn't meant to point, and his uniform, which had been so tidy last time, was badly torn, showing lacerations beneath.

"Guess that Ulfrik found you," Miles said.

The Commander looked up at Miles with his only working eye. He opened his torn lips to speak, but no words came out.

"I did," Ulfrik said, as he dropped from the walkway above, landing next to the Commander.

"Where is Thomas?" Miles asked, as Lauren and the desolates moved back, toward the stone door.

"Show him," Ulfrik commended.

Miles looked up as Thomas was kicked from the highest walkway. He tumbled over and over on the way to the ground next to Miles, a drop of several hundred feet onto hard stone floor. Miles leapt up, catching Thomas, and landing back on the ground a short distance away. The First Authority was hurt, but would live.

"Broken ribs, collarbone," Ulfrik said conversationally. "I think I collapsed his lung. He's a vampire, he'll live. He will be kept alive until William Fuller is brought before me. All who betrayed me will be punished."

"I think the First Priest has been feeding you spoonfuls of bullshit to suit his own agenda," Miles said. "Fuller wasn't even in America when your own people attacked you."

"Commander Bailey, the werewolf, and the witch were working together," Ulfrik said. "My talisman let me see everything the witch saw. They believe they can use my blood to destroy vampires, as if I would ever be easily subjugated so they could retrieve it. My library was not meant for humans. It was for our kind. The kind who should rule this world. This one here desecrated my library with his *human* filth." Ulfrik shouted the last part, the word echoing all around them.

"Torture is the last plan of the weak," Lauren said.

Ulfrik's gaze snapped toward Lauren. "You could have had it all."

"I don't want anything from you," Lauren said.

"Enough people have died here," Amelia said. "This has to stop."

Ulfrik laughed. "This will only stop when only the strong remain."

Miles laughed. "I think you might be pissing up the wrong tree with that idea."

"Aid me," Ulfrik said, ignoring Miles. "You will have a place at my side as we subjugate these pathetic creatures. You have my word that I will give you power and riches the likes of which you've never seen."

"Fuck you, and fuck your word," Lauren snapped.

"How dare you," Ulfrik said with a snarl.

Commander Bailey took that exact terrible moment to try to get away. Ulfrik caught him by the back of his head, with one swipe of his claw, removing a large part of the Commander's skull. "Your turn then," the Dusk said menacingly.

Miles rolled his shoulders. "Get ta fuck, ya wee bawbag."

Chapter Thirty-Seven

Miles didn't have the chance to attack first as the desolate slammed into Ulfrik like a wave of death, dragging him back toward one of the towers. Lauren stayed back, her eyes pools of darkness as she controlled the throng of desolate at her command, while simultaneously fighting Ulfrik to keep him out of her head. The talisman around her neck blazed red, and Miles hoped that she could keep up her control for long enough to give them the edge.

Miles watched for an opening to use his bloodline gift, but was unable to get through the mass of bodies that continued to assault the Dusk. The attack didn't last long, as Ulfrik tore into the desolate, sending them flying back, not always in one piece.

With an opening, Miles ran toward Ulfrik but was smashed into by something running toward him at speed. It took him off his feet, and only his own strength and agility managed to get him free of the attacker's grasp before he could be driven headfirst into the nearest tower.

A low growl emanated from beside Miles as Church barrelled into the huge desolate who had charged into Miles, taking the larger creature off its feet. As desolate poured past Miles, Church pinned the larger desolate to the ground, grabbed its leg, and tore a chunk free. The desolate screamed in pain followed by several nearby explosions from above that made everyone throw themselves to the ground. The walls of the cavern shook, and pieces of the ceiling fell, almost hitting Amelia, who used her magic to create a shield of roots above her head.

"We've got him!" Lauren shouted, removing the talisman and tossing it to Miles.

"You need this," Miles told her.

"The large desolate I controlled are dead; the rest will do what I say. Go get the Dusk."

Miles nodded and rushed over to Thomas, kneeling beside the injured vampire. "The First Priest?" he asked.

"Down there," Thomas said. "He knows how to put this big bastard back to sleep. I'm sure of it."

"We hurt it enough until it retreats," Miles said. "That's how they did it last time. Although last time, he had a sarcophagus here waiting for him to crawl into before they moved it. I doubt he built a second one."

Miles glanced around back toward the fight, where the huge desolate had gotten free and had thrown the rock at Church but missed by several dozen feet. It had one arm hanging uselessly by its side, and blood poured from a deep wound along its belly, but it was fending off the desolate controlled by Lauren.

"There are levels below here," Thomas said. "We can get him down there and blow the entrances to the city."

"There's a helicopter up there with a lot of fuel," Miles said. "If we can get it down here, we can use it as a bomb."

"It would collapse a large part of the city above us," Thomas said.

"So we make sure no one is up there," Miles said.

There was a rumble of noise as more desolate ran into the room.

"Go!" Thomas shouted as he created a shield of red energy in front of him, pushing it forward as he walked, trying to force the desolate back out of the door.

Roots and vines tore out of the ground, wrapping around the desolate, pulling some of them back down under the dirt. "I'll help here. Just stop them," Amelia said.

The large desolate hobbled by, followed by Church, who was certainly having the better end of that particular contest.

Miles ran, following Ulfrik, hating the fact that he was leaving his friends to deal with whatever trouble now came their way, although he was sure they'd be fine. He pushed it out of his mind as he reached the end of the hallway, kicking open the wooden door and revealing a large chamber beyond.

There were three large black stone columns on either side of the chamber, and a black throne at the far end, which to Miles looked as uncomfortable as a throne could possibly look. Two wooden doors were also in the chamber, both closed, leading deeper into the city.

He walked to the closest door and pushed it open, revealing a hallway beyond. The smell of fresh blood tinged the air, along with something else. *Desolate.*

He sprinted down the hallway and created a cushion of telekinesis in front of him as he hit the door at the other end of the hallway while running at full speed. He tore through it as if it were made of plywood, ready to catch whoever was beyond by surprise, and hoped that it would give him the edge.

Miles stopped running, and blinked in surprise himself.

The cavernous chamber beyond was like a dragon's horde. With hundred-foot-long walls, and fifty-foot-high ceilings, it contained a huge amount of jewels, gold, and silver, all in large piles. It also held the bodies of several dead desolate, all of whom were missing their heads, their blood splattered across the riches they lay among.

Miles heard footsteps behind him, tensed at the possibility of attack, but immediately calmed when Thomas entered the chamber. He looked worse for wear, although Miles was happy to see that he was up and about.

"That is a lot of stuff," Thomas said.

"The First Priest should be around here somewhere," Miles said as he walked across the room to the only exit there. "How goes the fighting?"

"The huge desolate is dead," Thomas said. "But more desolate arrived, so they're being dealt with. Everyone was okay when I left."

Miles was relieved that those he cared for were fine, although the idea of Ulfrik hiding out somewhere in the vampiric city left a bad feeling in his gut.

Miles pushed open the door and revealed a second large chamber.

"The library," Thomas said.

Miles nodded and stepped inside the grand room. It was a hundred feet long, with ceilings just as high. Blue-flamed torches sat every few feet, illuminating the large number of scrolls and parchments that littered the multitude of black stone bookcases. A spiral staircase sat at the far end of the library, leading up to the second floor, where balconies on either side of the central area overlooked where Miles and Thomas stood.

Miles took a long sniff of the air. "Blood," he whispered.

Thomas nodded. "I'll go up, you stay down."

Miles nodded and stepped to the side of the entrance, moving between the bookcases and discovering that the room went much farther to the sides than he'd expected. He moved quickly, but quietly, the musty smell of the library interfering with his sense of smell the farther he moved from the entrance.

The library was a maze of shelves and piles of old scrolls, most of which looked to be too fragile to even attempt handling. After a few minutes of walking, Miles heard a loud shout from back toward the entrance. He set off at a run, retracing his steps with ease, until he came out of the maze of shelves at the door again.

"Thomas!" Miles called out.

There was no answer.

Miles leapt up the thirty feet to the balcony above, pulling himself up and over, almost knocking over a stack of scrolls as he landed. He moved along the floor, the scent of fresh blood filling his nostrils the farther he got away from the dusty tomes, until he reached a black stone door, close to the staircase.

The door was open and Miles stepped inside, the scent of blood now so strong that he knew he would find the cause inside.

Thomas's body lay on the floor, his head several feet away, resting next to a pile of scrolls. The cut had been clean.

"Oh, Thomas," Miles said sadly, and looked to the far end of the room where a bloody First Priest Pedro de Moxica sat, holding a broadsword across his knees. Blood dripped from the edge of the sword in a steady beat against the stone floor.

"He wouldn't just let it go," the First Priest said. "He shouldn't have given me a chance to turn myself in. Should have just killed me. He never was one for the violence that sometimes needs to take place."

"Thomas was a good man," Miles said, looking from the body of someone he had come to like and respect, up to someone he very much wanted to tear in half.

"Good men tend to die quickly," the First Priest said. "I wonder, Arbiter, are you a good man? I'm pretty sure you're not."

"You woke Ulfrik up too early," Miles said, ignoring the barbed comment. "He's not at full strength."

The First Priest stretched and stood, keeping the broadsword down by his leg. "Doesn't matter."

"You know that Liam really did find something in here about using the blood of a Dusk as a weapon," Miles told him. "You all but gave the Magistrate access to a way to kill us."

"Liam and Stuart were traitorous, and paid the price for their betrayal," the First Priest said.

Miles removed the talisman from his pocket, and saw the *hunger* in the First Priest's gaze as it settled on it. "You want this?"

The First Priest laughed again. "You put it on, I assume. Didn't make you feel too good, did it?"

"It's made with magic," Miles said, voicing a guess he'd had for a while.

"Yes," the First Priest said. "I will take it from your corpse and gift it back to my king."

Miles slipped it over his neck, feeling a surge of power flow through him. Power that belonged to someone else. "Ulfrik is going to get to watch you die."

The First Priest charged forward, throwing several sharpened crimson daggers at Miles, who used his telekinesis to blast them apart, sending them flying around the room where they eventually dissolved once they'd hit something.

When the First Priest was only a few feet from Miles, his broadsword pulled back ready to strike, Miles blasted the blade of the sword with telekinesis, causing the fast-moving First Priest to shift his weight to compensate.

The First Priest's eyes widened just long enough to see Miles's elbow smash into his face. He kicked the First Priest onto the ground, placing a foot on his neck and pushing down, the broadsword clattering to the side. "I am so done with your bullshit," Miles snapped. "I am done with this fucking place, with all of this death and mayhem. I considered giving you a fight, a fair fight, but all I can feel is the power of the monster you unleashed, and the need to turn your body to pulp. You are old, but age doesnae make you powerful. I'm going to guess you ambushed Thomas, stabbed him from behind."

"He didn't deserve a fair fight," the First Priest managed to stammer.

"Exactly," Miles said, kicking the prone vampire in the ribs, feeling them break under the force.

The First Priest flew back across the room, smashing into the wall hard enough to bring pieces of stone down with him.

Miles picked up the sword and strolled over to the First Priest, who threw more crimson daggers at him, but they were easily avoided or parried with the blade.

The First Priest got to his feet and threw a wild punch at Miles, who blocked it, grabbing the wrist and snapping the elbow with his free hand. The First Priest screamed in pain, and Miles stamped down on the side of the House Idolator member's knee, shattering it. He leaned into the First Priest and whispered, "I'm going to burn all your plans to nothing."

"No," the First Priest said, now lying on the ground. "You're just a vampire, you're nothing special. You're not."

Miles placed the tip of the broadsword against the First Priest's heart.

"Please don't," the First Priest pleaded.

Miles pushed the sword into the heart of the First Priest hard enough that he felt the blade chip the stone on the opposite side of the vampire's neck. Miles pulled the blade free, covering the wall beside them in blood, before bringing it back down onto the vampire's neck, decapitating the First Priest.

When he was done, Miles stood over Thomas's body. "I'll tell your First Lord what happened here today," Miles said. "I'll make sure people remember that you were a good man."

He exited the library and headed back toward where he'd left the others fighting the desolate. Miles reached the room with the throne in it when he was greeted by Lauren and Amelia, the latter of whom was covered in dark blood.

"Thomas?" Lauren asked as a dozen desolate followed her into the room.

Miles shook his head sadly.

"Thomas," Amelia said, raising one hand to her mouth. "Oh, no."

Church ran into the room and went straight up to Miles.

"You okay?" Miles asked her.

Church barked once as he stroked her head, noticing that she too had a lot of blood on her, none of which was hers. "You have trouble?"

"A couple more of those large desolate decided to join the fight," Amelia said. "Hence the blood."

"Louisa arrived to help and her soldiers went that way," Lauren said, pointing to the door beside them. She stared at the talisman around Miles's neck as it glowed faintly. "You okay?"

"No," Miles said as he got to his feet, pushed the door open, and set off at a run. They continued along a long sloping hallway that took them farther and farther underground, only reaching a door after a few minutes, although the sounds of gunfire reached their ears much sooner.

Miles kicked the wooden door open hard enough to keep it from ever being usable again, and they saw that Louisa and her team of twenty soldiers had opened fire on Ulfrik, as a dozen more dead desolate, and even more soldiers, lay all around them. This was not a battle Louisa and her people could win.

Ulfrik moved between the humans at ease, practically ignoring the bullets and incendiary shells as they tore into his body. Each incendiary round caused a small flare effect as they hit the Dusk. Blood poured from the wounds that were inflicted on Ulfrik, but he jumped up, high into the air, landing on stone beams that crisscrossed the ceiling of the room nearly a hundred feet above where they all stood.

"We can't stop him," Louisa said.

"Get your people out," Miles told her, looking up at the darkness of the rafters above his head. He spotted Ulfrik, who was crouched at one end, a look of rage on the Dusk's face.

"The First Priest," Louisa said.

"Dead," Miles said.

Ulfrik dropped down, landing in the middle of a group of soldiers, tearing into them before Lauren could send her desolate to help. Everyone sprinted toward Ulfrik in an effort to slow down his murderous rampage, with Miles reaching him first, slamming into him, taking him off his feet, and throwing him back across the room into the tower. Black stone rained down over Ulfrik.

"Get back to the entrance," Miles said to Louisa. "Make sure we're ready to blow this shithole the second I'm done."

Louisa didn't need telling twice, and with several of her team carrying those still alive but wounded, they exited the room, leaving Miles alone with Amelia, Church, Lauren, and the dozen desolate that Lauren had with her.

"Miles," Lauren said, genuine concern in her voice. "I thought I could stop him, but I can hear him in my head."

"Go," Miles said. "Make sure nothing else bothers us while we're busy."

Lauren said nothing, but Miles heard her and the desolate leave the room.

"She should have stayed," Ulfrik said, standing upright and brushing pieces of stone off him. "I would have enjoyed watching her feast on you."

"You can either go climb back into your sarcophagus, or you can die here," Miles said. "Pick one."

Ulfrik laughed.

A low, angry growl left Church's throat as she stood beside Miles, her teeth bared, her lips pulled back in a snarl.

"You can't hope to kill me," Ulfrik said, stepping across the corpse of a desolate, crushing its ribcage as he did. "That talisman is mine."

Miles wanted to fight, to feel his fists connect with Ulfrik's body, to hurt the Dusk, to make him feel pain. Instead, Miles stayed calm. He pushed down the vampire's need for blood, the need for violence, and stayed where he was, in his vampire form, waiting for the opening he knew would come.

Ulfrik moved faster than Miles would have thought possible, slamming into him and throwing Miles back across the room. Miles hit the wall hard, dropping to his knees as Church and Amelia assaulted the Dusk. Church's speed and Amelia's magic—thorn-wrapped vines whipping out toward Ulfrik—managed to push the Dusk back, but as the vines wrapped around his legs, he laughed.

"Vines?" Ulfrik shouted. "You come at me with vines?"

The floor beneath Miles's feet shook as stone was ripped out of the ground and flung at Ulfrik, striking him across the head, causing him to bleed. In a rage, the Dusk charged at Amelia, but Miles moved to intercept, slamming into the more powerful creature, both of them knocked back across the room.

Miles landed next to Church and rolled to his feet.

"You fed from me," Ulfrik said, already standing, his wounds healed. "But it wasn't enough. I am a god. You are abominations."

Miles removed the talisman from around his neck and threw it to Amelia.

"That is mine," Ulfrik said as Amelia caught the talisman and immediately put it on.

"Come get it," Amelia said, the air around her shimmering with power.

Ulfrik ran toward Amelia, a roar of anger escaping his lips, but he never reached her as the ground beneath the Dusk's feet exploded up, throwing Ulfrik back across the room. Amelia tore more and more stone from the ground, throwing the large slabs at the Dusk, who was soon buried under a mound of rubble.

Amelia dropped to one knee, gasping.

"You okay?" Miles asked.

Amelia nodded. "This is . . . this is a lot."

Ulfrik burst free from the mound of stone and ran at Amelia and Miles, but Church intercepted, driving herself into his chest with furious speed and power. She knocked the Dusk off his feet, but he reached out, grabbing Church by her flanks and throwing her across the room. She hit the floor hard, with deep lacerations across her body.

"Check on her," Amelia said, standing tall once again, a hum of power all around her.

Miles ran over to Church, who was bleeding from deep wounds, but none of them looked to be anything that would bother her for more than a few minutes. Until she was healed, she'd be unable to fight, although she continued to try to get to her feet to help Amelia, only to find herself back on the ground.

"Stay here," Miles said, kissing Church's forehead. "Heal."

Church whimpered and licked Miles's face.

Miles turned to find that Ulfrik had Amelia by the throat, holding her aloft, her feet dangling above the ground.

Amelia flailed, and managed to grab her sheathed heat dagger, igniting it and driving it into the Dusk's forearm.

Ulfrik roared and threw Amelia to the side. She managed to use her magic to create vines that cushioned the impact, but the thud as she hit the wall still caused her to slump unmoving to the floor.

"I have had enough of you people!" Ulfrik shouted.

Miles ran at Ulfrik, throwing a wall of telekinesis at him, forcing the Dusk back only a few feet before he managed to shatter the wall, giving horrific feedback inside Miles's nervous system. Miles crashed to the ground, landing atop one of Louisa's dead soldiers, his head spinning. No one had ever managed to do that before.

The soldier had several UV grenades on his belt, and Miles hastily grabbed one, just in time as Ulfrik kicked Miles in the chest, breaking ribs from the impact as Church barked somewhere off to the side. Miles lost grip on the grenade, which skittered across the room in the opposite direction to where Miles fell.

"When I am done," Ulfrik said, placing a large foot on Miles's chest and pushing down, popping another rib in the process, "I'm going to kill your dog, your woman, and all of your friends. I will find those who created you, and I will burn them from this earth."

"No," Miles said.

Ulfrik removed his foot, picked Miles up by his hair, and punched him in the face, knocking him back to the ground. He smashed his knee into Miles's head, breaking his nose in the process, and sending Miles back to the dirt-covered ground.

"Weakling," Ulfrik said, as he picked Miles up by his throat, in the same way he'd held Amelia only moments ago. "You were not worthy to drink my blood, you wretch."

Miles spat blood on Ulfrik's face. "Fuck you."

Ulfrik brought Miles close to him. "I'm going to enjoy this," Ulfrik said.

"Me too," Miles told him, and slammed his hand into the Dusk's chest, unleashing his bloodline gift.

Miles expected it to weaken the Dusk, or maybe give him a few seconds of being human again. He hadn't expected Ulfrik to drop Miles while he screamed in agony.

The Dusk's eyes opened wide as he dropped to his knees and thick, black blood erupted from his mouth, covering everything around him in the tar-like substance. It sizzled on the ground, forcing Miles to take a step back.

"What the fuck?" Amelia asked, looking a little dazed.

Ulfrik's screams had become little more than a whimper, the toxic blood no longer pouring from his mouth, although it continued to stream from his eyes and nose, along with the dozens of deep wounds across his body.

"What did you do to me?" Ulfrik demanded to know as he scrambled back, putting distance between himself and Miles.

Miles shrugged. "I'm nae entirely sure. Figured I'd try it. I drank your blood, I can still feel the effects, I wondered if maybe it would do something to my bloodline gift. Don't know if House Venator's gift naturally does that, or what—we were meant to be the House that hunted other vampires. I figured maybe we hunted your kind, too. Whatever the reason, I'm glad it hurts."

"Sleep or death," Amelia said as she got to her feet, albeit a little wobbly.

Ulfrik grinned, showing bloody teeth. "You can't kill me. And I refuse to go to . . ."

Miles turned into his beast form mid-stride and punched one hand through the weakened—not quite human—form of Ulfrik, tearing out his heart, and crushing it in his grip.

The talisman exploded, throwing Amelia, Miles, and Church back across the room, as the power that it had contained flooded back into Ulfrik, who, despite having his heart ripped out, was still moving.

Miles, still in his beast form, walked toward the prone and twitching body of Ulfrik, and looked down at the bloody mess of the Dusk, who opened his eyes, to reveal that they were blood red.

"Both of you leave," Miles said.

"You sure?" Amelia asked.

Miles nodded. "I'll be right with you."

Amelia helped Church up and half carried her out of the room.

When he was alone with Ulfrik, Miles picked up the UV grenade, looked around and saw that another of the dead soldiers had one, too. He grabbed that one, took both over to Ulfrik, activated them, and dropped them one after another into the cavity where the Dusk's heart was.

Miles reached the doorway when the UV went off, searing the back of his arms from the flash. He ignored the pain and looked back in at the smouldering mound of ash that used to be a Dusk.

Miles caught up with Amelia and a healing Church as they walked back toward the exit from the city.

"Ulfrik dead?" Amelia asked.

"Very," Miles told her as Church licked his hand. "You okay?"

Amelia let out a long breath. "Nope. You?"

"Not really," Miles said. "I *really* want a drink."

"That sounds like a good way to cap this off," Amelia said with a slight smile.

They continued to walk through the city until they returned to where they'd first entered, which was now where Lauren and her desolate waited for them.

"He dead?" she asked.

"Yes," Miles told her. He felt no need to tell her more.

"You're burned," Lauren said, pointing to Miles's arms.

"I'll heal," he told her, stroking Church's head when she nuzzled against him. "I'm glad you're okay."

Church licked Miles's hand. She would be fine, her injuries already healing nicely.

Miles looked beyond them at the barrels of jet fuel that had been placed around the towers, along with what looked like several Claymore mines, each with a blinking detonator.

"We're really going to bury that library?" Lauren asked. "All that knowledge."

"None of this place should have been found," Miles said. "The library will still be there. I'll let Drest know about it; hopefully he'll be able to make sure it doesn't fall into the hands of the Magistrate. Besides, I'd rather not have anything else leave this hole."

Everyone left the city the way they'd entered, with Lauren telling her desolate to stay below. They would die when the city fell atop them, but they had died a long time ago, and deserved to rest.

The group left the facility and were back up toward the city itself, looking down toward the facility several kilometers away, when one of the soldiers pressed the detonator. The ground rumbled like a powerful earthquake, and then everything from the facility on toward the coast collapsed in a plume of smoke, dust, and dirt. Millions of tonnes of rubble buried the Dusk city, and Church laid her head on Miles's lap as they sat against the rubble of a long-destroyed building.

CHAPTER THIRTY-EIGHT

Sam, Amelia, the Major, and about a hundred soldiers and FBI agents descended on Brunswick a few hours later. Miles told Sam a brief and exceptionally different tale compared to what had actually happened, making out that Thomas had done it all and he'd just turned up at the end to mop things up.

The Major took control of Brunswick, primarily because no one else wanted to do it, and while a lot of people there were unhappy about having a vampire boss, most people decided that having someone in charge who knew what they were doing was preferable to having the US military or Assembly stationed there.

Lauren had said her goodbyes quickly, leaving the state before anyone else could ask about the Desolate Queen. There was a good chance Miles would have some explaining to do should the Assembly realise he'd let her live. Again.

Miles would make sure that Thomas got the funeral he deserved. He'd told Sam that Thomas had died killing the First Priest, that he'd been unable to survive his own wounds after a furious battle. That was the *official* stance from now on, the one he'd tell the Assembly and House Idolator when they inevitably asked.

The rest of the vampires had mostly all gone to rest for the day, returning after sundown to get everything in Brunswick sorted out so that hopefully everyone could live together in a more peaceful society. Or at least not one where one side hated the other so much they were willing to try to create a weapon that would murder a whole bunch of them. Miles hadn't found anything to suggest that Liam, Stuart, or Commander Bailey had managed to get a sample of Ulfrik's blood, and he wasn't entirely sure if using the Dusk's blood would have actually worked as a weapon, and hopefully that was the way it would all stay.

With everything seemingly dealt with, or at least ignored very strongly, Miles found himself sitting with Church outside of Brunswick on a comfortable patch of grass, watching the ocean in the distance.

Amelia sat beside him, resting her head on his shoulder. "I have a hell of a story," she said, removing the grimoire from her bag. "I reclaimed what I came here for, and stopped Stuart and Liam from hurting anyone else. Thank you for coming with me."

"You're very welcome. I was getting bored of all that peace and quiet at home," Miles told her wryly.

"So, what next?" Amelia asked.

Miles considered it for a moment. "I have no idea. But whatever happens next, it can wait a while."

Amelia kissed him on the cheek. "What happens to us? Was it just a fling brought on by being in such circumstances as all this?"

"I think I can take a little time off," Miles said.

"I think it would be nice to get to know you in a not terrifying and murderous background. Maybe a nice vacation somewhere quiet and in the middle of nowhere."

"I have a home in Scotland," Miles said. "It's lovely and quiet. Apart from the time a bunch of arseholes came and dragged me into some mess."

"Bastards," Amelia said.

"They really are," Miles agreed, and looked over at Church. "You agree?"

Church snorted, gave Amelia a lick across the face, looked between Miles and Amelia, snorted again, and walked off.

"I think she likes me," Amelia said.

"I agree," Miles said. "So, you want to come home with me?"

"I need to write this story," Amelia said. "You got Wi-Fi?"

Miles looked at her and smiled. "I've got everything you need." He kissed her softly on the lips.

"That was super corny," she whispered, a smile on her own face.

"I'm centuries old," Miles said. "At some point, super corny is all you have left."

Amelia and Miles sat in silence, and while Miles knew it wouldn't last, for the moment, he was just happy to let it wash over him.

Acknowledgements

There are always numerous people who have helped me get this book written, edited, and published.

My wife, Vanessa, and my daughters, Keira, Faith, and Harley. Their support can't really be measured. They're part of the reason I write; they're part of the reason I ever decided to try and get published in the first place. Thank you for everything you do.

To my parents, who have always been supportive of my writing and read every book I publish, thank you for being there all these years, and I am sorry (not really) for the amount of space the wall of my covers now takes up.

To my family, my friends, all of those people who have supported me, who have contacted me to tell me they've loved my work, who listen to me going on about ideas and complaining about how my brain won't shut up for five minutes to let me work on one thing, you're all awesome.

My friend and agent, Paul Lucas, thank you for all you do.

To everyone at Podium. It's been a genuine pleasure to work with you all and I look forward to what the future brings.

My incredible editor, Julie Crisp, who helps make my work better. Thank you for being awesome to work with.

To all of my Patreon members, your continued support is always appreciated. And a special thank you to members Lydia A. Dean and Daniel Humpage.

And last, but by no means least, to everyone else who picks up my books, whether this is the first one or those who have followed my work for years, thank you.

About the Author

Steve McHugh is the bestselling author of the Hellequin Chronicles. His novel *Scorched Shadows* was nominated for a David Gemmell Award for Fantasy in 2018. Born in Mexborough, South Yorkshire, McHugh currently lives with his wife and three daughters in Southampton.

JOIN THE FELLOWSHIP

follow us on our socials

 podiumentertainment.com

 @podiumentertainment

 /podiumentertainment

 @podium_ent

 @podiumentertainment